THE CHERRY PAGES

THE CHERRY PAGES

A NOVEL

GARY RUFFIN

THE OVERLOOK PRESS
NEW YORK, NY

This edition first published in hardcover in the United States in 2013 by
The Overlook Press, Peter Mayer Publishers, Inc.

NEW YORK
141 Wooster Street
New York, NY 10012
www.overlookpress.com
For bulk and special sales, please contact sales@overlookny.com

Copyright © 2013 by Gary Ruffin

Cataloging-in-Publication Data is available from the Library of Congress

Design and typeformatting by Bernard Schleifer
Manufactured in the United States of America
10 9 8 7 6 5 4 3 2 1
ISBN: 978-1-59020-235-7

THE
CHERRY
PAGES

PROLOGUE

CHERRY PAGE WOKE UP TO THE FEEL OF HER PERSIAN CAT'S ROUGH tongue. Marlon was vigorously licking her nose as he always did when she slept late. Cherry took his furry gray head in both hands, and kissed him on his nose in return. The vivid sunlight streaming in the bedroom window of her London townhouse was a welcome sight. The old city had been rain soaked for the entire past week, so the sun making an appearance on a Saturday morning was cause for celebration.

She scratched the fat cat's stomach, placed him gently on the down comforter, and yawned hugely before sitting up in her bed and stretching herself awake. Today was going to be a busy one, and after a four-month hiatus from work, she was eager to get out of bed and into the day. Tomorrow she was off to America to begin work on a new film, so she had to get all her affairs in order before leaving.

She walked to the loo, did what was necessary, washed her hands, and splashed cold water on her famous face. Taking down her old plaid flannel robe from behind the door, she wrapped it around the oversized men's pajamas she always wore to bed, and headed for the kitchen. Within a minute, the coffee machine was dripping the first cup. Normally, she would have had tea, but on days that required her to be alert from the moment she awoke, coffee provided the extra jolt she needed.

The aroma of the fresh coffee brought Marlon running, and Cherry poured him half a bowl of his dry food, then filled another bowl with water from the tap.

She called her neighbor, Mrs. Dimmock, and made arrangements to leave the house key in the large flowerpot near the front door. That way, Mrs. D could pick up the cat at her convenience. Typically, Cherry wasn't sure how long she'd be gone, but Mrs. Dimmock said not to worry, Marlon would be well taken care of in her absence.

They said their good-byes, and Cherry poured herself a cup of the strong steaming coffee, taking it black. Cup in hand, she moved to the living room to check her e-mail.

She turned on her laptop computer, waited for it to boot up, and saw the instant message box: *You will be sacrificed . . . In order to bring the Blessings of Baal, the sacrifice must be without spot or blemish . . . and you are the Only One who is truly worthy. I will be The One to set your Spirit free . . . You will be the Perfect Sacrifice. See you in Atlanta . . .*

At first, she thought it was her friend Vivian, who fancied herself a witch and was always teasing Cherry about being the "perfect woman." But Viv wasn't a practical joker. She was dead serious about her beliefs, foolish though they might be. Besides, Vivian used the name *wicca_woman_2012* when she messaged Cherry. The name at the top of *this* box was *not_so_shy_guy*.

Being a celebrity has its dark side, as Cherry knew all too well. There had been weird mail and boxes left on her doorstep several times before, and only last year, the studio had tracked down a sick young woman who had made death threats against Cherry by post.

But this was a new method of violating her space; to come right into her home this way was much more frightening. This person had to know her username in order to contact her. How in the world would someone know that?

After checking to make sure all the doors and windows were locked, she dialed the operator, and asked to be connected to Scotland Yard.

Part One
Lights . . .

1

MY FIRST CATCH OF THE DAY TURNED OUT TO BE A BICYCLE TIRE.

It was a Sunday morning, and I was making the most of it by surf fishing for the first time in months. Bum, my humongous German shepherd pup, was splashing in the chilly water of the Gulf, barking at the ridiculous spectacle of me reeling in the rubbery fruit of my three hours of labor.

I finally got the sodden old tire onto the beach, and Bum attacked: Biting it, growling, and shaking his head as he chomped down on it with all his puppy might. He actually has a *lot* of might, as he is the biggest ten-month old shepherd pup in the world, and I'm not kidding. He's from a long line of champion show dogs, and is exceptionally large for his age. Also, he can chew up stuff like you wouldn't believe.

I had to struggle to get the tire away from him so he wouldn't be hooked. Catching a bicycle tire is bad enough, but catching a puppy is just wrong.

I had been casting into the surf since six that morning, about two hundred yards east of the Gulf Front pier. The sun was hiding somewhere behind the pale gray clouds, nothing more than a big, dim lightbulb casting a dreary glow over everything. A soft drizzle was falling, and it was a little cooler than usual for an early-spring day in the Florida Panhandle, but we were having big fun just being out on the beach in the fresh salt air.

Bum was soaked and dusted with sand, and was having a grand time barking at the crabs that came into view before quickly disappearing. Earlier, he had chased a pelican that flew low overhead, and I wondered what he would do with one of the prehistoric-looking birds if he ever caught one. I knew what he would do if he caught a crab, because that happened last month during a walk on the beach. He quickly learned his lesson when a big one pinched the crap out of his snout. Barking at them was as far as he would go now, and several feet away was as close as he would get.

I unhooked the tire and tossed it on the sand, and he grabbed it in his teeth and ran down the beach about thirty yards, shaking his big head and growling the whole way. He settled down and began happily chewing on his trophy catch.

My next few casts brought nothing, but then something fairly large hit my line. I knew it was a fish this time, because it started to run parallel to the beach, and jumped out of the water. It looked like a pretty good-sized redfish, and it put up a first-rate fight for several minutes, going out as far as a couple hundred feet or so before I was able to start reeling him in towards the sand.

Just as I got the fish within about thirty feet of the shore, the line snapped, and my quarry got away. I reeled in the now naked line, and cursed the runaway redfish up one side and down the other.

Coming to the conclusion that the bicycle tire would be my limit for the day, I whistled for my buddy, and he came dashing towards me with the tire still in his mouth. He stopped just close enough to spray me with seawater as he shook himself dry. I thanked him for the shower, and wrestled the tire away from him.

I picked up my tackle box, grabbed the old canvas bag that holds towels, sunblock, keys, and my cell phone, and we walked in the damp sand up to the trash can that's next to the steps that lead to the public parking lot. I tossed in the tire, and we headed up the steps towards my patrol car, the broken line of the fishing rod catching the breeze.

Bum's claws clicked on the sun-bleached wood planks as he trotted up ahead on the walkway that leads to the parking lot, and seagulls called to each other overhead. Those were the only sounds until my cell phone rang in the bag.

Neal Feagin threw the saddle over Blue, his favorite of the four horses he kept stabled on the Feagin Farm near Cumming, Georgia. Neal, his wife Susan, and their three daughters had moved into the big new house just last month, and they'd never been happier as a family.

The Feagins had moved to Alpharetta when Neal retired from his job as a homicide detective in New Orleans after a particularly wild case just last year. Money was not a concern, as Susan had become a multimillionaire overnight several years back when her parents had died in a plane crash. She'd grown up an only child in a tony section of Atlanta near the governor's mansion, but now wanted to live far away from the urban areas of town. So, they had purchased the two-hundred-acre spread, and bought a horse for each family member but Susan, who had no interest whatsoever in horses. As she liked to point out, she had enough work to do with Neal and the three girls.

Neal had started his own private investigation business after passing the test for his license with the greatest of ease. He set up shop in Phipps Plaza, an upscale shopping mall in Buckhead, a suburb known as the Beverly Hills of Atlanta. He got the unusual idea of setting up a P.I. office in a shopping mall from Coop, his closest friend and former roommate at the police academy. Coop had said that there would be plenty of walk-in business from all the rich women who shopped at an upscale mall like Phipps, and it turned out that he was right.

Neal was in the middle of five cases involving surveillance of suspected adulterous husbands, and had hired three young investigators to help him deal with the overflow. Feagin Investigations was off to an excellent start.

Even better, the previous Friday afternoon, another client had fallen into his lap when a young Englishwoman happened to see his office in the mall. After he corrected her mispronunciation of his name ("Feagin" rhymes with "President Reagan"), she steered Neal to a job as a personal bodyguard for a celebrity who was coming to Atlanta to stay for a few weeks on business.

The commute into Buckhead from Alpharetta was a major problem, since the traffic in Atlanta is as bad as anywhere in America, so Neal only opened the office Wednesday through Saturday. The ride south on Highway 400 could be bumper-to-bumper for ten miles or more if you hit it at the wrong time, so he bought a new Lexus GS to drive to town, leaving his beloved Ford pickup behind at the farm. Besides, he couldn't follow someone inconspicuously in the huge red truck. Saturday traffic wasn't quite as bad as the workweek, so Neal's schedule was much less brutal than most commuters, who had to drive on Highway 400 five days a week. When you have a wealthy wife, you can live your life a little differently.

Early-Sunday-morning horseback rides around the property were Neal's major form of relaxation now, and he had settled into a routine. That was something he had never been able to even consider as a homicide detective in New Orleans. Now, he looked forward to the equine excursions, rain or shine, and often daydreamed of riding his horse down Highway 400 to the office someday. He usually dreamed of doing it as he was sitting in a gridlock.

Blue, a big black gelding, was still young enough to want to run a little each time they went out, and old enough to enjoy a leisurely stroll along one of the paths. Sort of like himself, Neal thought.

There was the threat of showers in the darkening clouds, so Neal put on his rain gear, including his waterproof Stetson. Spring hadn't quite sprung in Georgia, but it was just around the corner. It was a toss-up as to whether Neal liked spring or autumn in Atlanta more, because both of them brought gorgeous conditions.

The Feagin girls couldn't wait for their first spring on the farm after hearing their mother talk about how the dogwoods would look in full bloom. They wanted to plant flower and vegetable gardens near the big house, and were all considering becoming vegetarians. They also rode whenever they got the chance, and took care of the horses without complaint, honoring the deal they'd made with their parents when Neal and Susan agreed to buy the animals. The girls enjoyed riding almost as much as their old man. Almost.

Inside the barn, Neal cinched the saddle tight, fixed the bit in Blue's mouth, and led him outside. Then he stepped in a stirrup and took his seat on Blue's wide back. He gave the horse a pat on the neck and waved to Susan, who stood watching from the kitchen window, coffee cup in hand. Susan and the girls would head to church soon, but Neal and Blue were headed for the large pasture. Once they passed through the open gate, the big horse broke into a trot.

After half a minute trotting, Blue nickered when he saw the white rails that the girls had put together out in the pasture for jumping their horses. The top rail was only two feet off the ground, so there was no real danger involved.

Neal had never tried to get Blue to jump it, but he guided him in that direction, figuring that maybe the horse wanted to try. To Neal, the horse's nicker seemed to be a request for a chance at jumping the rail, so why not give him a shot?

Neal kicked Blue's sides, and said, "Giddy up, big fella, let's see how high you can fly."

The horse broke into a medium gallop, and headed straight for the rails. Neal leaned forward like he'd seen the equestrians do in the Olympics, and braced himself for the leap.

When Blue was within thirty yards of the rails, he sped up a little more, and flattened his ears like a thoroughbred on Race Day. Neal's hat flew off, and a thunderclap boomed just as Blue came within five yards of the jump. Startled, the big gelding dug his front hooves into the ground, and Neal went flying over the rail while Blue stayed behind.

When he hit the ground after what seemed to be a full minute, Neal's boot caught the ground in a way that caused his ankle to snap with an audible *pop*. He knew immediately that it was broken from the sound— that, and the fact that his foot was at an ugly angle in relation to his leg.

Blue stood on the safe side of the jump, looked at his master for a moment, and then turned away. He ambled twenty or so feet, and began to graze as best he could with the bit in his mouth. The bit didn't seem to hinder him too much; in fact, he was doing quite well, his big horse lips nibbling and pulling the short dry grass into his mouth.

Neal couldn't stand the sight of his twisted ankle, so he lay on his back and reached in his coat pocket for his cell phone. He'd argued with Susan for an entire day when she had demanded that he keep it with him while riding, his point being that he was trying his best to forget about phones when he rode. She wore him down as usual, and secured his promise that he would always carry it on his rides. Lying in the grass, he was glad yet again that he'd had the sense to marry her.

He reluctantly called Susan and told her what had happened, and was relieved that she didn't chew him out, but instead quickly called 911. He also knew his plans had changed, so he dialed Coop's number and waited for him to answer.

Bum stopped when he heard my phone ringing, and sat on his haunches as I put down the rod and tackle box, and retrieved the phone from my bag.

"Hello?" I said.

"Hey bud. You busy right now?"

I recognized Neal's voice, and asked, "Who the hell is this?"

"Oh, you're a riot, Alice," he said, and made a groaning sound.

"Hey, you okay? You don't sound so good."

"I don't feel so good, either. I'm lying on my back in a pasture with a broken ankle, looking up at a sky that's about to open up and drench me and my traitor of a horse," Neal replied.

"You're *what*?"

He laughed and groaned at the same time, and said, "You heard me. I took Blue out for our Sunday ride, and tried to get him to jump the—never mind, it's a long story. I need to know if you can take some time off and come help me with a job."

"Does Susan know you're lyin' out there with a broken ankle?"

"Yes, she does, but she hasn't made it out here yet. There'll be plenty of time to get cussed out by my charming wife." He barely got the last few words out through the pain, but I couldn't keep from laughing, even though I tried.

I pointed out, "Man, you are one sorry P.I. Aren't you guys supposed to spend all your time fightin' and lovin'? Just please tell me that you're not lying in a pile of horse manure."

Now it was his turn to try not to laugh. I could see him smiling through the pain as he said, "Will you just get your tail up here and help me out?"

"Well, I guess I can. If it won't take too long. And, if you need me to save your ass yet again."

"I do. And bring your Christmas gun."

I rarely wear my gun in Gulf Front, since it's such a small town. I had lost my ancient Smith and Wesson while working a case with Neal last year in New Orleans, and Penny, my on-and-off girlfriend and fellow police officer, had given me a new Glock .45 for Christmas.

"Will do," I said. "What's goin' on?"

"Another long story, but I'll make it short for now. I'll call you after I get my ankle taken care of, and fill you in. The deal is, I've got a celebrity comin' to town tomorrow who needs her body guarded. And lemme tell you, bud, this is one body you're gonna love guardin'."

2

"SINCE I'M THE CHIEF OF POLICE IN GULF FRONT, IT WOULDN'T BE A problem for me to take a little time off to go help Neal out of a jam," I said. "I know I took a few months off last year, but I still have a whole bunch of vacation coming to me. The town didn't blow up the last time I left, so there's no real reason I shouldn't go to Atlanta. Besides, you just don't leave a man in the lurch when he's got a broken ankle and eight mouths to feed."

I was practicing how I was going to tell Officer Penny Prevost about my Atlanta trip, and the above were my reasonable reasons. They sounded good as I said them out loud to my dog, and Bum looked at me as if he agreed with every word.

But I couldn't come up with anything to say after I told Penny that I was going to Atlanta to be *Cherry Page's* personal bodyguard. One thing was certain, I needed a really good reason for leaving before I confronted Officer Prevost with the news, because it's hard to come up with an explanation when you're running away from an armed woman at top speed.

Neal had said that the bodyguard job had fallen into his lap when Sally Allen, Ms. Page's personal assistant, had been shopping at Phipps Plaza, and noticed Neal's office in the mall. Sally had been "quite impressed, really" with Feagin's background as a homicide detective in New Orleans, which meant she'd probably be impressed with me, too, since I spent three years as a homicide detective in Tallahassee.

After talking with Neal for a few minutes and explaining that she needed a bodyguard for Ms. Page, Sally Allen secured his services on the spot. The studio wanted someone who could be under their employ, and at their beck and call. Neal assured Sally Allen that he was the man for the job, and she agreed. When Neal broke his ankle the following day, he called and secured my services on the spot.

The reason Ms. Page needed someone more qualified than just a standard bodyguard was that she had received a death threat online while in her London home. Scotland Yard had notified Interpol and the FBI, among others, and the Bureau had traced the message to a computer in Midtown Atlanta.

They'd stormed the place with a SWAT team, and found the body of a twenty-eight-year-old Caucasian male in the bathroom, his throat cut from ear to ear. His name was Daniel Cullen, an employee at a florist's shop by day, and a drag queen by night. Being dead, he was written off as a suspect, and a thorough examination of the premises had begun.

The only other fingerprints found in the house belonged to his parents and his live-in lover, a forty-year-old Caucasian male by the name of Peter Shelton. Shelton was the manager of Backdoor Cabaret, a Midtown drag club, and had met Daniel at the florist shop.

When Daniel applied for a job as emcee of the nightclub, Shelton hired him on the spot after seeing him dressed in drag as his alter ego, Danni Girl.

Peter Shelton was questioned, and released when he was able to prove that he had been in Miami at the time the online message was sent to Cherry Page. Shelton had phoned home the morning Daniel's body had been found, and left a message that was still on Daniel's voice mail.

The computer keyboard had been wiped clean, and no other trace evidence could be found, so the only thing the FBI knew for sure was that the stalker had sent the message from Daniel Cullen's home computer. They couldn't be certain, but they assumed the perpetrator was still in or near the area. How the perp knew that Cherry Page was coming to Atlanta to shoot her next film was not known.

Knowing all this gave me ample ammunition to fire at Penny about my leaving. Surely she could see that Neal needed me to come help on something so important.

"And, just because the client happens to be a beautiful movie star, well, that's purely incidental as well as coincidental. Right, boy?"

Right.

Another thing I was worried about is the fact that Penny is the world's biggest Cherry Page fan, and that would make it doubly hard to tell her about the bodyguard job. If it was just any woman, it would be bad enough, but her favorite movie star? Yikes.

I've seen Cherry Page a few times on late-night TV and other shows, but I've never actually seen one of her films. There's not a movie theater in Gulf Front, and I only have basic cable, so I don't see many movies except old ones, which are my first choice, anyway. One thing I *do* know about Ms. Page: Even though she isn't blond, she's known as the "British Marilyn Monroe," because her figure leans more towards the voluptuous as opposed to the stick figures that pass for movie stars in today's Hollywood.

Allow me to rephrase. Her figure doesn't just lean towards the voluptuous, it defines voluptuous. From looking at her, it's easy to tell her curves are all natural, too. That's another point for her, since I prefer real curves to man-made.

Appropriately, she's also known for her thick red hair, which she wears fairly long. It's a medium shade, and has a wave in it reminiscent of a star from the forties. Then there are her famous green eyes, which are large and wide set. She's consistently mentioned whenever the question arises as to who is the most beautiful woman in the world, and I can see why.

And another thing I know about her. She's gonna make Penny jealous like no other woman on earth could ever do.

I practiced my "Why I Must Leave Town, Penny" speech on my dog for a few more minutes as I packed my bags, and felt a little bit better after each run-through. Then I made a couple of fried-egg sandwiches, drank some chocolate milk with them, and took a shower so I'd look my best when I laid down the law to Penny.

My courage all screwed up, me and Bum headed over to Penny's beach cottage, which her uncle rents to her for a pittance. It's small, but sits right on the beach, and it's perfect for one or two people. Not that I have any plans to move in anytime soon, I'm just saying.

I left Bum in the patrol car with the windows cracked, and made my way around to the front porch, which faces the ocean. I knocked on the door, and listened to the wind chimes I'd given Penny when she moved into the cottage. I'd decided against bringing my dog inside, in case there were fireworks, because he's still young and I don't want to expose him to the ugly side of life just yet.

Penny was in bed since she didn't have to be on duty until the evening shift. After a minute or so, I could see her walking to the door through the leaded glass that covers the top half. I braced myself, and took a deep breath.

Penny opened the door, and said, "Hi, you. Whatcha doin' here before noon on a Sunday? Is somethin' wrong?"

"No, no. Nothin' is wrong. Lemme in and I'll tell you why I'm here."

She opened the door wider, and I walked in and took a seat on the sofa in the small living room. Penny remained standing in front of me, dressed in a tee shirt and a pair of my boxers, waiting to hear my reason for coming over. The look on her face left no doubt that she was suspicious of my intentions. She pulled her long black hair back over her shoulders as she waited for me to speak.

I said, "I just wanna run an idea by you, see how you feel about it. I need to leave Gulf for a week or so, maybe longer, and I just wanted to come by and give you a heads-up."

This didn't go over too well.

She roared, "*Now* where are you goin'? You've barely been home for five minutes! What could possibly make you wanna leave again?"

"Well, Neal called this mornin', and it seems he's gotten himself into a little jam up in Atlanta, and he needs me to come help him get through it."

"Don't you dare tell me that he's got another murder for you to try and solve. You know what happened the last time you two worked a case together. Are you tryin' to put me in an early grave? What could be so important that he has to have *you* come up there? He's a big boy—can't he find someone else this time?"

"Actually, no. This is a special job that requires someone with exceptional skill and ability."

Penny calmed down somewhat, smiled, and said, "Then why is he callin' you?"

"Very funny, Officer Prevost. Really. Now. I need to leave as soon as I can, and I have a few things to put in order before I head outta town. Would you be willin' to take over for me as acting police chief like you did last year?"

Penny glared at me for a moment before saying, "Not until you tell me what the deal is. This better be good, too. I'm not gonna sit around here on my butt worrying about you bein' on another wild goose chase. So, what's the deal?"

"Okay, you're not gonna believe this. And don't jump to conclusions. Just don't jump to conclusions. This is strictly business."

She crossed her arms over her chest, cocked her hip to one side and stared.

"Well?" she said.

The time had come. No more stalling. I jumped in with both feet.

"The deal is—what's happening is—okay, Neal got a job as a bodyguard for Cherry Page, yes, *the* Cherry Page, who's gonna be makin' a film in Atlanta, and he fell off his horse and broke his ankle this mornin', so he obviously won't be able to handle the work, so he wants to hire me to come up and take over for him and be her bodyguard because she got a death threat on her computer that the FBI traced to Atlanta, and I hafta be there as soon as possible to meet up with Ms. Page, so I can start guardin' her body. Like that."

Penny said nothing for a moment, then asked, "What are you really goin' to Atlanta for?"

"I just told you. Cherry Page got a death threat, needs a bodyguard, and yours truly is the only man for the job."

Penny then did something completely unexpected.

She flew across the room, jumped me on the sofa, hugged me tighter than she's ever hugged me, and screamed, "This is the coolest thing I've ever heard! I thought you were kiddin'! Cherry *Page*? She's only the greatest actress in the world, not to mention the most beautiful! This is unreal! I've gotta call my parents, Mama's gonna have a fit! Wait! Tell me all about it. Sit back—fill me in. This is absolutely fantastic. Of course I'll watch the town while you're away! Wait. There's one condition, and it's completely nonnegotiable."

Stunned by her reaction, I asked dumbly, "What's that?"

"You have to promise—and I mean swear on your mother's grave—you'll bring her down to Gulf Front so I can meet her. You know that she's my absolute favorite celebrity of all time. If I were a man, I'd marry her. I can't believe this. Wait here, don't you move. I gotta call Mama!"

She ran to the small kitchen, grabbed the phone off the wall, and feverishly dialed her parents' number.

I was shocked by her reaction, and I must admit, somewhat disappointed; a little touch of jealousy was what I had expected. Hell, a *huge* touch of jealousy was what I had expected.

Penny and I had gotten back together for the umpteenth time a week before the previous Christmas, after several months of being apart, and jealousy had been the culprit in our breakups more than once. Her jealousy or mine. Then again, a couple of times she had dumped me for reasons that, to my logical male mind, were unfathomable. Men are from Mars, Women are from Left Field.

I listened as Penny squealed while telling her mom the big news. When she finished, she came back and plopped down on the sofa like she'd just finished running a marathon, the adrenaline starting to ebb.

I said, "So. You think it'll be okay for me to take the job."

"O-*kay*? Listen. As acting police chief of Gulf Front, State of Florida, I'm giving you a civic order. You will take this job, and you will bring Cherry Page to meet your chief, meaning me, or I'll know the reason why. Is that understood, Officer Cooper?"

"Yes, sir, Chief Prevost, sir. Ma'am. Whatever. I must say, though, this was much easier than I thought it was gonna be."

She leaned back, gave me the once-over, and said, "Why is that? What made you think it was gonna be—ohhh, I get it. You thought I'd get all mad and jealous because you're gonna be a bodyguard for another woman, right? Jealous Penny would have a fit like she always does when you even look at another woman? But you don't get it. Cherry Page isn't a woman; she's an icon, a vision, an unreachable star. *You* couldn't get her into bed with a forklift. She's on another level, another plane entirely. She probably has an English soccer-player boyfriend, or a rock star, or some famous actor in tow. She could have any man on Earth. Not only that, she's so classy and sophisticated. Did you know that she's never done a nude scene? She even has it in all her contracts, no nudity of any kind. You can sleep *right in her bed* for all the good it's gonna do you. Oh, man, this is so exciting! Do you need any help packing? Have you got everything? Need some wash done real quick? Hurry, let's get you movin', big boy!"

Slightly peeved, I said, "No, I don't need any wash done, I'm all packed and ready to go. And just so you'll know, Adam's gonna keep Bum while I'm gone, so you don't hafta worry about that, either. Well, if you're sure everything will be okay here for a while, the studio is sending a plane for me to Pensacola that leaves in three hours."

"The studio is sending a plane! This is incredible!"

Looking for at least a little sympathy, I added, "You know how much I hate to fly. I hope everything works out okay."

Ignoring my ploy, Penny asked, "You need a ride to the airport?"

"No, Adam's gonna pick me up here in a while, and Neal's gonna pick me up in Atlanta. I'll leave you my patrol car so Adam and Earl won't hafta share."

"Okay. Good. That's great. I still can't believe it. This is so fantastic. Cherry *Page*! Unreal." She paused for a second, and then asked, "Oh, yeah. What's this about a death threat?"

"Some guy is threatening her on her computer by instant messenger, and—"

Penny interrupted, "You'll have Neal and the FBI behind you, so I'm not worried about your safety. Besides, you proved you can handle just about anything last year, right?"

"I guess I did, I mean, I'm not worried—"

"Well, listen, don't you worry about a thing down here, either. Adam and Earl and me will take care of everything. You just have a safe flight, and call me as soon as you get there." She paused again for a moment, and then said, "Oh, man, I just thought of somethin'. Wow! You'll probably be callin' me from *her room*! I can't stand it!"

I was beginning to feel like maybe I couldn't stand it either.

3

THE PLANE LANDED AT DEKALB-PEACHTREE AIRPORT IN ATLANTA AND
a stiff breeze met me as I walked down the steps of the Gulfstream.
I heard Neal call my name, and turned to see him on the tarmac in
a rolling wheelchair with a cast on his left foot. A young man who
was large enough to be an NFL lineman was pushing him towards
the plane. I would soon find out that my first impression of the
young guy was uncannily accurate.

We met at the bottom of the steps, and Neal said, "Hey, bud.
Welcome to Atlanta. How was your flight?"

"I have to say, there's nothing like the star treatment. What a life.
No lines, free beer and food, and a good-looking stewardess named
Brandy. Not a bad way to fly, considering that flying is insane."

He said, "Did you cry and whimper the entire time and embar-
rass your family like you always do?"

"Actually, it wasn't so bad. I only felt like I was gonna die in a
fiery crash a coupla hundred times. And I only made Brandy hold my
hand twice."

"Wow, that's a major improvement. Just so you know, Brandy is
a flight attendant. That's the proper term."

"I don't care."

"That's what I figured. Here, say hello to the newest addition to
Feagin Investigations. Coop, meet Joe Don Kendrick."

We shook hands, and both said "nice to meet you."

I recognized the name, and asked, "Didn't you play tight end at
Texas? All-American, right?"

Joe Don beamed, and said, "That's correct, sir. All-American my
junior year, then I missed most of my senior year with an ankle
injury. Atlanta drafted me in the sixth round because of my bad
ankle, so I didn't get much money up front. But, I made the team,
and got to play in the NFL as a Falcon. For one play."

I thought he was kidding at first, but he looked serious.

"Really?" I asked. "I don't get to see the Falcons too much down in Florida. Mostly the Bucs and Jaguars. One play? What happened?"

He replied, "Well, it was pretty bad. In fact, it may be the most embarrassing play in all the history of the NFL. My first play in the season opener against St. Louis, I caught a fourteen-yard touchdown pass on a corner route. Then—like a complete idiot—I got all excited and did the stupidest end-zone celebration of all time. I got up a full head a' steam, and ran over to try and dunk the ball over the goal-post. Well, I made it goin' up all right, but I had a little trouble with the comin' down part. A teammate ran over to hug me while I was up in the air, knocked me off balance, and I came down on that hard indoor St. Louis turf right on my dang knee. Two hundred and fifty-four pounds right on my left knee. I blew it out so bad that I've never stepped on a football field since. I had the knee replaced, and I still limp a little, but I can move pretty good nowadays, considerin'. I just hafta stay away from those big meanies on Sunday afternoons in the fall."

A young man had brought my bags over to me on a cart, and I began checking them while Joe Don was telling his tale. I said, "That has got to be the lousiest way to retire from football that I can imagine."

Neal said, "Well, the NFL's loss is my gain. Joe Don's gonna be an All-American private investigator, no doubt about it."

Joe said, "Thanks, boss. I really appreciate that."

After an awkward silence, Neal said, "Okay. Are we 'bout ready to blow this pop stand?"

"Ready and waitin'," I said. "Where we headed first?"

Neal replied, "Straight to the Ritz-Carlton Buckhead, which, according to this map, is only five or six miles from here. Ms. Page should be checked in by the time we get there; her plane landed an hour ago. By the way, you two will be stayin' in the same suite. Think you can handle that?"

"Same suite, hunh? I'll learn to live with it. Dirty job, et cetera. Say, should I address you as 'boss,' too? Or maybe 'master'? I know: 'King Neal the First.'"

Neal said, "Hmmm. I like 'King Neal' a lot. Tell you what, you can just refer to me as 'Your Highness.'"

"Fine," I said. "Okay, 'Your Heinous,' let's get outta here."

4

Watching Marianne from a corner table in the restaurant last night, it was easy to see she was right for the starring role in a little performance piece. Slightly taller, but her body is similar to that of the slut Cherry Page. Her hair isn't red, but that would be easily fixed.

Marianne handled her hostess duties flawlessly, and it had been easy to find out she was interested in computers and had recently purchased a new Dell. The flat-screen monitor had cost a little more than she really needed to spend, but what the heck. A girl has to spoil herself once in a while, right? Marianne moved easily around the restaurant, taking drink orders, and laughing with the customers. She was quite popular with the male customers, and more than one followed her with his eyes as she made her rounds in the tight little miniskirt. Wonder how differently she might have acted had she known it was the last night she'd be seen at work.

And now, less than twenty-four hours later, standing in the backyard of Marianne's Little Five Points home, watching through the bathroom window as she enters the shower. Hearing only the intermittent noise of the light traffic in the quiet neighborhood, waiting and watching the shower's steam clouding the window. Less than fifteen minutes later, the loud whine of a hair dryer, the perfect cover.

Marianne doesn't hear the pane of glass break and fall to the floor in the kitchen, nor does she see the gloved hand reach through and unlock the door. The other requirement is in plain sight: the new computer. Already online, no need to boot up. How nice of the pretty little bitch to make the job easier.

Down the carpeted hallway to the bathroom door, hearing the dryer blasting away, finding the door ajar. Yet more gifts from Baal! This is even easier than dispatching the faggot florist, who didn't try to fight back because he-she was pulling his-her dress over his-her head and couldn't see. Don't laugh at the memory!

The large hunting knife coming out of its sheath like a snake; a *snake prepared to strike once more for the divine cause. That awesome feeling coming on again, one of ultimate supremacy and righteousness. Knowing that the Powers would reward this devoted disciple very soon. And the reward would be everlasting. Not to mention extremely lucrative.*

The hair dryer suddenly no longer whining, and only Marianne's out-of-tune humming breaking the silence.

Two more steps to the bathroom door. A quick shove, and into the steam the knife slices its way, finding the target vulnerable. But it's not yet time for her to die. That will come later. Now is the time to terrify her into submission, to restrain, drug, gag, and blindfold her for transport. That done, the computer sits waiting in the living room, ready to send another message to The One.

Tomorrow, a message of another kind.

5

CHERRY PAGE WAS DRIVEN TO THE LOADING DOCK ENTRANCE AT THE back of the Ritz-Carlton Buckhead because crowds of screaming fans had somehow found out she would be staying there while in Atlanta. The two guest entrances were impassable due to the crowds, so the limo pulled into the delivery entrance, which lay below ground level.

As they got out of the car and walked towards the employees' entrance, Cherry's petite assistant, Sally Allen, apologized for the stench of the food that was rotting in the Dumpsters by the loading dock.

Pulling her carry-on bag up on her shoulder, Cherry laughed and said, "A little rotten food doesn't bother me in the least. The only bad thing is that it reminds me of my futile attempts at cooking."

The manager of the Ritz met them at the employees' entrance and welcomed them to the hotel, holding on to Cherry's hand a little too long when she offered it to him to shake. As they made their way through the bowels of the hotel, the employees who could speak English smiled and said welcome to Atlanta and the Ritz, and how much they loved her work. The others simply smiled and nodded. Cherry smiled in return, shook a few more hands, and stepped into the freight elevator that would take them to the back kitchen area of the ballrooms on the first floor.

After they finally made it to the lobby elevators that would take them to their rooms, Cherry said to Sally, in her London accent, "I hope this bodyguard turns out to be someone with whom I can have an intelligent conversation. I'd truly hate being stuck with a disagreeable type, especially for such a length of time as it takes to shoot a film."

Sally replied, in her equally British tone, "Mr. Feagin assured me that you will get on brilliantly with Mr.—let me check my notes—

'Mr. Samuel Cooper, chief of police, Gulf Front, Florida.' He also said Chief Cooper is highly qualified, having been a police officer for over twenty years, and a homicide detective as well. Mr. Feagin added that Mrs. Feagin adores Chief Cooper, and the three Feagin daughters regard him as they would a beloved family member. From the way he spoke of the man, I don't foresee any problems whatsoever."

"Well, that's nice to hear. It surely sounds as if we'll make a good match. I feel much better knowing that he's held in such high esteem by the women in Mr. Feagin's life."

The elevator opened, and they made their way down the hall to Cherry's suite. A policeman was standing guard by her door, and the women thanked him after he showed his identification and introduced himself.

He said, "I'll be right here, Ms. Page, until your bodyguard arrives. Feel free to relax in your room. I assure you you're in good hands."

"Thank you so much, Officer," Cherry said, and Sally opened the door with Cherry's key-card. They stepped into the suite, and Cherry carefully placed her bag on the carpet and then ran over and fell back on the sofa in the parlor like a thirteen-year-old.

Chuckling at her employer, Sally said, "The remainder of your luggage will be here shortly. Now that you're safe and sound, I'm going to retire for the evening. I've been running around all day like a madwoman, and tomorrow will be here much too soon, in my estimation. I'm just down the hall in 512, and Chuck, Lynne, and Lawrence are all on this floor as well. The crew are staying in a motel near the college where you'll be doing most of the location work. You're to be at the little theater the studio's rented for rehearsals at eight. The college has a theater, but they're in the middle of a production at the moment, so we can't use it. Let's see. That should cover everything for now. Come morning, we can breakfast here in your suite, and you and Mr. Cooper can go on over to the rented theater. How does that sound?"

"That sounds divine, dear. Thank you so much for taking such good care of me. You know it means the world to me."

"And *you* know it's my pleasure. Now, get your beauty sleep, not that you have need for it. Night-night."

"Night-night, Sally."

When Sally closed the door behind her on her way out, Cherry reached for the hotel phone and ordered steak and eggs with a pot of hot tea and a bottle of ketchup. Although it was only a little after seven in the evening in Atlanta, she was still on London time, and she often had a midnight supper. When she wasn't working, her usual bedtime was three or four in the morning, but she always found it easy to adjust her schedule once she was back on a film set.

The bag she'd brought up from the car contained her laptop, and she took it out and set it on the coffee table in the middle of the room. She turned it on and as she waited for it to boot, went into the bathroom and washed her hands.

When she came back, the message box was there on the screen.

This time, *not_so_shy_guy2* had written: *You are so close, I can feel you. Baal will soon be appeased as he accepts the Perfect Sacrifice. I say to you, Only One: soon your Spirit will be free.*

6

JOE DON DROVE WITH NEAL UP FRONT, AND I SAT IN THE BACK AS WE left the airport, headed for the Ritz in Buckhead. We'd been talking about football and fishing for a couple of minutes, when Neal's cell rang. It was an Atlanta police officer calling to say that Cherry had arrived, and that she'd been brought in through the back of the hotel due to the large crowds at both entrances. She'd made it upstairs without any problems, and was in her suite.

Neal hung up, and said to me, "Looks like you'll be on duty from the minute you get there, Coop. You ready to start guardin' that famous body and solving this case?"

"Well, I hoped to get a good night's sleep before the battle begins," I said. "Guess I'll just hafta sleep on the job, like always."

Neal chuckled, and replied, "Now wait a minute, here. You're representing Feagin Investigations, and this could make or break my business. You can't just sleep through the—wait, that's not quite right—I have a rich wife—never mind. Just don't get your tail shot off while you're sleepin' on the job. But seriously, folks, do you have any thoughts on where to begin with this freak that's threatening her?"

"Yeah, I had a thought on the plane: maybe this is coming from the inside. Maybe a studio employee who has a beef with her, or somebody that she trusts, like a makeup person or a driver or whatever. There must be studio types who came to Atlanta early, to do whatever it is they do before work starts on the movie. I think you oughta start tracing the backgrounds of her associates, Mr. Feagin, P.I. Besides, what else is a gimp like you gonna do while I'm out there on the front lines, puttin' my rear end in jeopardy?"

Neal said, "I had the same thought. We definitely need to check out the entourage and the studio people. Agent Carver—you'll meet him soon, I hope—has agreed to give me access to some of the FBI's resources, and seems like a good guy. I'll get on that as soon as we get to Buckhead. My office is right across the street from the Ritz, so I'll burn the midnight oil while you luxuriate in the presence of a world-class beauty. In the Ritz-Carlton. In a suite with anything you want at your disposal, on command. I'll tell you one thing, you owe me big-time for this experience, bud. In fact, I don't know if you'll ever be able to make it up to me. Hey, that reminds me. How are you gonna make it up to Penny? I wish I coulda been there to hear the explosion when you told her what you're gonna be doin' up here in the Big City."

"Actually, she was fine with it. I guess she trusts me to do the right thing," I said, heavily editing her reaction. "She even wants me to bring Cherry down to Gulf so they can meet. I really think that Penny has outgrown being so jealous about me. Maybe she realizes how lucky she is to have me."

This got a snort from Neal, and he said, "Yeah, maybe you're right, bud. Then again, maybe you've finally succeeded in driving her crazy."

"That's probably it," I said.

We rode in silence for a few minutes, then Neal said, "I forgot to tell you another great perk of this job: the studio had a Bentley flown in from London for you to use while you're drivin' Miss Cherry. A bulletproof Bentley."

"You're kiddin'."

"Nope. You're gonna be in luxury even while you're in danger." He sighed and said, "Aaah, the show business. Ya gotta love it."

Cherry wasn't sure how to handle the situation regarding the new instant-messenger threat; should she wait for her bodyguard to arrive, or open her door and notify the police officer immediately? She knew that there was most likely another murder victim somewhere in Atlanta, but also knew that the stalker would be long gone by now. She was still trying to make up her mind when room service knocked on her door, and set up the food on the dining table. She decided to wait for the cavalry to show up and save her; isn't that what always happened in America?

The steak was perfectly cooked, and the eggs with ketchup made her feel right at home. The tea was her favorite brand, so she knew that Sally had done her job flawlessly once again, but that was to be expected. Only in England could one get a proper cup of tea, unless of course, one had Sally Allen as a personal assistant.

Although the food was delicious, Cherry found herself unable to eat more than a few bites. She'd turned her laptop so she couldn't see the screen, but she knew the sick words were still there.

She pushed the plate away, walked over to the window, and looked down on the traffic behind the hotel from her fifth-floor perch. The sun was slowly going down, leaving a beautiful pale yellow and blue-gray sunset, and the street area was bathed in a golden glow.

Still unsure of what to do about the message, she called Sally's room and asked her what she thought. Sally was no help; she couldn't make a decision either.

As Sally was prattling on about the situation, Cherry continued to look out her window at the street below. She noticed a black sedan stop near the rear of the hotel, and watched as a man got out and said good-bye to the occupants. As he walked towards the same back entrance she'd been through less than an hour ago, he looked up and saw her at the window.

He carried his two suitcases with ease, and she could've sworn she saw him smile at her as he gazed upward.

Cherry broke in on Sally's long-winded monologue, and said, "Hey, it looks as if the cavalry has arrived. And at least from five stories up, he doesn't look half bad."

7

I MADE IT UP THE BACK WAY TO THE FRONT DESK, AND FOUND THAT I was already checked in. The clerk gave me a key-card to Cherry's room, a young bellman took my luggage, and we rode the elevator to the fifth floor.

He asked, "Are you like, a bodyguard for Miss Page, or somethin'?"

"Yeah, or somethin'," I replied. He smiled like a crocodile as he turned back to watch the numbers.

As we got off the elevator, he said, "Follow me, Mr. Lucky," and grinned widely again.

I followed him as he turned the corner and walked towards Room 521, pushing the luggage cart. There was a cop standing in the hall yawning widely. As we approached, a thick head of red hair poked out into the hall, followed by a barefoot body dressed in jeans and a white tee shirt that could only belong to a sex symbol.

She was shorter than I thought she would be, but what she lacked in height, she made up for in shape. She started to rub her temples as we came within twenty feet of the door, and the look on her face told me she was worried about something.

The bellman said, "Miss Page, I believe your guardian has arrived."

She stopped rubbing her head, and held her hand out for me to shake.

I took it and shook it, and said, "Hello, Ms. Page, I'm Chief Cooper."

"I'm so glad you're here, you have no idea," she said dramatically, and I thought, Great, every little thing's gonna be a crisis with this one.

The officer introduced himself, and we shook hands. He said, "I'll say good-bye now," and headed down the hall to the bank of elevators. The bellman was already in the suite, which left Cherry Page and me standing in the hall, face-to-face.

"Please, Chief Cooper, do come in," she said, looking back to see if the bellman was listening. She whispered, "I just received another message from the nutter on my laptop. What shall we do?"

Man, the job was starting with a bang. I whispered back, "As soon as the bellman leaves, I'll take care of everything. You just take it easy and leave it to me."

Under the circumstances, she had a right to be dramatic. In fact, she had a right to be frantic. I decided to reserve judgment on her personality for the time being.

To bring things down to Earth, I said to the bellman, "This room is bigger than my apartment. Just how big are we talkin' here?"

"This is a Ritz-Carlton suite, sir. It's fourteen hundred and forty square feet."

"That's a lotta feet. Well, thanks for everything," I said, and motioned with my head for him to go.

I pulled a ten from my pocket as the bellman was leaving, and put my finger to my lips to silence him before he could crack wise again about my being lucky. He took the bill, smiled, and silently rolled the cart out of the room.

I closed the door, and said, "Okay, Ms. Page, might as well get right down to it. Let's have a look at the message."

"Call me Cherry. What shall I call you?"

"Everybody calls me Coop."

She frowned, and said, "I don't want to call you what everyone *else* does." She looked thoughtful for a moment, and then said, "I shall call you 'Cooper.' That way, you'll always know who it is when you hear me call."

I chuckled, and said, "Call me whatever you want, but believe me, I won't have any trouble recognizin' your voice."

"Good. I shan't have any problem with that Southern drawl of yours, either. Now. Look here at the creep's latest missive," she said, taking my arm and pulling me towards the coffee table.

I asked, "This may seem like a dumb question, but is it the same person?"

She said, "Actually, that's not a dumb question a'tall. The name *is* slightly different this time. See where it says '*not-so-shy-guy2*' at the top of the box?"

"Yes. You said 'slightly different.' In what way?"

"The first message didn't have a 'two' after 'guy.' That's easily explained, of course, as I'm sure you know."

"I may be the most computer-illiterate person left on Earth," I said. "My secretary and officers take care of all the computer stuff. I'm just not plugged-in, so to speak. Explain it to me, and talk reeeaaalll slow."

That earned me a smile, and she said, "Well, the thing is, when you go online using an instant messenger, you can create up to six identities on some of them. I *think* that's right. I could be proven wrong, but I'm fairly sure that's the way *this* messenger works. Anyway, since he used '*not-so-shy-guy*' on the first computer messenger, if he tried to use it again on a different computer, it would tell him the name was already taken." She frowned, and continued, "But, he *could* have used the same computer, and simply have added the 'two' to confuse us. But why would he do that? I think we should assume it's a different computer, don't you?"

It made sense to me, so I nodded my assent.

She went on, "So, since it's probably a different computer, he adds a 'two,' and the messenger sees it as a different name, and allows it. Know what I mean?"

Women with English accents really do it for me. Especially when they have a pleasant voice, like this one. The way she pronounced *Cooper*, it came out, 'Coo-puh.' I could've listened to her blather on about anything, but the amazing thing was, I actually understood what she'd said about the computer messenger.

I said, "Okay, so he most likely used a different computer; and stating the obvious, a different location. First things first. Let me call and report this so the Feds can locate the address. I guess it's too much to hope for, but maybe there was no one killed this time. Relax for a minute, and I'll call my boss."

Cherry sat down on the sofa for a full five seconds before she stood back up and began pacing. Normally someone pacing bothers me, but since there were so many interesting things about her to watch as she paced, I let it slide.

I got Neal in his car and filled him in about the latest message. He told me he'd get back to me as soon as he knew anything.

After I hung up with Neal, an idea came into my head, and I said to Cherry, "You know, maybe we could have you do an interview with CNN, and just casually mention that your computer died and you're offline now. Maybe add that you're tired of it too, whatever. CNN's home base is here in Atlanta, and they could do an interview in a heartbeat. Really get the word out there and hopefully, stop this computer messaging. And killing."

She stopped pacing, and said with a distracted tone, "I'm willing to try anything at this point."

"I know what you mean."

She went back to pacing, this time mumbling to herself. I couldn't make out what she was saying, but I heard the words "killer" and "murder."

Wanting to keep her mind occupied with something other than the stalker, I asked, "Cherry, could you do me a favor and go online and find out if the media has caught wind of what's happening to you? Is it possible to do that without losing the message?"

Laughing softly, she said, "You really *are* a babe in the woods when it comes to computers, aren't you, Cooper?"

"I tried to warn you."

She walked over and sat down in front of the laptop again. After staring at the screen for a moment, she looked up and caught me standing by the table, gazing at the leftover food.

"Cooper, have you had your supper yet?"

"As a matter of fact, I haven't, but I've had my eye on that steak ever since I walked in. You gonna finish it?"

"Oh, no, we can do better than that. Wouldn't you prefer to order something else from room service?"

I said, "As a police chief, I know that wasting food is a crime. Besides, who knows how long it might take to get another order up here. Seriously, is it okay if I finish it?"

"Well, if you really want it, be my guest. I wasn't much in the mood to eat after I saw the latest message. There's tea in the pot, and—hey, I just realized there's not a bed for you. I'll call down and have them send one up."

"Don't go to any trouble on my account. I can sleep on the sofa. It's no big deal."

She gave me a look that said, "Don't make me hurt you." I said, "Okay, okay. Sheesh, what a grouch."

Smiling, she reached for the phone and ordered a bed. I ate the steak down to the bone, put the cold eggs and ketchup on a roll, and devoured them, too. I washed it all down with a cup of warm tea, which was better than I thought it would be. In fact, it was pretty tasty.

The bed soon arrived and I asked them to set it up near the window; I like to have the sunshine coming in on me while I try to wake up in the morning.

When we were alone again, Cherry asked: "Cooper, what do you know about this 'B-a-a-l' person? Have you any idea what all that means?"

"First of all, I think it's pronounced 'Bail'—at least, Southerners pronounce it that way—but I've heard other pronunciations too. Other than that, I don't remember much about him. You've got the computer. Look him up."

"Will do."

She tapped the keys for a moment, and said, "Right. Here he is. It says that Baal was a god that was worshipped by the ancient Israelites. Jezebel introduced him to the Israelites after she married Ahab and became their queen."

Because of her age, I wasn't sure if she knew who Jezebel was, so I asked, "Are you familiar with Jezebel?"

Cherry pushed her hair back from her face and said, "Yes, I know what she represents. Do you think Jezebel has something to do with all this? I mean, could this person see me as a Jezebel?"

"Whoever is doing this is probably not much of a thinker. I think."

"Well, while you're thinking, do you think this person wants to sacrifice me for real? Or is it just some sick game?"

"It's sick no matter *what* they want. They may just be trying to scare you with the 'sacrifice' bit—as if the threats weren't enough—but typically, these creeps are harmless. They usually just want attention, but it's obvious that we have a real killer on our hands. I don't believe the Baal stuff is real, though; sounds phony to me. I'm in the dark about a lot of what's happening, but one thing I *do* know: we're gonna find whoever's doin' this, I promise you that. Another thing I can promise is that you're in good hands with the FBI. Not to mention me."

I gave her my best reassuring smile, and she said, "You know what? I believe you."

I said, "Good. You should. But as I said, and proved, I know very little about the Web and computers. My—one of my officers showed me how to Google when I got back from a case in New Orleans last year, but that's about the extent of my knowledge. The case got a pretty good amount of media coverage. I was famous for a week or two. Put in 'Samuel Cooper police chief Gulf Front Florida' and see what you get."

She said, "'Cooper' is such a good, solid, English name. Do you know much about your family history?"

"I hardly know anything at all about it, but I assume there were a few barrel makers climbin' around in my family tree."

"Mmm, I suppose so," she replied, now occupied with the computer again. After a moment of typing on the keyboard, she said, "Hey, you're still here. Six hits out of ten on the first page are about you. The others are about some confederate general bloke."

"See? I was famous for a while. Now. Look for any news about your stalker."

Cherry said, "But I want to read all about your exploits."

"There'll be plenty of time for that. Now, let's get back on track here. Find out if the media is aware of your 'situation.'"

"Okay, whatever you say, Chief. But I'm going to check up on your recent history the first chance I get."

She searched the Internet for a while, and found nothing to indicate that the media was aware of the situation. I knew it wouldn't be long before the news got out, but we had at least one more night before all hell broke loose.

And I do mean "hell."

8

After three solid hours of applying makeup and putting different wigs on, there was still no resemblance to Cherry Page whatsoever. You'd think there would be at least some minor similarity, but it was clearly hopeless. The finished look was more like a demented caricature than a twin.

The tiny dressing room was so damned hot with all those lights around the mirror, and sweating like a pig was not helping the situation. In fact, it was ruining any chance for inspiration. Not to mention having to wear the surgical gloves.

So, with a mighty heave, the makeup tray crashed against the wall, spilling its contents on the blood-covered floor. Lipsticks, mascara, brushes, powders; they were all useless!

One by one, the lights surrounding the mirror became dark, as they were smashed with the heel of the Manolo Blahnik open-toe pump. The exact model of the ridiculously expensive shoe that the fabulous Cherry Page had worn in her last film. The model that was supposedly her favorite shoe of all time; whether it was her favorite or not, it made an excellent hammer, popping the lightbulbs easily and completely.

As each bulb exploded, the room darkened a little bit more. That made it easier to bear looking at the face that had failed so miserably to achieve the famous "Cherry Page Look." The look that was known all around the globe. The look belonging to one of the most beautiful women who has ever lived. The look that was not happening.

If only she had taken the time to listen.

9

THE SHRILL RINGING WOKE ME AT 6 A.M. AFTER THREE RINGS, I GOT UP in all my naked glory and answered the living-room phone. Cherry hadn't answered because she was in the shower, as I could tell by the sound of water coming from the bathroom. I thanked the lady desk clerk for the wake-up call, and got back in bed.

A knock at the door made me grab my bedspread to cover myself as I answered it. A cute little brunette stood in the hall with a bellman and a breakfast cart for three. He set it up on the dining table as Sally Allen introduced herself to me. She was all business, with her hair in a bun and designer glasses. She opened her slim black briefcase and tipped the bellman, as she'd probably done a thousand times before.

When he left, I said, "Excuse my attire, but it beats meeting me in my birthday suit."

"I'm not so sure that's true," Sally said with a smile. "I'll call down and have a robe sent up for you immediately."

She made the call, and we both sat down to breakfast. Me in my bedspread, Sally in her black business suit.

She said, "How was your flight, Chief Cooper?"

"I think memorable is the word, Sally, and please call me Coop."

"And how did you sleep—Coop?"

"I slept like a log. How 'bout you?"

"I was tossing and turning all night, so worried about Cherry and this madman. Please don't tell her though, she'll only fret needlessly."

"You're secret's safe with me," I said, reaching for a croissant. "I don't want to worry her either. She's got enough on her plate, what with the movie and this jerk playin' games."

"Well, she likes you, Coop, told me so herself not fifteen minutes ago. I'm so glad that you were the one chosen to watch over her."

"Me, too. I can assure you that she'll be just fine until we catch this guy."

Sally said, "After speaking with Mr. Feagin and the FBI, and meeting you, I'm confident of that," and joined me in buttering a croissant. She poured herself a cup of tea, and asked, "Coffee?" I nodded as I chewed, and she poured me a cup.

She said, "So sorry about the sleeping arrangements, but the FBI were adamant about it. We could rent two suites that connect by a common door, but then there would be two ways in, as opposed to having just the one this way. I hope you're all right with that."

"I'm fine with it. It's safer with just one door, and I slept comfortably through the night on the bed they provided." I took a sip of coffee, and said, "What's this I hear about a bulletproof car?"

She said, "The car—a Bentley—is out back behind the hotel, near the loading dock. They've graciously allowed us to keep it parked there, so you and Cherry can get in and out without alerting her fans, hopefully. It's good luck them letting you park there, because the employee parking lot is down the hill a bit, and underground, sort of. Looks like it could be quite spooky late at night. Oh, before I forget, here are the keys."

Taking them from her, I said, "Thanks, Sally, especially for the parking arrangement."

"My pleasure."

We ate in silence for a moment, and then the sound of the shower stopped. Sally excused herself, and went into the bedroom. I heard some hushed talk and giggling, but who knows what it was about. I just hoped they weren't making fun of the Yank.

A knock at the door signaled the arrival of my robe. After thanking the bellman, I closed the door, dropped the bedspread and put the robe on quickly. Not a second too soon, as Cherry and Sally came in at just that moment.

Cherry was barefoot and in her robe, too, and her wet hair was down in big curls around her shoulders. She looked as good without her makeup as she did with it, I thought. And the legs weren't too shabby, either. In fact, I was staring at them as I tied my robe shut.

"Oh, dash it all, Sally, we've missed the show," Cherry said, which brought more giggles.

"How old are you people?" I asked in my mockest fatherly tone.

Yet more giggles, then Cherry said, "Shower's all yours, Cooper." To Sally, "I'm completely famished. Let's tuck in."

With that said, they both sat down and started filling their plates with eggs, sausages and tomatoes.

Cherry said, "What a lovely fry-up, Sal. Just what the doctor ordered. Thanks for getting my tea, you darling girl."

"Just doing my job," Sally replied.

They started eating, so I threw the spread on the bed, grabbed some jeans, clean boxers, and a tee shirt from my suitcase, and headed for the shower. The condition of the bedroom surprised me more than a little bit; Cherry's bed was made, and all her clothes were put away. I knew for a fact that no maid had been in there to clean up yet. I thought, This one's okay for a pampered movie star.

When I was finished showering, I dressed and came back to the table. There was still plenty of food, and I filled my plate. Sally poured more coffee for me, and said, "Coop, I was just reminding Cherry you're to be at the Candler Community Theater by eight o'clock. It's located in a section of town known as Little Five Points. From what I understand, it's a small Bohemian community, lots of art and music. I've printed directions and phone numbers, so you should have no trouble. I'm quite sure—or, I assume—there's a directional system in the Bentley, as well. There are also some brochures on the coffee table—local food delivery, shopping, that sort of thing. I always make sure whenever we travel to have local places to go, and—hmm, that's not such a good idea now, is it? Right. Well, anyway, I must handle some errands, and meet with some very boring people. Call me if you need anything a'tall, Coop."

She stood, kissed the top of Cherry's wet head, and smiled at me as she walked over to and out the door.

I checked the directions, and saw that Sally was obviously very good at her job. The directions were a computer printout, with every turn designated, along with the mileage between each one. There were also phone numbers for everyone in town from the looks of it.

Cherry said, "The studio has rented the theater so we can have a few days of rehearsal before we begin filming."

"Oh, okay. That makes sense. I'm interested to see how the process works. Do you always rehearse before you start to film?"

"It depends on the director. A few like to just go out and start banging away, but that's rare. Our director, Chuck Guinness, likes to have all his ducks in a row before shooting. He's very much like Hitchcock in that way."

I said, "I'll start my acting career right now, and act like I know what you're talkin' about."

She smiled, took a drink of her tea, and said, "I'll bore you with the facts concerning Hitchcock when we're not in such a bind time-wise. I have a feeling we're going to be spending a lot of long days and nights together, and we shall have need of subjects for conversation."

"You're the boss."

She looked me over, and said, "Oh, am I now? Hmmm. I know only a very little bit about you, Cooper, but one thing is obvious: your acting skills are impeccable."

We made our way down to the back of the Ritz in the service elevator, and as we were almost to the loading dock, I realized I'd left my wallet in the suite. I leave my apartment back home without my wallet at least once a week, if not more—must be old age setting in.

I said, "I forgot my wallet. Be right back."

"I'll go with you," Cherry said.

She looked nervous, so I touched her arm and said, "No need." I stuck my head in the door of the small security office, and motioned to a big black guy whose name tag identified him as Lewis. One of several people hired on as extra security, he was armed and looked plenty dangerous. He came out and I left Cherry in his charge; Lewis was more than happy to watch her, and I knew she was in good hands.

I took the service elevator up, retrieved my wallet, and stepped back into the hall. A few doors down, I saw a pretty, plump brunette dressed in a businesslike gray suit. She was wearing small earphones and dancing wildly to music only she could hear. Humping and pumping to the beat, she put her key-card in the door, then stopped immediately when she turned and noticed me watching. Embarrassed, she smiled, shrugged her shoulders, and slipped into her room. I made it back down to the security office in a matter of minutes, and after Cherry finished signing autographs, we left and got in the Bentley.

It was a gorgeous spring morning in Atlanta, a real Chamber of Commerce special: sunny, warm, with low humidity. The drive to the theater was easy and pleasant, Cherry and I talking as if we'd known each other forever. She sat up in the front seat with me, refusing when I tried to open the back door for her. For a young international movie star, she was really much more down-to-earth than I had expected.

The Bentley was an Arnage T, deep blue in color and ridiculously luxurious. It had a burr walnut dash and light gray leather seats that felt like butter. The tremendous surge of power I felt when I accelerated was something I could get used to with no problem. There was indeed a navigational system, and every other gadget a guy could want. The sound system was extraordinary, so I found a classical station for our soundtrack, and we motored along like royalty.

Halfway to the theater, I realized that I hadn't called Penny yet, and mentally braced myself for the butt-chewing I would receive when I *did* call. But that would have to wait. The company, the car, and the day were all too fine for me to worry about my girlfriend killing me.

We arrived at the theater right on time, and found a group of thirty or more photographers and reporters in front. Another twenty or thirty Cherry fanatics were behind a line of security men, and they all started yelling and waving when they recognized the object of their affection.

As we got out and headed towards the front door, I held Cherry's arm, and she said, "I usually talk to the fans at a moment like this."

"Not today. Sorry, boss."

She nodded, and smiled and blew kisses as we passed the throng.

Inside the theater, Cherry introduced me to her director and several members of the cast. No one mentioned my gun, or asked why I wore it. Everyone was friendly except for Guinness, who seemed to be in a world of his own. Before I mentioned it, Cherry said, "Don't mind Chuck, he's not a rude man, just very involved and on edge right now. First day, and all that. Everyone wants a piece of the director, and there's only so much of him to go 'round."

In the lobby was a table with doughnuts, muffins, bagels, fruit, coffee, and tea, and several members of the cast were standing around it eating and drinking. Cherry and I went over and got a tea for her and a coffee for me.

A young man with a clipboard entered the lobby from the auditorium and boomed loudly, "Okay, people, time for the first table read."

The cast gathered around and sat down at a long table in the center of the stage, and began running over lines as Guinness made suggestions and offered encouragement. There was a lot of laughter and good-natured ribbing, and Cherry held her own. Preoccupied with the stalker, I had no idea what the movie was about from hearing them read their lines. All I could tell was that Cherry was unquestionably the star, and everyone seemed to love her.

I had hoped that I might see something or someone suspicious, but nothing caught my eye. It was just a happy bunch of actors going about their jobs, as far as I could tell.

Then it hit me that they were just that—actors—and wouldn't give anything away even if one of them was the stalker.

I decided to just listen and guard my employer's body.

At a little after noon, the same young clipboard guy who had boomed earlier called for the lunch break, and Cherry came over to the side of the stage where I was sitting on a folding chair.

I asked, "Would you like to go get some lunch, or do you have time?"

"Craft service has set up lunch in the lobby. Come on, let's get there before it's all gone."

"And 'craft service' would be . . . ?"

Cherry pulled me from my chair, and said, "They're the good people who supplied the food and drinks that were set up on the stage earlier. When we go on location, we'll have a chef and catered meals as well. Lunch on location will be even better than what we have here, and what we have here is quite nice."

We walked down the steps of the stage and headed for the lobby, where a remarkable spread was set on the tables. There were several types of eats, including vegetarian fare, all kinds of sandwiches, fruit and salad fixings, the ever-present English tea, quite a few brands of bottled soft drinks on ice, even some Mexican dishes. I was in hog heaven, and I do mean "hog." Free food always makes my day; I'm a man of simple tastes. Just give me a buffet and a room full of actresses, and I'm happy.

The executive producer, who'd seemed nice during the table read, came over to the back row, where Cherry and I were sitting with our food, and tried to horn in on our conversation. He was a real dandy, or at least *he* thought so. He was wearing black leather pants and a shiny purple shirt, and was doing his best to hit on Cherry. Obviously British, his pick-up lines sounded better than most would-be playboys, but she was not impressed.

At one point, she turned to me, her back to the Limey Casanova, and crossed her eyes as she denied his third request for a date of some kind after rehearsal. I didn't laugh, but it was difficult to keep a straight face.

When he finally gave up and walked down to the front of the stage, I asked what his name was.

Cherry said, "That creature is Lawrence Lyndon-Bowen, a marginally successful producer, and a true pussy-hound."

Chuckling, I said, "Why Miss Page, such language. I was very impressed with Lawrence what's-his-face. He's quite charming. If you're an idiot."

She said, "I'm always amazed at men like that, who think no one sees through them. But I guess there are women who find that smarmy approach appealing. Actually, I don't know of anyone who has ever fallen for his tired pick-up lines, but I know he always hits on the women with whom he works. I think he's overcompensating for a lack of confidence."

I agreed, and we went back to eating. Cherry to her turkey on whole wheat, and me to my plate of Mexican everything.

Almost the entire cast was sitting here and there inside the theater in small groups, munching away happily, when a bloodcurdling scream came from somewhere backstage.

I stood, pulled my gun and told Cherry to drop her food and get down on the floor. She quickly complied, and was looking up at me from her crouching position when one of the actresses—still screaming

—came running out from the backstage area and fainted on the stage.

From behind a curtain, smoke began pouring into the stage area, and someone yelled, "Get a fire extinguisher!" and the place basically went nuts. A few male members of the cast ran towards the stage, and everyone else headed in the opposite direction at top speed. I noted that Mr. Lyndon-Bowen quickly moved away from the danger.

Cherry and I headed out to the lobby, and I got Neal on my cell as fast as I could. Within a couple of minutes two Atlanta police officers and four FBI agents were on the scene, guns drawn, moving towards the backstage area. In another few minutes, more police had set up a defensive perimeter around the theater.

We watched as a couple of firefighters came in the front door and hustled inside the theater to assess the situation. It turned out to be a small fire—mostly smoke—and was easily handled with the fire extinguisher on hand. The stage manager with the clipboard came out and nervously told us that all was under control, so Cherry and I went inside the theater again and sat in the back row, watching the action as if it was a play. We didn't say much, and I was just about to ask her what the film was about, to take her mind off of the action, when my cell rang.

"Hello?" I said.

"Hey bud, it's me again," Neal said. "The FBI found out where the last threatening message came from. It's a house near Little Five Points, owned by one Marianne Ensberg. We're trying to contact her, but haven't been able to. At least we didn't find a corpse this time. And her place is even cleaner than the last; not a shred of evidence has been found. I'll call you as soon as I know more."

We hung up, and I knew more almost immediately.

10

Watching the action from a parked car thirty yards up the street was such an amusing way to pass the time. The crowd was growing by the minute, additional morons attracted by the noise and activity.

If only the firefighters could have been wearing black coats with yellow stripes, like the ones in New York City. That would have reinforced the notion that the place was nothing more than a hive, with all the mindless little bees droning around in circles.

Clearly, no one was in control of the situation. There was simply seemingly endless movement. The effect was hilarious, and every few minutes the horn of the parked car sounded when the hilarity was especially effective; it simply couldn't be helped!

Like when a pair of FBI agents arrived, and one of them tripped over a fire hose that had never even been used, as the small backstage fire had been extinguished ten minutes before the truck had arrived. Or when a particularly affected young woman who was probably an actress had run out and vomited on the sidewalk. The looks of disgust on the faces of some of the bees near her were priceless, and the car horn hooted in response as if it had a mind of its own. Not one of the idiots ever turned to see who was honking the horn, or acknowledged the bleats in any way.

Hilarious.

Setting the blaze and walking away unnoticed had proven again how easy it was to move undetected among these imbeciles. And, it was definitely fun watching all the mayhem that had been inflicted with the fire, and all, but the big question still remained unanswered: Where was the Queen Bee herself?

Was she in the old theater bathroom with the corpse, holding in her own sick? Was she crying from the pressure of knowing that her refusal to allow herself to be sacrificed was directly responsible for another person's death?

Or was she—and this was the most likely scenario—inside the theatrical hive, surrounded by her drones, unaffected by all the commotion? Yes, that must be it. Nothing affected the Queen.

The next message would have to hit even closer to home.

11

THE DIRECTOR'S ASSISTANT, A TALL, SLENDER BRUNETTE OF AROUND twenty-five, came hustling up the aisle from the stage towards us, and Cherry introduced her to me as Lynne Prather. Wringing her hands nervously, Lynne asked if she could have a word with me in private.

I looked at Cherry and she said, "Go on, Cooper, I'll be fine here for a minute or two. But don't go too far."

Lynne and I walked out into the now empty lobby, and her nervous hands moved to her short hair, tucking both sides behind her ears. She said in a low voice, "There's a dead woman in the backstage ladies' room."

"Oh, great. I knew somethin' bad was goin' on, but not that."

"It gets worse," she said. "Her throat has been cut, and the body has been dressed and made up to resemble Cherry. It's the most gruesome thing I've ever—her eyes are closed—but her eyelids have—they have green 'eyes' painted on them, to look like Cherry's, I guess. She's also dressed like Cherry was in her last film. Same outfit: little black dress, handbag, right down to the shoes. The woman has—*had*—a similar body type, and she's—there's a red wig. Should we tell Cherry, or what? I just don't know what to—"

"How many other people know about this?"

Trying to remember, she looked at the floor, and said, "I—I don't know. The police are there. Her throat is—the green eyes—you have to do something!"

"Calm down," I said, looking around to make sure we were still alone. "Stay with Cherry while I go backstage, and tell her that the police want to talk to me. Do *not* tell her anything else, understand?"

"Yes, sir. I won't say anything."

She started to cry softly, so I said, "Listen, forget about staying with Cherry. Go outside and wait 'til I come for you, okay?"

She nodded her head yes, and walked towards the front door like a zombie.

I walked back to Cherry, and said, "Listen. The cops wanna talk to me backstage, so sit here and wait. Don't move, I'll be back as soon as I can."

"No way I'm sitting here without you," she said. "I want to know what is going on here, and right this minute! Now, I mean it. Let's go talk to the police together."

"Cherry, listen to me. I'm sure it'll be nothing more than routine questions and stuff. You'll just be a distraction. To them, and to me."

"I'm going with you, Cooper. I am putting my foot down here; I'm going to find out what is going on. After all, it has to do with me, yeah?"

We glared at each other for a moment before I gave in, and said, "Okay, you win. But don't say I didn't warn ya."

We went backstage, and the smoke that remained from the fire made us both cough. I identified myself to a young male officer who directed us to the man in charge, Sergeant Traylor. He was standing in front of the ladies' room door, making notes on a pad. A burly man of around forty, he looked at Cherry, and said, "I don't think you oughta be seein' this, ma'am. It's not a pretty sight."

"All right, sir, I'll not get in your way. I just want to know what is happening."

I said, "Cherry, there's a dead woman behind this door, and she's most likely the latest victim of your—your fan."

Cherry backed up slowly, shaking her head as if it was all too much for her. She found a seat in an old wooden chair, and put her face in her hands. I asked if she was okay, and she waved me off, her eyes closed. The sergeant and I entered the restroom and I got my first glimpse of just how sick the stalker really was.

Marianne Ensberg's body was propped up on a toilet seat, her legs spread wide, the black dress hiked up to expose her naked privates. Her head was at a weird angle, due to the fact that the cut to her throat was so deep. There was blood only on her body and clothes, which meant that she'd been killed somewhere else and brought to the restroom. A wavy bright red wig was on her head, and just as Lynne had said, her closed eyelids were colored with bright green circles around black dots, representing Cherry's famous eyes. Written on the stall beside the body in black magic marker were three words: "Baal's Only One."

Traylor asked, "You have any idea who this poor girl might be?"

"Yes, I'm pretty sure her name is Marianne Ensberg. The FBI just traced another death threat to her house. I assume you know about the threats Ms. Page has been getting?"

"Yeah. I'm part of the task force lookin' into it."

At that moment, two men walked in carrying large metal briefcases. Traylor said, "These guys are part of the task force."

I nodded.

He said, "Let's get outta here and let 'em get to work."

As we walked out of the ladies' room, Traylor led me out of earshot of Cherry, and said, "The fire was started in a dressing room down the hall that's usually used by someone who isn't too important, according to the building manager. That's why it's so small. Whoever did this musta been in here last night. I'm no expert, but I've seen enough corpses to know this one's been dead quite awhile. But the fire was started only a short time ago, so it's obvious that the perp likes to live dangerously. Takes a lot of nerve—or not much brains—to pull a stunt like this. That gives me hope that he'll screw up sooner rather than later. It also points a finger at anyone who was in the theater this mornin'. I called you back here 'cause I want you to be on the lookout for anyone involved with the film who acts strange. And, I wanted to let you know that we're doin' all we can to catch this bastard."

I could read the sincerity in his eyes, and it gave me a good feeling to know he wasn't just going through the motions. Sometimes, *wanting* to get the job done—as opposed to not caring about it—can go a long way.

I said, "Thanks for everything y'all are doing, Sergeant. I'm sure we'll see each other again, and we'll figure this thing out before too long. I'm gonna go ahead and take Ms. Page back to her hotel. Here's my card, call me anytime you need me or have news."

He looked at my card and said, "Will do, Chief Cooper. You take real good care of that young lady. We don't want Atlanta to be her final restin' place."

12

I TOOK CHERRY BY THE ARM AND LED HER TO A QUIET SPOT IN THE BACK corner of the theater, and we sat down, as far away from the noise and action as we could get. She was quiet and withdrawn after going through the ordeal of another dead body being found, and I gave her a few minutes to be alone with her thoughts. I was putting my own thoughts together, trying to decide the best way to discuss what had happened over the last few days, and especially the last few minutes.

Before I could speak, she slid down in her seat, and said, "That idea you had about telling the media I no longer have a computer simply won't work."

"Why not?"

"I don't know why I didn't think of it before, but I suppose with everything that's been taking place, I merely forgot. When I first started to gain recognition in Britain several years back, I mentioned on a chat show that my cell phone had been destroyed when I dropped it in the street and a taxicab ran over it. I thought it was an amusing story, and told it only because I had run out of things to say. I was oblivious to the incredible power of the telly, having had almost no experience whatsoever with it before that night. The next day, the movie studio and the chat show each received over a dozen brand-new cell phones from all the big-name manufacturers—and 'small-name' as well—hoping I would be seen using their product in public. So you see, if I were to say on CNN that my computer is no longer working, well, I'm sure you can see where I'm going with this, yeah?"

I said, "Yeah, I see what you mean."

"Maybe we could say that I deleted the instant messenger from my computer, and can no longer receive messages."

I thought for a moment, and said, "That might be hard to slip into an interview. And besides, our sick friend would only come up with an even sicker way to get his messages to you. And at least the FBI has a chance, no matter how slim, of finding evidence at one of the murder scenes."

Cherry said, "I still can't believe there's someone out there murdering people simply to get my attention. It's just not something one thinks can ever happen."

She leaned forward in her seat and put her head in her hands again, clearly exhausted from the stress of it all. I wanted to comfort her, to give her a hug and tell her that everything would be okay, but I decided not to cross that boundary.

Instead, I said, "That whole 'tell the media your computer died' was a dumb idea, anyway. We can't trick this monster into just giving up. I think we're dealing with a much more intelligent and dangerous creature than I first thought. But you can't allow it to get to you like this. There may be some really rough days ahead, and you hafta hang tough. I know that's easy for me to say, but it's true."

She slowly stood up from her seat, and like a child, crawled into my lap. She put her head on my shoulder and her arms around my neck. Her famous red hair smelled of peaches.

So much for boundaries.

We sat in silence that way for ten minutes before a young female police officer came over and said, "Sorry to bother you, but someone has obviously told the news crews what's going on with the stalker, because they're asking about the threats and the murder victims." She smiled weakly, and said, "I want to make it clear to you that it wasn't me who told. I just thought you should know."

"Thank you, Officer," I said, and tried to gently pull Cherry's arms free from my neck.

She was having none of that.

"Cherry. Listen, kiddo, we need to get outta here. The vultures have you in their sights, and if we don't move fast, we could be under siege in no time. You really gotta help me out here; you're the expert at avoiding crowds of fans. Got any bright ideas?"

She looked up at me groggily, and I realized that she had fallen asleep in my arms. I felt so sorry for her at that moment. It really made me aware for the first time how deeply she was being affected by the horror that was following her. The only escape she had from the constant pressure she was facing was sleep, and I felt her sadness as she could barely summon the energy to move.

There I was, sitting with a world-class beauty curled up in my lap, and all I could feel was sympathy. I selfishly wished that Penny was there to see it, so she'd quit being so jealous. Cherry was fast becoming like a little sister to me. At least, I guess that's what I was feeling, being that I'm an only child. I do know that it felt really nice to be so close to a woman without wanting to without trying to . . . let's just say it was a nice moment.

Yawning and releasing me, she said, "Cooper, did you say something about 'avoiding fans and vultures'?"

"Yes, Cherry, I did. Somebody has leaked the information about the death threats and the murders to the newshounds. We need to get you outta here, and fast."

She shook her head slowly. Thinking of her bright assistant, I asked, "What would Sally do if she was here?"

"Not to worry," she said, suddenly clear-eyed and calmer-looking. She stood up and stretched before taking a seat next to me. "Put out a call for Will Underwood. He's my secret weapon and my brilliant hair and makeup artist. We shall use a little trick Will and I keep up our sleeves for moments like this. He's probably outside with the police, as far away from the danger as possible. Would you please go and see if Lynne can find him?"

I stood, and said, "At your service, m'lady."

She groaned softly, and rolled her eyes.

"Sorry," I continued, "It's just that I've always wanted to say that to a beautiful British broad."

This got her to smile, and even laugh a little. Cherry was looking at me and still smiling when I reached the aisle and checked backed to see if she was watching.

Maybe I was being a bit hasty with all that "little sister" stuff.

13

I FOUND LYNNE AND TOLD HER WE NEEDED THE MAKEUP GUY, AND SHE said to follow her. Cherry had been correct in her assumption regarding his whereabouts: Will Underwood was out front standing so close to a policeman that the two of them looked like Siamese twins. Except for the fact that the cop was about two feet taller.

I walked up to him and got Lynne to introduce us, then filled him in on the situation. In a heavy Cockney accent he said he knew exactly what Cherry wanted, and he walked over to a large SUV and opened the back.

He reached inside and brought out a substantial black case, and said, "This is where I keep what she's looking for. I have it with me at all times. Never know when she'll feel the need to disappear."

"Disappear?"

"You'll see what I mean soon enough," he said. "Inside this case is all I need to do the magic; it's mostly filled with the 'disappearing act.' Most actresses demand that their poor makeup people carry tons of stuff 'round with them, but since Cherry requires so little makeup, I don't need a lot of cases for my tools and product. She also requires very little hair styling most days, so I do that for her as well. Two jobs in one."

"Must be pretty nice doin' those two jobs," I said.

"Oh, it's *brilliant* having these two jobs. The only thing that would make them better would be if she was a he."

He took the case, which was nearly as big as he was, and we walked into the theater.

Cherry was waiting on the steps of the stage, and Will handed me the case before trotting down the aisle and giving her a bear hug. Well, maybe not a bear hug. The guy probably weighs a hundred pounds soaking wet. More like a poodle hug.

They seemed to draw courage from each other as they held

hands, and walking up the steps to the stage, they moved towards the backstage dressing-room area.

Cherry turned and called out, "Cooper! Hurry up with the case! Don't you dare leave this lady-in-waiting!"

It was my turn to groan, and I followed the happy duo back to the dressing room area. Whatever it took to make her feel less afraid and more secure, I was going to do it.

Watching her makeup being done actually turned out to be a lot more interesting than I thought it would be.

Cherry, Will, and I made our way past the police and crime scene workers to one of the upstairs dressing rooms. It was a struggle for me to get the makeup case up the old iron spiral staircase that led to the second floor, but I managed.

Cherry seemed to have caught her second wind, emotionally, and reacted only slightly when we passed the ladies' restroom before climbing the stairs. Will really had a calming effect on her, and he kept her mind off of the events of the morning by chatting and joking, telling her how terrible she looked without his handiwork. It was obvious that they were close friends, and watching her come back to life was a great relief.

As soon as we were in the dressing room, Will told me to place the case on a chair by the door, and he started to pull things out of it. A gray wig was first, followed by some tattered clothes and shoes, and what appeared to be a rubber or plastic mask.

The mask turned out to be an old lady's head that had been made from a mold of Cherry's face; when Will put it on her and applied makeup and the gray wig, she aged fifty years. Ten minutes later, Cherry was dressed in a padded suit that added sixty or seventy pounds to her figure. The end product was a shabbily dressed old woman that no one on Earth would recognize as Cherry Page.

Will looked at me and asked, "Now do you see what I meant by 'disappearing act'?"

"I sure do. You're a master of your craft, Will. She could walk out of here and look straight in the cameras and never be noticed. If I hadn't seen it with my own eyes, I never would've believed it."

Cherry said in an old lady's voice, "Well, sonny, what's our next move? I ain't got a lotta time left in this world. Don't wanna waste it sittin' around in some musty old theater."

"Amazing," I said. "Okay, lemme think a minute."

Will adjusted Cherry's gray wig, and put a pair of gigantic, thick-lensed black eyeglasses on her prosthetic nose while I was planning our escape. The final touch was an old, battered hat with big flowers on top. It was clear that they'd done this many times before; Will had it down to a science.

Cherry would turn her head, or look up or down as he worked, knowing exactly what came next. It was an interesting thing for a Florida police chief to witness, that's for sure. I couldn't wait to tell Penny about it.

I came up with an idea, and said, "Will, you go out first, and get your SUV started and ready to go. I'll walk Cherry out the door, and over to you. Drive her up to the grocery store at the end of the street. It's called the Piggly Wiggly, you can't miss it. Park in the lot and wait for me. I'll get the Bentley, and come pick her up as fast as I can. Does that sound like a plan?"

Will said, "I love it when a man takes charge, don't you, Miss Cherry Page?"

"I surely do. Especially this man."

I carried the case down the spiral staircase for Will, and he kissed Cherry on the cheek and headed for the exit, case in hands. As Cherry and I made our way past the same officers and workers that we'd passed no more than thirty minutes earlier, not one of them gave her a second look. The transformation was absolute, and if it fooled the police, the news people would pose no problem.

Cherry had the walk down, too; she bent over slightly, and shuffled like an elderly woman, putting a hand on her back every few steps. It was good stuff.

When we got near the front doors, she asked, "Cooper, do you think I'll be able to get work when I'm this age?"

"Cherry, I think you'll be able to get work at any age—no wonder my girlfriend loves you so much."

"Girlfriend? Why, Cooper, do tell."

"Later, old lady. I promised her I'd introduce you to her, by the way, but for now let's get you outta here and back to the hotel."

"My, my. You young people. Always in such a hurry."

I opened the door, and we stepped into the bright sunlight. The lot was packed with news vans, camera crews, a fire truck, cop cars, and a big crowd of onlookers. Everyone turned to see who was coming out of the theater, and Cherry began coughing and hacking, making a terrible racket. All eyes turned away quickly, no longer interested.

I held her arm as if she was on her last legs and we slowly walked and shuffled through the crowd without a single person saying a word to us. Cherry coughed and hacked the loudest as we passed right in front of a video news camera, and the poor cameraman backed away in disgust. It was hard to keep from laughing, but I saw Will's SUV idling by the curb, and led Old Lady Page over to it. She played her part to the end, grunting loudly, and yelling at me in her old-lady voice as I put her in the car.

It was an award-winning performance.

14

IT TOOK AWHILE FOR ME TO LEAVE THE THEATER, AND BY THE TIME I got the Bentley down to the Piggly Wiggly, Cherry had taken off her disguise and was back to her gorgeous self. She jumped into the passenger's side, and we waved to Will as I pulled into traffic.

She was quiet for the first few minutes, and I didn't disturb her. I've had a lot of experience with real live killers, but I knew she hadn't.

As we slowed for a red light, she finally said, "I'm sorry if I caused trouble for you today."

"What? What trouble? You didn't kill anybody that I know of."

"I shouldn't have pressed you to take me backstage with you. I acted like a real brat, and I'm terribly sorry."

"Cherry. Get this through that thick red mane of yours. I'm here for you, not the other way around. You have nothing to be sorry for. In fact, I'm the one who should be sorry. I shouldn't have let you know what was going on until we were safely away from there. You have enough to worry about as it is." I paused for a moment, and then said, "Tell you what. Let's both forget about it, and move on. Whatta ya say?"

"I say that's a fine idea, and let's move on."

The light changed and I said in my best cheesy British butler voice, "As you wish, madam. Will there be anything else?"

"That's the worst excuse for an English accent I've ever heard."

"Critics. You're all alike."

We rode back to the hotel, keeping the conversation light. Cherry had gotten over the gloominess that she'd shown in the theater, and was talking up a storm. We were discussing what we should order from room service for supper, when she sat up straight in her seat, and said, "Oh, no! I can't believe it!"

"Can't believe what?"

"I have to make an appearance tonight at a function for my charity foundation. I completely forgot about it until just this instant! *Balls!*"

Hoping to help, I said, "Looks like I'm not the only one who forgets stuff." When she didn't respond, I asked, "Do you really have to go? Can't you make some lame excuse and bow out gracefully?"

"No, no, *no*! The foundation is very important to me. It's one of the only things I do that makes me feel like my life has any real value. It's a cause that's very dear to my heart: children's leukemia. You'll hear this again later tonight, but when I was fourteen, my best friend died from leukemia after a horrible period of almost a year. Her name was Poppy, and she was the best friend I've ever had. It almost killed me, too, when she passed on."

I said, "Now I see where your username on the instant messenger comes from."

Cherry replied, "Exactly. And I'm sure you can also see why this evening means so much to me, yeah? The money we raise goes not only to research and development, but pays medical bills for children who've contracted the disease. It's *so* much more important than some silly film or play that I might be doing. If I don't show up there tonight, it would be like throwing money away that's badly needed for research. It's not an ego thing; it's just that we make five to ten times more money when the 'big movie star' makes an appearance. I simply *must* go, there's no getting around it. There'll be makeup to put on, hair to be done, and a stupid designer gown to squeeze into as well. Bloody *hell*!"

Not knowing what to say, I tried the reality approach, "I sympathize, but I don't know what to tell ya. Looks like we'll hafta suck it up, and go to this deal. Where is it, by the way?"

She frowned, and said, "I'm not really sure. Some sort of museum that's high, as I recall. Sally will know all the details and have everything under control, so there's no worry there. She reminded me of it this morning over breakfast while you were in the shower, but it just completely escaped my mind."

I said, "Well, with everything that's been goin' on—especially what happened at the theater—you're allowed a brain freeze. Just take it easy, and we'll get you through the night without too much pain."

She stared out the window for a moment before saying, "This happens more than I'd care to admit, me forgetting things, that is to say. My schedule can be utterly ridiculous at times, and it's just—I *so* wanted to have a nice, quiet evening in the suite. Maybe watch a DVD, or some telly. No cameras, no makeup, no people, no appointments. Just a few hours to myself, some quiet time, know what I mean? Sometimes I just wish—oh, I'm such an idiot at times! Forgive me, Cooper. You must think me a stupid, spoiled child to carry on like this, but after the events of today . . ."

She rubbed her temples and took a deep breath, no doubt trying to summon the strength it would take to put the day behind her and face the night ahead. I drove the next few minutes without speaking, waiting for her to calm down. I almost felt sorry for her, but this was the path she'd chosen, and all that other philosophical gibberish. And besides, she'd made a ton of money doing something millions of young women would kill to do.

Then I felt sorry for myself when I realized that if she had to dress formally, I probably had to wear a tuxedo.

Balls, indeed.

Cherry's cell rang as we were pulling into our special parking spot in back of the Ritz.

"Hello? Yes, Sally, I just remembered. No, sweetie, it's certainly not your fault. You told me this morning, don't blame yourself. It just completely slipped my mind. Oh, good, that will do nicely; I love her designs. Yes, I'll tell him. Okay, my love, we'll see you there. Bye."

She sighed deeply, and said, "Sally's bought you a tuxedo and had it altered to fit. She took your suit from the suite, and gave it to wardrobe so they could make you look presentable. Everything you need is laid out on your bed for you."

"Oh, joy, a monkey suit of my very own. This day just keeps gettin' better and better."

"At least you don't have to wear hideous makeup and have your hair pushed and pulled for hours on end."

"Says who? I'll have you know I expect the full treatment from Will. Makeup, hair, the works. The hideouser, the better."

Trying her best to look mean, she said, "Oh, let's get on with it. Put me over your shoulder and carry me to my suite. I'm grown tired from all your silly demands."

"No way, sister, carry your own self. Get your vacant, forgetful head out of the clouds, and let's go make some money for Poppy."

Cherry looked as if she might cry for a second, then a huge smile came onto her face, and she leaned over and gave me a big kiss on the cheek.

"You're a darling man, Chief Cooper. And you're absolutely right. This night's for Poppy."

Back in the suite, we found everything that Sally had promised. A tux for me on my bed, a gown for Cherry on her bed, and a full set of maps and phone numbers for the High Museum of Art, where the soiree was to take place. Cherry had been right, in a manner of speaking; it was "some sort of museum that's high."

She went into her bedroom as I checked the map and found that the ride wouldn't be too bad. The Ritz was turning out to be pretty much centrally located as far as our itinerary went. We were expected to arrive no later than eight thirty, which gave us plenty of time, as it was straight-up five o'clock. Or at least, it gave *me* plenty of time—Cherry was another story.

I turned on the TV to a local station, and saw that our little escapade at the theater was the lead story on the news. The cat was out of the bag. Cherry Page was in Atlanta, and was being stalked by a serial murderer. I tried the other local stations; two more also had the news on, and were breathlessly telling the story of Cherry's situation.

I called her in to watch, and just as she came into the room, the screen was filled with Cherry in her old-lady costume walking in front of the camera. The sheer lunacy of it all had us both laughing, and we forgot for a moment that a madman was hunting her.

I switched around to the other stations, and each one had a glimpse of us walking through the crowd, acting our brains out. Cherry laughed until she cried, and then she cried until she laughed, finally dropping to the floor in a heap. She lay on her back, staring at the ceiling, and said, "Get me to a nunnery. I surrender."

I took her hands and pulled her up to her feet, and gave her a swat on her rear end.

"Get that thing in gear, young lady; you have a show to do tonight. Lemme call Sally and see if Will is on his way."

A knock at the door, and a singsong voice calling "Miss Cherry Pa-age" announced Will's arrival.

I walked over and let him in, and he blew into the room. Well, maybe that's a bad choice of words. Anyway, he was ready for action again, this time carrying a smaller case.

He asked, "How are you, mister bodyguard man? I see you got my girl home safe and sound."

"I'm fine, Will. Get our star ready for her big night, will ya?"

"That's what I'm here for, cowboy," he said, and sidled over to his gal pal.

Cherry had quickly recovered from her attack of near hysteria, and they went into her room to get her ready for the evening.

A moment later, she called to me, "Cooper, would you care for a haircut? Will is dying to get his hands in your hair."

My hair *is* always a little long and shaggy, so I agreed, and fifteen minutes later I had a really sharp new look. Will is an expert, and I wondered how much it would have cost me to get a haircut like that in London. I thanked him; he said it was a pleasure, and went back into the bedroom to attend to Cherry.

In a few minutes, I heard the shower running, so I checked out my tux and accessories while I waited for my shot at the hot water. The tux was an Armani, and while I don't know a lot about fashion, I know enough to appreciate quality. The wardrobe people had done a great job with the alterations, and it fit me as well as my one and only suit.

I went to the prom twice in high school, like most people, but unlike most people, I didn't wear a tuxedo because I was too cool for that, being on the football team. We all went dressed in our Gulf Front letterman jackets, and looked like complete idiots, unbeknownst to us at the time.

But those unfashionable days were behind me. I was escorting an international movie star to an affair catering to the hoity-toity types of Atlanta, and I was wearing Armani, my friend.

I made a mental note to have my picture taken with Cherry at the museum. Penny would kill me twice if I didn't record the event for posterity.

15

THE HIGH MUSEUM OF ART STANDS BACK FROM THE STREET A WAYS, and the one it stands back from is the world-famous Peachtree Street. It's painted a brilliant white, and to me, it looked like what an architect might have designed in the thirties if he was trying to build something ultramodern.

From reading the brochure Sally left for me, I knew that it had won several architectural awards, and deserved each one. From the outside it looked very clean, with its rounded, partially glass front. Sophisticated is the word that came to mind. In the moonlight it shone like a big, white, Miami Beach hotel.

There was heavy security in the parking lot and at the front door, and I was relieved to see so many uniforms and weapons in attendance. I also saw several guys and one woman who I thought were probably FBI. Surely the stalker-freak wouldn't show up at such a gathering, but the extra help was appreciated.

The officers helped keep the news people away as we parked and headed towards the entrance. What had been a small group had now become a small mob. There must've been fifty photographers calling out to Cherry as we entered the museum.

Once inside, I was impressed even more. Part of the main floor is a four-story atrium, and wide, circular ramps go upward and around at a not-too steep angle. As you walk up you see art on the walls, and the people below. It's the perfect place for rich people to hang out with a movie star.

Cherry was absolutely stunning in a pale silvery gown that looked like something Marilyn herself would've worn. It had a low back, and showed off her cleavage just enough to draw every man's eye to that vicinity. Her glowing red hair was down, with her trademark wave in it. Cherry looked every bit the international star, and I looked pretty good myself, I must say, decked out in my Armani tux and new haircut.

In the ground-floor area, where most of the guests were gathered, there was a bar almost everywhere you looked. Any other time, I would have been tempted, but not while I was on duty, so the bars didn't really matter to me. What mattered was that several waiters were walking around passing out food, and there was a long buffet table in the back as well.

Huge mounds of giant shrimp, hor d'oeuvres of all kinds, and a big ice sculpture of three cherries with stems attached were in the center of the table. I mentally marked my territory as we came in. As soon as Cherry started her speech, her bodyguard was going to be gobbling.

Three photographers, and guests both male and female quickly surrounded Cherry. The interesting thing was that both genders seemed to want to be near her. The men were a given, but it's been my experience that gorgeous women usually are not warmly welcomed by other females. Especially when the gorgeous woman has the undivided attention of every husband, boyfriend, and male escort in the vicinity.

But I would find as the night went on that all the ladies' comments I overheard about Cherry were complimentary. In fact, they were all as taken with her as Penny is. It was definitely not what I had expected, but there it was: Everybody loves Cherry Page.

Except one sick bastard.

I stayed close to Cherry most of the time, constantly scouring the crowd around her. It was fascinating to watch her work the crowd, and I saw what she meant about her having to be there to make the big bucks for her foundation. If she had stayed away, the party would've been insufferably dull and lifeless. Half of the people looked like they were not long for this world; "Old Money" were the operative words. But with the fabulous Ms. Page in their midst, I could almost hear the rustling of paper in the checkbooks as they opened. The wealthy folk of Atlanta made more than generous donations in the name of their object of desire. We would find out later that the night was a huge success monetarily.

I even managed to get the official foundation photographer to snap a couple of pictures of Cherry and me standing by a Rothko, whoever he is. The photographer promised to send copies over to the Ritz as soon as possible, and I could see Penny hanging the framed prints on her living-room wall, smiling at me and not killing me.

The only thing that made it less than perfect for me was the awful music being poorly played by a four-piece combo. Their leader was a heavyset woman of probably sixty-five or so, dressed in a vast black dress that thankfully covered her entirely, who sat banging away on an ancient electric piano. The sound of the piano was so distorted that it sounded like it must have been dropped on concrete about a thousand times. That's the only thing that could've made it sound so bad, in my unprofessional opinion. But I seemed to be the only one who noticed. The big piano woman certainly didn't seem to care.

To the right of the big piano woman sat a guy of fifty or so in a metal folding chair, playing an electric bass. He looked like some derelict she'd picked up off the street, and was wearing what looked to be a forty-dollar tuxedo. I don't believe I've ever seen a more bored-looking human being, but he was actually the only good player in the band.

The drummer was tippy-tapping along, seemingly striking as many parts of his drum kit as he could at any given moment, and the effect was more confusing than rhythmic.

Last, and fighting for least, the diminutive guitar player wore large white Elton John-type glasses, and strummed a big, fat electric guitar that was half as big as he was. He was in dire need of talent, and a good tuning. His alleged playing left almost everything to be desired, and what I loosely call his "singing" was made even more annoying by the cheap, distorted P.A. system. But, to their credit, they seemed to know every song in the book—especially the irritating ones—and hardly took a break the entire night.

The crowd ignored them completely, and if anyone danced, they didn't bother to applaud. Just for laughs, I went up to them as they were taking one of their short pauses, and told them they'd "never sounded better." They all smiled and said thanks.

I don't think they got it.

Throughout the evening, nearly every guy in the place made a pass at Cherry, and I heard a lot of the lines they tried on her. Cherry defended herself brilliantly, and I don't think any of the dreamers were offended. Disappointed, definitely, but not offended. She often would use me as an excuse, explaining that I was her escort for the night, and if that didn't work, I became her boyfriend. In a couple of extreme cases I was designated as her fiancé, so a couple of the fellows really disliked me after that. Cherry would take my arm, or hold my hand when the water got rough, and I was, without question, the most despised man at the ball.

Let me give you an idea of what Cherry was dealing with the entire night:

Fat, bald guy, maybe fifty-five or sixty used this approach: "My business has me here in town for three more days, and I'd love to take you up in my helicopter."

Cherry said she "suffered terribly" from airsickness.

A fellow of perhaps thirty-five, athletic-looking, with a mass of curly gold locks, tried these lines: "Remember me? We've met before, last year in London at another of your charity foundation gatherings. I was able then—as well as now—to make huge contributions because I made my fortune in dot-com stocks, and was smart enough to cash out before the bubble burst. Maybe we could have dinner one night while you're in town?"

Cherry said, sorry, she didn't remember him, but she meets so many people, and no, her fiancé wouldn't like the idea of her going on a dinner date with another man. Especially a strong, handsome, rich, *smart* man.

The girl is good.

Short, stout, fortysomething guy tried a different tactic: "My mother just *adores* you, and she would be *so* happy if you would come with me to the nursing home for a visit. I could pack a picnic lunch, and the three of us could eat out by the lake at Greenwood. Can I call Mother and tell her it's a date?"

Cherry pulled me over next to her, and said (to me), "Darling, I want you to meet—I'm sorry, what was your name again? Oh, yes. Harold. Meet Harold, dear." To Harold: "Harold, this is my lover, Butch Hardmon." She got a hundred points for my new name.

Tall, slim dude, dressed in a formal western outfit, cowboy hat in hand, tried to rope the filly with these words: "Ma'am, I live on a nice spread just outside of town, near Marietta. I'd be honored if you'd let me take you to breakfast in the mornin', after we take in all the sights Atlanta has to offer tonight. Country-and-western music is my specialty. You like to line dance?"

Cherry said she had no line-dancing experience whatsoever, and skillfully denied his next request to "just relax and let him guide her into the land of rhythm and pleasure." I was introduced as her body-guard this time, so I looked at Cowboy Guy as menacingly as I could. He decided to hunt for another mare to corral.

Older gentleman, very short, probably eighty, distinguished-looking, thick silver hair, was one of my favorites, and Cherry's: "Young lady, my private jet is only a thirty-minute limousine ride away, and my yacht in Palm Beach only a short flight from there. I lost my wife last month, and am now free to offer you a life of lux-ury and excess beyond your wildest imaginings. Don't give me your answer now. Think it over and let me know before this evening is but a memory." With that said, he bowed, kissed her hand, and left with-out another word. Cherry waited until he was out of earshot before asking me which of the gentlemen she should choose to be her escort while in Atlanta.

I said, "Well, I can't decide between the cowboy and the little old chap you just talked to. You can't go wrong choosing either one of those guys."

"Mmm," she said. "It truly is quite a dilemma."

"Go with the old guy. You'll be a rich widow in no time," I said.

"Cooper, you're a true romantic."

At that moment, the lady in charge of the gathering came over and told Cherry that it was time for her speech. Cherry thanked her, excused herself, and went to the ladies' room to freshen up, which was totally unnecessary in my mind. But it was nice to see her feel-ing safe and happy in her natural environment, preparing herself to be the center of attention.

I was sure there would be plenty of time to feel unsafe and unhappy in the coming days.

16

LOIS LANGLEY ORDERED HER SECOND GIN MARTINI FROM THE BAR-
tender in the Ritz-Carlton Buckhead Lobby Lounge, and settled her
tab by charging it to her room. The day had been a long and trying
one, and she'd eaten at a Burger King on the way back to the hotel
after her downtown meeting. All she wanted to do now was finish
the martini and head up to her room for a long, hot soak.

A voice from beside her asked if she would mind passing the
bowl of spiced nuts, and Lois reached for it and placed it in front of
her neighbor. They struck up a genial conversation, and within ten
minutes were laughing and joking together like old friends.

Lois felt the stress of the day melting away as the discussion
turned to things of a more risqué nature. Maybe she wouldn't have
to be alone tonight after all.

Having intended to make the second martini her last, Lois surprised herself when she accepted the offer of a third, then a fourth,
and finally a fifth. It was nice to have someone else pay for her
drinks, so she wouldn't look like such a barfly when she handed in
her expense report back in Minneapolis. Besides, the companionship
was welcome, since she'd been through quite a long dry spell in the
romance department. Three and a half years without sex was too
long for anyone, especially when you were used to being in a relationship. A relationship that had been the best two years of her life.
And two out of four wasn't bad, she liked to say.

The barroom was becoming a bit fuzzy, so Lois asked her new
friend to come upstairs so they could continue their conversation
and see what else they might find to do. Two hundred-dollar bills left
on the bar by her new friend covered the tab and tip nicely and they
walked to the bank of elevators, Lois leaning on her escort for sup-
port.

When they got to her room, she had trouble inserting the key-card, and they both had a good laugh. Finally, it was in the slot and they were in the dark room. The only light came through the open curtains from the streetlights outside, and the light from the hall.

She closed the door, and as she turned back around, she found herself in an embrace, her lips being kissed softly. She kissed back, harder, and they staggered to the bed, still locked at the lips. Her new friend turned on a bedside lamp and smiled at her, looking her up and down.

As a rule, Lois was shy about undressing in front of other people. She was what her mother called "full-bodied" and her ex called "fat." Uncertain about her looks, she had always wished she were slender, and blond instead of brunette. But the martinis had washed all those feelings away. The two quickly undressed, and were in a clinch before Lois could catch her breath. There was nothing subtle about it, no need for any more talk or attempts at seduction. They both wanted the same thing, and they both wanted it five minutes ago.

Half an hour later, as they lay spent and entangled on top of the bedspread, Lois asked, "Now, what was it you wanted me to Google for you again? That last drink seems to have made me a little scatterbrained. Not to mention what my second orgasm did."

Chuckling, her lover said, "I was hoping to find some information on a character called 'Baal.' I saw that program on the History Channel about ancient deities, and it got me interested, remember?"

"Oh, yeah, now I remember. That sounds interesting to me, too. Just let me boot up my laptop, and we'll have all we ever needed to know about Baal in no time."

"Great. But that can wait for a little while longer. Let's stay here in bed and try and get you orgasm number three."

Lois said, "Three? Hell, let's go for five or six!"

"Sounds good to me. Let's do it like it's the last time we'll ever do it."

17

CHERRY SPOKE FOR TEN MINUTES TO AN ENTHRALLED AND HUSHED audience, and did herself and Poppy proud. The speech was entirely off the cuff, and obviously straight from the heart. When she finished, the crowd stood and cheered for a full two minutes. Everywhere I looked, I saw women crying, and men trying not to. She was passionate and articulate, and I was as proud of her as I possibly could have been.

Even with all the emotion in the room, I still managed to eat about fifty bucks' worth of shrimp. You can't let emotion get in the way of free food.

When the applause died down, Cherry graciously chatted and posed for pictures with the crowd for about fifteen minutes. Then an officer came and told me that the path to our car was clear, so I signaled Cherry. She said good-bye to the crowd and the lady in charge, and we headed out the side door to another round of applause. The paparazzi tried unsuccessfully to get closer, and their frantic attempts to get my date to acknowledge them continued.

Cherry looked absolutely radiant in the light of the full moon as we walked the short distance to the Bentley. She took my arm, and asked me what I thought of her speech.

"Boss lady," I said. "You were sensational, and I know Poppy is smiling down on you from heaven tonight. I couldn't believe you didn't use any notes. I'm extremely proud of you, and very impressed."

She stopped me, stood on her toes, gave me a short kiss on the lips, and said, "Oh, Cooper, that's so sweet of you. Thank you very much for saying that. I meant every single word I said, and truly felt every emotion. I just hope we raised stupendous amounts of money. I simply love the people here in Atlanta. The audience were so well behaved and attentive, I could have gone on for hours."

I said, "And they would have let you go on for hours, believe me. Another thing, I don't think you hafta worry about how much money you raised. I bet you set some kind of record for a single night in this town. It was a great night, any way you look at it, and you should feel very proud of yourself, young lady."

"I must say, I feel like a million bucks. Maybe a billion!"

As we got to the car, I took hold of her hands, and said, "Well, you *should* feel that way. And I bet Poppy feels like a couple of billion herself."

We had managed to avoid the TV news crews all night, which would not have been possible without the aid of the Atlanta police. The same officers who'd met us when we arrived gave us a police escort back to the Ritz, with two motorcycle cops in front of the Bentley, and two behind. Cherry and I had a ball cruising through all the red lights, acting like big shots. It was a cool way to end an extraordinary evening.

Back in the suite, Cherry changed into her usual jeans and a tee shirt, and I did the same. I called room service, and we both had her favorite midnight supper again. Steak and eggs, a pot of tea, and a bottle of ketchup.

We watched a bad old movie, but anything would have been better than to have seen all the news reports concerning Cherry's circumstances. The amount of coverage had become ludicrous, but it was to be expected. How many movie stars have a cyber serial killer stalking them? Talk about hitting all the hot-button topics: Sex and Death and Fame and Fortune. It was fast becoming a true media-frenzy whirlwind on all of the news channels, and would soon dominate every entertainment news show as well. I don't know the names of those shows, but Penny likes to watch them, so I'm aware of their existence through her.

Anyway, we ate and talked and watched the movie, and left the news to people who weren't living right smack in the middle of it.

After we polished off our chow, I lay on the couch while Cherry made a few phone calls in her room. I thought about calling Penny, but decided against it yet again. I think I was still a little miffed at her for not being jealous when I told her about what I'd be doing in Atlanta. Hell, I *know* I was still miffed.

Like her, I sometimes wonder if I'll ever grow up. Also like her, I'm not holding my breath.

I was beat to the socks, so to make sure I didn't doze off on the couch, I got up and knocked on Cherry's bedroom door, and said good night. I undressed down to the skin as usual, and climbed into my bed by the window, leaving the curtains cracked just a little. If someone got into the room during the night, I wanted to be able to see them before they saw me. That was the plan, at least. If someone actually had gotten in, I probably would have slept right through it. I sleep the sleep of the dead once I'm totally out, which is great for an off-duty policeman, but not so great for a bodyguard.

I was in that twilight state I go into right before I fall asleep when I felt the covers slowly pull up, and caught the light scent of peach shampoo. Was I dreaming, or was a beautiful British redhead climbing into bed with me?

Sleepily, I asked, "Are you by any chance a serial killer?"

Giggling, Cherry said in French-accented English, "No, I'm the French maid, come to make your bed, monsieur."

"What are you doin' makin' my bed, and me in it?"

"Please don't be cross with me, Cooper, but I just don't want to sleep alone tonight. Especially after all that's happened today. I just felt so alone in my room."

Since I had my back to her as she got in the bed, her pajama-clad butt rubbed up against my naked one. She said in her accent again, "Ooh, la *la*. The police man sleep *au naturel, oui?*"

"No, the policeman is *trying* to sleep *au* whatever. And I'm unclothed because I usually sleep with my girlfriend, or alone, miss—miss whatever-the-French-word-for-Cherry is." I yawned big, and asked, "Are you sure you can't sleep alone?"

"Yes, I'm sure. No, I can't. I'm a big chicken. I need a warm body to feel secure. Marlon usually has that job, but I didn't bring him because of all one must do to get around that bloody quarantine business."

"Your boyfriend has to be quarantined?"

Laughing, she said, "No, silly. Marlon is my big fat Persian cat. He sleeps with me at night, and keeps me warm. Well, sort of."

"So, I'm nothin' more than a warm body to you. Thanks a lot." Another huge yawn.

"No, of course you're more than a warm body," she said as she snuggled her rear end closer to mine. "C'mon, Cooper, don't be difficult. Come to bed with me, won't you please?"

That got my attention, and the need for yawning disappeared suddenly. In my mind's eye, I saw a picture of Penny hoisting me into Cherry Page's bed with a forklift.

I said, "Well, okay, I guess. Your bed is a lot more comfortable, I'm sure. But no more talkin'. We need to get some sleep. You have another big day tomorrow."

After being invited to share the bed of one of the most beautiful women in the world, it was hard to believe that I was saying those words, but I was.

"Oh, goody!" she exclaimed, and jumped out of my bed and ran towards hers.

I wondered how many guys would give their right arm to be sleeping with Cherry Page in a fancy hotel suite. I stopped mentally counting at 3 billion.

Checking to make sure that she couldn't see, I quickly pulled on a pair of clean boxers, and a clean tee shirt as well. There was no way I was going in that bedroom without some form of defense.

The light from her bathroom was on, and it gave the bedroom a nice subdued lighting. Surely she wasn't trying to seduce me, right?

She was sitting on top of the bedspread with her back against the headboard, dressed in the most ridiculous pair of oversized men's pajamas I've ever seen. There was enough room in them for two Cherrys, and the print was some cartoon characters on a light blue background. What kind of man wears pajamas with cartoon characters on them to bed, I don't know. But I do know this: sexy, they weren't. I put all notions of seduction out of my mind, and climbed under the covers next to her in the spacious bed.

"Can we go to sleep now?" I asked.

She ignored me, and said, "Cooper, the entire cast and crew like you very much, you know. Will thinks you're the 'cat's meow.' He told me so himself while we waited for you at the Wiggly Piggly."

"Piggly Wiggly."

She ignored me again, and said, "Tell me your girlfriend's name."

I sighed deeply, and said, "Penny Lee Prevost."

"How remarkable! My name is Cherry Leigh Page!"

"That *is* remarkable," I muttered. "You must be related." I couldn't believe I was in Cherry Leigh Page's bed, talking about my girlfriend instead of trying out my best lines. Not that I have any best lines, but I mean, come *on*. Thank God, there was no one there to witness my pathetic behavior.

Cherry asked, "And what does Penny Lee look like?"

Realizing I wasn't going to get any sleep until she was finished interrogating me, I said, "Well, Penny is gorgeous, a real looker. She has long, straight black hair, and deep brown eyes. She's maybe a little taller than you, but you two share the same body type. I mean, you're both—voluptuous. Unlike you, she has a suntan all year round, and like you, she makes men's heads turn whenever she walks by. Is that enough?"

"You forgot the most important thing about her. She's a very fortunate girl. She has you."

"I wouldn't go so far as to say that."

Cherry said, "You don't have to say it. A woman knows these things."

I said, "That's very nice of you to say, but we've only just met, Cherry. You hardly know anything about me."

"That's not true. I know that you're sweet, and smart, and funny. Not to mention good-looking. And I know that I feel safe and secure when you're around."

Okay, I admit that I'm sweet, and pretty smart, and that I can be funny at times, but good-looking? I'm average-looking at best, with a slightly crooked nose that I got playing high-school football, and my height and weight are average as well. My brown hair is always a little too long, except when there's a gay hairdresser around, which is never, and my green eyes are nothing special. I guess you could feel safe with a guy who carries a weapon, but the rest of it was a little too much. I was beginning to think I had a woman with a schoolgirl crush on my hands, and an unmerited crush at that.

Sitting up and leaning back on the headboard beside her, I asked, "How old are you?"

"I'll be twenty-seven November next—the tenth, to be exact. How old are you?"

"I was forty-five last January first."

She said, "Oh, a New Year's baby, yeah? That makes you what, a Capricorn?"

"Oh, no," I groaned. "Don't tell me you believe in all that stuff."

"Lord, no. Only the good parts," she laughed. "Like the part about us Scorpios being quite sexy, and all. The bad stuff I forget as soon as I read it."

"Well, you're definitely sexy. The stars got that part right."

"I'm not all *that* sexy. When we know each other better, I'll let you in on a little secret," she said. "So. What are the characteristics of a Capricorn?"

"I have no idea, but you reminded me of a show I saw last year. This debunker guy—you know what I mean, he's always tryin' to expose frauds—debunk 'em, I mean—he did a test with a class of college kids, as I recall, maybe high schoolers—twenty-five or so. Anyway, he gave 'em all an astrological reading done expressly for each individual in the class. A single page describing what a person born on the same day as each one of them would be like. In other words, the girl born on June sixth got one for *that* day, the boy born on October twenty-fifth got one for *that* day, and so forth. Next he asked them to take their time reading the personalized information, and then tell him how accurate they thought the descriptions were. Somethin' like eighty percent of them swore that the readings were highly accurate, and described them to a tee. There was only one thing wrong with the test."

I paused for effect, and after a few seconds, she couldn't stand it. "Tell me!"

I chuckled, and said, "He gave them all identical information. Each page was exactly the same, and eighty percent of 'em bought it. That pretty much tells ya how accurate astrology is."

"I love it!" she said. "We need a lot more debunkers, wouldn't you say?"

"Yes, I would. And that concludes the astrology portion of the evening."

Cherry said, "Not just yet. Do you think a Scorpio and a Capricorn might make a good match?"

"Cherry, even if they—we—*did* make a good match astrologically speaking, I'm old enough to be your—your—uncle. A young uncle."

"So?"

"*So?* So. So, look, I know there's a 'so' in there somewhere. You and I could never be, well, you know, together."

Cherry turned to look me in the eye, and asked, "And why on Earth not?"

"Because we live in two completely different worlds. You're always flyin' off to some faraway part of the globe, and I'm a police chief in a drowsy little town in Florida."

"Well, maybe you could come and be a part of it. My world, I mean. You could be my permanent bodyguard, and protect me from all the bad people in my world."

"Cherry. Kiddo. Let's get serious about this thing. I think you're doin' what the shrinks call 'projecting,' or 'transference,' or somethin' like that. You're makin' me out to be some kind of knight in shining armor because I've been there to look after you during some scary moments. You're projecting qualities on to me that aren't really there. And, on top of all that, I already have a girlfriend."

"Are you two engaged to be married?"

"Well, no, not exactly, but—"

"Well, there you go, then. If you're not engaged, that makes you fair game. 'All's fair,' and all that. Besides, if you *were* a knight, you certainly wouldn't be in shining armor. I should think your armor would be slightly shabby," she said, laughing her sweet laugh. "Cooper, my knight in shabby armor."

"That's not funny," I said joining in on the laugh.

After a pause, I said, "You're not really serious about this stuff, wanting me to stay on as your bodyguard, and whatever."

"Oh, I'm quite serious. Truth be told, I'm seriously serious. Someday, you might grow to truly like me. One never knows with affairs of the heart."

With that accent of hers, "heart" sounded a lot like "hot." It was certainly getting warmer in that bed, lying next to her like that.

Keeping the heat on, Cherry asked, "Cooper? Seriously, now. Aren't you attracted to me in the slightest?"

I looked at her as if she was nuts, and said, "Cherry, of course I'm attracted to you. What man in his right mind wouldn't be attracted to you?"

"Ah, there's the rub," she said. "'Right mind.' Well then, if any man in his right mind would be attracted to me, and you're not attracted to me, then it's plain to see that you're not in your right mind."

I put my hands on my head, and moaned, "You're givin' me a pounding headache. And, just for the record, there are other reasons I could never be with you. Like, for instance, you wear really, really, ugly pajamas to bed."

Reaching for the buttons of her pajama top, she said, "I can remedy that."

"No! I mean, that's not necessary, I mean—"

"I know what you mean," she said, giggling. "I was only winding you up."

"Whew. You're gonna give an old man a heart attack. Now, how 'bout we wind *down*, and get some sleep?"

"Oh, you're no fun a'tall, Chief Cooper."

Lying back down, I said, "I know, I know, I'm a stick-in-the-mud. But you're killin' me over here. And tomorrow's another busy day, ya know."

She sighed dramatically, and said, "Oh, all right then. I'll be a good little girl."

Closing my eyes as I turned away, I replied, "That's what I like to hear. That's nice. Now, g'night, Cherry."

"Night-night. Uncle Cooper."

18

NEAL FEAGIN WAS IN HIS PHIPPS PLAZA OFFICE ACROSS THE STREET FROM the Ritz talking with special agent John Carver of the FBI's Violent Crimes Unit. Neal was seated at his desk, and Carver was sitting in a chair beside the desk so he could see the television that was suspended several feet off the floor in the corner. They were watching the early-morning news reports on the Cherry Page stalker case, Neal switching back and forth between channels with the remote. Neal had arrived at the office at 5 a.m. in order to beat the traffic. Since his left foot was the one in a cast, driving was not too much of a problem.

He usually didn't come in on a Tuesday, but Neal wanted to glean any information that Agent Carver may have had, and to ask him what the FBI profilers were saying about the stalker. Neal showed his thanks to Carver for meeting him so early by bringing some of Susan's homemade cinnamon rolls and hot coffee from a thermos.

Neal opened the conversation by saying, "So, tell me. What do the legendary FBI profilers have to say about our killer?"

Carver swallowed the last bite of his cinnamon roll, and said, "Their best guess is that it's a white male, thirty to forty. Probably affluent, able to make his own hours. They also suggest that he may have ties to a satanic cult of some kind, or may be trying to join one. It's entirely possible that the murders are part of an initiation rite. That narrows it down somewhat if the satanic stuff is true, but take that away and it could be hundreds of men in this city alone, not to mention the country. Truth is, we don't have a make on this guy yet, due to the lack of evidence left at the crime scenes. Also, he may have a thing against homosexuals, or be one himself, since he targeted Daniel Cullen. Or, that could have just been a crime of opportunity. No one at the drag club where Cullen worked saw anything out of the ordinary. Nothing unusual at the flower shop, either. Add to all that the arson at the theater in broad daylight, and we've obviously got a nut job on our hands, a full-blown psychopath. But in reality, it could be any one of a thousand guys. That's what's so frustrating about the whole thing."

Neal said, "Sounds to me like this case has more than a few unusual things about it."

Carver replied, "It really does, and it keeps getting stranger by the minute, or at least by the killing. In a normal stalking case, you might have a perp show up at your home, or harass you at your job, something of that nature. Or, he may follow you around wherever you go, like the freak who attacked the female tennis player a few years back, right out in front of God and everybody while she was in the middle of a match. Then there are stalkers who want to be as famous as the people they stalk, or the ones who are jealous, or just plain crazy. But this guy seems even less human than most serial killers. At least serial types usually have some reason for killing, no matter how twisted it may be. This bastard is killing innocent people just so he can have access to their computers. It's as if their lives are just a hurdle to be overcome. No rhyme, no reason, just people in the wrong place at the right time. That makes it really difficult because there's no discernible pattern. And still another thing sets this one apart from the pack. Most serial killers take time off between killings, sometimes years, but this one is knocking off victims almost every day."

Neal said, "You're right: there are more questions than answers at this point. I have another question to add to the mix: Why do you think the killer just doesn't try to get to Cherry in a more conventional way, like just shooting her? Not that I want her to get hurt, but why bring all these others into it?"

"Who knows with these sickos? Maybe it's just a case of trying to get Cherry Page to take notice. Maybe she means something to him that we haven't been able to perceive yet."

"Hmmm," said Neal.

"Right. It gets curiouser and curiouser," Carver said, staring into space.

Noticing a pack of cigarettes in Carver's pocket, Neal said, "I usually don't allow smoking in here, but since you made a special trip, go ahead and light up if you want to."

"That's okay. I need to cut back anyway. These cinnamon rolls are hitting the spot."

"They're the best, if you don't mind me bragging on my wife. So,

I guess you've considered that the stalker might be an acquaintance of Cherry's. Possibly a coworker, someone here for the filming?"

Carver said, "Yeah, we've been looking into that, but so far, nothing. It makes sense, seeing as how Cherry's being contacted through her personal computer."

Neal reached down to try and scratch under his ankle cast, and said, "You know, John, I've been wonderin' if there might be more than one person involved. I mean, if this cult thing pans out, why couldn't there be two or more people involved? It seems to me that it would be difficult to move a body from a house to a theater without help. Do the profilers have anything to say about that?"

Smiling weakly, Carver said, "That's the main problem we have here. Too many questions and opinions, and not one particular answer that covers all those bases."

Neal took a cinnamon roll, and asked, "Do you think it could be a woman?"

Carver paused, and said, "Well, if we were just talking about normal stalking, it could easily be a woman. But female serial killers are rare." He sipped his coffee, and continued, "Only about one or two percent of stalkers actually kill. Mostly they just drive their victims crazy."

When Neal took a bite of his roll without elaborating, Carver asked, "What made you ask about a woman?"

Neal finished chewing, swallowed, and said, "Just a thought, no real reason. When I worked homicide in New Orleans, we tried to look under every rock."

Carver replied, "Personally, and off the record, I think you may be right about a group possibly being involved. And even though, like I said, it's rare, there's always a possibility that the killer is a woman. I guess just about anything is possible these days. But until we find something physical, evidence-wise, at a scene, it's all speculation. I know that the profilers can be amazingly accurate at times, but they need more hard data to be effective. And our killer, or killers, just aren't cooperating."

Neal said, "Maybe we should add that to the list of attributes our stalker has."

"Add what?"

"Our stalker is completely uncooperative."

19

I WOKE UP IN CHERRY'S BED ABOUT THIRTY SECONDS BEFORE THE DESK clerk rang the room with our wake-up call. I answered in midring, thanked the clerk for calling, and lay back on my pillow. I was alone in the big bed, and I could hear the shower running. Cherry was up and at 'em early again.

The bathroom door was slightly open, and steam was coming into the room along with the light. Again, I thought of how many men would love to be in my position, less than twenty feet away from a wet, naked Cherry Page.

To keep from becoming too stimulated by my surroundings, I thought about anything else: baseball, World War II, fishing, et cetera. But the thought that really cooled me off was an image of Penny aiming her Glock at my boxers.

Just as I was feeling proud of my self-control, the shower stopped, and I heard the sound of Cherry humming as she toweled off. A few moments later, she came out in just a bra and panties, and headed into the outer room, unaware that I was awake. She was unaware that I was awake because I had my eyes almost closed. With the room only slightly lit, I must have appeared to be asleep when she glanced at the bed before moving to the other room.

After that display, I had to visualize Penny in triplicate, with each of the fuming Pennys aiming shotguns at my fun zone. It seemed to be working, until Cherry reappeared in the bedroom, reached behind her back to take off her bra, and replaced it with another one. She turned away from me to do it, but the sight of her naked back in the dim light was too much. I kept my eyes shut—well, almost—and watched through the slits as she went back into the bathroom. The shotguns were no longer working at that moment.

To let her know I wasn't sleeping, I fake-yawned loudly, and turned away towards the wall. She stuck her head out and asked, "Are you awake, Cooper?"

"Mmmph," I said. Trying to yawn, and failing, I said, "Are you already up and about? Boy, I was sleeping like a teenager in study hall. I dozed off after the front desk called."

"Study hall? I suppose that translates to 'you were sleeping soundly,' yeah?"

"Yeah."

"I'll be out in just a few."

"Great," I said. I needed a few.

A knock at the door signaled Sally's arrival with breakfast, and I went to answer it, closing the bedroom door behind me. Had to keep up appearances. "Just a minute," I said, as I pulled on my jeans and opened the door to the suite.

Sally said cheerily, "Good morning, Coop. How's the boy? Did you sleep well?"

"The boy is doin' just fine. I slept very well. Come in and make yourself at home. Cherry should be out in a minute, and I'm gonna shower and be right with y'all."

"Splendid. I'll have the table set and ready for you."

"Thanks. Be right back."

I grabbed a tee shirt from my suitcase, and walked towards the bedroom. I knocked, and entered when Cherry said, "Come in." Cherry was in her robe, combing her wet hair in front of the dresser mirror.

She said, "Shower's all yours, Cooper. Hurry so you can have your breakfast hot."

"Yes, ma'am, be right there."

The first minute of my shower was under cold water.

As Cherry and I cruised in the Bentley to rehearsal, I asked, "Why are you guys filming in Atlanta? Why not Hollywood?"

"Okay, first things first. You're aware that the studio in charge of this film is called Stonestreet?"

"Yes," I said. "They flew me here."

"Right. Well, Stonestreet is the studio that I most often work for in Britain, and they have used Atlanta before on a picture that was set in America. And this film happens to be set in a small town in America, at a college. The interesting thing is—depending on how and where you shoot—Atlanta can be made to look like many places, which makes it quite nice as a location. Or so I've been told. Also, there is rather a lot of rural area nearby, and that can be a plus as well. *And,* it's closer than Hollywood. Add to all that the beauty of the city itself, and you have quite a few reasons to film here."

"Are many movies shot in Atlanta?" I asked.

"I'm not sure where the city ranks in film production, but it's certainly not unheard of to be filming here. The main location for us is a college that was used in a very successful horror film several years back."

"How 'bout that. I had no idea that movies were made here. Of course, my knowledge of moviemaking is almost nonexistent. What's your movie about?"

"Didn't you listen at rehearsal yesterday?" she asked with a smile.

"Um, to be honest, my mind was elsewhere."

"I hope so. You're not being paid to listen to a bunch of hacks reading lines."

"I'll try again," I said. "What's your hack movie about?"

She giggled and said, "I play a first-year college professor from England who falls in love with the dean's son."

"Well, I can definitely see you playing an English chick, but I don't know about that 'professor' stuff."

"Shut up."

"Yes, ma'am. Continue, please?"

"*Anyway,* the dean doesn't approve of the match, because, you see, it turns out he was engaged to my character's mother years before, when he was a student at Oxford. Had they actually gotten married, he could've been my father, so he feels the whole thing to be a bit unseemly, me marrying his son, and all. He's a widower now, and my mother is a widow, so she comes to America to straighten him out, and they too become involved. And then, naturally, the hilarity ensues. It's a romantic comedy. At least I hope that's what it turns out to be."

"What's it called?"

"*Teaching English*. It's based on the best seller by the same name."

"Not a bad title. Anyway, I'm sure with you as the star, it'll be a big hit, and I know Penny will drag me kickin' and screamin' to see it, so you better be good."

Frowning, she said, "'Kicking and screaming?' Haven't you seen every one of my films?"

"Well, you see—the thing is—I haven't seen even one of your movies. Does that mean I hafta give back the Bentley and my suite at the Ritz?"

Cherry looked at me coolly and said, "Of course it does. If you haven't seen even one of my films, I shan't pay you for services rendered."

"Oh, but you *shan*," I said.

"I *shan't*!"

"Shan!"

Laughing, she said, "Oh, all right, you blithering idiot, I shall keep you on the payroll for the time being. But cross me even once, and you'll never work in this business again."

"Whew. That's a huge relief. I don't know what I'd do if I could no longer act. It's in my blood now."

"Oh, shut up and drive, Jeeves."

"Yes, mum. Whatever you say, mum."

Cherry threw her perfect nose in the air, and said, "That's more like it."

I was enjoying my job way too much. I needed to call Penny.

20

ACTING POLICE CHIEF PENNY PREVOST WAS BOILING MAD AT COOP, BUT she was determined not to call and check up on him. She'd seen the endless news reports on CNN and all the entertainment news programs about Cherry, and she'd also seen Coop in his tux walking from the museum with her, looking a little too happy. His hair looked better than she'd ever seen it, and she wondered who had cut it for him. She knew who had talked him into having it done, but it wasn't Cherry who was making her so angry.

The freshly shorn son-of-a-bee should've called her five or six times by now, but she could just hear him if *she* called and asked what the hell was going on: "Oh, that was nobody, Cherry. Just one of my officers needing me to straighten out a mess they made."

If he were with anybody else in the entire world, Penny would have called and blistered his eardrum over the phone the first day, but she would rather die than have her heroine think of her as a shrew. Cherry Page and Penny Prevost were going to be the best of friends: of that she was certain. Having her revenge with Coop would have to wait.

As soon as Coop brought Cherry to Gulf Front, she and Cherry would become bosom buddies, forming a lifelong bond that could never be broken. They would stay in touch constantly by instant messenger—well, maybe not at first, considering the circumstances—and the two of them would become closer than sisters, promising to stay in touch after Cherry had to leave Gulf Front and go back to—

Penny's daydream was rudely interrupted when officer Adam Ingmire called on the patrol-car radio to tell her that there was trouble at the barbershop. Two of the elderly gents who hung around there were squaring off out in front on the sidewalk, and it looked like fisticuffs were inevitable.

Penny told Adam she was on her way, and sighed deeply as she turned Coop's patrol car around and headed back to town. She checked her watch, and made a mental note of the time: 10:12 A.M.

When she arrived at the scene, there was no one in front of the barbershop other than Adam and Bum, Coop's big German Shepherd. Adam was leaning on his patrol car, cleaning his finger-nails with a pocketknife, and Bum was sticking his nose through the partially opened window of Adam's car.

Penny slowed to a stop in the street, waved at Bum, and asked, "Where'd everybody go? Anybody get hurt?"

Adam walked over to her window, and said, "Naw, the show's over. Mr. Hinckley and Mr. Nicks were about to go at it, when Miz Hinckley came up and grabbed Mr. Hinckley by his ear, and pulled him down the block to Doc's office. She was in the waiting room when somebody told her about the fight that was brewin'. It was pretty much all over after that."

"Did you write out any citations?"

"Naw, didn't seem to be any need. If one of 'em had actually thrown a punch, I was ready to put a stop to it, but old guys like them two wouldn't have caused much damage, anyway." He smiled, and said, "Hey, listen, I got an idea. Maybe you should deputize Miz Hinckley while Coop's away."

Penny thought, Maybe I should deputize Miz Hinckley and send her to Atlanta.

21

SPECIAL AGENT JOHN CARVER WAS AT HIS DESK GOING OVER THE PROFILERS' latest report for the third time, when his desk phone rang. He picked up, said hello, and listened as Sergeant Traylor of the APD task force told him he was needed at the Ritz-Carlton Buckhead immediately. A maid had discovered a dead female body in one of the rooms at 11 A.M.

Carver asked, "Did you find anything helpful in the way of evidence this time?"

Traylor said, "You need to come see this for yourself, Agent Carver. This is, well, bizarre is the word I might use. There's a lot of—you just really need to see this for yourself."

"I'm on my way."

Carver glanced at his desk clock, saw that it was 11:25, and told his secretary where he was headed. He hustled to the elevator and took it down to the parking lot.

At 12:05, he parked in the loading dock area of the Ritz and flashed his badge to the security guard as he entered the hotel. A uniformed officer was there to meet him, and they took the stairs to the fifth floor.

Sergeant Traylor was standing outside the open door of Room 506 talking to a crime scene investigator, both of them wearing plastic shoe covers. After the introductions were made, Carver put covers on over his shoes and entered the room. Whatever hopes he had for finding evidence quickly faded as he surveyed the space.

Almost the entire room, including the body, was covered in fire extinguisher foam. There were five extinguishers just inside the door, and they were small enough to all fit easily inside a large suitcase. Judging by the amount of foam, it was likely that they had all been emptied in the room. The foam had subsided somewhat, but still covered every inch of the room and its contents, except for one thing: the victim's laptop, which was sitting on the dresser.

Carver stepped gingerly over to the laptop, and saw that there was an instant message from *not_so_shy_guy3* to the username he recognized as Cherry Page's. It read: *Baal calls to you through me. . . . You are The One . . . I am your Deliverer. Come home . . . the time for Sacrifice draws nigh.*

The message box wasn't the only thing on the screen; a website devoted to Baal worship was visible behind the box. The image of a weird three-headed creature stared out from the screen. One of the heads was an ugly man wearing a crown; the second head was a cat; the third head, a toad. The chest was that of a human, while the legs were those of a spider. Carver shook his head at the disturbing sight, and turned his attention to the corpse.

Even more disturbing was the sight of the victim's foam-slimed body. Her throat had been cut, and blood had mixed with the foam to make a sickly pink. She had been sliced open from her pubis to her breastbone, and a sixth extinguisher had been left lying on her exposed entrails. The killer had also violated Lois Langley with one final insult, and had left the police a final taunt.

Carver sighed deeply, and said, "This freak is one sick sonofabitch, but surely isn't stupid enough to forget to wear gloves or to wipe everything clean. Do we know where the victim was last night?"

Traylor said, "Not yet, but my guys are questioning the hotel staff. If you've seen enough, we need to move so the crime scene team can get to work."

Carver said, "I've seen more than enough. They're obviously not gonna find much in the way of evidence. I'll be interested to see if they can estimate how long it's been since the killer left the scene. My guess is he waited until almost checkout time, so the maid and the manager would find the body covered in foam. This guy likes to live dangerously."

When they were in the hall, Traylor asked, "You ever see anything like this?"

Carver ran his hand through his hair, and said, "Nope, can't say that I have. One thing's for sure, whoever's doing this is getting bolder by the day. We'd better focus on the guests, as well as the hotel staff. It's possible whoever's doing this works here, or is staying here."

Sergeant Traylor nodded and made notes on his pad as Carver closed the conversation. "Thanks for your help, Sergeant. I need to call my contact, and bring him up to speed. With this happening just a few doors down from her room, Ms. Page needs to know this whack job is closing in on her."

22

WHEN CHERRY AND I ARRIVED AT THE THEATER, THERE WERE SEVERAL news vans and camera crews set up near the entrance, but there were also enough police officers on duty to get us into the lot, into a parking space, and inside the building without too much trouble. The reporters were yelling questions at Cherry about the stalker, and how she felt about the murders, and who was I, and anything else their little pointed heads could think of to shout. The paparazzi were back with a vengeance, and a couple were knocked to the ground in the battle to get a good angle. Cherry smiled at them all, and I scowled at them all.

Everyone in the cast and crew tried to keep things light, and no one talked about the stalker or the murders with Cherry. They all wanted the day to be as ordinary as possible under the extraordinary circumstances.

I was sitting in the aisle seat of the middle row of the theater, listening to the actors rehearse, when my cell rang. I got up and walked out to the lobby. It was around twelve fifteen, and craft service had set another nice spread on the tables. I had my eye on the lasagna as I answered the phone.

"Hello?"

Neal said, "Hey, bud, you sittin' down?"

"As a matter of fact, I'm not. Should I be?"

"You might want to, after you hear the latest. There's been another murder, and this one is a little too close for comfort."

I said, "Don't tell me it's somebody we know."

"No, it's not quite that bad. It's more about location this time."

"Gimme the bad news."

"Okay, here it comes," he said. "At eleven A.M. today, a maid at your hotel found a dead woman in a room right down the hall from yours. The victim is Lois Langley, from Minneapolis, down here on business. Caucasian, thirty-seven, brown hair and eyes, never been married, no kids."

I recalled the plump brunette from the day before, dancing as she unlocked her door down the hall. It took a moment before I could get back into detective mode and say, "Damn, bud, that *is* a little too close for comfort. Did they find anything in the way of evidence this time?"

Neal said, "This is where it gets a little weird—not that it hasn't been weird from the get-go. The entire room, including the victim, was covered with foam—fire extinguisher foam. There were six empty canisters in the room. You can imagine the mess that would make of the crime scene. There was only one area left untouched. Ms. Langley's laptop was sitting on the dresser with an instant message from the killer to you-know-who, and was on a website about Baal. I guess our stalker wanted to have a little fun with us, show the police how smart he is. The victim's throat was slashed, just like the others, and she'd also been basically gutted. And, there was a sick little twist."

"Do I wanna know?" I asked.

He said, "Well, let's just say that there was an extinguisher lying on top of her open guts, and the nozzle was stuck inside her—in a place it shouldn't be, if you get my meanin'."

"Sadly, I'm pretty sure I do." I tried not to picture the grisly scene, but was unsuccessful. Suddenly, the lasagna with its meat and red sauce didn't seem like such a good idea anymore.

I sighed, and said, "That obviously makes it impossible to determine if there was a sexual assault, or even consensual sex, for that matter. No doubt about it, this freak is gettin' sicker by the minute. I guess y'all checked out what the victim was doin' last night."

Neal said, "Yeah, they found out she was in the lounge for a couple of hours, sitting at the bar getting loaded. We talked to the bartenders who were on duty, and neither could tell us much. They also said it was much busier than usual because of a convention. They didn't notice when the victim left, or with who, or much of anything. One of the bartenders—who was on duty at the time she left—said he'd gone to use the men's room, and when he got back, the victim was gone. What else. Oh, yeah. Atlanta detectives are hooking the bartenders up with a sketch artist. I'm not expecting anything to come of it, but who knows?"

I said, "So Cherry has a message waitin' for her on her laptop."

"Yep. Tell her I'm sorry, and that we're all doin' the best we can. I think it might be best to leave out most of the gory details, don't you?"

"Yeah, I'll try and give 'er the news as gently as possible. I gotta tell ya, Neal, I'm a little worried about her state of mind. Another dead body and another message might push her over the edge. I'm not even sure if I should tell her about 'em, the way she's been actin'. And I don't mean professionally. I guess we'll find out what she's really made of after she hears this bit of news. I better keep her away from the television and radio for now."

Neal said, "Good idea. I'll call you as soon as I hear anything. Speaking of calling, Penny called Susan this mornin' to see how you're doin'. Haven't you called that girl yet?"

"No. I feel like livin' dangerously."

"Well, if I were you, I'd be more worried about *dyin'* dangerously. And not at the hand of some serial killer."

23

WHILE I WAS TRYING TO DECIDE JUST HOW MUCH TO TELL CHERRY, AND when, lunch was called, and everybody came out to the lobby. The hungriest of the group hit the tables like locusts, but I was slow to move, and Cherry noticed.

She asked with a smile, "Aren't you going to fill your plate to overflowing?"

Trying to keep it light, I said, "Of course I am. You ever see me turn down free food?"

"Not yet. What do you fancy today? I think I shall have a light lunch. The pasta salad looks yummy."

She led me to the tables, and we began to walk through the line. As soon as I got near the food, my nose took over. All of a sudden I was hungry again—slashed throats, viscera, and fire-extinguisher nozzles notwithstanding. Soon we were walking back into the theater to grab a seat on the back row, my plate packed with lasagna, Cherry's with a reasonable amount of pasta salad.

She looked so peaceful that I didn't want to tell her the latest bad news, so when she asked if I'd heard anything, I told her we'd talk about it after lunch. That seemed to satisfy her, and we finished our meals while talking about nothing in particular. Cherry kept glancing at me every so often, as if trying to get a read on what I was thinking. I just concentrated on my plate and kept stuffing my face.

I think she knew there was something going on, but she didn't try to pry it out of me. Penny came to mind as this was happening. She would've known everything *I* knew in a matter of seconds. I smiled at the thought, and continued stuffing until my plate was clean.

Cherry hopped up when she finished her salad, and said, "I'm going to get some biscuits—oh, sorry, *cookies*—shall I bring you a handful?"

"I'd rather have a brownie. Does that translate?"

Chuckling, she said, "Barely." She looked pensive, then asked, "Who was it that said: 'England and America are two nations separated by the same language?' Or however it goes. Was it Oscar Wilde? Churchill, perhaps? I'd Google it if I could face my computer."

That reminded me that she had a new sick instant message, but instead of telling her about it, I merely replied, "I don't know who said it, but it's true. You Englishters sure do talk funny."

"No, my dear, we don't. You insufferable colonists are the ones who speak oddly. We speak the King's English, and don't you forget it."

"Oh, yeah? Well, Carl Reiner said, talkin' about you Brits and your fancy speakin': 'If you wake 'em up in the middle of the night, they talk just like everybody else.' Take *that*, Limey!"

Cherry walked off and said over her shoulder, "See if you get your brownie now, Mr. Man."

I actually did get a brownie. In fact, I got two. I had been trying to think of a way to soften the blow about the latest instant message while Cherry was getting dessert, but I couldn't come up with anything. When she came back, she threw the wrapped brownies in my lap with a smile, and sat down to eat her cookies. She looked so childlike, I wished I could have kept her in the dark, but there was no easy way around it: She was just going to have to hear the news, and take it like a man, in a manner of speaking.

When we finished eating, the cast went back to work until almost six, and then the director thanked everyone and called a halt to the action. Cherry talked to the oily producer again, Lyndon-Bowen by name, and I could see her deftly parrying each advance he made. After a minute, he gave up, and tried to give her a kiss good-bye. She pulled back and offered her hand for him to shake, and he gave up gracefully and shook it.

As she headed up the aisle to my back-row seat, she crossed her eyes like she'd done the day before when he'd hit on her, and I had to once again keep a straight face while the dork followed her with his eyes.

I had decided to tell her the bad news as soon as possible and just get it behind us.

As we made our way out the front doors, I was surprised to see that there were still a lot of news people waiting outside. Don't these people have lives?

Officers had them all safely behind barricades, so it wasn't too bad. The police were doing a great job as far as security went, I thought. But, the commotion and bellowing started as soon as the reporters spotted Cherry, and she smiled, waved, and said nothing as we walked down the steps. I wondered how she dealt with all the fanfare that surrounded her every time she went out in public. At least they hadn't heard about the latest killing, so they didn't yell any questions about it.

We had reached the bottom step when a gunshot rang out above the clamor of the crowd.

I immediately took Cherry down to the ground by the steps, and covered her body with mine, drawing my gun. I stuck my head up, looked around, and saw the media types screaming and scattering in all directions, some being trampled in the frenzy.

Unbelievably, three video cameramen stayed put, and aimed their cameras in the direction of the gunshot. A second shot blasted, then a third, and finally two of them ran for cover as best they could with their big cameras in tow. One intrepid soul just kept filming as an officer drew his gun and ran alongside the building towards the back of the theater, barking into his handheld, "Shots fired, Candler the-ater! Request backup immediately!"

While all this was going on, Cherry and I were on the ground by the steps, basically in the missionary position. I suddenly felt Cherry's hand slide under my shirt, and slowly make its way up my back. I tensed, and she started to lightly scratch my back.

It was one of the sexiest things that has ever happened to me, but I went against everything that my body was screaming for me to do, and pulled away from her touch. I had to remind myself yet again that I already had a girlfriend, and was happily entangled with *her*. Not to mention, we were under fire. I quickly unlocked our loins before I lost my resolve, and got to my feet, my gun aimed safely at the ground, but still ready for what might come.

There was a commotion going on behind the theater, and I could hear policemen and policewomen calling out to each other, but couldn't make out what they were saying. Luckily, the brave video cameraman had moved towards the action behind the theater instead of focusing on Cherry and me. I was glad that he wasn't as interested in her as he was in the officers' situation. There was already enough news footage of me to last a lifetime.

I turned and glanced down at Cherry. She was smiling up at me as she lay on her back, her left arm now under her head as a pillow. The stretching of her arm had caused her tee shirt to ride up on her belly, exposing her navel and the bottom of her bra. The same bra I had watched her change into earlier that morning. I swallowed hard, and went back to looking towards the action, my poor brain frying to a turn.

A moment later, an officer called, "All clear!" and two other cops walked up by the side of the building towards the front of the theater. Each officer had two young boys by the arm, leading them towards a squad car.

I holstered my weapon, and asked, "*Those* guys were the shooters?"

One of the officers, a large black man of thirty or so, said, "These knuckleheads were the shooters, all right, but it wasn't gunshots you heard. They're goin' downtown for setting off illegal firecrackers, which is just the beginning of their troubles. Skipping school is another charge. They thought it would be kinda funny to make everybody think that there were shots fired. Take a look at the name on these firecrackers."

The name on the package was "Gunshots." There was a picture of what appeared to be a .357 Magnum under the name. They were "Guaranteed to sound just like real gunshots!"

I said, "Truth in advertising, for sure." Giving the boys my meanest chief-of-police glare, I asked the officer, "What're you gonna do with these guys?"

"We may just throw 'em *under* the jail," he replied.

The boys, two white and two black, looked to be ten or twelve. They tried their best to look tough, but as soon as they got close to the squad car, tears started to flow, and the begging began. They were in huge trouble, and I was glad it wasn't me going to jail. I was also glad that the shots had turned out to be nothing more than a prank.

The relief of it all was so great that I forgot about what had just happened with Cherry for a second. That's about how long it took for me to turn back and see Cherry still lying on her back on the grassy spot, smiling at me.

She stretched her arms up, and showing me her red fingernails, said, "Are you sure you don't want me to scratch that itch for you, Cooper?"

There aren't enough red fingernails in the world to scratch the itch I felt at that moment.

24

The report about the kids and the firecrackers was just too funny! The news cretins had a field day with it, some reporting the story so earnestly, and others taking a lighter approach. It was all over the TV and in all the papers, and the Internet stories covered all the bases: Sympathy, outrage, lampooning, seriousness. Cherry Page certainly was a lightning rod for the media. Everyone had an angle and an opinion.

Come to think of it, maybe the kids' false attempt on her life would take her over the edge, and she'd be an easier target. If she had to be hospitalized, it might make the job of getting to her easier. But in reality it probably made it harder to get to her now. All her protectors would be on an even higher alert.

But come on, it was pretty damned funny. Kids setting off firecrackers!

And what fun Lois had turned out to be! No doubt the display of that stupid bitch covered in fire extinguisher foam was a sight to see for those pathetic, dim-witted cops. Wonder how they liked the positioning of the nozzle-slash-sex-toy left for their perusal? Probably some of the morons even got a little excited by that, especially the crime scene monkey who was given the job of taking it out of the barfly-bitch's hole.

What did the slut expect, letting a stranger buy her martini after martini? Some kind of romantic interlude that would lead to a deeper relationship? Possibly a life-changing affair filled with excitement and joy? Could she really have been as desperate as her eyes had shown? Such an obvious target, sitting there at the bar all alone. She deserved everything she got, and more.

Besides, she shouldn't have advertised the fact that there was a laptop in her room when asked about it. She chose herself to be the messenger, and that's all there was to it. It was almost as if her *actions were preordained, as if her destiny was to end up in that hotel room exactly as she did. Living all those empty years before that night, each day bringing her closer to that exact location, at that precise time.*

Speaking of exact locations, it was time to move even closer to home.

25

I PULLED CHERRY UP OFF THE GROUND BY HER MANICURED HANDS, AND watched as she brushed the dirt off her backside. There were a few blades of dry grass in her hair, and I reached over and pulled them out. As I removed the blades, I was trying to think of something to say that would be completely asexual after our little moment in the grass. The scent of peaches on my hand reminded me of a question I wanted to ask, so I did.

"Do you always use peach-scented shampoo?"

Pulling her hair back, she said, "Actually, no. I generally use an apple-cinnamon scent, but when I heard I was coming to Georgia, I thought peach might be more appropriate. Don't you like it?"

"I like it very much." Looking at her in the late-afternoon sun, I completely forgot my asexual approach, and stupidly said, "I don't think I'll ever catch the scent of a peach again without thinking of you."

She leaned into me, kissed my cheek, and said, "Cooper, if you really want to keep me at arm's length, that is definitely not the way to go about it."

"Well, see—I mean, I'm not tryin' to—I still think—"

Laughing softly at me, she put her arm in mine, and said, "Down, boy, you'll have a stroke. Now would you please get me out of here before the horde returns?"

I smiled and took hold of her hand, and we ran to the Bentley and were away before the crowd could follow. I took a different route back to the Ritz just in case.

I turned on the classical radio station, and she said, "After today's events, what would you say to a little rock and roll?"

"I'd say 'rock on, Red.'"

She fiddled with the radio till she found John and Paul belting out "Eight Days a Week."

"Ooh, I love this song!" she said as she sat back and started to dance in her seat.

I asked, "How would a young'n like you know that song? I barely do."

"Mum used to play them all the time when I was growing up. She loves them more than anyone I know. Besides, it's pretty hard not to know about the Beatles when you grow up within a stone's throw of Abbey Road."

"You're kiddin'."

"No, my dear, I'm not. You're riding with—or should I say, you're *driving*—the youngest daughter of Pamela Jayne Cherry and James Hubert Page III. My older sister and I grew up in a beautiful home in St. John's Wood, in London, and spent many happy days at our glorious family manor house and estate in the Lake District. I also bought myself a townhouse in London a few years back, where I now live quite happily with Marlon. Truth be told, I was born with a silver spoon in my mouth. Or as Sally likes to say, 'A complete silver service for twelve.' You would've found out sooner or later, so I might as well admit it to you now. I was born to a life of privilege. Since he was an only child, my father inherited everything from my fabulously wealthy grandfather Page. I've always had the absolute best of absolutely everything, and I'm now quite certain you're absolutely bored with me."

I did my best fake sigh, and said, "You're absolutely right. Whatever chance we had for absolute happiness just went up in absolutely the most absolute smoke in the absolute—help me out here."

She laughed, and said, "Oh, shut up, you dreadful old man, I'm trying to hear my neighbors sing." She sang along with John and Paul, in perfect tune.

I said, "Well, I'll say one thing for you, missy. You're full of surprises. Never in a million years would I have taken you for a rich girl."

"And for exactly what would you take me?" she asked with a sexy look in her big green eyes.

I looked at her for a second before asking, "Will you please quit leavin' the door wide open with all kinds of innuendo? Or should it be 'leavin the *window* wide open with' . . . never mind, just knock it off, will ya?"

My fake scowl didn't work, and she said, "You love it, and you know it. You may be an ancient geezer, but there's still a part of you that's young enough for me. And I don't mean *that* part, either. Get your mind out of the gutter. Anyway, you might just as well give up, Cooper. We Pages can be quite determined when we see something we want."

The Beatles ended their tune, and she turned off the radio. She said, "We shan't hear anything better than that today. Or anything more appropriate."

I liked the Beatles before I met Cherry Page, but at that moment, I loved them.

Trying yet again to keep things aboveboard, I said, "So, your mom's maiden name is Cherry. I just assumed like everyone else you got your name because of your hair."

"You're right, that *is* what everyone assumes. In truth, my name was chosen before I was even a twinkle in me dad's eye. Had I been a boy, I was to have been called Oliver. Please tell me you prefer driving Cherry Page rather than Oliver Page."

"Hmmm, let me think. Yep, I'd hafta say that I prefer drivin' Cherry rather than Oliver." Pause. "I'm relatively happy, but I'm not gay."

"Awfully glad to hear it. Glad that you're happy, and that you're not gay."

26

LAWRENCE LYNDON-BOWEN HAD BEEN WATCHING THE RELENTLESS MEDIA coverage concerning Cherry and her stalker, and had come up with a plan to take advantage of it. He was stuck in traffic near Agnes Scott College, the location for much of the film, when he hit upon an idea that made him smile and pull out his cell phone. He soon had his director, Chuck Guinness, on the line, and was trying to persuade him to join in on the scheme.

"Chuck, we're already getting tons of publicity from these dreadful killings, and if we were to let Cherry disappear for a few days, it would become an utter deluge of ink being poured out on to paper worldwide. Think of it, the headlines would write themselves: 'Missing Movie Star' this, 'Missing Movie Star' that. Surely you can see my point?"

Seated at the desk in his suite, Guinness said, "There already is a deluge of ink. As well as video. I don't know, Lawrence. The whole idea seems a bit ghoulish to me. I mean, using the suffering of innocent people, as well as our star, purely for financial gain? It just doesn't feel right somehow."

Lawrence replied, "I understand your point of view, Chuck, really I do, but you need to look at this through my jaundiced eye, and see that we can make something good come from all these terrible things. The more money the film makes, the more we have to share with all those who have a vested interest in it. Not just you and I, but everyone from the grips to the stars will benefit. You see that, don't you?"

"Yes, Lawrence, I can see that, and your point is well taken. But I'm also worried about what taking time off will do to the feeling of camaraderie that is forming within the group. It can be quite a delicate balance, and I don't want to muck it up while all is going so well."

Lawrence said, "If that's your major concern, I hardly think that a few days will change the dynamic of the group. In fact, it might even make them *more* inclined to rally 'round our girl. But obviously, I'm looking at it from a purely monetary standpoint: you know, add a little more mystery to the already boiling pot, and it can only help our cause. 'Where Is Cherry' and 'Cherry Is Found' stories will keep us on the front page, no pun intended, for weeks, I tell you. Weeks."

Guinness paused for a beat, and then said, "I actually *could* use a little more time to work with my leading man, and scout the college location a bit more. And—I must admit—more free publicity is not something to which I'm opposed." He sipped his vodka tonic, and said, "All right then, Lawrence. I'll set the wheels in motion. How does three days sound? Is that enough time?"

Lyndon-Bowen said, "Why not keep her hidden until next Monday? That way, we shall have five full days of utter madness, and we can spring her on the media at the beginning of the week, when everyone's back from their weekend gatherings, and whatnot. Believe me, it's always best to be the big news at the week's start, as opposed to its end. Remember, I was in the publicity department at Stonestreet for nine years before I ever produced a foot of film. Just leave it all to Uncle Larry."

Guinness didn't want to leave it all to Uncle Larry, but he really could use more time. Any filmmaker at any level could always use more time. He said, "I'll call Cherry's girl when we hang up, and tell her that Cherry needs to disappear until next Monday. Call me first thing tomorrow morning. I want to discuss the location shooting and run some ideas past you."

"Splendid. I'll call you bright and early. Oh, one more thing. Let's keep our plan a secret from the cast and crew. I don't want any leaks to the press."

"Fine by me. The less who know, the better. I'll wait for your call."

They hung up, and Guinness told his assistant, Lynne, what was happening, and what needed to happen. She immediately got on her cell, and Guinness immediately went back to his vodka.

27

CHERRY AND I HAD A VERY PLEASANT DRIVE BACK TO THE RITZ, AND managed to get there without being spotted by any news types. I pulled into our reserved spot behind the hotel, and there were the usual ten or twelve photographers standing above us on the sidewalk, yelling and snapping pictures.

The loading dock area of the hotel is actually well below street level, so they can look down on us from their perch on the sidewalk. Cherry smiled up at them, and blew a kiss, so I did, too. This made them yell questions at me, and I did the old 'I can't hear you' routine, cupping my hand to my ear and shaking my head. Cherry then did the same, and we walked up the ramp that leads to the lower part of the Ritz.

I made up my mind about whether or not to tell her about the latest message and murder on the ride up in the elevator.

I said, "Listen. There's been another killing, and another message from the stalker."

She closed her eyes and slumped against the back wall of the elevator, and said, "Oh, no, please don't tell me that. I simply cannot bear another person being killed because of me."

I took hold of her arm, and said, "Cherry, look. It's not your fault. This maniac could be after anyone who's famous. You just happen to be the target this time, that's all. You're not the cause, so stop saying that you are."

She kept her eyes closed and didn't speak again until the doors opened onto the fifth floor. As we walked out, she said, "Please don't tell me what the message said, or who was killed."

"I have no intention of letting you read the message, and you don't need to know the details. As far we're concerned, there isn't a laptop within fifty miles of this joint. We'll have a quiet evening in the suite, and go about our lives as if nothing happened. Okay?"

Smiling weakly, she said, "Whatever you say, Cooper. You're the chief."

"That's more like it."

We had just walked into the suite when she got a call from Sally Allen. She listened for a minute or so, and said, "Well, you'll get no complaint from me, dear. I could surely use a vacation from this whirlwind we wake up to each day. You're certain Chuck is on board with it? He usually likes to—oh, okay, then. I guess I'd better start planning my vanishing, then. Love you, too, dear. Bye-bye."

I took a seat in one of the armchairs, and asked, "What's this about vanishing and a vacation?"

She said, "You remember Lawrence? The smarmy creature that keeps trying to get a date with me? Our executive producer?"

"How could I forget Old Leather Pants? How does he figure into your going on vacation?"

Cherry flopped down on the sofa, took off her sneakers, and said, "Lawrence has decided that if I 'disappear' until next Monday the media will go insane, and the resulting publicity will boost interest in the film."

"Hmmm, so what he's sayin' is: daily coverage in every newspaper in the world and on the Internet, and twenty-four-hour-a-day coverage on every channel on TV in every nation in the world just isn't good enough."

"Precisely," Cherry said, leaning back on the sofa. "I suppose he wants thirty or forty hours a day devoted to my stalker and me." She looked at the unopened laptop on the coffee table, and said, "Honestly, it *would* be nice to take a little break from this madness, even if just for a short while. I have to say, sometimes I feel as if I may go into hysterics and never come out."

I got up and put the laptop on the shelf in the closet, and said, "Well, we can't have you dissolving into a pool of tears, now, can we? Anyplace special you have in mind?"

Cherry leaned forward and put her elbows on her knees. "As a matter of fact, I do have a place in mind. And I should think you'd be right at home there," she said.

I walked over and sat on my bed by the window. "Let me guess, Jolly Old England?"

"No, silly goose, I was thinking more along the lines of some-where a bit warmer."

"Oh. Okay, then. Someplace warmer. Let's see. I know what would be good. How 'bout Bermuda? I hear they really like Brits out there. Especially you privileged types."

"No, not Bermuda. But you're on the right track."

I thought for a moment, and said, "I've got it. The Bahamas. We can even gamble down there."

"Nope."

"Las Vegas?"

Cherry laughed, and said, "No! I want to have a bit of a rest, not a wicked, sinful gambling spree."

"Okay, I give up. Where, then?"

She said, "I *told* you. Somewhere you would feel right at home."

I got it then. "Oh, no, Cherry, you don't mean . . ."

"Oh, yes, Cooper, I *do* mean. Gulf Front, here we come!"

Part Two
Camera ...

28

Penny was about to blow her top.

The day had been a nightmare from the moment she got out of bed. First, the toilet overflowed, and Binny couldn't get there to fix it until after two o'clock, because he was going to his wife's uncle's funeral. So, Penny had to mop up the water and make arrangements to leave him a key so he could come by and do the repairs when he was free.

Then the power went off as she was in the middle of drying her hair, because some moron made a mistake on a work order. Her nearest neighbor's power was supposed to be turned off because he was leaving for six months, but hers was cut off instead. It took over an hour to straighten it all out, and that made her late for work, and cranky to boot.

She spent her first half hour at the office apologizing to Doreen for snapping at her. Coop's secretary was the sweetest woman in the world, at least to Penny, and said to just forget it, but Penny couldn't.

Then, at 2:15, when everything seemed to be going smoothly, Binny called and told her she was "lookin' at about five hunnerd dollars' wortha work" before she could use her bathroom again.

She told him to go ahead and fix it, and then had to phone her landlord/uncle in New York and get him to wire her the money. She felt guilty about asking Uncle Stan for the money since he rented her the cottage for a pittance, but as he had told her more than once, the landlord was responsible for maintaining the rental property. And besides, a woman without a bathroom is no woman at all, she thought.

So when she found herself refereeing a domestic brawl in the boondocks, she saw it as the perfect end to a perfect day.

Danny Shannon and his wife Serena were at it again, having one of their drunken knock-down, drag-out fights, and it was fifteen minutes past quitting time. Penny had taken the call thirty minutes earlier, and ever since had been trying to get the two combatants to calm down and go back inside their trailer home, which sat two miles outside the city limits. But every time it looked as if the fight was over, one of them would say something nasty about the other, and it would start up all over again.

Danny had a huge lump over his left eye caused by a cast-iron frying pan that Serena had smashed upside his head, and she had a bloody nose caused by Danny's buttocks. He had turned his back on her to plead his case to Penny, and when Serena tried to sneak up on her husband to hit him with the frying pan again, she stumbled and fell, ramming her face into his bony backside.

After wrestling the frying pan from Serena's grasp and putting it the patrol car, Penny had literally sized them up. She figured that Serena weighed about two hundred and twenty-five pounds, and Danny one-twenty in his clothes and boots, so their tally came to almost three hundred and fifty pounds of pure meanness. Add a couple of quarts of cheap booze to the equation, and no doubt about it, you had a fun day all the way around.

Just as Penny thought for the umpteenth time that the fracas was finally coming to an end, Danny called Serena a "hillbilly pig," and she took off her shoe and began to beat him about the head and shoulders with it.

So, acting chief Prevost was about to lose it, and lock them both up and be done with it, when fellow officer Earl Peavey pulled up next to the trailer. Penny took a deep breath and relaxed because Serena had a huge crush on Earl, and would always instantly stop fighting if he took the call.

Twenty minutes earlier, Earl had just started his shift when Penny called and told him to drive out to the Shannon trailer. There had been a slight delay because while Earl was stopped at one of the three traffic lights in Gulf Front, Heather Gilley drove her old Toyota into the back of Miss Wallace's new Saturn. Had it been anyone else, the matter would have been settled quickly, but Miss Wallace was impossible to deal with when she wasn't angry, and she was very angry at that moment.

Now that her Earl was finally on the scene, Penny could go home and forget the worst day she had experienced in months.

She watched as Serena and Danny shook hands with Earl, both of them immediately calming down as if nothing had happened. Serena calmed down because she didn't want Earl to dislike her, and Danny calmed down because he didn't want the much larger Earl to cream him.

Penny said, "Carry on, Earl, I'm gone," got into Coop's car, and left at a high rate of speed. She slowed down when she was nearing the city line, and relaxed for the first time all day.

The tension in her neck was driving her crazy, and she cursed Coop loudly for not being there to give her one of his patented shoulder rubs. Then she cursed him for not calling her, cursed him for being on TV with Cherry Page, and then she cursed him for living. She was all knotted up and all cursed out as she pulled into the graveled parking area behind her beach cottage.

The only things she wanted at that point were a beer and a bath. She opened the door of the screened porch, made her way to the kitchen, and dropped her keys on the counter. After grabbing a Rolling Rock from the fridge, she went into the tiny bathroom and checked to see if the toilet flushed correctly. It did, and she moved to the tub and turned on the hot water for her bath.

As she waited for the tub to fill, Penny wondered yet again what was keeping Coop from phoning her; she decided to give him one more chance to call before losing her patience completely.

But, if he didn't call *tonight*—well, he had just better call tonight.

29

"Cherry. Kid. Pal. Can't you think of another place you'd like to go? Maybe Hawaii, or Tahiti? I've always wanted to go to Ta—"

"Cooper, why don't you want to go to Gulf Front? I thought we could kill two birds. We could disappear, and you could introduce me to Penny. You promised her that you'd introduce us, didn't you?"

"Well, yes, I mean, I did, but—"

"No buts about it. We can leave first thing in the morning. How long of a drive is it?"

Once again resigned to my fate, I flopped dramatically on my bed and said, "Depending on traffic, it's usually five and a half or six hours. It won't be too bad of a drive, but I *really* wish you'd choose some other spot to visit."

"Oh, come on, now, it'll be wonderful. I can meet your beloved, see your home, and learn more about you. I think it will be brilliant!"

I wanted to argue, but knew it wouldn't change her mind. "Okay, I know when I'm whipped." As I lay on my back, I got an idea, and ran it past her. "I have a plan as to how we can get outta here without any problem. You call Will and get him to bring your old-lady-disappearin'-disguise stuff. I'll call Neal and get another mode of transportation. If we try to leave in the Bentley, we'll never get away without being followed."

She jumped up and said, "Now you're talking, big boy! I'll let Will in on our plan. I'll even get him to bring a disguise for you, too."

She danced off to the bedroom, and I called Neal on my cell.

A young female voice answered at the Feagin residence. "Hello?"

"Julie? Jill? Joy?" I asked.

"Coop! Hi! It's me, Joy! How are you? When are you bringin' Cherry out here? We've been watchin' you on TV all day and night! Your hair looks *so* good! We can't believe you finally got a decent haircut. Are y'all comin' over tonight?"

Laughing at her excitement, I said, "No, darlin', we're not

comin' over tonight. And thanks. I do look more respectable, don't I? Listen, sweetie, is your old man there? I need to talk to him as soon as possible."

"Aw, c'mon, can't y'all come over for just a *little* while? Just for a little while, please-please-*please*?"

"No, not tonight, but we'll try and get out there soon, okay?"

She said in her disappointed voice, "Okay, I guess. I'll get Daddy. And Coop?"

"Yes, sweetie?"

"I know that you and Daddy are gonna catch that psycho killer before he can get to Cherry. All my friends are scared for her, but not me. I told them that she has my dad and Coop with her, and that's all she needs."

I said, "Thanks, Joy. That means a lot to me. And you're right, we'll get the killer."

"I know y'all will. And another thing. Your hair really does look great. Lemme get Daddy for you. Come as soon as you can, okay?"

"I promise."

Neal came on the line, "I thought it was you when I heard the squeals of teenage delight. What's up?"

"Long story short, Cherry and I are headin' outta town tomorrow, and I was wonderin' if I could use the Lexus. You can drive the Bentley while we're gone and feel like a big shot. Whatta ya say?"

"I say fine. Cherry's assistant called me just a few minutes ago and filled me in. I thought you might wanna change cars. I'll probably just park the Bentley back at the Ritz so they don't come to me askin' about y'all. What else do you need?"

I said, "I have it all figured out. Here's the deal."

We talked for a few minutes about my plan, and a moment after I hung up the phone, Cherry called from the bedroom, "Will wants to know what time he needs to make me disappear tomorrow."

"Tell him ten o'clock."

"Righty-o."

As I waited for her to come out of the bedroom, I looked at the room-service menu, and decided it was time for a change. Delivery pizza, or Chinese?

Pizza.

Cherry came out a minute later, and asked, "What shall we do this evening?"

"I was thinking pizza and TV in the suite. Is that okay by you?"

She said, "That's sounds divine, Cooper. Nothing would please me more right now. What do you fancy on your pizza?"

"Well, I know you'll probably hate this combination—all my officers do, they never let me order it—but I would really like mushrooms and anchovies. Does that disgust you like it does everyone else?"

She smiled, and said, "You've been talking with Sally, haven't you?"

Puzzled, I said, "Actually, no. What does Sally have to do with it?"

"You swear you haven't spoken with her?"

"I swear."

She said, "Well, this settles it. I'm the only person I know who *ever* asks for anchovies. I absolutely adore anchovies. It's quite obvious: you and I were meant to be, Cooper. Might as well give in now, and be done with it."

"Can I eat my pizza first?"

Giggling, she said, "Yes, you may, but then it's off to the church immediately after."

"Deal," I said.

"And get some beer, too, will you?"

"Yes, ma'am. Any special brand? Light? Dark?"

"Get whatever *you* like. I'm sure I'll love it too."

"Your wish, et cetera."

I looked through the brochures Sally had brought the morning we met, and found a nearby pizzeria that would deliver. Forty-five minutes later, Cherry and I were sitting next to each other on the sofa chowing down on a giant pizza, swilling beer, and watching *The Pink Panther*. It was about as good as it gets. I'm a huge Peter Sellers fan, and it turned out she was, too.

I was so comfortable with Cherry that it made me uncomfortable. Penny and I have been together for about nine years, off and on, and I do mean off and on. She keeps a journal, and did the math last year, and found that we've been together almost exactly as much as we've been apart. I've never been unfaithful to Penny while we're together as a couple, but when we've been apart, I've strayed a few times. With the pizza, and the beer, and the laughing, and the redheaded movie star sitting next to me, straying had never looked so good before.

I needed to call Penny.

Cherry must be a psychic as well as an international beauty. The moment I thought of calling Penny, she said, "I'll wager you and your lady friend spend evenings like this together quite often."

I just stared and said, "I'm sorry, what?" not wanting her to know that she was reading me like a script.

"I was just saying—never mind, it was nothing, really. Did you have enough to eat?"

"I had way too much to eat. And drink."

She inspected her fingernails, and asked, "Does Penny like anchovies?"

"No. As a matter of fact, she despises them."

"Hmmm. Then I guess we shall have to stay away from pizza while we're in Gulf Front, yeah?"

"Yeah. That might be best," I said. After what felt like an awkward moment, I said, "Lemme tell you what I have in mind regarding our great escape."

"Oh, please do, I'm dying to hear your devious plan."

For the next five minutes, I filled her in, and Cherry listened and clapped her hands when I was finished.

"Bravo, Cooper," she said. "I love an adventure, and I'm so glad that you're allowing me to impose on you this way. I promise to be a good girl, and behave like a lady the whole time we're there. I'm so excited, I shall probably be up all night!"

I looked at my watch: 11:52. "Yikes," I said. "We better hit the sack. Tomorrow's a bigger-than-usual day."

"Awww, Cooper," she whined. "Can't we stay up for a little while longer? There's another Peter Sellers movie on. See? *Revenge of the Pink Panther*." She turned those big green eyes on me, and resistance was out of the question. I couldn't resist her *and* Chief Inspector Clouseau of the Sûreté.

"Okay, we can watch a little bit longer, but then it's straight to bed, and no more whining, young lady."

"Yay! You're the best!" she said, and leaned over and kissed my cheek.

I really needed to call Penny.

30

No wonder so many people sought fame! It was so energizing, so exhilarating! Even being famous in an anonymous way was nothing short of fantastic. Watching the news day and night and knowing that you were the star was something you had to experience, it couldn't be explained.

So much energy was available to you when you were doing that which must be done! That which was demanded from the higher power! The mind worked with such ease, driven by unseen powerful forces that fed you when you were most hungry for answers. The only requirement was to ask the forces for help, and then things happened almost on their own. Doors opened, paths became clear of obstacles, and moves were made as on a giant chessboard.

This next move was truly inspired, and when it got out that the last murder had happened so close to Cherry, right in her hotel, it would put the media in a frenzy yet again!

But there was no time for self-congratulation or to rest on laurels. The time had come to attack even closer to home, and this assault would no doubt be the crowning achievement in the Battle so far. No one would see this move coming, not in a million years!

Everything must be in place; there would be no room for slipups. This would be more difficult to pull off than the others, but what really good thing ever came easy? The satisfaction afterward would be deep and long lasting. Maybe then a break would be in order; let the heat die down for a day or two—maybe even a week—then strike back harder and closer still!

But for now, what a beautiful spring night to go to work. The moon still fat and bright, even though no longer quite full. A breeze cooling down the warm evening; as midnight arrived, the sweet smell of honeysuckle in the air. Lightness around the heart of the one chosen to do the most important task of them all, the weight of the *responsibility lifting as the action began. The silence on the street as everyone nestled in for the night, snug in his or her bed and safe from sacrifice.*

Well, almost everyone.

Okay, enough savoring the moment: time to settle down and get to work. Make sure everything was in the car and head out for the hunt.

Gas? Check. Dark suit and mask? Check. Appropriate shoes? Check. Duct tape? Check. New toy, the thing that will be the most fun yet? Double check.

Start your engines!

The midnight hour, the moon as companion, the feeling of power as the car roared to—shit!

Almost forgot the knife.

31

PENNY WAS IN A FOUL MOOD WHEN SHE WOKE UP. SHE HAD TOSSED AND turned half the night, and was in the middle of an unpleasant dream when her alarm clock sounded.

All the unpleasantness of yesterday was made worse by the fact that Coop still hadn't called. What possible excuse could he have? Were all his fingers broken? Had he been kidnapped and taken to a land where no phones existed? He'd better hope that his excuse was good enough to appease her; otherwise, he was going to be looking for a new girlfriend when he finally *did* call.

The stupid dumbass.

She showered, dressed, and headed to Matthews Cafeteria for breakfast. Penny only ate in the restaurant four or five times a month, as opposed to Coop, who ate there every day he was on duty. She moved through the line, speaking only to order biscuits and eggs with coffee. Her mood kept everyone at arm's length without her having to say a word. Anybody who knew her was familiar with her "I hate Coop" expression, and no one said anything more than good morning to her as she ate at a table by the front window alone.

Fueled by the food and coffee, her mood lightened and she bid everyone a cheery farewell: "Okay, everybody, y'all can relax now. Chief Cooper is safe for at least one more day."

This got her a rousing cheer from the patrons, and she smiled broadly as she left.

One of the town mutts came up to Penny as she opened the door to her borrowed patrol car, and she petted his head for a moment before getting in the car and heading to the office. Once there, she spent the first ten minutes apologizing again to Doreen for her actions the day before, then sat in Coop's chair behind his desk, going over the monthly reports. She drank two more cups of coffee as she worked, and finished the reports a minute before Doreen called out, "Penny, line one. It's Blanche."

Blanche was calling from O'Kelly's, the smaller of the two grocery stores in Gulf Front. Penny did all her shopping there, since it was closest to her cottage. Blanche had worked the only cash register for as long as anyone could remember, and was the main source of gossip in town. Penny smiled to herself as she picked up, knowing it must be pretty juicy if Blanche felt the need to call her at the office.

"Hey lady," Penny said. "What's new?"

Blanche replied, "I think this is somethin' you need to see for yourself. It just come in a few minutes ago."

Penny looked at her watch: 9:04. She was surprised that she'd been working on the reports for almost an hour. She asked Blanche, "What's so important that I hafta come over there and see it? Can't you just tell me what it is?"

"Honey, you need to see this for yourself. Cain't choo take a minute and come on over?"

Penny sighed and said, "Okay, but you're bein' mighty mysterious about this. I'll be there in a minute."

They hung up, and Penny told Doreen where she was going as she headed out. This had better be good, she thought as she started the engine and drove to O'Kelly's.

Blanche met her as she walked into the store, her hands behind her back, hiding something.

Penny chuckled, and said, "All right, you're under arrest for disturbin' my peace. Show me whatever it is you've got back there, and no sudden movements."

Blanche brought her arms forward, and handed Penny one of the tabloid papers that were on sale in the market.

Penny stared at the cover in disbelief.

Cherry Page and Coop were in living color on the front page, Coop in a tuxedo, Cherry in a formal gown, their lips locked in a kiss. Another, smaller picture below showed them in the same attire, laughing as if they were sharing some secret joke.

The headline blared, in large yellow print: BRITISH BOMBSHELL'S BRAND-NEW BODYGUARD BOYFRIEND. Below the headline another, less significant line read, "Has This Cherry Been Picked?"

Penny opened the rag to the article about Coop and Cherry, and read the first line: "Who is the hunky guy who has been spotted around Atlanta closerthanthis with the fabulous Cherry Page?"

That was all Penny needed to read, and she rolled it up and gripped it in her right hand like a nightstick.

Blanche said, "You know, these so-called magazines come out Wednesday mornin', and they deliver 'em right as we're openin' the store. When I seen it, well, I knew I had to call you and show it to ya before it got around town. You know how people are: they see a picture, and go off the deep end. But, ya gotta admit, it *is* quite a picture." She went and got another copy, pointed at the cover, and asked, "Are you believin' that? I liked to have *died* when I seen it!"

Penny tried to smile, and said, "Oh, come on now, Blanche, you know these rags make up stuff like this all the time. I'm sure there's a perfectly innocent explanation for this photo. This coulda been taken with a dozen people around. Besides, Coop would never cheat on me. He's as loyal as they come."

Blanche replied, "He's as loyal as *men* come, Penny. That's the problem."

At first I didn't know where I was, then I realized that Cherry and I had fallen asleep on the sofa watching the movie. I was still in a sitting position, and she had curled up on the sofa, her head in my lap. I looked at my watch, saw that it was 2:51 A.M., and slowly moved out from under Cherry, placing her head gently on the sofa cushion.

I turned off the TV, and quietly called the front desk from Cherry's room to cancel the wakeup call since we would be sleeping late. Then I went back and picked her up, brought her to her bed, and placed her on top of the covers.

I debated for a full minute whether or not I should undress her, and decided to let sleeping movie stars lie. Her shoes were already off, so I pulled the covers from the other side of the bed over her, wrapping her like a calzone. I yawned deeply and walked back to my room, so tired that I didn't bother to undress; I just took off my shoes and got into bed, still somewhat woozy from the beer and pizza. Sleep came quickly and heavily.

When I woke up again, I found that Cherry had climbed into bed with me during the night, and was sleeping with her back to my front, dressed only in her legendary bra and panties. No pajamas after a night of beer, I guessed. I was spooning her, my arm across her breasts, and she was holding my hand in hers. It was a good thing that I still had my clothes on, or something might have happened during the night.

Or right then.

Anyway, I did the last thing in the world that I wanted to do at that moment: I removed my hand from hers, and withdrew my arm. Another chance squandered, I thought, and smiled again at the notion of all the guys who would've loved to be in my position. Especially *that* position.

She stirred as I moved, and made a small moaning sound, but didn't wake up. I got my watch from the windowsill where I kept it, and saw that it was 9:22. We had slept through the night, and obviously we'd both needed it. In fact, I wanted to turn over and catch a few more winks but knew we should be up and at 'em, so I made a conscious effort to stay awake.

About ten minutes later, Cherry stretched lazily and said, "I hope you took advantage of me last night. I promise I won't tell, if you won't."

My eyes still closed, I said, "I did unspeakable things to you. Things I would be arrested for in twenty-nine states. Terrible things that we shall never speak of again."

"I knew you couldn't resist me forever, Cooper," she said, still stretching. "Was I any good?"

"A gentleman never tells."

She yawned, and asked, "What does that have to do with the likes of you?"

I chuckled, and said, "You're pretty funny for a sex symbol. Now, get out of my bed and go get dressed. We hafta order breakfast and get Will in here. It's time to implement my most devious of plans."

Yawning wider, she asked, "Can't we lie here for another hour or two? Or three? We have all day to be devious. What say we be sleepious?"

"No, ma'am, we need to get up and get going. I wanna be in Gulf before dark. But, if you wanna just lay around here and—"

Excited, she said, "I forgot! Right, I'm ready to go, sir! Won't take a mo' to get my bag packed!"

With that, she jumped from the bed and ran to her room, leaving me with an eyeful of her celebrated rump.

I didn't need to call Penny. I needed to call a psychiatrist.

When I heard the shower running, I got up and called down for breakfast. They informed me that Sally had already taken care of it, and that it would be delivered at ten on the button. That gave me twenty minutes to shower, dress, and get Cherry to call Will and tell him to come over at ten thirty, instead of ten. It also gave me plenty of time to call Neal, which I did. Everything was in order, and all was right with the world.

Except for that whole serial killer deal.

32

PENNY THOUGHT SERIOUSLY FOR A MOMENT ABOUT BUYING UP ALL THE copies of the tabloid rag, but knew it was hopeless. The news would be all over town in no time, no matter what she did. So, she smiled at Blanche and told her halfheartedly that everything would work out fine, and headed back to the office.

Halfway there, she decided instead to make her rounds, and called in on the radio to tell Doreen. The spring air would make her feel better, she thought, and she was right. Ten minutes after she passed the city line she was in high spirits again, even able to laugh at herself for worrying about the tabloid photos. Her friends would know it was all a bunch of nonsense, and the ones who didn't know weren't much good to her as friends, anyway.

Everything was calm on the highway that led north from Gulf Front, and she waved back to the drivers who waved as they saw her. As usual, traffic was light, and she drove at a leisurely pace as she surveyed her borrowed kingdom. Truth be told, Penny Prevost could get used to this chief-of-police arrangement; it was actually kind of nice to be in charge.

Feeling slightly antsy, she got on the interstate and headed towards Pensacola. Once there, she went for an early lunch at a soul food restaurant that she and Coop frequented at least once a month. "Ludie's Soul Kitchen" opened for lunch at eleven, and Penny was the third person standing in line when the doors opened.

She talked easily with the customers and the servers, and sat down to eat with the owner's recently married niece at a table in the center of the small room. They talked about married life, minivans, and police tactics, and Penny felt her anxiety melting away with each bite of lunch.

After a meal of fried chicken, turnip greens with corn bread, baked yellow squash, and sweet-potato pie, she was ready to take on the world.

On the ride back to Gulf, she felt so much better that she decided to give Coop a pass on his reluctance to pick up a telephone. Maybe there really *was* a reasonable explanation for his not calling. The day before, Susan had put her mind at ease when they had talked, and she knew from the news reports that he was at least alive and well. Maybe a little *too* well, if the tabloids were to be believed, but she didn't really think that there was anything improper happening in Atlanta.

But—if she didn't hear from him by tomorrow, he was in for an earful, which she would deliver at high volume.

The sweet boy.

Cherry and I were showered and dressed and had long ago finished breakfast when we finally heard from Will at 11:40.

He said he'd be right over, and arrived a few minutes later with his Cherry-Page-Disappearing-Case, and a few items to make me disappear also. This was made necessary by the fact that I was fast becoming a recognizable face to the photographers. Like my new-found "success" with women over the last year, my newsworthiness had increased greatly over the same period as well. Last year's New Orleans murder case had put me near the national spotlight for the first time in my long career, and of course, now I was worldwide. It was beginning to look as if I might get sixteen minutes of fame.

Will came straggling in a little after noon, causing us to be over ninety minutes late for our getaway preparations. He looked like he'd slept in his clothes in an alley somewhere, but maybe he was just being fashionable.

Putting his big case down in the middle of the room, he said in his thick Cockney accent, "It turns out your Atlanta has quite a gay nightlife scene, know what I mean?"

I said, "Actually, no, I don't know what you mean. But if you had a good time, who am I to question it?"

He laughed, which made him cough, and said, "I woke up in some bloke's house in Midtown with a—never you mind. No need for sordid details. Let's just say old Will had a right laugh, and get on with the bleedin' disappearin', yeah?"

"Yeah," Cherry and I said in unison.

Thirty minutes later, Cherry was her "old" self, and yours truly was dressed in a light blue running suit with wraparound sunglasses, a gray wig and moustache, and an Atlanta Braves baseball cap. I must admit Will's a genius at disguise. Our closest friends wouldn't have recognized us.

As we stood in the middle of the big suite admiring Will's handiwork, someone knocked on the door.

With a sly smile on her wrinkled old face, Cherry asked, "Would you mind getting the door, Cooper?"

Suspicious, I said, "I don't mind in the least. What's with the devilish look?"

"Nothing. Nothing a'tall." She and Will exchanged a glance, and both looked at me as if waiting for me to move.

Another round of door knocking.

"Just a minute," I said, and went over and opened the door.

An old cliché became true: You could have knocked me over with a feather.

Standing in the hall smiling at me was an absolute dead ringer for Cherry. The body, the hair, the resemblance was astonishing. I thought she was a twin sister until she spoke.

She asked, in what I would learn was an Australian accent: "I do have the right suite number? I'm looking for Cherry Page." She obviously didn't recognize me, but maybe she would have, had I not been disguised by Will. She said, "I don't believe we've met. Are you a relative?"

I closed my mouth before flies started moving in, and said, "Uh, no, I'm Cooper. I mean, Coop. I'm the bodyguard. Uh, won't you come in?"

She said, "Oh, yeah, now I see. Will has already done a job on you. You look much younger on the telly."

She walked in and when she saw old lady Cherry and Will, they all came together in a group hug. I stood by and stared like an owl. Except I wasn't wise to the situation.

They unclenched, and Cherry said to me, "Cooper. Meet Bev Morgan, my stand-in and body double. We called her in early just for this occasion. Isn't she the loveliest thing ever?"

"She sure is," I said, and shook her hand. "You look so much like Cherry, it's amazing. The eyes, the hair—almost identical."

Bev touched her chest and said, "Well, there is a little padding up top to fill me out like our girl, and the eyes are colored contacts—my eyes are blue. And the hair? Actually, my hair is the exact same color as yours. But Will cuts it just like he cuts Cherry's, and with a little red coloring added, we come out looking much the same."

"You sure do," I said, still staring. "Where'd they find you?"

"Australia. Tasmania, actually. I worked at a resort in Wynyard, near the beach, and met Sally when she was on holiday there a few years back. She stole me from my boss, and here I am."

"Uncanny resemblance," I said, unable to take my eyes off her.

Cherry laughed at my astonished look, and said to Bev: "We found a chap who works here in the hotel to play the part of Cooper in our little farce." To me: "Will is going to make him look just like you, and then we can all go our merry ways."

Another knock at the door, and a guy who was roughly my size came in and introduced himself as Justin. He looked like he was about eighteen years old, so I took it as a compliment that he had been chosen to impersonate me.

Will burst my bubble when he said, "Blimey, I don't think I have near enough product to make *this* bloke look like Coop. Maybe I better send out for a few cases of pancake makeup."

Everyone chuckled, so I had to act like I thought it was funny, too. Actually, I did.

I said, "Just try to keep your roving hands to yourself, Will old buddy." To Justin: "Make sure you don't fall asleep in the chair while he's workin' on you."

Justin looked nervously at Will, then me, and said, "They told me if I came up here and followed the program, there was five hundred bucks in it for me, and a small part in the movie. But, hey, if there's gonna be some kind of—"

Cherry took Justin's arm in hers, and said in her old-lady voice, "Don't you worry one little bit, Justin. I'm Will's grandmother, and he does everything I tell him to do. And nothing more."

That calmed the kid down, and fifteen minutes later, Justin was me, Bev was Cherry, and we were ready to put our plan into action. Cherry made us all lock pinkies and swear to remain silent, and we all wished each other good luck.

We were gonna need it, as it turned out.

Suitcases in hand, Cherry and I went down the hall to Sally's room—in case cameras were trained on Cherry's window—to watch our look-alikes escape. Sally opened her door, laughed, and said, "Are you a pair, or what? Coop, you've gone gray overnight."

"The pressures of my job, Sal."

We walked to the window and opened the curtain just enough to see the action play out five stories below. From our vantage point, Justin was a passable replica of me, but Bev was a dead ringer for Cherry in her sunglasses and tennis visor. Justin really didn't have to be all that much of a copy of me, since all eyes are always on Cherry. Even when it's not her.

The photographers were fooled, waved at Bev, and called out with the usual clamor: "Cherry, over here! Cherry, look up! Cherry, how do you feel?"

Justin and Bev got into the Bentley, drove away from the Ritz, and the usual three or four paparazzi-mobiles inevitably followed. Justin headed down Lenox Road as if the destination was the theater, and that made the coast clear for Cherry and me to make our great escape. We were already more than a couple of hours behind schedule, but if we hit the road, we could still make it to Gulf Front before dark. I was hoping to give Cherry a little tour of the town, and then take her to meet Penny at the beach cottage.

Sally called down for a bellhop, and when he knocked at the door, I said to the ladies, "Okay, I think it's safe to go now. Sally, have a nice vacation, and call if you need anything."

Sally hugged Cherry, and said, "I intend to be as still as possible for the next few days, Coop. Take good care of Miss Page, and have a safe trip."

Cherry and I made it to the elevators, the unaware bellhop following behind with our suitcases. We rode down with a young couple, and Cherry's coughing and hacking routine kept them as far away as they could get in the elevator. The bellhop kept his eyes locked on the numbers, no doubt hoping time itself would speed up. I moved away from Cherry, too, my face twisted in disgust.

When we got to the lobby, we both shuffled out of the elevator,

Cherry coughing as if she might lose a lung at any moment. I patterned my walk after an old guy who lives in my apartment complex. I thought if my landlady, Mrs. Wiley, had seen me, she would have fallen for me on the spot. They say your mind's the first thing to go when you start to age, or is it your legs? Whichever, I had both bases covered.

People moved aside as we made our way to the hotel's back entrance; it may have been Cherry's coughing act, or it may have been my light blue running suit. Baby blue just isn't my color. It washes out my complexion terribly.

Kidding.

When we got outside, I tipped the bellhop, dialed Joe Don Kendrick, Neal's P.I. associate, and told him we were ready for take-off. He had been waiting in the upper parking area in the Lexus, and drove to where we stood. He left the car running, and headed inside the Ritz without a word. Cherry got in the passenger's side; I tossed our bags in the backseat and got behind the wheel.

Cherry asked, "Who was that big fellow?"

"Name's Joe Don Kendrick. He works for Feagin Investigations."

"Glad he's on our side. Well, drive on, old man."

"Yes, mum."

I put the car in gear, and we drove out of the Ritz and into traffic, luckily hitting it at just the right time. Highway 400 had an entrance ramp within a hundred yards or so of the Ritz, and I got on it with no problem. We made our way to I-85 south, which would take us to Alabama, where we could take smaller highways and back roads south into Gulf Front.

It was a beautiful day, the traffic was moderate, and driving the Lexus felt pretty good. Of course, it was no Bentley, but I was willing to sacrifice luxury for a little privacy.

As Cherry said, I'm the best.

When Justin and Bev arrived at the Candler Community Theater, Justin parked the Bentley in the assigned spot next to the front steps. Two large male police officers opened the car doors and escorted them inside. The reporters and photographers were kept far enough away that they didn't notice that two impostors had replaced Cherry and her bodyguard. The officers didn't notice either, as they were too involved with getting the look-alikes safely into the building.

Chuck Guinness met them as they walked in, and said to Justin, "Stay away from the stage, and keep out of sight." Chuck pointed to the balcony stairs and Justin nodded and walked across the lobby. He took the stairs to the balcony and Chuck took Bev down the aisle to the stage, where the table was set up for the reading of the script, and addressed the cast and crew.

"Good morning, boys and girls. I'm afraid Cherry won't be joining us today, she's turned up missing." When several cast members looked concerned, he said, "Don't worry, nothing dreadful has happened to our star, it merely appears that she may have made a break for it. Can't say as I really blame her, what with all the pressure she's been under of late, but we need to keep working as if she were here. Let me introduce Bev Morgan to those of you who don't already know her. She is Cherry's stand-in and body double, and will be reading for her today. Hopefully, we shall know more about Cherry's whereabouts soon, but for now, let's get on with it, shall we? I want us all to pull together and treat this as any other day. We don't need to put in a full eight hours, but I want to work on a few things we discussed yesterday. Please turn to page fourteen, and let's start with you, Molly. Begin with your first line."

Molly Harkins, who played the college dean's assistant, began to speak her lines, and everyone got over the fact that Cherry was not there, and got down to the business of rehearsing. Lawrence Lyndon-Bowen, who was sitting in a chair a few feet from the table, smiled at his director, and Guinness nodded in recognition.

Everything was falling smoothly into place, and the disappearance of Cherry Page was now on the record.

33

ONCE WE WERE OUT OF THE ATLANTA AREA, CHERRY CLIMBED INTO THE backseat and began to take off her disguise. Under all the camouflage, she was dressed in black shorts and a yellow tee shirt. She climbed back to the front, pulled down the passenger's mirror, and spent a few minutes fixing her face, as if she needed it. Finished, she put the mirror back in place, and asked, "Isn't that running suit a bit warm?"

"Yes, it is. Help me get out of it."

She pulled on my sleeve as I got my right arm out, and then helped me pull it off over my left arm. I took off the wig and the cap, and we settled back to enjoy the ride. Alongside the interstate, flowers were blooming and trees were beginning to fill out. We saw a few cows and horses, too, and Cherry seemed to be enjoying herself. I know I was.

I'd been thinking and driving silently for five minutes or so, when she said, "Penny for your thoughts about Penny."

"How do you know I was thinkin' about Penny? Maybe I was thinkin' about gas mileage, or where to stop for lunch. What are you, psychic, or somethin'?"

"I am, as a matter of fact, but it doesn't take a mind reader to know that she's the focus of your thoughts today."

I said, "I *was* thinkin' about her, actually, but nothing too deep. I was just thinkin' how happy she'll be when she meets you. And that's the truth."

She looked out her window, and said wistfully, "I wish I had a man like you thinking about me. It must be very nice indeed to be the object of a good man's affection."

I said, "You gotta be kiddin' me. You're the object of a billion men's affections. And that's a conservative estimate."

"Being the object of a man's lust is not the same thing, and you know it." She turned to look at me, and said, "I know I sound like such a ninny when I get serious, seeing as my life appears to be so easy and glamorous to those who don't know me, but I have never truly been loved for my self. Even before I became famous, which again, sounds so egotistical and stupid, even when I was just a girl growing up in London, I could never be sure that I was liked for myself alone. The fact that my father was so bloody wealthy made me suspect the motives of all the boys who came 'round during my teen years. Again, it sounds so stupid! Complaining about being rich! Complaining about being famous! It's so—asinine.

"But, sometimes I wish I had been born to a shopkeeper, or a farmer, or anything other than a rich father. Being born into wealth can be a curse as well as a blessing, believe it or not. In fact, I often think I'm cursed, I really mean that. And, as dreadfully trite as it might sound, I want to be loved for myself, for what's in my heart, what's in my soul. I want to be special to someone, and not because I make movies, or have a rich daddy. I want to be special to someone the way Penny is special to you, the way you're special to her. I want—I want to be special. That's all, really."

I noticed a tear in her eye, so I said as reassuringly as I could, "Cherry, you're gonna have to trust me on this, but I know you'll find someone to love you the way you want to be loved. You're such a good person, and a good friend, it's bound to happen for you, and sooner than you think. Look at me, I liked you immediately, and I hate everybody."

Laughing and crying, she said, "No, you don't. You get on with everyone. You most certainly do *not* hate everybody."

"I most certainly *do* hate everybody. I hate everybody all day long. But—like I said—with you, it was different. Hell, I hate Penny half the time, and she hates me almost all the time."

She laughed and wiped her eyes with the bottom of her tee shirt, and said, "Penny loves you all the time. She just can't stand you all the time. There's a difference."

"Tell me about it. I'm lucky she even talks to me half the time. But, to be serious for a moment, you'll find a guy to love you some-day. Take it from a guy who thinks you're *very* special. And I haven't even seen one Cherry Page movie. So take that, and put it in your pipe."

At that moment, the left rear tire blew, and the car swerved as I got it back under control. Luckily, there wasn't a car within half a mile of us. I pulled off to the side of the highway and came to a stop in the middle of nowhere.

Cherry said, "See? That's what you get for being nice to me. Like I told you, I'm cursed."

34

BACK IN THE OFFICE, PENNY THOUGHT THAT MAYBE THE TABLOID pictures would turn out to be no big deal. Then the calls of sympathy started coming in from all her "friends."

Mrs. Norberg called and said that it was a *such* shame that Chief Cooper had moved on without her, but it was best that Penny find out now what kind of a man he was, rather than later. The gall of the woman amused Penny, because Mrs. Norberg's husband had been cheating on her for over twenty years, and everybody in town knew it, including Mrs. Norberg. Being given advice on relationships by the town's relationship laughingstock was the height of irony, Penny thought. She thanked the fiftysomething woman for her concern, and hung up in the middle of Mrs. Norberg's blathering.

Angie Coletti of Angie's House of Beauty chimed in a few minutes later with a message from all the girls who were under a dryer, getting a cut, or waiting for their color to take effect: "You're better off without him." Penny thanked her, and told her to pass along her deepest thanks to the girls, who had been kind enough to take time from their busy schedules to worry about Penny and her love life. It just meant so much to her, they had no idea. Penny was reminded of the old proverb that if your ears are burning, people are talking about you. She now knew it wasn't true, because if it were, her ears would have burst into flames the moment the tabloid reached the women at the beauty shop.

Althea Silbey, a waitress at the Colonnade Restaurant who had just been through a nasty divorce, called to say that all men are scum, and that being alone was the greatest gift she'd received in years. Penny agreed, thanked her, and told her she had to take an emergency call, since Althea had started to cry. Penny hung up just as the dam ruptured.

DeWayne Berry, a mechanic at the town's only gas station, came by on his lunch break to make sure Penny was all right. Ten minutes after he left, she was still cleaning the grease and oil off the chair in which DeWayne had parked his ample rear end.

Over the years, DeWayne had tried at least thirty times to get Penny to go out on a date with him when she and Coop were apart. The only reason she never took him up on his offers was that he was the smelliest, grossest, fattest, and yes, the least attractive man in Gulf Front. Not to mention, he chewed tobacco. Not to mention, he was a racist pig. Not to mention, he spent time in prison for passing bad checks. Penny thanked him for his concern, and was able to get him to leave without actually having to touch him.

Josie Cutler, the town slut, called to say that men were like buses, and another one would be along soon. She also asked would Penny mind if she (Josie) called Coop when he finally got back? Penny stifled a laugh, recalling things Coop had said about Josie's character and lifestyle. Penny listened for a moment and then said that Josie was a free woman in a free country, and whatever would be, would be. The song "Que Sera, Sera" came into Penny's head and stayed there for quite a while after she hung up with Josie.

The phone rang yet again, and she picked it up to find her mother on the other end. Penny told her mom about the calls she had received, and Mrs. Prevost told her daughter that the tabloid was good for nothing except wrapping fish, and to call home if Penny wanted her father to come over to Gulf Front and punch anybody in the mouth. They both laughed, Penny said to give Daddy a big kiss, and they hung up.

There were several other calls meant to help Penny come to grips with the fact that it was over between her and Coop, and good riddance to bad rubbish. The only call that actually made her feel better was from Coop's elderly landlady, Mrs. Wiley. She said that anybody with half a brain knew that Coop and Penny were made for each other, and that the tabloid picture could have easily been doctored to make it look like they were kissing. Mrs. Wiley wasn't even sure if the man in the picture was actually Coop. It might be his head on another man's body, you know.

She also said that Penny should talk to Coop before letting it upset her, and asked if Penny would like to come over and have supper with her after work. Penny thanked her for her kind words and the offer, but politely declined, saying that she already had plans for the evening. That wasn't true; she just wanted to be alone after the events of the day. Mrs. Wiley said to forget about all the busybodies in town, and to call if she needed anything.

When they hung up, Penny smiled at the old lady's kindness and wisdom, and told Doreen to hold all her calls unless they were actually police business.

Then she sat back in Coop's chair, put her feet up on his desk, and watched the clock slowly tick off the seconds.

By 3:45, she'd had enough, told Doreen she was going on patrol, and headed out to Coop's patrol car.

She spent the rest of the day driving back and forth on the old highway that runs parallel to the town, lost in her thoughts.

35

I said, "Cherry, you are most definitely not cursed. In fact, you're about the most un-cursed person I know. Now, this is just a small setback on the highway to happiness, and I'll have us back on the road in no time."

"Highway to happiness?" she asked with a grin. "That sounds really good to me right about now. What can I do to help?"

"Just sit there and look beautiful. Actually, you might wanna get outta the car. It may get warm in here."

"I believe you're right," she said, and we both got out of the Lexus. First, I pulled off the running suit pants, revealing the khaki shorts I wore under them. Tossing the pants in the backseat, I opened the trunk and got out the small replacement tire. Cherry walked over to a grassy knoll by the road and sat down.

I said, looking at the crappy little tire, "We're gonna have to double back a little, and go into Montgomery. I refuse to drive Cherry Page into my town on one of these punk tires. We can get some lunch while we're there, too. Pick up a drive-thru burger, or somethin'. I don't want anyone to spot you and alert the media."

"Don't get another tire on my account, Cooper. And I don't need to eat again anytime soon. Besides, if we double back, won't that make us awfully late?"

"We're already late, and it's not just because of you that I want to get another tire. I really can't stand these things. Not to mention, I'm hungry, and I was gonna stop and eat anyway. Just relax as best you can. We'll be back on the road to Gulf before you know it."

She smiled, saluted, and said, "Yes, sir, Chief Cooper, sir."

"You're dang straight, 'yes, sir,'" I said, and got down to business changing the tire.

Fifteen minutes or so later, we were on the highway heading to Montgomery. Cherry put on my Braves cap and her sunglasses, and piled her hair under the cap. As soon as we reached an area that had a convenience store, I stopped and found a tire place in the phone book. An hour and ten minutes later, we were headed south again with the new tire in place.

I found a McDonald's, and we went through the drive-thru without her being spotted, and left with a sack full of burgers, fries, and Cokes.

The ride through southeast Alabama was nice, and we talked when we felt like it, and listened to the radio when we didn't. It was a very enjoyable experience, even considering the flat tire and backtracking we had to do. I did a quick mental projection, and figured we'd hit Gulf Front right about sundown, or a little after.

I shared the information with Cherry, and she said, "Well, I don't know about you, Cooper, but I'm well chuffed with that bit of news."

"Uh, okay. I feel a little chuffed myself," I said.

And I'm pretty sure I was.

36

GUINNESS CALLED AN EARLY END TO THE REHEARSAL AT 3:30, AND EVERY-
one said their good-byes. Everyone, that is, except Bev, Justin, Will,
and Lyndon-Bowen.

It was time to implement the next stage of the plan, which meant
that Will had more work to do on the impostors. He dressed Justin
in a maintenance worker's uniform that he had borrowed from the
Ritz, and made up Bev with some body padding and a short, dark
wig. The two of them walked out with Will to his SUV without a single member of the press giving them more than a casual once-over.

Lawrence waited until they were safely away, and then went out
to address the media. The cameras started flashing and recording,
the questions came in bunches, and he raised his hands to quiet the
crowd. All eyes, ears, and cameras were on him as he opened his
mouth to speak.

"Ladies and gentlemen, I have a brief statement, and then I shall
take questions for five minutes or so. I'm afraid I have a confession
to make. Cherry Page and her bodyguard have gone missing."

That got a collective gasp from the crowd, and the questions flew
immediately, drowning out Lyndon-Bowen's attempts to speak. He
was able to keep from smiling, and to maintain a look of concern,
all the while enjoying the firestorm he was creating. If this was any
indication of the interest that his words held for these people, his
intuition was spot-on, he thought.

Raising his arms again, he was able to get them to quiet down,
and he continued his tale.

"First of all, let me say, there is no evidence of foul play of any
kind."

Again, the crowd erupted, and he basked in the glow of their
white-hot efforts to get his attention. The cameras saw a man who
was clearly distraught, and fighting valiantly to keep from showing

his emotions regarding the situation. Lyndon-Bowen saw dollar signs and box-office records being broken.

He waited for them to stop bellowing, and then said, "The couple you saw arrive in Cherry's car this morning were actors hired to do nothing more than mislead you, and for that I am deeply sorry. I just didn't know what else to do when I heard that Cherry had—had—well, disappeared, and I made a bad job of it by deceiving you good people of the press, and for that I sincerely apologize. At this time, I shall be happy to answer any questions that you may have."

Instant pandemonium, as everyone began to try and shout his or her question louder than the next person.

Lyndon-Bowen said, "Please, please, one at a time. You there, the pretty blonde with the 'five' on your microphone."

"Denise Brooks, Fox Five news. Has Ms. Page ever left a movie set without telling anyone where she was going?"

"To my knowledge, this is the first time anything like this has ever occurred. Cherry Page is known for her consummate professionalism. But under these rather extraordinary circumstances, well, I can easily see why she might feel the need to jump ship, as it were. Next question? You, the gentleman with CNN."

"You stated earlier that there is no evidence of foul play. Do you have any idea as to where she might have gone, and have the authorities been notified?"

Lawrence lied, "We have our own people checking the airports in the area for any activity, and yes, the proper authorities have been notified. My guess would be that she's headed home to England, but that's only speculation on my part."

For the next twenty minutes, Lyndon-Bowen answered all manner of questions, lying through his capped teeth, and enjoying every second of his time in the spotlight. Playing the media crowd like a fiddle was something he had never experienced, and he didn't want it to end. He felt as if he could go on for hours, but he called a halt when the questions became absurd.

All in all, it felt wonderful to be the one on whom all the attention was focused for a change, and he lapped it up like the double cream he always poured on his strawberries.

An idea hit him as he was turning to walk away. He now had a name for the stalker and another way to stir the pot. He turned back to the microphones and asked for their attention one more time.

"Ladies and gentlemen, I have one additional thing to say before I go.

"Stonestreet Studios is prepared to pay a five-hundred-thousand-dollar reward for information leading to the capture of the 'Computer Killer.'"

37

THE SUN HAD JUST GONE DOWN WHEN PENNY ARRIVED AT THE BEACH cottage after driving out on the highway all afternoon and into the early evening to avoid everyone. She went inside, took off her uniform and slipped into her favorite cutoffs and one of Coop's old Florida State tee shirts. She let down her long black hair, and brushed it out in front of the bathroom mirror.

Deciding that a salad would be perfect for supper, she went into the kitchen, raided the refrigerator, and laid the ingredients out on the butcher-block island in the middle of the small room. She was chopping carrots for the salad with her big chef's knife when she heard a knock at the front door.

Putting down the knife, she wiped her hands on a dish towel and walked towards the door. She couldn't see anyone through the leaded glass, so she turned on the porch light and opened the door. Still seeing no one, she pushed the screen door open, and stepped out onto the porch.

A searing pain jolted her exposed left thigh, and she was on her back on the porch instantly, flopping around uncontrollably. A blow to the head left her unconscious, but still twitching. Her ankles were duct-taped together long before the spasms stopped.

When she came back to consciousness, Penny found herself on her back on the living-room floor, unable to move, due to the fact that she had been taped up like a mummy from her ankles to her waist, her wrists taped to her hips. She couldn't see or speak, since tape also covered her mouth and some kind of blindfold covered her eyes. She felt lucky when she realized that the taping stopped at her waist, because it would have been impossible to get duct tape out of her hair without cutting it. And Coop loved her long hair.

Then she thought, why am I thinking about my hair at a time like this? She had no idea how much time had passed since that attack, and couldn't tell if the lights were on, but she could hear someone moving about the small cottage. She listened to see if anyone else came in, but heard only a single set of footsteps walking into the kitchen, and then back to the living room. Then she heard the footsteps move towards the small corner table in the living room.

Her computer table.

Her thigh burning from what she was certain was a stun gun, Penny tried to relax as best she could and let her head clear as whoever was in the cottage sat in the chair in front of the computer and turned it on. Penny heard the familiar hum as her PC booted, and within another few minutes heard the tapping sound of the keyboard.

Still in a fog, she thought: why would someone want to attack her and then use her computer? What kind of nut—?

Penny froze as the realization of who was inside the cottage hit her. Only one person that she knew of could be in her house acting that way. She began to mentally calculate how many minutes she had left. The sound of the keyboard was all she could hear, and she realized that each tap brought her closer to the end of her life. Then she thought of how terrible Coop was going to feel when he heard what had happened.

She wished she could take back every last mean thing she had ever said, and tell him just one more time how much she loved him. The last memory on Earth that she would have of him would be that stupid picture on the cover of the tabloid.

Too weak to struggle, she was afraid she would lose consciousness again at any moment, and the fogginess in her head was increasing with each passing minute.

A tear formed in her right eye behind the blindfold, and trickled out from under it. She decided to play possum and hope for the best. The killer had to know that she couldn't make an identification, so maybe she could survive.

"Maybe" was all she had left to hold on to, and her grip was slipping away with each and every tap of the keys.

Suddenly, the tapping stopped. She heard the chair squeak as the intruder stood, then heard footsteps coming towards her. Just as the killer came within a few feet of her, she heard the sound of the footsteps quicken, and run out the door and down the steps, headed for the beach.

38

It was barely dark when Cherry and I reached Gulf Front, and I turned on the headlights. Even though I wanted to give her a quick tour, it was actually better that the sun was down because if it had been earlier, someone might have recognized me.

In no time, we were past the city limits and turning off the road on to Penny's driveway. I pulled into the parking area, and turned off the Lexus.

I waited until the headlights went off, then turned to Cherry, and said, "Well, here we are. Penny's cottage by the sea. Whatta ya think?"

"Oh, Cooper, it's just lovely! I simply *love* the sea air. It's such a tonic for whatever ails you."

"Yes, it surely is." Looking at the cottage, I said, "Hmmm, both cars are here, but there aren't any lights on. Maybe she's walkin' on the beach. She does that sometimes after work. Oh well, it doesn't matter, I know where she keeps the key."

"Don't you have a key of your own?" Cherry asked.

Smiling, I said, "We've had to take them back, and *give* them back so many times over the years, we finally decided to just keep our own keys to ourselves. I know where she keeps her spare, and she knows where I keep mine. C'mon, let's go see if she's inside."

We got out and walked around the side of the cottage to what we refer to as the front porch, which is really the back porch, but since it faces the ocean we call it the front porch.

When we walked up the side steps onto the wide porch, the porch light wasn't on, but the moonlight was bright enough to see that the screen door was wide open, as well as the front door. No lights were on inside, either. Knowing Penny wouldn't leave the cottage that way, the hair on the back of my neck stood up, and I motioned to Cherry to be quiet, and stay still. She did, and I hurried back to the car. I got my Glock from under the seat and crept towards the front door as quietly as I could, the waves and the wind chimes the only sounds.

As I moved towards the open door and looked inside, I saw Penny on the floor, and my heart sank. I silently moved inside, my gun out in front, and looked around in the darkness. The only light came from the computer screen in the corner. It took a few seconds before I realized what that meant.

Rage and adrenaline combined with sheer terror caused my gun hand to start to shake. I took a deep breath, and calmed down enough to steady my hand.

There was no blood visible on or near Penny, so I leaned down and whispered in her ear: "It's me. Don't move. I'm gonna check out the rest of the house."

She nodded.

I searched the cottage, my heart pounding. I didn't want to turn on any lights, but finally realized there was no way around it. I went into each of the small rooms, turning on lights, and searched every inch. I opened the closets, and even pulled back the shower curtain.

When I was satisfied that there was no one in the house other than Penny and me, I got her knife from the kitchen and hurried back to her side. I removed the tape slowly and gently from her mouth, and she said groggily, "The killer's getting away. Get out there and see if you can find any tracks in the sand."

I said firmly, "Penny, I'm not leavin' you alone. We don't know how many people are involved. Just hold still, and let me get this tape off."

As I was sawing my way through the duct tape, Penny said in a slurred voice that could have come from a drunk, "I cannot *believe* that you've been gone all this time, and haven't even called me once. Why didn't you call? Do you, do you, know how that makes me look? It makes me look like some damn—I don't know what. Listen—why haven't you called? You haven't even called *once*. I am royally pissed. In fact, I'm royal."

I said, "Penny, this is no time to pick a fight. I didn't call because I just never had a chance, simple as that. Now hold still and let me get this tape off."

Still slurring her words, she said, "Get out there and get the killer. What are you *doing*?"

"I'm trying to get this damn tape off. Now hold your horses."

Penny remained quiet and still until I cut all the tape away, then she suddenly jumped up and ran out the open door. I quickly followed and saw her collapse and fall on her face in the sand about twenty yards from the cottage.

She wasn't moving, so I jumped off the porch and ran to her side. I picked her up carefully, carried her into the bedroom, and carefully laid her on the bed, on top of her grandmother's quilt. I pulled the small chair from her vanity over next to the bed, and sat down.

Cherry had come in by then, and stood in the door, uncertain of what to do. I'd completely forgotten about her during the insanity of the last few minutes.

I said, "Good Lord, Cherry, are you okay? I'm sorry, I just—"

Cherry said, "I know. It's okay. I'm fine. I admit I was petrified at first, but I'm over that now. Well, mostly. Anyway, when you first went in, I saw someone dressed in black run down the beach and disappear into the darkness."

I asked, "Which way?"

"If you're facing the sea, to the left."

East. Towards town, probably the public parking lot.

I said, "Thanks, that might be helpful. I'll check the parking lot over that way later, see if I can find anything."

She nodded, and anxiously ran her hand through her hair. "I noticed that the computer was on. I looked at what was on there. The instant messenger was up, and—I quit reading as soon as I recognized the name."

"It can wait for now. We'll have a look at it when Penny wakes up."

Cherry laughed nervously, and said, "Quite a reception we got, yeah?"

Softly stroking Penny's hair, I said to Cherry, "I'll say it was. This is some way to start a vacation. Oh—I almost forgot—welcome to Gulf Front."

39

That was way too close!

Luckily, it had been dark, so the car pulling into the yard had its headlights on, or it could have been a hairy situation. There had been no other indication of anyone driving up; that car must be really quiet. But all things go well for the true believers.

What an amazing turn of events! The trip down to get the chick cop had been an inspiration, no doubt from Baal himself. A quick Google of Cherry's bodyguard, and there in living color was this Penny Prevost person, standing by her man after a case in New Orleans last year. Was it blind luck that the bodyguard cop had come when he did? It had to be, no doubt about it. How could he have possibly known that his precious bitch was in danger?

Amazing how the forces work to help the chosen servants, providing a path to escape, keeping them safe, even when the enemy is right there!

And to top it all off, Cherry had been standing by, watching! It was dark, but there was enough moonlight to recognize that figure. Her bodyguard had brought her home with him for some reason, with literally everyone in the world out looking for them!

Now what? Wait around for another chance? Staying around could be dangerous. Attacking the dragon on his home turf was never a good idea. Best to leave while still safe, and live to fight another day.

But how wonderful it would have been to use the woman cop to get at him! His own true love, if the townspeople were to be believed. How simple they all were, so generous with their information. Ten minutes after arriving in town, by pure chance sitting at a long table in the local breakfast spot.

A minute after the policewoman left, all it took was asking the old guy in the next seat if he knew where she lived. The old moron answered without thinking, "Oh, she lives in a cottage right on the beach a few miles west of town. There's a pink flamingo on the mailbox. You can't miss it."

Such a shame this blow could not be struck. But there would be other days, and other chances.

And the sacrifice would be made, no matter what.

40

As we waited for Penny to wake up, I asked Cherry to go to the kitchen and get a glass of water. I noticed there were two identical marks on Penny's left thigh, and recognized them immediately. The stalker had used a Taser on her, or something like it; the marks were definitely made by a stun gun. I touched them gently and felt the rage again, and it took a supreme effort to calm down and remain rational.

A moment later, Penny stirred, and moaned as she opened her eyes. She looked at me as if she was underwater, struggling to bring the world into focus.

"Coop, I had the strangest dream. I was running outside and thought I saw Cherry Page on the porch." She rubbed her temple, and asked, "What are you doin' here? Did you get fired?"

Laughing softly, I said, "No, Chief Prevost, I didn't get fired. And you weren't dreamin', either. Do you remember being attacked and taped up?"

She looked at me for a moment, and then said, "Oh. Wait. Yeah, I do, but that's about all I remember."

At that moment, Cherry walked in with the glass of water, a wet washcloth, and two aspirin. I said, "Penny Prevost? Allow me to introduce Miss Cherry Page."

Penny looked like a five-year-old on Christmas morning, her eyes like saucers as she tried to sit up in bed.

I pushed her gently down, and said, "Now, no. No getting up for you just yet."

She lay back down, staring at Cherry as if she was seeing a specter standing at the foot of her bed.

Cherry handed me the water and aspirin, sat on the bed, and carefully placed the washcloth on Penny's forehead. Taking Penny's hand in hers, she said, "My mum always put a cool, wet washcloth on my head when I felt feverish. It never failed to make me feel better."

Penny said, "It feels really, really nice. But I wanted to meet you under better circumstances—I must look like such a mess. If only I'd—"

Cherry gently shushed her, and said, "You look absolutely beautiful, Penny. Cooper told me you were gorgeous, but that doesn't do you justice. I think he was trying to keep me from getting my feelings hurt, downplaying your beauty. Everyone goes on about me being such a beauty, but I have to say—you're stunning. Not to mention, completely fearless. I would've died from fright alone had someone attacked me in the manner—well, let's not say another word about *that*. I'm just so pleased to meet you, and to see that you're all right."

Penny said, "You have no idea what a pleasure this is for me, and thank you for your sweet words, but *c'mon*. I look like a boy compared to you!"

That got a big laugh from Cherry, and she said with a smile, "I see now why Cooper is so mad for you. You're a treasure."

Penny said to me, "She calls you Cooper! How cool is *that*?"

I said, "It's very cool. Totally and completely cool. Now—sit up slowly, and take a sip of water. Take these aspirin, too. I want you to get some rest, and we can all have a big time later, when you're feelin' better. I need you to be sharp and help me get whoever did this."

Barely able to keep her eyes open, Penny mumbled, "I don't wanna get some rest, I want to tell you I really, really like your new haircut. It makes you look younger. And another thing—looks like—now—we're even."

She went out like a light.

41

I GOT AN AFGHAN FROM PENNY'S CLOSET, COVERED HER WITH IT, AND whispered to Cherry, "Let's go sit and wait for Penny to sleep it off."

Once we were in the living room, Cherry said, "As I told you earlier, I looked at the computer to see if there was a message."

"And?"

"The stalker had opened the instant messenger, and had set up the username *not_so_shy_guy* again. Probably, he heard us drive up, and left in the middle of sending me another message."

I said, "Thank God for small favors."

"I realized too late that I shouldn't have gone near it, but I'm not used to observing proper crime-scene etiquette. I hope I didn't destroy any evidence."

"Hell, Cherry, I pretty much trampled the whole house when I saw Penny on the floor taped up like that. I contaminated the scene myself—big-time. So just forget about your minor breach of crime-scene etiquette. Luckily, this particular time, it's not a problem. Just don't make a habit of it," I said with a smile.

Cherry asked, "But what if one of the neighbors saw the stalker running away? Mightn't that be a problem?"

I said, "You couldn't tell in the dark, but this cottage is pretty isolated; the nearest neighbor to the east is maybe a hundred yards off, and the nearest to the west is even further. Like a lot of Gulf Front, this stretch of land has been owned by the Milo family for years, and there hasn't been any real development. So, the neighbors wouldn't have seen anything. I'd stake my life on it. Penny's uncle, who owns this place, is a good friend of the Milo family, and that's why he was allowed to build here. And, besides, there may not even be anyone in those homes. They're owned by some rich folks who are hardly ever down here. Anyway, while I was sitting with Penny, I came to a decision. It goes against everything I've been taught, but

I think we should keep this evening's events to ourselves. I have a feeling that Penny will agree with me this one time. After all, we are the law in Gulf Front."

Cherry said, "Well, I'm sure you know best."

"Not always. Hell, hardly ever. I'll talk to Penny about it when she's up and around, but like I said, I think she'll agree with me. What's more, I don't want the media comin' down here and attacking Gulf, and Penny won't, either. I may regret it, but I just don't think it's worth it. Now—I think we should try to settle down."

Cherry nodded in agreement. I turned on a lamp, opened the front windows, and turned to see Cherry sitting on the sofa. She patted the seat next to her, and I accepted her invitation. I put my Glock on the end table, and my legs up on the coffee table in front of me like I always do. It felt good to calm down and take my first real breath since I'd found Penny lying on the floor, blindfolded and bound. The Gulf of Mexico waves provided the background music, with the wind chimes adding their bright musical notes occasionally. We didn't speak for several minutes, enjoying the concert and the sea air.

I was trying to think of a mild topic of conversation when Cherry said, "Were you born in Gulf Front, Cooper?"

That was mild enough.

"As a matter of fact, I was. I came into this world in Dr. Brawley's office, right on main street. There was no hospital within twenty miles of town in those days. Almost everyone I know from my youth was born in that office."

"How nice it must be for you to live in a place where you're so deeply rooted."

I said, "It's a real nice place to grow up in, and live. Knowing everybody in town has its advantages."

"I can see why you love it so. From the little bit of it I've seen, it's brilliant."

"The little bit of it you've seen is pretty much all there is to see."

She said, "Maybe that's why it's so wonderful."

"No argument here."

"Where are your parents? Do they live here, too?"

"My Mom died years ago, and my father left us when I was three. So I guess the answer to your question is no, they don't live here."

She touched my arm, and said, "Oh, I'm so sorry—I had no idea. Forgive me for being so stupid."

"You had no way of knowing. Don't worry about it."

"It was still insensitive of me. I just am curious about you, knowing so little about you as I do."

"The less you know, the more you'll like me," I said.

She smiled, and said, "I don't believe that for a minute." We sat in silence for a while, and then she asked, "Do you mind telling me about your parents?"

"No, not at all—whatta ya wanna know?"

"Why did your father leave you and your mother?"

I paused for a moment, then said, "I really don't know. I'm sure that's hard to believe, but Mom never actually told me, and I never actually asked. The subject was kind of like an elephant that just sat quietly in the corner. We both knew it was there, but we both ignored it."

"That's so sad. My dad has always been there for me. Always. I can't imagine how that would feel, to always wonder about his whereabouts."

I said, "But that's just it. I never wondered about his whereabouts. I was a tough little kid; I didn't cry or show my feelings very much. At least, that's what Mom told me."

"She must have loved you very much."

"Yep, she sure did that. She had to love me for the both of them. I was all she had, and she didn't let a day go by without telling me how special I was to her. She was the best."

"Well, she did a fantastic job raising you, especially since she did it by herself. I'm sure she looks down from heaven and knows what a fine man you've become."

I said, "I hope she feels that way. All we had was each other, but she was enough family for me."

"Speaking of family—have you never married, Cooper?"

I took a beat, and said, "No, I've never been married."

"Why not?"

"Are we really gonna get into this? I mean, my girlfriend was just attacked by a homicidal maniac, and is unconscious on her bed less than thirty feet away."

"I simply want to know why you've never been caught, that's all."

"Well, if you must know—and it looks like you must—the reason is simple. I'm an idealist."

Cherry stared at me before saying, "What in bleeding hell does *that* mean?"

I laughed, and said, "Well, it means that I have very high standards concerning the kind of woman I would take to wife. I'm not interested in marryin' just any woman out there, ya know. She would have to be smart, funny, honest as the day is long, beautiful, and insane."

"Insane?"

"Yeah. She'd be marryin' me, wouldn't she?"

"Oh, shut up, and tell me the truth."

I said, "Actually, I *was* telling the truth. I need a woman with all those traits, plus, she has to be madly in love with me. As impossible as they are, those are my requirements."

Cherry said, "But you already have that right here. Penny meets all those requirements. Why have you two never married?"

I didn't know what to say to that, so I tried to change the subject. "Don'tcha just love the cool night air?"

Cherry sighed, and said, "Message received, loud and clear. It's none of the movie star's business."

"No, it's not that. Really. My problem with being married is I like being alone. I like being alone a *lot*. It's kinda hard to be married and be alone, too."

"Ohhh, I see. You want to eat your cake, and have it, too."

I said, "Hey, I like that. It makes more sense."

"What makes more sense?"

"In America, we say: 'You want to have your cake, and eat it, too.' That never made sense to me. I mean, the expression is supposed to be used for something that's impossible. But it's not impossible the way we say it. You *could* have some cake for a while, and then eat it. But the way you guys say it, it really is impossible. You can't eat it, and still have it."

Cherry said, "You're truly a master of avoiding the question at hand. Maybe that's what drives Penny mad."

I said, "The truth is, I don't have a good answer for your question."

Cherry looked at her nails for a moment, then said, "Maybe you think you are your father's son, and you're afraid to find out if that's true or not."

I hate it when women make sense.

I said, "Let's go see how Penny's doin'."

Cherry sighed dramatically, and said, "Okay, Mr. change-the-subject man. We'll go into this in more detail later."

"Yes, we will."

(No, we won't.)

42

WE GOT UP FROM THE SOFA, WALKED TOWARDS THE BEDROOM, AND met Penny as she was coming out.

I felt her forehead, and said, "Hey, Chief. You feelin' better?"

"I feel *much* better, thanks. My thigh is a little sore, but my headache's gone. I'll be fine after I eat somethin'."

Cherry said, "Speaking of eating—I hope you can cook, Cooper. I'm absolutely the world's worst in the kitchen. And Penny is in no shape to cook, so it's all on your shoulders, I'm afraid. So—what's on the menu?"

Penny took my arm, and said, "Coop is an excellent cook, Cherry. It's one of the good things about long-time bachelors. They learn to cook out of self-defense."

I said, "I'm better than excellent. I'm nothin' short of fantastic. Especially when it comes to the grill. And on top of all that, I'm quite humble, too. Whatcha got in the fridge, Chief Prevost?"

"Well, I was gonna have a salad, but now I'm in the mood for somethin' a little more substantial. Hmmm, lemme think. Oh, I know! There are two big sirloins in the freezer. Cherry and I will thaw 'em in the microwave, and you fire up the grill."

"Done," I said. "You two amateurs make the salad, and I'll take care of the rest."

Penny asked, "By the way, how were you two able to get away and come down here?"

Cherry and I smiled at each other, and I said, "I guess you haven't been listening to the news today."

"No, as a matter of fact, I haven't, not since this mornin'," Penny replied. "I spent a lot of the afternoon cruising the highway because —well. Anyway, what news are you talkin' about?"

I said, "All will be revealed in time, all will be revealed. For now, let's get supper started."

"Okay with me," Penny said, and we all went in the kitchen to start fixing the meal.

I was slightly amazed at how Cherry was handling the events of the past hour. Not to mention how Penny was already up and about, since only a short time ago she was about to become the next victim of a serial killer. But I didn't want to discuss the attack at that moment, either, so I went along with their denial. Besides, grilled sirloin sounded like a really great idea.

I was lighting the charcoal in the bottom of the grill when Penny and Cherry came out to bring me a beer.

Penny said to me, "You think we should eat inside?"

I looked at Cherry, and before I could answer, she said, "You know, if this madman really wants to kill me so badly, he could do it at literally any time. He could get one of those high-powered rifles and shoot me from half a mile away, if that's what he wanted to do. Or strap a bomb to himself and run at me. I can't possibly be made safe from every nutter out there, twenty-four seven. No one can be totally secure at all times, not even a queen or a president. When I was in danger last year—you may have heard about that, Penny?"

Penny nodded. I hadn't heard, but wasn't surprised.

Cherry went on, "Well, as scary as that situation was, and this situation *is*, I've been thinking about it all. While I was on the porch alone, watching someone dressed in black—who had just attacked Penny—run down the beach, it hit me: I can only try and live my life as best as I can, without cowering in fear. I mean, I can't be looking over my shoulder every minute of every day."

"That's what I'm here for," I said.

"Me, too," Penny said, and took Cherry's hands in hers.

Cherry grinned, and said, "Enough of all this for now. Let's just be on our toes, and go on with our lives, shall we?"

I wanted more than anything to tell Cherry she was wrong, and that there was no way she could get hurt—or killed—while under my protection, but she was right. If a whack job is willing to die to kill you, well—good luck with that. All I could do was do my best to keep her safe. And I was definitely going to do my best.

An hour or so later, we were all sitting at the picnic table beside the cottage, Cherry on one side, and Penny and I on the other. Candles on the table lit up the evening, and the girls looked gorgeous in the soft light. We were stuffed to the gills with meat, salad, bread, beer, and Penny's favorite dessert, chocolate-mint ice cream. And, to top it all off, not once during the entire meal had a killer tried to kill any one of us, which was pleasant.

So, since we were all fat and happy, I decided it was time to bring up the matter of how we were going to handle the attack on Penny, but she beat me to it.

"Coop," she said. "I've been thinkin'. Whatta ya say we keep the attack under wraps? At least for now, I mean. This goon is *long* gone by now, and I doubt that anybody saw anything, or they would've called to check up on me. Now, I know what I'm suggesting goes against everything you believe, and everything you've been taught, and everything you've taught *me,* but—can't we bend the rules a little just this once?"

Cherry and I grinned widely at each other, and Penny asked, "What's so funny?"

I replied, "You basically said exactly the same things I said to Cherry while you were asleep." To Cherry: "See? Did I tell ya?"

Cherry said, "Yes, you surely did. Penny, you're even braver than I thought. You're my new hero, no doubt about it. You astonish me."

Penny beamed, and said, "Well, I just think, as chief of police, that Gulf doesn't need to get involved in all this crazy stuff. We're such a small town, I don't know how the locals would react if suddenly Gulf became a news hotspot again, even after last year. And besides—I want you two all to myself."

I said, "Exactly what I said. Then it's a deal. We'll keep it secret for now. I know damn well the creep won't hang around. Any stranger in town would stick out like a sore thumb."

"That's for sure," Penny agreed. "I'll discreetly ask around town tomorrow and see if anyone has seen a stranger or two."

I said, "Good idea. Especially the discreet part."

"I'll be very sneaky." Pause. "Okay, that's settled. Now. What brings you two down here?"

Looking at Cherry, who nodded her approval, I said, "The producer of Cherry's movie cooked up a publicity stunt. He wants to make it look like she's disappeared. As far as the world knows, Cherry's left the movie, and is in the wind."

Penny stared openmouthed, and before she could speak, I said, "We know it's ridiculous, but Cherry could use a break from all the craziness, and this way, we both get to come down here and relax for a while."

Penny said, "I don't claim to understand, I'm just happy you're both here. How long are y'all stayin'?"

Cherry said, "We're expected back on Monday morning, ready to go to work and face the media. Can you stand us for that long?"

"I'm not so sure about *this* guy, but you can stay as long as you want, Cherry Page," Penny said with a smile.

There was silence among us for a few moments before Cherry said, "The sound of the waves is so soothing. I could sit out here all night, just taking in the natural beauty. There's no place on Earth I'd rather be tonight."

Penny and I concurred, and we all sat and enjoyed the evening. The sound of the surf took the place of conversation.

After a few minutes, Cherry stood and said, "You two sit still while I take the dishes in and give them a good washing."

Penny was on her feet in a flash, then woozily sat back down, and said, "Cherry, you will not be washin' any dishes while you're my guest. I won't hear of it. Now just gimme a minute, and I'll be—"

"No, you won't be anything," Cherry said. "Except tranquil. I'm going to earn my keep around here, so you might as well just do as I say. I'm a big star, remember? I always get my way."

"She's right, Chief Prevost," I said. "You better do what she tells you. It can get pretty ugly if you don't."

Penny started to object, but Cherry shushed her, and began gathering most of the plates and glasses onto the tray for her trip to the kitchen.

When she walked away and entered the cottage, an idea came into my fevered brain. Having been so close to Cherry for the past few days, I felt the need to—I was beginning to want—I was beginning to sprout horns is what I was beginning to do. I turned to Penny, gave her my best come-hither look, and said, "Little girl, why don't you sit on my lap. I have somethin' I want to show you."

She looked at me as if I came from another planet, and asked, "Are you out of your mind? I can barely stand up, I was just attacked, I'm stuffed to the gills, and you actually think—whatta ya want me to do—strip off my shorts and lay back on the table so you can have your idiot way with me? Is that what you want?"

"Well . . ."

Laughing, she showed yet again that she knows me inside and out when she said, "Being in such close quarters with Miss Cherry Page has put a little lead in your pencil, am I right?"

Actually, it was a lot of lead.

I lied, "No, it's not that at all. I've just been missin' you, and I was hopin' that—"

"I think I know what you were hopin'," she said, moving closer to me on the bench. She put her head on my shoulder, and her hand on my pencil.

"Coop, if you be a good boy tonight, I promise you that when Cherry takes her shower in the mornin', I'll do anything you want."

"Anything?"

"Anything."

I thought about her offer for a moment, which wasn't easy, considering the location of her hand.

I sighed, and said, "Okay, Chief. I guess I can wait."

"Good boy. And it'll be worth the wait, I promise. When I get you alone tomorrow mornin', I'm gonna ride you like a—like a—bicycle."

I laughed, and asked, "A bicycle?"

She frowned, and said, "Hey, now. It's all I could come up with on such short notice. Gimme me a break here, I just got hit with about fifty thousand volts of electricity, remember?"

"Yeah, I remember, but—you really think of me as a bicycle? Can't I be a wild stallion, or a buckin' bronco, somethin' like that?"

"Nope."

"Okay, then, acting chief Prevost. I just hope I'm a good bicycle."

Penny said, "You're a mighty fine bicycle," then leaned over slowly, put her mouth on mine, and kissed me for about thirty seconds, her right hand moving slowly over my deprived area.

She pulled her lips away, her face an inch from mine, and said, "You know, it's not exactly easy for me right now, either.

You saving my life has put me in the mood, too. *Way* in the mood."

Her hand was proof of that.

I said, "Then how 'bout you and me sneak off and—"

Her mouth found mine again, with even more enthusiasm.

It was my turn to pull away. I tried a different approach, "If you don't mind me askin', what are the sleeping arrangements for tonight? I was thinkin' you and me in your bed, and Cherry on the sofa."

Giggling in my ear, she said, "Now, no, Coop. You and me will not be sharin' my bed. Me and *Cherry* will be sharin' my bed. You'll be on the sofa. You hafta stay up and guard the place in case the deranged killer man comes back."

"I thought we agreed that the deranged killer man wasn't comin' back," I griped.

She removed her hand, and said, "We did—and he won't—but we better be prepared and act like the creep might come back. And— I can't stand guard, because I hafta go to work tomorrow so nobody gets suspicious and comes out here lookin' for me. Now that that's settled, let's take the rest of the dishes in and help our movie star finish up."

Again, her mouth was on mine, kissing me even deeper than before, literally taking my breath away for a moment.

When she finally stopped, I said, "Maybe you better go inside. I can no longer guarantee your safety."

43

I LINGERED OUTSIDE FOR TWENTY MINUTES OR SO, LISTENING TO THE surf and the sound of two beautiful women becoming fast friends. The kitchen window was open, and I could hear Penny and Cherry talking like old buddies, though I couldn't make out much of what they were saying.

The conversation ebbed and flowed, with laughter breaking out every few minutes. They seemed to be having a good time, so I just sat at the weather-beaten picnic table and watched the waves and the moonlight on the water. I had my cell on me, so I called Neal to see what was what.

When he answered, I asked, "Hey, P.I.–type guy. Did you get beat up by any cheatin' husbands today?"

"No, bud, I didn't," he replied. "I've just been sittin' around the house most of the day, watching news reports about you and *her* on television. You in you-know-where?"

"Yep, I'm in you-know-where with you-know-who. Did Carver or any other law-enforcement types try and get information from you?"

"Carver called with some pretty funny news. Some whack-job woman in Buckhead made a false report, claimin' that the killer had attacked her. She's in jail now, but I seriously doubt that hers will be the last phony report. Carver didn't ask if I knew where y'all are, he just thought I'd get a kick outta hearin' about the false report. I think he knows better than to ask me about what's goin' on. In case he calls again, and does ask, is there anything you want me to say in particular?"

"No, just use the old 'privileged information' line and dummy up—which should be easy for the likes of you."

Neal said, "Just for that, I'm tellin'. And not just the law—I'm callin' the news creeps, buddy boy. Like I said, you two are all over the TV news. You know that, right?"

"I've purposely avoided all types of media so far, but I can imagine what's goin' on. So after all I've done for you, you'd go and turn us in. And here I am, takin' care of Cherry, and living in the same luxurious Ritz-Carlton suite with her, and drivin' her around town in a Bentley, and goin' out on the town to big charity balls with her, and—"

"Okay, okay. You've made some incredible sacrifices, and I consider myself lucky just to know you. You're a credit to your race and gender, and so forth and whatnot."

"This is what I'm sayin'."

Neal snorted, and said, "That English guy—the producer—what's his name? Little Bo Peep?"

"Lawrence Lyndon-Bowen."

"That's him. He was all over the news today, talkin' this disappearance thing up. He can really spread it, and deep, too. And—he came up with a catchy name for your stalker."

"Oh, boy. What is it?" I asked.

"The Computer Killer. Not too bad, I say. Whatcha think?"

"I've heard worse. It's better than the Cherry Pitter, or somethin' like that."

Neal agreed, "That's for sure. Oh, he's also offering five hundred thousand bucks for information leading to the capture of the killer. You may end up a rich guy like me, you know it?"

"I may end up a rich guy like your wife, you mean. Damn, that kinda money should bring *all* the fruits and nuts outta the woodwork. It's probably why that woman filed a false report."

"You're right about the fruits comin' out, but the woman in question was more interested in getting her ex-husband arrested for murder. Anyway, how are you guys doin'?"

I said, "Oh well, we're safe and sound for the moment." I thought of the attack on Penny, and realized the unintentional irony in my statement.

Neal said, "Glad to hear it, bud. Has anything interesting happened to you since you left? Was the trip largely uneventful and relaxing for Cherry? You didn't have any car trouble, didja? My Lexus still in one piece? Oh—and the burning question of questions—did Penny beat your ass for you not callin'? C'mon, come clean. You're makin' this call from the emergency room, am I right?"

That got a small chuckle from me, and as I was chortling, the thought of telling Neal about the killer attacking Penny flashed into my head. I decided to keep the secret from him, knowing he'd understand. "I did have a little car trouble. A flat tire, but I got you a new one in Montgomery. Actually, I'm callin' from the picnic table while the babes are in the kitchen, cleanin' up after one of my famous steak dinners. From the sound of it, they're gonna be best pals before the night's over."

Neal said, "Well, anybody in their right mind would love Penny, and from what I've seen and heard, ol' Cherry ain't so bad her damn self."

"You're right on both counts. Speaking of great women, how's my darlin' Susan doing?"

"She's fantastic, as usual, and sends you and Penny her love. She took the girls out tonight to see the latest movie with that guy they all love so much."

"Good for them. Tell 'em all hello, and that Penny sends her love right back. Me, too."

"Will do, bud. Keep in touch."

After we hung up, I noticed that the voices from the cottage had become quiet, and the laughter had stopped. In fact, I couldn't hear anything. Curious, I dragged my stuffed stomach into the cottage's kitchen, and saw Penny holding what appeared to be a supermarket tabloid in Cherry's face, shaking it violently. She was speaking in what I can only describe as a screaming whisper, and Cherry had the look of a terrified child.

Whatever Penny was saying, it wasn't: "I'll be your best friend."

44

A MINUTE AFTER NEAL HUNG UP WITH COOP, HIS WIFE, SUSAN, AND their three daughters came noisily into the living room where he was sitting on the sofa. They were all talking a mile a minute about how great the movie was, and how many Oscars it would win. Each of them leaned down and gave Neal a hug, and then stood in front of him in a line. Susan started the interrogation, "Have you heard from Coop?"

This got all three girls in on the cross-examination, and the questions were flying faster than Neal could think, much less answer.

Laughing, he said, "Whoa, hold on a minute. All I know is what you guys know. The last report I saw an hour or so ago said there was nothing new to report, which basically made it not so much a report, but more a waste of my valuable time."

Susan gave him the once-over that always made him glad she had no jurisdiction. Because if she did, he'd be in jail for lying to his wife six months out of any given year.

"Neal Feagin, are you gonna sit right there, and tell me that you have no idea where Coop took Cherry, and that you're not involved in any way with their disappearance?"

Neal gave his best "I can't believe you said that" look, then asked, "Why do you find it so hard to believe that your lovin' husband is not privy to everything that goes on in Coop's life? Not to mention a famous movie star, who, by the way, I haven't even met yet. How would I know what some crazy actress would do, or where she would go? All I know is that Coop's not here, and I suppose, like everybody else, that he's with the famous Miss Page." He leaned down and massaged the area above his cast to stall for time, and hopefully, get a little compassion.

No dice.

"Neal Feagin, I *know* you know where they are. Do you think

I'm goin' to call the news and report 'em? Do you want the girls to leave the room so you can tell me? Are you afraid they'll tell all their friends, is that it?"

This brought a chorus of "we won't tell anybody" and related remarks from the girls, and the decibel level went up accordingly.

Neal put his hands over his ears as all four of his girls pleaded with him to spill the biggest beans of the year.

He kept his hands over his ears, closed his eyes, and hummed loudly in the face of the female verbal assault. The girls and Susan finally gave up, and he opened his eyes to find his daughters all standing in front of him in the classic begging pose, and his wife putting her fists on her hips in the classic "boy, are you gonna get it" pose.

Neal said, "Even if I *did* know where they were, you know I couldn't tell. There *is* such a thing as ethics when it comes to bein' a private eye, ya know. A little matter of employee-client privilege, remember?"

The girls all whined, and Susan tried to keep her mean face on but couldn't, and smiled at her husband before leaning down and kissing him.

"You're father's right, girls. We can't have him actin' in an unethical manner. But it was worth a shot."

The girls all gave their dad a kiss good night, and headed upstairs to their respective bedrooms. Neal and Susan had moved into the downstairs guest room until his ankle healed so he wouldn't have to climb the stairs.

Susan sat down on the sofa beside Neal, put her arm around his shoulder, and whispered in his ear, "You know, your havin' all this inside information is mighty sexy stuff. How 'bout you pull yourself together and use those crutches to come to bed?" She stood up and headed for the guest room, and said over her shoulder, "By the time you get there, I'll be ready and waitin' to show you just how sexy I think all this privileged information really is."

45

Leaving the crappy little beach town without finishing the job on the chick cop was a drag, but better safe than sorry. The attempted hit on the bodyguard's girlfriend was satisfying enough for now, even if the results were less than perfect. At least, it scared all of them to death figuratively, if not literally.

Literally would come soon enough for all of them.

It was nice to think about the confusion that the three had experienced, especially the moronic bodyguard. They were all probably huddled in that hovel on the beach, shaking in their sandals, and jumping at every strange sound. That would have to be satisfaction enough for the time being. There were more plans to make, and people to do.

Finding the news/talk radio station out of Pensacola had been easy enough. Now there was a name to live up to. The Computer Killer! And a reward of five hundred thousand bucks for information leading to the capture; a bounty on the head of Baal's servant! No doubt the police and the FBI would be inundated with calls and messages from hundreds of idiots giving false leads, hoping to be the one to get paid.

It was becoming more fun by the minute.

But now the radio station was starting to fade in and out as the vehicle made its way north, back to the Atlanta area, the cruise control making it seem as if the car knew the way home. The movie star's so-called disappearance was big news at the top and bottom of each hour, second only to the reports concerning the latest White House scandal, which had knocked Cherry down from number one. Something about a member of the cabinet misusing his power, or some such nonsense.

They probably had to make that the lead story to keep up appearances, but anyone listening was more interested in the where-

abouts of Cherry Page than any political scandal, whether they would admit it or not. Washington was a sewer, and everyone knew it. Where was the news in that?

It was so hard to decide what to do next! Wouldn't it be fun to make an anonymous call to CNN, or Fox, and let them know where the two targets were? Give them the exact coordinates, right down to the flamingo on the mailbox.

The thought of all those news trucks and vans suddenly showing up in that crummy little town, wreaking havoc wherever they went, driving the bumpkins crazy, was fun to consider. That alone would almost make it worthwhile to tell the true story of the vanishing act that was consuming all the cretins who had no lives of their own.

But, it seemed somehow better to keep the truth from the masses. For now, at least.

Having the power to dictate the news was another electrifying experience, but having it and not using it seemed even sexier! All those media snakes out looking under every rock for clues, and the only knowledgeable person was driving north on I-85 headed for Atlanta, listening to them blather on about this and that.

All the useless speculation, the guessing games being played by the "experts" was entertainment at its finest when you knew it was all nothing more than a huge waste of time. Driving past town after town, completely unnoticed, utterly omniscient.

Knowledge was power, and power was absolutely addictive.

46

PENNY HAD CHERRY BACKED UP AGAINST THE STOVE IN THE TINY kitchen, waving the tabloid magazine in her face and hissing at her in that weird whisper. Cherry was staring at the floor, apparently unable to make eye contact as the accusations flew. The film star was obviously no longer Penny's favorite woman in the world; in fact, the star was suddenly in danger of becoming a punching bag.

Penny's voice became loud as she said in a hateful, accusatory tone, "And since you're such a big, bad, *movie star*, I guess you think you can just have any damn man you lay your big green eyes on, is that it? All you have to do is pick out the man you want at any given moment, do your little sex symbol act, and every man is fair game because you're gorgeous, and famous, and it's your God-given *right* to have whatever you want, whenever you want it! Right? The whole world—no—the entire stinkin' *universe* revolves around you and your desires, and everybody else's feelings be damned! It's all about what *Cherry* wants, what *Cherry* needs, and to hell with whoever gets hurt, right, Miss British Marilyn Monroe Bombshell? Well, let me tell you somethin', movie star. You messed with the wrong man this time!"

Still keeping her eyes on the floor, Cherry tried to defend herself, clearly cowed by Penny's verbal assault, "Penny—I never realized how much—if I *knew* you—I never in a million years would have done the things I did. I'm just so, so sorry."

"Sorry? *Sorry?* You move in on my man, doing God knows what in that hotel room of yours, and all you can say is you're sorry? Oh, lemme tell ya, bitch, you're sorry all right. You're about the sorriest excuse for a role model I've ever seen! I cannot believe that I ever thought you were someone that I could look up to. What a stupid little fool I've been, sittin' here waitin' for Coop to call, when you probably kept him as far away from a phone as you possibly could.

And to think that I *wanted* him to take the job as your bodyguard. I must've been out of my mind!"

Cherry continued to stare at the floor, completely defenseless, as Penny glared at her, daring Cherry to say another word. The tension in the room was palpable, and I was afraid that Penny was going to lose it and do something she'd regret for the rest of her life. That's how serious the scene had become.

I decided to make my presence known.

"Uh, Penny? Cherry? What's goin' on here?" I asked in a tone I hoped wouldn't turn Penny's wrath towards me.

Wrong tone.

Penny wheeled around and shrieked at me in an even louder voice, "Well look who's here! If it isn't the British Bombshell's hunky bodyguard! The 'Cherry Picker' himself, in all his two-faced glory! Why don'tcha come on in here and make your new girlfriend a cup of tea, or whatever it is that hunky bodyguards do for their bomb-shells!"

The situation was escalating by the second. I was actually begin-ning to fear for Cherry's safety. Trying to calm Penny down, I asked in my most soothing tone, "Penny. What in the heck are you talkin' about?"

Throwing the tabloid at me, she screamed, "This is what I'm talkin' about, you thoughtless bastard!"

The paper hit me in the face, and fell to the floor. I picked it up, saw Cherry kissing me, and read the lurid headlines. My heart liter-ally stopped for a beat, and I felt the sweat begin to form on my fore-head, just waiting for its chance to start sliding down my reddening face.

Staring at the supermarket rag in disbelief, I figured I'd better try a new tone; I struggled to sound as innocent as possible. I said, "Penny, you can't be serious. This, this piece of, these stupid tabloid things are, they're all just a bunch of made-up lies. The people who buy this trash are either idiots, or they know damn well that these so-called newspapers are nothing more than . . . they're like comic books for adults. You know better than to believe any of this."

Penny shrieked, "I believe what I see, buster! And what I see is the two of you goin' at it in formal wear, in front of the whole damn world! *That's* what I believe! Couldn't you at least have waited until you got back to your fancy hotel suite before you started kissing her? Did it have to be right out in public for the entire planet to see? Not to mention *photograph*? And, not only do I believe what I see, I also believe what I hear! Your floozy movie star whore told me everything!"

Uh-oh.

Everything?

My swimming head tried valiantly to come up with some kind of explanation for "everything."

Talk about being caught with your hand in the cookie jar. And the cookie jar was being no help whatsoever. Cherry was still staring at the floor, unable or unwilling to come to my rescue. What had she told Penny about our relationship? Wait. There was no relationship. Not really. I just needed a minute to think, to get my mind right. But it was impossible to think, what with Penny throwing daggers at me with her eyes, and Cherry hanging me out to dry.

Should I come clean, and tell Penny the truth? That it was all Cherry's doing, and that I was completely innocent in regards to "everything"? Inform her that I was on my best behavior at all times, at least on the outside, and that I was a victim of circumstance? Should I tell Penny about the sleeping arrangements, or Cherry scratching my back, or me seeing her half naked in the dim bedroom? Or tell her that I had managed to keep what was left of my virtue intact, even though the temptation was there twenty-four hours a day, and that the temptation was staring at the floor as we spoke?

I tried to state my case, but a stammer was the best I could manage: "Penny, I—see?—the thing is—if—if you knew—I never—it was . . ."

Staring me down, Penny barked, "Well? It was what?"

I stood there openmouthed for a full ten seconds, stunned into silence.

Then, the two of them suddenly collapsed into each other's arms, laughing their beautiful asses off.

I'd been had. Big-time.

I tried to look as angry as I could, which only brought more laughter. They separated, and were holding their stomachs, Penny slapping the butcher-block island, and Cherry leaning back against the stove.

I said, "Very funny. I mean, reeeaaallly hilarious."

More laughter, more stomach holding, more butcher-block slapping.

I tried to gain some sympathy, "You know, the only reason I fell for your little performance is because I trust you both so much."

They actually went to the floor on that one, tears in their eyes brought on by all the hilarity at my expense.

Barely able to breathe, Cherry said from her seat on the floor, "We really got you good, Cooper! The look on your face! Priceless!"

Penny chimed in, "Oh! Oh, my stomach hurts! That was too much! What an egomaniac! You really thought I was—I *told* you, Coop—there's no way you can get with my girl! Ow! My side! It's killin' me!"

I let them laugh themselves out, acting as if I was angry, when in fact I was relieved. What if Cherry had actually felt the need to confess to Penny about our sleepovers? I inwardly celebrated, but kept my pissed-off face on as they helped each other to their feet, still giggling like maniacs. I walked over and tossed the tabloid into the trash can.

Penny caught her breath, and said, "Oh. Man, Coop, I wish I had a picture of your face when—oh, man—too funny. Whew! I'm dyin'."

Cherry said, "*I* wish I had my film crew here."

That started another wave of laughter, not as hard or as long, because neither of them had the strength for it anymore.

Finally, after another minute or so of mirth, Penny said, "Whew. I needed that."

Cherry hugged her, and said, "Me, too, darling. Oh—I almost wet my pants."

That brought on yet another bout of howling.

When she was finally able to speak again, Cherry continued, "I'm sorry, Cooper. Penny put me up to it. It was all her idea."

Penny leaned away from her, and said, "Thanks a lot! Go ahead, blame me—oh—I'm dyin'. My jaw is killin' me. My head's still a little foggy. Let's go sit down, before I fall down."

Arm in arm, they pushed past me into the living room, and fell out on the sofa. Penny whispered something in Cherry's ear, and the laughter started up again.

I took it like a man, and joined them in the living room, sitting in the stuffed armchair across from the sofa.

I said, "Well, I hope you two brats had fun givin' me all that grief, and only minutes after I slaved over a hot grill for y'all."

Cherry wiped the tears from her eyes, and said, "So sorry again, Cooper, but it was just too easy. And, again, I have to say, all the fault of your lovely better half."

I said, "Better half? Ha! That's a good one. Your behavior—the both of you—inexcusable."

Penny said, "We both know I'm your better half, so just be glad I was only kidding, or I'd be your 'used-to-be' half. Yet again. Cherry explained about the kiss, that you had said somethin' nice about Poppy, and that it was only a friendly peck, so you're off the hook. For now. But come on, it was pretty damn funny, you gotta admit."

"Okay, I begrudgingly admit it."

"She also told me about your bed by the window in the parlor, as she calls it. Didn't I tell ya you'd probably end up in her suite? Maybe now you'll listen to me when I predict the future."

They were both lying back on the sofa, their bare feet propped up on the old coffee table. It was nice to see them getting along so well, but it was even nicer to know that the whole thing had been a joke.

Whew, indeed.

We sat in silence for a few moments. Then Penny giggled, and put her head back and closed her eyes.

Cherry looked to make sure Penny's eyes were still closed, and got my attention by waving her hand slightly. Then she pantomimed locking her lips with a key, and throwing it away, indicating to me that she would never tell Penny about our "relationship."

Knowing that Cherry was keeping quiet about our time together only made her more attractive. And if there was one thing I didn't need in my mixed-up life, it was a Cherry Page that was even more attractive.

Still, it was nice to know that she hadn't told Penny about our relationship. Which really *wasn't* a relationship.

Or was it?

47

THE SUN WAS JUST COMING UP WHEN I FINALLY DOZED OFF IN THE
living-room armchair, my Glock in my lap. True to her word,
Penny had shared her bed with Cherry, and had made up the sofa
for me with a sheet, quilt, and a pillow. But I was too wired after
the attack to sleep, so I kept watch while gazing at the muted
TV, flipping around looking for any sporting event. Twice during
the night, I thought I heard something or someone outside, but
when I checked, there was no one there. I was pretty sure that the
murderer (I refused to use the moniker "Computer Killer") was
long gone after all, but being pretty sure still left plenty of room
to worry.

I was not only worried about a repeat performance of the attack
on Penny—or one on Cherry—I was also worried that the moron
might contact the media and give them our location. Penny doesn't
have cable, being so far from town, but she does have a satellite dish,
so I had access to CNN and Fox.

I periodically checked to see if they had been informed as to
where Cherry and I were, but they never revealed our hiding spot.
There were just the usual reports of the missing movie star, and endless replays of Lawrence Lyndon-Bowen's speech to the press gathered outside the Candler Theater in Atlanta. Thankfully, I didn't hear
him.

Penny came in and woke me with a soft kiss while Cherry was in
the bathroom showering, but I was too tired to be her bicycle. I'm
pretty sure Penny was secretly relieved by my refusal of her offer,
what with her idol in the house, and all. She promised to take care
of me the first chance she got, kissed my forehead, and headed to her
room to get dressed for work.

After a night of more TV than I watch in a week, I wanted to
avoid it—and the radio—all day if possible, since it just made the

day so much more pleasant. So I got up, walked to her door and said to Penny, "Call me if the our killer friend has ratted us out to the press."

She said, "I've been thinking the same thing, that he might tell on you guys. I'll call right away if there's any news."

At that moment, thunder started to sound, and dark clouds began to form out over the Gulf. Within five minutes, a full-blown thunderstorm was pouring buckets of rain on the cottage, and heavy wind and lightning joined the show. The wind was blowing the rain at an angle, causing water to come in the open windows. I went through the cottage and made sure all the windows were closed, and turned on the three overhead fans so we wouldn't burn up in case the storm lasted awhile.

After placing my gun on the coffee table, I took off my jeans and lay down on the sofa. I found myself in dreamland almost instantly, the sound of the rain on the tin roof lulling me to sleep. Penny was gone by the time the smell of bacon frying woke me up for the second time. Or should I say the smell of bacon burning.

Trying to remember where the fire extinguisher was, I pulled on my jeans and stumbled into the kitchen to find Cherry dressed in Penny's black bikini, desperately trying to get the smoke out of the now-open kitchen window. I instantly regretted that I had not taken Penny up on her offer of a morning ride, but managed to keep my eyes off of Cherry's barely clad body for the most part.

I needed a vacation from my vacation.

The bacon was a total loss, so I walked over and took the frying pan off the stove, and dumped the greasy mess in the trash can on top of the tabloid paper. The Bombshell-Bodyguard Kiss was now officially dead and buried. And greasy.

Cherry whined, "I'm absolute crap in the kitchen, but my intentions were good. I wanted to pay you back for your grilling, but I've only made a dreadful mess of things, as usual."

"It's not a problem, boss, your job is to be beautiful and say your lines when it's your turn. And speaking of beautiful—you look almost as good as Penny does in that thing." The black bikini looked terrific against her cream white skin, and it made her hair seem even redder.

"My, what a wonderful compliment, Cooper. I'll settle for second best whenever Penny's around. What an extraordinary woman she is. I'm so very glad we got the chance to travel down here so I could meet her. Last night was a right good laugh. You almost had a heart attack when she lit into you, yeah?"

"Well, maybe a small palpitation here and there."

She washed her hands in the sink, and said, "Did it cross your mind that perhaps I'd been telling tales out of school about our sleeping arrangements? Was that why you stood frozen to the spot with your jaw on the floor when she went after you?"

She smiled her sexiest smile, and I reached over and opened the refrigerator to cool off.

Finding the bacon, I said, "I'll admit I was pretty worried there for a minute. Okay, I was pretty terrified there for a minute. At least now I know you don't sleep and tell."

"Never," she said. "I threw away the key, remember? Seriously, I would never say or do anything to jeopardize what the two of you have. Especially since there's nothing to tell, really. I hope you know that."

Putting five strips of bacon in the pan, I replied, "I know that for sure now. And by the way, it *was* pretty funny. It was nice to see you and Penny getting along together so well, like I knew you would. Now. Scrambled eggs and toast with your bacon sound all right?"

"Wonderful. I'll make some tea. That I can do."

"I'll have some coffee, if you don't mind, and there's OJ in the fridge."

"Coming right up."

We ate sitting at the little table in the small dining room, which is really more like an alcove set off from the living room.

Looking out at the lightning, black clouds, and pouring rain, Cherry said, "Damned bloody downpour! It feels like London instead of sunny Florida. I was so looking forward to a quick swim after breakfast. Penny said the sandy bottom is clean as a whistle, and the water temperature ideal in the morning for bathing—nice and cool. With my skin, I can't stay out in the sun for too long in the middle of the day, especially when I'm working. It simply wouldn't do for me to show up for work with a sunburn. Guinness would pitch a fit."

I said, "Sometimes, these storms are over before you know it, so don't give up just yet. Of course, sometimes, they last all day."

"Oh, well," she said. "At least the company is pleasant."

Lawrence Lyndon-Bowen woke up in his Ritz-Carlton Buckhead suite at a few minutes after 9 A.M. He called from his bed down to the desk, and found that he had more than thirty messages from various reporters, news agencies, and television programs. He thanked the clerk, smiled to himself, and reached over and roughly shoved the young man sleeping next to him in his bed.

Michael, a young black hustler Lawrence had picked up at a gay bar in Midtown, turned over towards the wall and pushed his pillow into a mound under his clean-shaven head.

Lawrence said, "Look. Get out of here, and right this minute, you muscle-bound cretin. That's what I paid you for, to get out. And make sure no one sees you leaving, as I might need you again while I'm here. But only if you keep this quiet, is that understood? It wouldn't be good for your heath if I find out that you've told anyone about our little tryst. Now, move your arse, and be quick about it."

Michael grumbled something about old closet queens under his breath, but was dressed and out of the suite in less than two minutes. He managed to make it downstairs and out of the hotel without being noticed by the staff or any of the hotel guests. The old English tart was obnoxious as hell, going on and on about what a great movie producer he was, but he paid well. A cool two grand for the night was more than twice the price that most of these old guys were willing to pay, so it was a profitable night, if a boring one.

Lyndon-Bowen called Lynne Prather at the theater, and told her to tell Guinness that he was calling to check in, and that he was available if needed. The rehearsals were going on as planned, with Bev reading Cherry's part. Lynne said she would inform Guinness, and they hung up, leaving Lawrence with nothing more to do for the day than to try and stir up more publicity. And that was something he could do quite well, thank you very much.

He took a shower after ordering breakfast, and turned on the television to a news channel as he toweled himself dry. There was only a wait of a few minutes before he saw himself dazzling the press corps; it had to be the twentieth time he'd seen it since yesterday, but it seemed to just get better with each viewing. There was simply no doubt about it, L. Lyndon-Bowen was a natural, a born star. And if everything went as planned, he was going to prove it again today.

A brainstorm had come to him in the night, while he was trying to ignore the snoring of his hired bedmate. What if he could some-how fake an attack on himself? Maybe go to the theater and scream bloody murder during the lunch break, just like the other day. Perhaps make a cut in his hand, or make some rope marks on his neck, or both? Then tell the cops that he had no idea about the Computer Killer's size or weight, because he had been attacked from behind. The cut on his hand was a—what was it called?—a defensive wound.

There would be sympathy to go along with the publicity, not to mention the admiration that would be created by such a heroic act. More face time on all the news channels, Lyndon-Bowen moving ever closer to becoming a household name.

But the plan had its downside, too. What if it could be proven that he had faked an attack? What then? The investigators were usu-ally very good at their jobs; at least they were on all the crime shows on the telly. Was it too risky, too mad a scheme even for the likes of an expert publicity-generating machine such as Lawrence Lyndon-Bowen?

Maybe.

But, then again, maybe not.

Part Three

Action . . .

48

Penny drove towards town with a lightness in her heart she hadn't felt since Coop had left town on his big adventure. Last night had been such a grand occasion: meeting her idol and finding her to be just as beautiful and charming as she had imagined her to be. More, even.

And it was so great to find out that the kiss between Coop and Cherry was nothing more than a friendly peck on the lips, not that Penny had ever believed it to be anything other than that. Not really. Well—*maybe* there were a few moments when she'd thought that it might be barely possible there was something going on between Coop and her new best friend. Okay, so there were *more* than a few moments. All *right*—she wasn't sure until she actually saw them, and talked to them, that there was no relationship outside of business between them. But she was convinced now that all was well, and she had to fight to keep a smile off of her face as she pulled up and parked in front of Matthews Cafeteria.

If the patrons saw her smiling like an idiot, they'd know something was up, and that was the last thing that anybody in Gulf Front needed to be thinking today.

She sat in the patrol car for a while as the rain continued to come down in sheets, already overrunning the gutters as the thunderstorm made its way through town. The memory of last night's practical joke on Coop had her smiling again, and she actually laughed out loud as she remembered the look on his face, and the release the wild laughter had brought her. Luckily, the rain kept anyone from seeing her laughing, or there would have been concern among the citizens about the state of their acting police chief's mental well-being.

She realized that she'd forgotten her umbrella, but then remembered that she was in Coop's car, and that he kept one under the front passenger's seat.

The darling man.

Penny reached under the seat, retrieved the umbrella, and made a mad dash to the front door of the cafeteria. Everyone waited to see what kind of a mood she was in before they said anything, and all were greatly relieved when she greeted them with a friendly hello. But not too friendly—she was on a mission.

As she made her way through the line, she took two biscuits with honey, one piece of link sausage, and a cup of coffee from the servers. When she got to Willene at the end of the line, and paid her bill, she asked if they might talk for a minute when Willene took her break.

"Why, sure, sweetie," Willene said. "I'll be over at your table in, let's see, twelve minutes. Would that be all right?"

"That'd be just fine," Penny said, paying for her breakfast with a ten and taking her change. She then walked over and took a seat at a table not far from the cash register.

The conversation among the customers had returned to its normal din, and Penny knew then that the good people of Gulf Front had decided the tabloid picture was just exactly what it was: yesterday's news.

She enjoyed her meal, and was almost finished when Willene turned the register over to Thelma, and sat down across from Penny.

"How's them biscuits today?" Willene asked with a smile, knowing they were the best biscuits for miles around.

"They get better every time I come in here, Willene. How does Annie do it?"

"You're tastin' about fifty years wortha cookin' experience. That's how she does it. Now, how you doin'? Everything okay? You and Coop talk yet? I seen on the TV last night that he and that movie star has gone missin'. Have you heard from 'im?"

Penny lied, "No, I haven't, but if he was in any trouble, I know he'd call and let me know. But that's not what's worrying me. There's another reason I wanted to talk to you. But this has to be just between you and me. You okay with that?"

Willene slyly looked around the room, and said, "I ain't like Blanche over at O'Kelly's, sweetheart. Anything we talk about don't go no further than this table."

"Good. I knew I could trust you. Here's the deal. Did any

strangers come in here yesterday during the time I was havin' breakfast? If you can think of anything, no matter how big or small, I need
to know, 'cause a lot of times the smallest details can lead to the
biggest clues."

Loving the conspiratorial nature of the conversation, Willene
took another look around before she said anything. She looked
down at the floor, then up at the old clock on the wall behind Penny,
trying to picture in her mind yesterday's breakfast crowd.

She finally said, "They was a guy looked like a truck driver, big
fella, I ain't never seen before, and a family with two cute little boys
that was drivin' their mama crazy, and a woman sittin' by herself,
maybe thirty, thirty-five, who just had coffee and a cinnamon roll,
and two young black guys dressed in real sharp clothes, like they
hadn't been to bed yet, and one fella and another young lady I've
never seen who sat at the end of the table with all the regular old
men there in the middle of the room, but they didn't talk to 'em. At
least not that I seen. Let's see, what else?" She stared at the clock
again for a moment, and then said, "Darlin', that's about all I can
remember right this minute. Did that help any?"

"Willene, it helped more than you'll ever know," Penny said as
she finished off the last bite of sausage with a little mustard on it.
"One other thing. Did any of those strangers come in again this
mornin'?"

Willene thought for a moment, and said, "Nope. Not a one."

Penny said, "That's good. I only asked about strangers because a
call came in yesterday afternoon concerning a stolen car over in
Pensacola. But nobody you described fits the report. So, see? You
were a great big help."

Willene smiled and said, "I'm just so glad I could do my civic
duty, sweetie. You let me know if there's anything else I can do to
help, okay?"

"I sure will," Penny said, and watched as Willene got up and
went out the back door to smoke a cigarette.

Penny thought that only three of the people Willene described
could have possibly been involved, unless there was a new satanic
cult that included the whole family. Maybe the two little boys *were*
the killers. Lord knows the young ones today know more about
computers by age five than their parents do, she thought.

But realistically, the single male and the two single females were the only plausible suspects, and more realistically, she was never going to find out if any of the three of them had anything to do with the attack last night. But, you never know, maybe she'd catch a break.

As she looked around the room at all the regulars, Penny knew that every one of them wanted to know if she'd heard from Coop. She also knew that as soon as she left, they'd be all over Willene, asking if Penny had told her where he was.

If Willene told them that she hadn't heard from Coop, it would actually save her from having to answer the question all day long, so she secretly hoped that Willene *would* tell.

She sat and finished her coffee, wishing the rain would let up a little.

49

After breakfast, Cherry and I opened all the windows in the cottage because even though the rain was still pouring steadily, the wind had died down. It wasn't blowing the rain at an angle on to the windows anymore, so there was no longer any danger of the inside of the house being flooded. I turned off the fans, and we went out on to the porch to sit in the swing and talk.

Penny's uncle Stan originally built the beach cottage as a vacation home for his family while they were living in Pensacola. When he was offered a job in New York City, Stan and his family moved there, and he began renting the cottage to Penny for a ridiculously low monthly fee. Otherwise, there would be no way she could afford to live right on the beach.

There are several things about the cottage that make it special, not the least of which is the tin roof. When it rains, there's nothing better than to fall asleep to the sound of raindrops drumming on the tin. The screened back porch is another great feature, especially when a cool breeze is blowing through.

But the best thing her uncle did was to make the porch twice as deep as you would expect it to be, and to leave it free of railings that would block the view. Maybe even better, he positioned the porch swing so that it faces the ocean, as opposed to the normal way, which is to have it on the end, at a ninety-degree angle from the house. Swinging in that swing while looking out at the ocean is one of my favorite things to do at the cottage.

The rain was so dense, it was hard to tell where the horizon was. Everything from the water to the sky was one big gray wash. The drops hitting the tin roof delighted Cherry, and she said the rain might not be so bad after all, since we would have time to relax and talk. After all the lunacy of the past few days and nights, I agreed with her wholeheartedly.

Looking out at the gray, I said, "Hopefully, tomorrow will be sunny, and you can take that morning swim. I promise you'll be really impressed with how clear the water is, and how gentle the waves are. And, another thing. You'll get to feel that smooth, clean bottom out there. No rocks, no seaweed, it's just like walkin' on the beach. Also, not that you can tell it right now, but our sand is clean, white, and soft. You're gonna love it."

Cherry wiggled her toes, and said, "It sounds absolutely sublime. I can't wait to get in and bathe in the Gulf. I've always loved the sea, and would absolutely weep when we left the seashore to go home to London. It really is one of my favorite things in the world, being in and around the ocean."

"Good to hear. I take it for granted, bein' around it all the time. It'll be nice to experience it through your eyes."

Cherry said, "I know what you mean about taking things for granted. When people who've never been to London come there for a visit, it always rejuvenates my love for the place when I take them 'round to all the touristy places. It's a magnificent old city, really."

"You gonna take me to those touristy places someday?" I asked.

"I'll take you anywhere you want to go, and maybe even a few places you don't want to go," she said with a smile.

"Deal," I said.

Cherry started the swing with her foot, and said, "This truly is a perfect day for a chat, don't you agree?"

"Depends on what we talk about, I guess, but it's definitely relaxing."

"Well, there is one thing I'm dying to ask," she said. "No, it's not as bad as all that. Don't pull such a face. I only wanted to know how you got your start in law enforcement. What made you want to become a police officer? Was that always your dream growing up?"

I yawned, stretched, and said, "No, it wasn't my dream job. I wanted to be a professional football player. And not soccer, either, missy. I mean *our* football. Real football."

She chuckled, and tossed her hair back from her face. "Okay. Believe it or not, I do know the difference between the two. So, tell me. What drew you to the law as an occupation?"

"Well, first of all, I wasn't good enough to even play college football, so the pros would never get a chance to see me play. So, that was out. I got into the law—you sure you wanna hear this? It's kind of a long story."

"We have nothing but time. And yes, I really want to hear the story of why you became a policeman."

"Well, okay. It all started with vodka and orange juice."

She stopped the swing with her feet, and looked at me. "Vodka and orange juice?"

"Yep. A screwdriver led me to the law. Let's start at the beginning."

"Yes, let's," she said, and started the swing again.

"I had a friend who I grew up with who moved to Pensacola when we were both fifteen, name of Barry Payson. I used to go over and spend the night at his house on Friday nights during the summer as often as I could, and he'd do the same at mine. We would always sneak out until almost dawn, and then we'd go home to whichever house we were stayin' at. One Friday when we were at his house, he said he had somethin' to show me, so we went up to his room, and he locked the door. He had stolen a fifth of vodka from a neighbor's house while they were havin' a big party, and had managed to stash it in his room."

"This sounds like trouble to me," Cherry said with a grin.

"That's putting it mildly. So I knew this was going to be a Friday night to remember. I asked what did he have planned, and he told me."

"A wicked plan, no doubt."

"No doubt. Barry's house was in a new subdivision called Nottaway that wasn't quite completed at that time, so there was a lot of construction goin' on, and a lot of empty lots. Down the street from his house was a cul-de-sac, and there were no houses down there, just empty wooded lots. One of the lots was up on a fairly high hill, and his plan was to tell his parents that we were going to camp out up on that hill and spend the night in his tent. His mom and dad were fine with it, and said we could do it, just be careful and all that. Of course, we said we would, and in the late afternoon, his dad drove us down to the woods—it wasn't even a quarter of a mile— and we took the tent and our food up the hill, and waved good-bye to Mr. Payson. Then Barry showed me how he had stashed the booze in the cooler under the ice, and we had a big laugh about it. We set up the tent, but didn't build a fire, because we had other plans for the evening. Big plans."

Cherry said, "Do tell."

"Well, after we set up the tent, we ate the sandwiches Barry's mom had made, and sat around waiting for it to get dark. At that time of year, the sun didn't go down until almost nine o'clock, so we had a pretty good wait ahead of us. And we weren't going to go out until late, maybe midnight or so, to make sure that there were no people out and about. Well, finally, at a few minutes before midnight, Barry pulled out a quart of orange juice and two big plastic cups. He poured—now, get this—he poured enough vodka into each cup to fill it about a quarter of the way. Then he poured in an equal amount of OJ, which came to about four ounces of vodka and four ounces of juice in each cup. Now this was the first time either of us had ever tasted liquor. We'd never even had a beer."

Cherry said, "Babes in the woods."

"Definitely. Anyway, we now have two big glasses of vodka and orange juice, and it's time to drink 'em down. So, being completely inexperienced, we decided to just hold our noses, and guzzle the entire cup down as fast as possible."

"*No*," Cherry said.

"Unfortunately, yes. We swilled them down in maybe five seconds or so, and looked at each other. I guess we expected something different to happen, but we didn't really feel the full effect at first. So he made two more quickly, even bigger than the first two, maybe six or more ounces each, and we drank them down the same as the first, and then—*WHAM*. Within seconds, we were both knee-walkin', completely bombed out of our gourds."

"Oh, no, Cooper, this sounds a bit dodgy. Then what?"

"Well, behind our hilltop campsite there was a creek, maybe fifty feet away once you got to the bottom of the hill. Beyond the creek was the objective that Barry had in mind: the Nottaway Community Swimming Pool. So we were now completely gassed, and naturally, we started to walk down the hill towards the creek. Or, stumble and fall down the hill is more like it."

"Here we go."

"Yep. There we went. Okay, so we headed in the general direction of the pool, but we got off course, and ended up next door in the church parking lot. There was a standing metal figure of a cop with his hand up, maybe five feet tall, with 'stop' on his chest. It looked sorta like those flat pictures of famous people at tourist spots you can stand next to and be photographed, only it was metal, and more of a caricature. The church used it to control traffic, and it was just standin' in the middle of the parking lot mindin' its own business. So, for some idiotic reason, I went over and punched it in the face. The punch didn't knock it over, so I took another swing, harder than the first, and I fell down on my butt on the asphalt. The next day, my hand and my butt were both pretty sore, naturally. Anyway, that's the last thing I remember until the next morning. I only know what happened that night because Barry told me. I have to take his word for it, 'cause it's all a blank to me until the next morning."

Cherry said, "So punching the metal cop made you feel guilty, and that's why you became a policeman, is that it?"

"No. There's much more to the story. According to Barry, we went next door and broke into the swimming pool. All it took was me boosting Barry up, and him climbing over a wall, and letting me in."

"According to Barry."

"Right. According to Barry. So, now we're inside and we start throwin' trash all around, then tossin' the trash cans in the pool, stupid stuff like that. Next, all of our clothes come off, and we start diving off the lifeguard stand, which was probably a good three feet from the pool."

"Cooper! You didn't!"

"We did. We could have easily broken our necks, but Barry swears that's what we did. It's a wonder we both lived through the night. Anyway, after several hours, Barry wanted to leave and get back to our campsite before somebody caught us."

"Smart Barry," Cherry said.

"Right again. But I didn't wanna leave, so Barry said he tried to force me to go, and I told him that if he didn't leave me alone, we were going to fight. So, still totally bombed, he managed to get dressed and leave, but instead of walkin' back to the tent, he headed for his house. The problem was he only made it about halfway home. He fell asleep in a ditch," I said.

Cherry chuckled and asked, "Where did you sleep?"

"On a bench in the men's locker room. Buck naked, of course."

"Woo hoo!"

"Indeed. Anyway, I slept for a while, then the sun started to come up, and I heard someone coming. It was one of the lifeguards, and luckily for me, he was one of the smaller ones, little skinny guy. It was real lucky for me, in fact."

"Why was it so lucky for you?"

"Because before I even saw him, I yelled that I would beat anybody's ass that came in the locker room. Anyway, he goes outside to the pay phone to call the cops, and I get up and start lookin' for my clothes. So, I'm walkin' around naked with a massive hangover."

"Your first," Cherry said.

"Right. So, I walked out to the front entrance of the pool, and there stood about twenty or more eight- and nine-year-old kids of both sexes, who were there at the pool for their Saturday-morning swimming lesson."

Cherry stifled a laugh with her hand, and said, "No . . ."

"Again, yes. Anyway, I'm naked, hungover and pissed off, 'cause I can't find my clothes, so I go back to the men's locker room and lay back down on the bench. About five minutes later, a cop walks in with my muddy clothes in his hands, and says, 'Are these yours?'"

"Oh, Cooper. And you said?"

"'Yes, sir, they're mine,' and I took them and put 'em on. He saw that someone had been—well, had gotten sick all over the place, and asked, 'You been drinking, son?' 'No, sir,' I said. He asked, 'What's your name?' With the purest adrenaline flowing to my now wide-awake brain, I said smartly, 'Curtis Anderson.'"

"Curtis Anderson?"

"It was a combination of two of my friends' names, Curt Kiefer, and Steve Anderson. See, I had quickly devised *another* plan," I said.

"And the plan was?"

"Well, the plan was to tell him I lived in a nearby subdivision. A friend of Barry's lived there, and I knew the directions. So my plan was, when the police officer takes me to the friend's house, and goes to the door to ask if they know a Curtis Anderson, I was gonna jump outta the police car and run off. They would say they didn't know anybody by that name, and by the time the cop figured out that something wasn't right, I'd be long gone. Then I would make my way back to the campsite, and no one would be the wiser. Cool plan, hunh?"

Cherry said, "Sounds cool to me. Did it work?"

"In a word, no. There was something that I wasn't aware of that made my plan null and void."

"Yeah?"

"Yeah," I said. "What I didn't realize at the time was, police patrol cars don't always have door handles on the inside in the backseat. That one didn't. Once you were in, the only way out was if they opened it from the outside."

"Poor Cooper."

"'Poor Cooper' is right. Anyway, back to the pool. The cop asks me why I'm in the neighborhood of Nottaway, swimming illegally, so I told him I was spending the night at Barry's house and we had camped out in the woods nearby. At that moment, I still thought my plan would work. But, he puts me in the backseat of the patrol car, and drives me over to Barry's house, and that's when I found out the car's back door won't open, and that I'm in big trouble," I said, laughing again. "We get to Barry's house, and the officer goes and knocks on the front door. Mr. Payson opens the door, so I slid down outta sight in the backseat, and the cop comes back and says that Barry is down at the end of the street."

Cherry asked, "So Barry made it back to the campsite safely, after waking up in the ditch?"

"No. I found out later he woke up in the ditch, ran home as fast as he could, snuck upstairs to his room, and made it into his bed about ten minutes before his mother knocked on his door. We were supposed to be back in the morning, so she knocks and says that after breakfast, she needs Barry to help her get some rocks."

"Help her get some rocks?" Cherry asked. "For what purpose?"

"She wanted some for her garden. And naturally, she wanted to go to the empty lot where we'd camped to get them."

"Wait. What did Barry say about your not being there?"

"He told her we got into a fight during the night and I stormed off. There was a convenience store near the entrance to the subdivision, and he said I called my mom to come pick me up."

Anyway, the cop drives me down to the end of the street, and sure enough, thirty yards or so from where the cop parks, there's

Barry and his mom lookin' for rocks. The cop gets out, walks over
to 'em, and begins to question Barry. That's when I knew I was dead,
'cause Barry's shaking his head no to all the questions, and denying
any knowledge of the pool break-in, or any acts of vandalism that
may have occurred in Nottaway the night before. In fact, he was
probably denying everything he'd ever done in his life up to that
moment."

"It doesn't look good for young Cooper," Cherry said.

"No, it doesn't. So the cop comes back and asks in a real mean
cop voice, 'What's your name, boy?' I said meekly, 'Samuel Cooper,
sir.' He said, 'You're goin' to jail, son.' 'Thank you, sir,' I said."

Cherry laughed and said, "Uh-oh."

"Yep." I continued, "So, it's straight to juvenile detention for
young Coop, no way out of that backseat, no chance to put my
genius plan into action, no nothin'. And to top it all off, I had a monster hangover."

"My poor little teenaged Cooper," Cherry said, and gave me a
peck on the cheek.

"It was not a very good mornin' for me, as you can imagine.
Anyway, I won't bother you with the details of my six hours of incar-
ceration. I'll save that story for another time."

"I can't wait."

I looked at her and said, "I guess you're wonderin' how all this
made me wanna become a cop?"

Cherry said, "Yeah, I am."

"Okay, here's what happened. Mom came and got me out, and
they told us to show up in court the following week. The first thing
the judge said to me was 'They let you go to school with your hair
like that, boy?' My hair was a little shaggy, as always, and he
didn't like it. He was a well-known hardass, Judge Oscar Mitchell
by name. He was famous for givin' out really harsh sentences, and
everybody hated him, from what I heard. I said, 'Yes, sir, Your
Honor, I'm on the football team.' He looked at me like I was pond
scum, and after bad-mouthing me for a while, gave me a year's pro-
bation and thirty days washing police cars in Pensacola. That was
a drag, since it was June, and Mom had to make arrangements to
get me over there Mondays through Saturdays for five weeks. But
it coulda been a lot worse, so I said 'Yes, sir' a few hundred times,

and took my punishment. Then the judge said, 'I don't ever wanna see you in my courtroom again, boy, you hear me?' I said another 'Yes sir', and Mom asked, 'He's free to go? He doesn't have to come back to court?' And Judge Mitchell said, 'That's correct. He's free to go.' So we both thanked the old so-and-so, and drove home to Gulf."

"And that was it?"

"No, it wasn't. The next night, Mom made me go and apologize to the Paysons, and Barry sat there looking innocent as an angel. We were both trying not to laugh the whole time I was apologizing. Then Mom made me go and apologize to the president of the Nottaway Neighborhood Association."

Cherry said, "Well, all in all, that wasn't so bad, yeah?"

"No, none of that was too bad, but it gets worse. Six weeks later, a county sheriff showed up at my house, and arrested me on a bench warrant."

"Whatever for?"

"Well, a bench warrant means that you were supposed to show up in court on a certain date, and didn't show."

"I don't understand," Cherry said. "The judge said—"

"Right. The judge *said* not to come back, but he put in the record that I was *supposed* to come back."

"Unreal," Cherry said.

"Unfortunately, it was real. So, Mom called an attorney, and he called the judge and told him that there was some kind of mistake, and Judge Mitchell said, 'There's no mistake. You tell that boy to cut off that damn hair, or I'm sending him to the Okaloosa Juvenile Detention Center for six months.' He did all that just to make me cut my hair. And my hair wasn't even that long."

"You're joking."

"Nope. That was his whole purpose. Imagine the money spent: the sheriff; Mom payin' a lawyer; getting me to Pensacola to wash police cars. It was ridiculous. And you know, he didn't force me to get a haircut. I mean, he gave me a choice. I could go to a juvenile home for six months, or cut my hair."

Cherry said, "I hope you got a haircut."

"Oh, *hell* yes. I liked my hair, and so did my girlfriend, but go to jail for it? No way."

"What a bastard, your judge," Cherry said.

"Well, you'll be happy to know that he was beaten in the next election, and never had a seat on the bench again."

"Hooray!" Cherry said, throwing her hands up.

I laughed, and said, "That experience made me see the power that a judge has. I saw that they can do outrageous things if they want to. I mean, he could've made me wear a red dress for six months, or made me quit the football team, or quack like a duck on a street corner if he'd wanted to. Wait, he couldn't *make* me do any of that stuff. But he could've said, 'You either wear a red dress to school for six months, or go to juvenile detention for six months. It's your choice.' I saw the abuse of power, and that's when—"

"You decided to become a police officer!" Cherry said triumphantly.

"You got it. I know it may sound corny. Does that translate? Corny?"

"Yes, it does. I'm simply mad about corny," she said.

"Anyway—corny as it is—that's why I became a policeman. I wanted to balance out at least one bad guy like Judge Mitchell."

Cherry said, "That's quite a story."

"You know what? I've never told that story to Penny. Neal knows, but not her. She'd never let me live it down. I guess I felt free to tell you because I won't be seeing you every day."

Cherry stopped the swing, and said softly, "I don't want to think about that. You'll be gone soon enough."

I was quiet for a moment, and then I said, "I guess I will. Be gone soon enough. I mean, I know I will."

"Thank you for sharing that story, Cooper."

I said, "My pleasure, boss lady."

Cherry started the swing again, and said, "Remember when I said that I'd tell you about Alfred Hitchcock someday when we had the time?"

"Sure do."

"It's seems that you two have something in common, after all."

"You mean besides both being heavily involved in filmmaking?"

Cherry smiled, and said, "Yeah, something like that. Your story reminded me of something he said years ago. Hitchcock was being interviewed, and the reporter asked him a question I'm sure he had to answer a thousand times or more in his lifetime. I thought it interesting when I heard his answer, and even more so in light of your experience. The interviewer asked him something like, 'Since your films are so famous for scaring the daylights out of everyone, tell our readers: What scares you?' Hitchcock answered, 'The police.' I guess he knew what you know."

I said, "He was right. Abuse of power is a really frightening thing, especially when it involves the law. It happens in every country on the planet, every single day of the year. It can be the scariest thing in the world, being at the mercy of a bad character in a uniform. And they have the whole power of the law behind them. It's your word against theirs. And guess who gets believed most of the time. I'm serious about what I said—I really want to balance out one or more police officers that abuse their power. I guess when all is said and done, I'm a corny copper."

"You're a wonderful copper, Cooper."

"Good one."

Cherry looked out to sea with a wistful look, and we sat silently swinging for a while, the rain still falling steadily. After a couple of minutes or so, she said, "It's funny the way our lives take certain paths, almost as if we have no control over them."

I stretched, and said, "I know what you mean. Sometimes the smallest incidents can turn out to have the biggest effect on who we become."

She nodded in agreement, and then asked, "Do you ever feel you want to go back and relive your childhood? Would you do anything differently, if given a chance?"

I replied, "Oh, man, would I ever. When I think of some of the really stupid things I've done, it makes me nuts. Like the hundreds of times I hurt someone by being mean, or broke almost every Commandment in the Book, or just made a stupid decision in my life that I regretted later. I've never understood these people who say they wouldn't do anything differently, that they wouldn't change a thing about their past. Hell, I'd change a million things if I could."

When she didn't say anything for a few moments, I asked, "What about you? Was your childhood really as idyllic as you made it out to be?"

She looked down at her hands, which were on her bikini-bottom lap, and a tear formed and trickled down her cheek.

I said, "Hey, Cherry, come on now. I'm sorry, I was only trying to make conversation."

She smiled, and said, "You just hit a nerve, especially with the tale of your late-night sneaking out with a great friend. And, well, it's just that there is something I've always wanted to tell someone, but I made a promise."

I patted her bare knee, and said, "Look, I don't want you to break any promises. We can just sit here and enjoy the rain if that's all you want to do, no questions asked."

She wiped the tear from her eye, and said, "No, Cooper, I think I really *do* want to tell my story. And you're the one person I want to hear it."

She stopped the swing with her feet, took a deep breath, and told me the story of her secret.

50

AFTER LEAVING MATTHEWS, PENNY DROVE HER USUAL PATROL ROUTE, the rain still coming down in sheets. The windshield wipers were barely able to keep up with the deluge, and the overall grayness of the day made it difficult to see. Luckily, she knew the route so well that it didn't matter. No amount of rain could dampen her spirits after meeting Cherry last night, and while finishing her coffee, she had come up with a good plan for the evening.

The first order of business was to buy plenty of groceries. Her refrigerator was almost empty, and that was unacceptable with a houseguest. But she would be damned before she set foot in O'Kelly's again while Cherry Page was in town. Blanche would get suspicious if Penny bought enough food for three, and word would get around in a matter of minutes that something was going on at the cottage. She thought about going to the other grocery store, Milo's Whole Foods, but decided against it. Milo's is bigger, and more impersonal, but people knew her there, too, so she decided to do her shopping in Pensacola.

Her plan for the evening's entertainment would also be easier to execute with a trip to Pensacola, so after making her rounds, she called the office to let Doreen know where she was going.

Penny had decided that tonight was a good time to introduce Coop to Cherry's movies, and the Blockbuster in Pensacola would be sure to have a much bigger selection than the tiny video store that sat on the highway just outside Gulf Front.

Bub's Video had only two Cherry Page selections, and Penny had seen each of them three times. And besides, all Bub had were VHS tapes, which simply would not do. Coop had given her a DVD player for Christmas, and they hadn't even used it yet; it was time to break that baby in.

The drive to Pensacola was difficult, but she was so excited about the thought of watching a Cherry Page movie with Cherry Page *sitting right next to her*, that she was unaffected by the downpour. She changed her mind, and decided to go and get the videos before the groceries. She couldn't wait another minute to get her hands on a Cherry Page DVD. Or four.

Then she remembered that someone had told her one could buy used tapes and DVDs from Blockbuster. Should she just go ahead and buy them? No, she'd rather have brand-new ones. As soon as she got home, she'd go online and order the complete Cherry Page collection.

She pulled off the interstate, headed for a Blockbuster she'd noticed one day, after a meal at Ludie's Soul Kitchen. She parked and once again was happy that her sweet Coop always kept an umbrella in his car.

Inside, she got herself a membership card, and asked where she could find Cherry's movies. A nice young man took her right to an aisle that contained nothing but Cherry Page movies, taking advantage of all the free publicity the murders had generated.

Penny thanked the guy, and smiled to herself as he walked away, wondering what all the store patrons would say if she told them that she knew where Cherry was at that very moment. Not to mention, that the Computer Killer had tried to add Penny to his list of victims last night. No doubt about it, life was a lot more exciting with a fugitive movie star in your house.

She looked at each of the selections, trying to decide which one would make Coop the least unhappy. He was a pretty romantic guy sometimes, when the moon was right, but chick flicks were something he avoided with malice.

What was the title of that World War II movie Cherry had made a few years back? It had enough killing and things blowing up to keep Coop's manly attention span interested for a couple of hours. What was the name of it?

Success! At the end of the aisle, she saw it: *The Cliffs*. The title referred to the white cliffs of Dover, and Penny remembered enjoying it in spite of the guns and killing, because it had a lot of romance and a big dance scene in it. It had been nominated for a slew of international awards, and Cherry looked absolutely gorgeous in the clothes and hairstyles of the 1940s. Guns, bombs, and a bombshell. Perfect.

Penny took it, and three other Cherry films, and headed to the checkout line, wishing she could tell everyone in sight what she was going to be doing later that night.

Back in the downpour, she realized she had no way to record Cherry's visit. Coop's digital camera was at his place, so that wasn't an option. Even though she knew where he hid his extra key, she might have to deal with his elderly landlord if Mrs. Wiley saw her entering Coop's apartment. Then, Mrs. Wiley would want to ask questions about Coop and Cherry's whereabouts, and that just wouldn't do.

Luckily, there was an electronics store right up the street, so she headed there to buy a camera. No way was Cherry Page going to stay at Penny's house and not be photographed at least a hundred times.

When she got to the store, she found a camera she liked, and then it hit her: Why not get a video camera too? There were a million good reasons to get one, including the fact it might come in handy on the job someday. At least, that's how she convinced herself to buy it.

Penny almost maxed out her credit card buying the video camera, a video card, and a digital camera with printer. Outside the electronics store, she used her bank card in the ATM and got cash for groceries.

Now all she had to do was go back down the street to the Publix and buy enough food, Cokes, wine, and beer to last the three of them through Sunday.

And enough popcorn and candy to get them through four Cherry Page movies.

51

It was nice to be home again, out on the prowl in the late-morning sunshine, searching for what might turn out to be the most important chess piece of them all. After the all-night drive from that crummy beach town, it felt good to sit still and keep an eye out for the perfect prey in the small park. The amphetamines were just kicking in, smoothing out all the rough edges caused by the near tragic consequences in Florida. Near tragic? Maybe a bit melodramatic, even under the circumstances.

Okay, time to concentrate on locating and securing the perfect dumb animal for the job at hand. Another sacrificial lamb, blemishes accepted this time. A complete nobody, another so-called human that wouldn't be missed by society, or bring the police into the mix.

Eyes peeled.

Not that one, though—not big enough. No, that one is too big. There's an interesting-looking creature, the one talking to what must be a close companion. That might be a problem if they are too close, but it doesn't seem that way. Now, if the companion will only go away and leave the coast clear. Once again, Baal brings the ideal victim to the web, right on time, and ready to be taken.

The smoothness of each operation so far, excepting the chick cop, showed that it truly did matter where you put your faith. If you believe something will happen, it will, as long as you remember who is behind the scenes pulling the strings that make the puppets dance.

Yes, this one looks to be a perfect choice to fill the role. Focus becoming sharper as the drug reaches every nerve ending, bringing with it confidence and strength. Now if only the rabbit could be alone for a few minutes, just enough time to stalk and capture the worthless creature.

There goes the companion walking away, done as if by order! The rabbit, alone now, taking a seat on the bench out of sight of the *few people in the small park. No one left to call for help now, and nowhere to hide. No angels watching over this scene, ready to lend a helping hand.*

Look at the dull expression on the fresh victim's face, the heavy form; there really couldn't be a more perfect choice. Strong, yes, but soon that strength would be reduced to nothing more than dead weight. Well, not dead weight.

Not yet, anyway.

The new toy had been more fun than anticipated down in the beach boondocks, and would truly come in handy with this big creature.

Zap!

Down to the ground, duct taped and hog-tied, and another very important piece of the puzzle would be in place.

The rest of the day to take it easy, and yet still take care of the business that must be done before nightfall. Tonight and tomorrow will be a delight, even more pleasurable than the next few minutes!

Once again, the timing couldn't be more perfect.

Okay, slowly out of the car, quietly, quietly. Stun gun in the pocket at the ready, and all the signs pointing to another triumph. Time to make the move that will—damn it!

What made the rabbit suddenly run? Why would—oh, there was the reason. The companion came back, and they've left together.

No problem. There will be another chance, and soon. Baal must have changed his mind about this move, and he certainly knew best.

Time to forget about this one, and go on to the next appointed meeting.

52

Twelve-year-old Cherry Page was under the covers in her big bed, fully dressed and waiting for the ancient downstairs clock to strike eleven. Her parents had checked on her an hour ago, and she knew they were fast asleep by now.

The clock chimed, she jumped from the bed, formed her pillows into the shape of a body, and pulled the covers over them. Satisfied that her ruse would fool anyone who looked in, she slowly opened her bedroom door, stepped out, and closed it quietly.

Creeping past her parents' bedroom, she heard her father snoring loudly, and giggled softly as she tiptoed down the long upstairs corridor. The antique Oriental carpet runner softened the sound of her footsteps as she walked past the portraits of long-dead Pages, each of them following her with their eyes as she made her way to the top of the stairs. The large old mansion in St. John's Wood in London had been in the family for generations, and its size made it easy to move about undetected.

The house was not as cold as it would have normally been on a night in late October; a freak warm spell had come to town, and the temperature was more like an evening in early August. Earlier that day, Cherry and her best friend, Poppy, had decided to take advantage of the nice weather and have one last late-night adventure before winter came to London. It being Friday, they had no school the next morning, and they made plans to meet at their special place at eleven fifteen, as usual.

The past summer, they had slipped out after hours almost every weekend, and each time had been more fun than the last. They would nick cigarettes from their parents, and had four or five apiece to smoke during their late-night trysts. They both were *so* good in school, *so* proper in church, it was fun to be a little bad now and then, and they looked forward to the get-togethers with great excitement.

The household staff were dead to the world by ten, so there was no chance of being caught going out or coming in. Even if they did catch her, Cherry was sure she could talk her way out of trouble.

Downstairs, she took her bright yellow scarf from the coat rack and wrapped it around her neck, throwing the end over her shoulder with a flourish. She silently opened the big front door, stepped outside, and felt the exhilaration of freedom. She quietly locked the door, took the front steps in three jumps, and walked quickly down the street towards the park.

There had been a short rain shower during the earlier part of the evening, and it made everything seem brand new, all shiny and clean. The night air invigorated her, and made her feel as if the night would never end. The red and white lights of the cars were reflected in the wet surface of the street, the colors running together like a watercolor.

Cherry couldn't wait to get to the meeting place and share the perfect night with her dearest friend. Poppy was so much fun, so smart and nice. Best mates since the first day they met at school, they were now inseparable, sharing each other's secrets and looking out for one another at every turn.

There had been quite a transformation in Cherry's behavior since the summer; she had been timid on her first few late-night jaunts, but now was confident and not the least bit afraid. She ignored the looks and stares of people who wondered what such a young lady was doing out in the street alone so late of a Friday night, and smiled to herself at what they might be thinking.

She hastened to the park, and waited at the appointed spot by the brick wall near the entrance. Within five minutes, Poppy showed, and they held hands and ran into the park. They ran across the large open green, stopped when they reached the wooded area that had become their favorite place in the world, and stepped off the path into the trees. The leaves were almost all gone, but the girls couldn't be seen because of the hedges that bordered the path, and the thick undergrowth all around.

Out of breath from running and laughing, Cherry said, "I couldn't get any of Mummy's ciggies. Were you able to get some?"

Poppy said excitedly, "I got an entire package from Daddy's desk while he was out golfing!"

"Well let's have them, then!"

Fishing through her pockets, Poppy said, "They're right here. Or, they were."

Cherry asked, "What, can't you find them? You *did* bring them didn't you?"

Poppy moaned, "I must've left them in my other coat. Bloody hell! I've got to go back. We can't stay out here without a fag or two. Back in a mo'!" With that, she bolted across the field.

Cherry wrapped herself tighter in her coat as the wind started to pick up. It was colder than she had thought it would be, but being with Poppy was worth a little cold. Plus, this would be the last chance they would have until next summer to get out and 'go on the prowl,' as Poppy called their late-night conduct.

After several minutes of waiting and pacing, Cherry looked up at the night sky and made a wish upon the first star she saw. She just knew that her wish would come true, having been made on such a glorious night. The nearly full moon was shining brightly, causing the wet, leafless tree branches to glisten like diamonds floating in the air. She couldn't remember seeing a more beautiful sight ever in her young life, and felt as if the park were the center of the universe. Smiling broadly, she twirled around three times, and snapped a large twig that was beneath her feet.

A man walking by on the path stopped, and said, "Who's there?"

Startled, Cherry quickly crouched down behind a hedge. Her scarf caught on the top of it, and she pulled on it.

The man came straight at her and grabbed the scarf before she could get it free.

"Well, well," he said. "What have we here?"

Cherry turned to run, but he caught her by her long hair, and clamped his gloved hand over her mouth before she had a chance to scream. She tried to bite his hand, but the thick leather gloves protected him, and he laughed as he squeezed her mouth shut.

He pulled her by her hair around to face him, and slapped her hard, knocking her to her knees. She tried to scream, but his hand found her mouth again as he pushed her onto her back in the damp grass. He lay on top of her, his weight nearly crushing the air from her lungs. Cherry squirmed with all her might, but she couldn't budge him even an inch. He removed his hand from her mouth for a second, and she managed to shriek, "Help!" before he slapped her hard again, splitting her lip.

Cherry blacked out for a moment, and when she opened her eyes, he snarled, "Make another sound, girlie, and I'll straight-on kill you."

Tasting her own blood, Cherry went limp and gave up, something she had never done before. But she had never been so completely and utterly powerless before.

Now satisfied that he had her under control, the man pulled back her coat, and tore her shirt open. Cherry tried to cover herself, but he roughly pulled her hands away, crushing her fingers together so hard it brought tears to her eyes.

He leaned down to kiss her neck, and Cherry realized that he wore the same brand of cologne as her father. She remembered going to the shop with her mother to buy a bottle for Daddy's last birthday. How could someone similar to her dad be treating her in this manner?

Her attacker continued his sick attempt to make love to her, and Cherry escaped into her imagination. Pretend this is a movie, pretend that he isn't there, pretend it isn't happening, she told herself. But it was happening.

The man pulled himself up and said, "Remember what I told you. Not a sound."

Grinning down at her, he wrapped Cherry's yellow scarf around his neck, undid her belt, and roughly opened her corduroy trousers. He grunted as he ripped her knickers off and tossed them aside. One hand on her throat, he choked her as he began to undo his belt. With a laugh, he said, "Now you're going to grow up fast, little girlie."

When he let go of Cherry's throat to pull down his pants, Poppy struck the back of his head with a large rock she had found nearby. The blow stunned him, and Poppy smashed the grapefruit-sized stone down on his head again with all her might.

He fell off to one side, still halfway on top of Cherry, and Poppy bent down and struck his face with the big rock, causing blood to spurt from his nose and trickle from his mouth. Cherry struggled to get out from under him as Poppy smashed the stone down on his head another five times, each blow harder than the last.

Cherry finally managed to get out from under the now dead

man, quickly pulled her pants back on, and jumped to her feet. Poppy dropped the bloody rock beside the corpse, and the two girls fell into each other's arms, hugging tightly as they broke into tears.

After a moment, Poppy pulled back, and asked, "Are you all right? Did he hurt you? He didn't—"

"No! He didn't, thanks to you. It—it all happened so fast."

"Let's get out of here!" Poppy said, breathing hard.

Cherry said coolly, "First, we must get rid of the stone." She picked it up, and asked, "Where are the ciggies? Did you bring them?"

Poppy said, "Yes, but I dropped them when I saw what was happening."

"Look for them while I get my scarf off of this pig," Cherry said, as she reached down and pulled the bloody scarf from the man's neck.

Poppy said, "I've found them," and showed the cigarettes to Cherry.

"Good. Now, we must get rid of all these things. Come on!"

They made their way through the bushes, and took off running across the open field, headed for the small lake at the other end of the park. When they got to the water's edge, they stopped to catch their breath.

After a moment, Cherry said in a melodramatic tone that could only come from a preteen girl, "Poppy, my dearest friend, I shall never, ever forget what you have done for me. *Ever.* We must make a pact that not a living soul shall ever know what has happened here tonight. This will be our secret. 'Til death do us part."

They put down the things they were carrying, and shook hands to seal the pact. Then Cherry reached down and picked up the bloody stone, and flung it as far out into the lake as she could. They watched the ripples form into rings and move away until the water was almost still again.

Cherry said, "Now we must do something about all this blood that we have on us. We need to find something that we can use to wash—oh no, Poppy! I forgot my knickers! I have to go back and get them. You wait here. No. Go behind that big tree, and wait. I can't believe I almost left them! I'll be back as soon as I can."

That said, Cherry flew across the field again, then slowed to a walk as she approached the area that would no longer be her favorite spot in the whole world. She scanned the area to make sure no one was looking, and then stepped off the path, making her way behind the row of hedges. She kept her eyes averted from the grisly corpse, afraid the man might somehow still be alive. Panic overtook her when she couldn't find her panties, but she quickly calmed down when she saw them several feet away from the dead man's body.

She made her way out from behind the bushes, made sure she wasn't seen, and ran back to Poppy, no longer feeling any pain, unaware of her bleeding lip.

Back at the lake's edge, Cherry bent down and soaked the cotton knickers in the cold water. Poppy came over from behind the big tree, and gently took them from her.

Poppy tenderly washed the blood from Cherry's face, and then bent down to rinse the panties in the water. She twisted them dry, then stood and handed them to Cherry, who soaked them in the water and washed Poppy in the same manner, taking special care with Poppy's bloody hands.

After they were as clean as they could get, they hugged each other tightly for a full minute, then ran to their homes without another word. Each made it home without being discovered, and the sun rising found them wide awake in their beds.

A year later to the day, Poppy was diagnosed with leukemia.

53

AFTER SHE FINISHED TELLING ME HOW POPPY HAD SAVED HER FROM certain rape and possibly being murdered, Cherry was quiet for a moment. She started to speak, then closed her mouth and stared out to sea. I was surprised by her story, and wanted her to finish it, but waited until she was ready to continue.

Finally, she said, "When Poppy was diagnosed, my world felt as if it were closing in on me, and I was far more scared than she ever was. I convinced myself that she would never have gotten sick if not for me. So you can see that I feel a terrible sense of guilt over what happened that dreadful night."

I took hold of her arm, and said, "Wait a minute. You don't mean . . . surely you don't think that you being attacked was the reason Poppy came down with leukemia?"

With a weak smile, she said, "At thirteen, I was convinced it was the reason. As the years have gone by, I'm a little less sure."

I shook my head, and said, "Let me tell you somethin', kiddo. It is *not* the reason, and this will be the last year you ever feel that way. And that's an official order."

Cherry looked lost in thought, but tried to smile.

She said, "When Poppy was in hospital the last two months of her life, I visited her most every day, and always brought her a yellow tea rose. They were her favorite, and now they're my favorite, too. Poppy had read somewhere that a tea rose means 'I'll remember always' in the language of flowers. Nothing could have been more true, and still is to this day."

I said, "Havin' a friend like Poppy is the best thing in the world, and I know you miss her every single day that goes by. You were both very lucky to have found each other at such a young age, and I gotta tell ya, it's amazing that she saved your life the way she did." I paused for a moment, then said, "There's one thing that I wanna know, probably because I'm a cop. You said y'all met later to get rid of the clothes? How'd you do that?"

"We both managed to hide them that night, in the back of our closets. Our maids never did more than hang up our clothes unless it was absolutely necessary; they had enough to do around the house without worrying about our closets. Poppy and I met that afternoon, and threw the clothes into a big trash receptacle at a nearby construction site."

"Didn't your parents wonder what happened to them?"

Cherry replied, "Heavens, no. We both had so many clothes they simply weren't missed. Nothing was ever said about them a'tall. There was always a clothing drive at school or church, and we both frequently donated all sorts of clothes."

"Man, if I had lost a coat, I woulda been in big trouble. We weren't poor, but we sure weren't rich, either."

"I guess that was a perk of being a rich kid," Cherry said.

"What about your bloody lip?"

"Easily explained. Children's games."

I asked, "Was the killing of a man in the park big news?"

"Oh, my, yes. In St. John's Wood? A man found bludgeoned to death with his trousers half off? Everyone was appalled. It was the biggest news in London for a week or more. I remember my parents talking about it over breakfast, lunch, and dinner for several days. No one could figure out what had happened to the—gentleman. There was great speculation as to why he was killed, and by whom. It was so strange to be in the middle of something like that, and be one of the only people who knew the truth."

"Hmmm," I said. "Sounds kinda familiar."

"I've been thinking the exact thing since all this madness began. I've wanted to tell you about that night since my current troubles became news."

"Another question: Who was the guy who attacked you?"

"He was a doctor who was going through a divorce, and was about to lose everything. His home, his family. The family were living in their home near the park, and he'd moved out and taken a flat in the neighborhood. His wife told the police he had been threatening suicide, and that's probably why he was out walking so late that night. Trying to forget his troubles and figure out what to do next.

Anyway, that's what I've never told anyone. That's what I've been holding in for all these years," she said, and sighed deeply.

"Well, you've told me now, and I'm glad you did. Your secret's safe with me."

She nodded and looked me in the eyes. "I know it is, and thank you, Cooper."

She was silent again for a moment, then said, "Speaking of secrets, there's more. Only my closest friends and family know what I'm about to tell you."

She looked at her hands for a moment, then asked, "Remember the other night when we were in my bed, and I told you I'd let you in on a secret when I knew you better?"

"As a matter of fact, I do. You mean there's another secret?"

"Yes. I didn't tell you the complete story. Poppy and I made more than one pact that night." She paused once more, and closed her eyes.

After another few moments went by silently, I asked, "Are you gonna tell me, or what?"

Cherry said, "The second pact we made that night was also 'til death do us part, so I guess I'm free to tell someone now. And I think Poppy would approve of me telling you. In fact, I'm sure of it."

"That's a nice thought. I hope she wouldn't mind."

She said, "After what almost happened to me that dreadful night, Poppy and I swore to each other that we would never make love until we were married to the man of our dreams."

I thought about that for a moment, then asked, "You mean . . . ?"

"Yes," she said. "That world-famous sex symbol—Cherry Page, the British Marilyn Monroe—is a virgin."

54

NEAL WAS SEATED AT HIS DESK AT FEAGIN INVESTIGATIONS, TALKING ON the phone with Susan, when a potential client walked into his office and took a seat in the chair in front of his desk.

Neal said into the phone, "I'll talk to you about it when I get home, someone just came in. . . . I hope so. . . . I love you, too."

He hung up, and asked, "How can I help you?"

"I was shopping for a birthday gift when I noticed your office, and I thought I'd take a chance and see if you could help me with a problem."

Neal asked, "What's your problem?"

"Right to the point. I like that. I'll get right to the point too. I was wondering, do you handle all types of surveillance?"

Neal said, "We can pretty much handle anything that's legal. What exactly did you have in mind?"

"Actually, I'm just sort of weighing my options. I guess you could say I have my suspicions about my business partner. There are some people who are saying—well, it's really only secondhand, it may just be gossip, or it might be jealousy among the people who work under my partner. It's entirely possible that they're just making up things to try and cause friction in the company. Maybe try and move up through the ranks. Know what I mean?"

Neal smiled, and said, "Unfortunately, I do. I understand completely, maybe even more than you do. I was with the New Orleans Police Department for over fifteen years, nine of them as a homicide detective. I know more than I ever wanted to know about backstabbing, rumors, and false accusations. Especially the kind that are intended to make someone look bad so that another person can look good. So, let me ask you, does your problem center on one individual in particular?"

"Yes. And now that I think about it, I'm not sure if 'surveillance' is the right term for what I need. Maybe what I'm looking for is someone who could—what's the word—*infiltrate* the situation. Someone I could actually hire. Well, not actually hire, but put them on the payroll for appearances' sake. A person who could come in and help keep an eye on my bad apple. Be my eyes and ears, that sort of thing."

Neal sat back in his chair, and said, "We're not really set up for that kind of covert action just yet. To tell you the truth, I'm new to the business. I just opened this office recently. So far, we've been doing mostly mundane investigative work. Surveillance of suspected cheating spouses mainly, along with serving papers on people, tracking down a couple of deadbeat dads, those kinds of things. I even have one of my guys working a bodyguard job. But what *you* need, I don't think we can handle. I hate to turn you away, but, the truth is, we're just not set up to handle your particular situation at this time. I'm sorry as I can be, but I don't see how I can help you."

"I understand, and I appreciate your honesty. Some people might try and fake their way through something like this, just so they could fatten their bank account. It's refreshing to find someone in your business—well—don't take this the wrong way, but the impression most people have of private investigators is that they can be a little shady sometimes, if you'll pardon me saying so."

Neal chuckled, and said, "I'm aware of that impression, and a small percentage of private investigators are a little shady, and will work outside the law to get the job done. Unfortunately, or fortunately, I just can't do that."

"Well, you're to be commended." After a pause, "Say. Could you do me a favor?"

Neal replied, "If I can, sure."

"Would you take an hour or so, at your convenience, of course, and try and find out who I could call to get some help with this? I'd be more than willing to pay for your time, whether you find someone or not. And money is not a problem."

Neal said, "Sure, I could do that. If I can't find someone, or point you to someone who can, there won't be a charge. I'll know in less than an hour if I can help you. How's that sound?"

"That sounds wonderful. It really would be such a help, you have no idea."

They both stood to shake hands, Neal holding on to the desk to keep from falling on his ankle. He said, "Here's my card. Call me after lunch tomorrow. Around two o'clock."

"That will be fine. Thank you again for all your help, and good luck with your business. I'll call tomorrow at two."

Only seconds later, Joe Don Kendrick walked into Neal's office, and asked: "Was that a new client I almost bumped into?"

"Could've been, if we were into corporate espionage. Think you could pass yourself off as a businessman for a month or so?"

"Let's see. A businessman, hunh? Naw, I'm not so sure that I'd be good at that. I might be a little too noticeable, size-wise. Besides, I'm not very good at being sneaky. I guess that has to do with my bulk too."

Neal said, "Yeah, I don't think stealth is your strong suit. You're better at knocking things down than going around 'em. Even if we got you a pair of bona fide gumshoes, I don't think you could creep up on anybody. Actually, I don't really know if any of us could handle the job; it takes a certain kind of mind-set to pull off the spying stuff. So, what brings you in? I thought you were on cheatin'-husband patrol today."

Joe Don said, "I was, but I got Brown to take over for me. He needs the extra money, and I need some extra time."

"What for?"

"Well, I got a call from one of my old Falcon teammates. He was also my college teammate, and we roomed together for the short time I was a pro. There's a big party for all the single players tonight out at a house in that fancy subdivision, the 'Country Club of the South.' You know the area, right?" Joe Don asked.

"Yeah, I know it well," Neal replied. "Some of the Braves and Falcons live out there, and a few big-time musicians, too. Probably a Hawk or two, as well. Takes a lot of bread to buy a house in that subdivision, if you can even call it a subdivision. It's more like a little city within the city."

"I know from personal experience." Joe Don looked at the floor, as if the memory gave him pause. He looked back at Neal, and continued, "Anyway, one of the young, single Falcons—Quintavius Sanford—just bought a house out there, and he's throwin' a big bash. There's gonna be lotsa food, booze, and probably women. Okay, definitely women, so I really wanna go. Problem is, if I *do* go, there's no way I can drive back home tonight in the shape I know I'll be in, so I wanted to check with you and see if I could take tomorrow off too. Brown says he can do my job with no problem, so I'm just makin' sure that it's okay with you."

Neal said, "It's fine with me. Just be careful with all those women up there. You're a big guy, don't break any of 'em."

"I won't," Joe Don said with a grin.

Neal asked, "Why isn't this guy havin' his party on a Friday or Saturday night like everybody else?"

"Well, first of all, he's not like everybody else when it comes to parties. No player is. During the off-season, players hafta get in as many parties as they can, 'cause once summer comes along, what with working out and practices and preseason games, there's not a lotta time for partyin'. And second of all, it's not just a housewarming party, it's Sanford's birthday today."

Neal said, "That all makes sense, I guess. Been a long time, but I remember what it was like to be your age and single. Okay. Well, have a good time."

"I'm sure I will. Thanks again, boss. And, hey—if you don't hear from me within forty-eight hours, send an ambulance out there, will ya?"

55

AFTER CHERRY AND I HAD TOLD OUR STORIES, WE WERE BOTH SUD-denly exhausted, and decided to go in and have a nap. If we had been in Atlanta at the Ritz, I would have offered to sleep with her, and hold her—as a friend only, of course—but the thought of Penny coming home unannounced kept that from happening.

I could tell that Cherry felt the same, about wanting company, and about not wanting to hurt Penny. She said as much, and smiled when she said we didn't need a replay of last night's "Penny attack" on me, especially if it was for real. We went our separate ways in the cottage: Cherry lay down on Penny's bed, and I went and took a quick shower and put on clean clothes before my nap.

The sound of the rain on the tin roof made it easy to fall asleep again, and a gentle breeze blowing through the house made for a perfect naptime. Within five minutes, I was sleeping soundly on the sofa, making up for lost time. I slept through the day, and didn't dream at all, something that's unusual for me. I must have really needed the rest.

When I woke up, the sun had finally broken through the clouds, and there was a blond glow to the sand in the late afternoon sun. I could hear Penny and Cherry talking and laughing in the kitchen, and cabinet doors opening and closing. The sound of plastic bags rustling and various thumps and thuds were evidence of a trip to the grocery store. I stretched, and sat up on the sofa, preparing myself for an attack on the produce. Napping through lunch had me ravenous.

When I walked into the kitchen, I received a peck on the cheek from both of the women, and took an apple from Cherry's hand, and a paring knife from Penny's. Cherry was now dressed in her own halter top and shorts, and Penny had changed from her police uniform into her customary cutoffs and one of my tee shirts, her hair down.

"Thank you, ladies," I said as I began to try and peel the apple without breaking the peel. "Looks like you bought out the store, Penny. Glad to see you went to Publix instead of O'Kelly's. Blanche would already be here if you had brought this much stuff home from there."

"That's what I was thinkin'," Penny said. "Sorry you missed lunch. I got plenty of Cokes, beer, and wine to make up for it. Besides being gossip central, O'Kelly's doesn't have the precooked stuff that Publix has; look at these rotisserie chickens I got. One is a lemon-herb, and the other is barbecue. They looked so good I couldn't decide which one to get, so I got both. We can have one tonight, and y'all can make sandwiches from the other tomorrow for lunch. Which one tonight, barbecue, or lemon-herb?"

"Barbecue sounds good to me for tonight. How 'bout you, Cherry?"

"That sounds delicious."

Penny said, "Good. I got three beautiful baking potatoes and there's cabbage for your coleslaw in the fridge. I want this meal to be light."

I asked, "What about dessert?"

"What'd I say? I want this meal to be *light*. No dessert, that comes later. I also bought all kinds of microwaveable stuff for the freezer and pantry. I know you'd prefer that I cook fresh food, but I thought I'd try and keep outta the kitchen as much as possible while y'all are here. That okay?"

"It's fine. I can take a little junk food now and then. I eat plenty of it as it is, and I'm still here." I looked through the bags, and spotted grapes, apples, bananas, and oranges, so I said, "There's plenty of good stuff here. You did a great job as far as I'm concerned."

Cherry agreed: "One thing's certain, we won't starve or die of thirst while we're on the run."

I said, "From the looks of it, I'd say you got that right." To Penny: "Lemme get my wallet and reimburse you for all this stuff."

Penny shook her head, and said, "No way, buster. This stuff's on the house. I'm gettin' a bigger paycheck while you're away, remember? So don't you worry about my bankbook, just eat like I know you can."

Cherry said, "Penny, at least let us pay for a portion of it. You shouldn't—"

Penny put her hand on Cherry's mouth, and said, "Hush up, movie star. You may be the boss of *him*, but you're not the boss of me."

"Bnn ah thnk we shoo hllpp pay frr thh foo," Cherry tried to say through Penny's hand.

I chimed in: "Yeah, what *she* said. We'll settle up with you later, Chief."

Taking her hand away from Cherry's mouth, Penny pointed her finger at us, and said, "Now look, you two. I'm the law in this town, and in this house. What I say, goes. Do I make myself clear?"

Cherry said, "Yes, sir."

"Sheesh, what a grouch," I said, and went back to peeling my apple.

Penny said, "I also have a little surprise for you, big boy. I have some world-class entertainment planned for after supper."

"What kind of entertainment?" I asked.

"It's a *surprise*, sweet cheeks. If I tell you what it is, it's no longer a surprise. What are you, a cop or somethin'?"

"No, ma'am, I'm a just a lowly bodyguard. I guess I'll just hafta be surprised. I can hardly wait."

Penny said to Cherry, "This one hates to be surprised. He has control issues, in case you haven't noticed."

Cherry chuckled, and said, "You can't be serious. Cooper? A control freak? Never."

They went back to the business of putting away the groceries, and I leaned on the island and finished peeling my apple. As usual, I didn't quite get the entire peel off in one piece, but it tasted just fine. I sliced it and ate slowly, feeding each of the girls a chunky slice when they came over and opened their mouths, like baby birds.

Five minutes later, the groceries were all put away, and Penny ran to her room. She came back with a plastic bag, took out a camera, and said, "Ta-dah!"

I asked, "Is that new?"

"Yep," she said with a grin, and aimed it at me. Before I could protest, the flash went off, and I was the first subject for Penny's new toy.

Penny said, "You two stand by the refrigerator."

We did as we were told, and Cherry put her arm around my shoulder. We smiled, and Penny took the shot, and then made us stand by the window, and pose for another.

"Okay, Paparazzi Prevost, that's enough for now," I said, and Penny put down the camera.

She reached in the bag and pulled out a new video camera. I asked, "What'd you do, go nuts and buy out the electronics store, too?"

She said, "We can use this on the job, so don't get all mad about it. Besides, how many times are we gonna have Miss Cherry Page here in my house?"

Cherry said, "I hope I'm here an awful lot."

Penny hugged her and said, "You better be here an awful lot. You're welcome anytime, any day."

"Good," I said. "No more cameras until after supper, I'm starvin'."

"Oh, all right," Penny said. "But later, there's gonna be all kind-sa taping and picture-taking goin' on around here."

"Fine. But for now, give me my instructions so I can get started on supper."

Penny told me the menu for the evening, got a bottle of chilled white wine from the refrigerator, opened it, and poured three glasses. Then the two of them went out on the front porch to drink and swing, and I started to put supper together.

I preheated the oven, and then put the barbecue chicken in to warm. Next, I washed and forked the potatoes, put them in the microwave, and got the cabbage out of the refrigerator. I make a mean coleslaw, with mayo, vinegar, salt, sugar, and celery seed. I stole the recipe from Susan Feagin, and mine is almost as good as hers. I chopped and mixed and poured and stirred, and in five minutes there was beautiful bowl of coleslaw chilling in the fridge, and three microwave-baked potatoes sitting on a plate on the counter.

I joined the girls on the porch, took a seat in one of the rocking chairs, and we drank our wine and passed the time talking as we waited for the chicken to warm through.

The sun was setting, and the golden glow of the fading sunlight was made even more special when a rainbow formed out over the ocean.

On his way to the party, Joe Don stopped at a liquor store to get some beer for himself and his friends, and wine for his host. Even though he knew that Sanford would never touch the wine, there was sure to be a bevy of young ladies in attendance who would appreciate a good Chardonnay.

He found a cart just inside the door of the large store, and headed to the refrigerated beer section. He selected a case of longnecks for himself, two more cases of bottled beer for the party—one American, one German—and then asked the clerk to select six bottles of the best chilled white wines the store carried.

When he got to the counter to check out, he realized that two cases of bottled beer might not be such a good idea at a gathering of young, rowdy males. Especially around a swimming pool where there was sure to be a lot of cement and rock surfaces. So, he wheeled the cart back over to the refrigerated section, and put back the two cases of bottles that he had bought for the party, and replaced them with cans. He kept his longnecks, though, knowing that he could be responsible for his own behavior. Those other guys—who knew?

At the counter, he purchased six bags of ice, and with the help of the young clerk, wheeled the cart out to his Jeep and opened the back. Together, they iced down the beer and wine in the three large coolers Joe Don had brought along. The coolers had been collected over several years of high school and college drinking. Joe Don had a fourth one, but couldn't find it in his cluttered garage when it came time to pack the Jeep.

He tipped the clerk a five, got into the front seat, and checked the map one more time. According to the directions, the party house was less than three miles away.

He pulled out of the parking lot and merged with the traffic, resisting the temptation to open one of the longnecks. He knew that Georgia had an open-container law, and it would be just his luck to get pulled over on his way to the party with a beer in his hand. Besides, he would be safely at the party house in a matter of minutes, and then it would be time for "serious drinking to commence," as his father was fond of saying back in Texas.

Within ten minutes, he stopped at the small office in the entrance to the exclusive gated community, showed the guard his invitation, and was waved through. Joe Don thought of what Neal had said earlier, that the large elite subdivision was home to several well-known Atlanta athletes and musicians. Doctors and lawyers and anyone else who could afford the price of the big homes lived there as well.

Among the amenities homeowners enjoyed were the usual community pool and clubhouse, but there was also an eighteen-hole private golf course. Owning one of the large homes was a signal to the world that you had arrived.

Joe Don had looked at a house in the neighborhood when he was drafted by the Falcons, and had thought at the time that if he played a few years, he might have been able to afford it. He felt a tinge of sadness as he slowly drove through the immaculate streets. He usually managed to keep the past from interfering with the present, but every once in a while, what might have been would slap him in the face. All the dreams he had of playing in the National Football League and living the lifestyle of a wealthy young athlete were now just that: dreams.

He sighed loudly, took a deep breath, and slowed down as he saw the well-lit party house come into view. This was no time for what-ifs and what-could-have-beens.

It was time to party.

56

WE ATE OUTSIDE AT THE PICNIC TABLE AGAIN AS THE SUN WENT DOWN, and the lack of bread and dessert—and lunch—had me picking the chicken carcass for every shred of meat I could find. However, I'm not even in the same league with my girlfriend when it comes to eating poultry.

Whenever there's a chicken to be had, Penny always eats the dark meat, paying special attention to the legs. She can make the leg bone look like it should be in a museum, it's so clean when she finishes with it. I'm serious; there isn't even the tiniest hint that there was ever anything on the bone, particularly any kind of flesh. It's a remarkable thing to watch, and Cherry got as big a kick out of it as I do. Good thing for us we both liked white meat.

When we were finished, Penny said, "You two take care of the dishes, and by the time you're done, I'll have the surprise all ready. Deal?"

"Deal," Cherry said, and I nodded my assent, my lips wrapped around the wishbone.

Penny headed for the front door, and Cherry and I gathered the dishes onto the trays, and went around to the back and into the kitchen.

I asked, "You have any idea what this surprise is all about?"

Cherry grinned, and said, "No, 'sweet cheeks,' I don't. And it wouldn't *be* a surprise if I told you, remember?"

"You've been around Penny too long," I griped, and turned on the hot water.

"How shall we do this?" Cherry asked. "You wash, I dry?"

"Sounds good to me. We can't show up back in Atlanta with you havin' dishpan hands."

"Good. Let's hurry and finish, I'm dying to know what the surprise is."

We washed and dried, and in ten minutes the dishes were clean and put away.

I called out to Penny, "Can we come in yet?"

"No! Go sit on the screened porch for a while."

"Okay, okay, we're goin'," I snapped, and Cherry led the way to the back porch. I turned on the overhead light, and we sat in the wicker chairs. We could hear Penny rummaging around in the kitchen, and a couple of minutes later, the smell of popcorn came sidling out to the screened-porch area, and my not-quite-full stomach growled in anticipation.

Cherry said, "Mmm, that smells divine. I haven't had popcorn since the last time I went to . . . never mind."

"Since the last time you went to where?"

"Never *mind*. I have an idea as to what the surprise might be, and I don't want to tell you."

"Great. Women," I said, and Cherry stuck her tongue out at me.

In a couple of minutes the *beep-beep-beep* of the microwave announced that the popcorn was done, and I called, "Penny? Can we come in *now*?"

"No!"

"Then *when*?"

"Just a few minutes more. Now hush, and entertain your boss."

"She's the movie star. She should entertain me."

"Shuddup!" Penny said from the kitchen, and Cherry laughed at my helplessness.

"What are you laughin' at?" I asked in my surliest manner.

"Oh, I wasn't laughing *at* you," she said. "I was laughing *near* you."

I tried not to smile, but couldn't help it. The smell of another batch of popcorn wafted out to my hungry nose, and it was my turn to say, "Mmm."

Cherry and I sat in silence until the microwave beeped again, and then Penny called out, "Okay, you guys, it's showtime!"

Curious, I looked at Cherry, and she acted as if she had no idea what Penny was talking about. I followed her into the kitchen, and took two large bowls of popcorn from Penny.

"I mixed 'em together so that one bowl's not hotter than the other," she said, and led me into the living room, Cherry close behind.

On the coffee table were four DVDs. Penny picked one up, opened it, and put it in the player. I put the popcorn bowls on the coffee table, and picked up one of the other DVDs. On the cover was our guest, dressed in period clothes from what I would guess to be Victorian England. The title read *A Matter Of Honor*. I showed it to Cherry, and she said, "That's one of my favorites. We made it in London a while back. It did quite well, actually."

Penny said, "It's really great, Cherry. I loved the scene where you slapped the old guy's face at the dinner table. That was a hoot."

Cherry replied, "We had such a brilliant time working on that film. The actor in question is just the dearest soul; it was truly difficult to let him have it. To make matters worse, the director made me do it eight or nine times before he was satisfied. I almost beat the poor man to death."

A look of horror showed in her eyes when she realized what she'd said, but luckily, Penny was turned away fiddling with the TV, and didn't see.

I quickly joined in, "It was a good thing the old guy is a dear soul, or he might've slapped you back."

Recovered from her unfortunate misstep, Cherry asked Penny, "Which film did you choose to show our Cooper? This will be his first, you know."

"I know. Can you believe it? We'll just hafta show him what he's been missin'. I chose *The Cliffs*, 'cause it has the most violence and explosions in it."

"Superb choice," Cherry said with a laugh. "That's my favorite of the lot of them."

Penny said, "Oh, cool! It should be your favorite. You were fantastic in it." To me: "Coop, Cherry was nominated for a Golden Globe for this one, and won a couple of awards for it in Europe."

"You guys don't hafta convince me," I said. "I know from watching rehearsals our girl here has talent. Plus, I've seen her rebuff the advances of several dozen men with a smile on her face. This chick can flat-out act." Pointing to the TV, I said, "I'm glad to see you finally hooked up the DVD player; now we can watch all the movies I've missed since last year. Was that what you were doin' while we were washing the dishes?"

"Yep." Pulling her new camera from the pocket of her tee shirt,

Penny said, "Let me get some more pictures. Coop, put your arm around Cherry."

I did as instructed, and after four or five shots, took several more of the girls in various poses. Then Penny broke out the video camera, and we spent another ten or fifteen minutes posing and mugging. When she felt we had a good start on recording the event for posterity, Penny directed us to take our seats. It was movie time.

Penny turned out the lights and said, "Cherry, you sit in the middle, so Coop and I can both say we watched a Cherry Page film with the star sitting beside us."

We all took our appointed seats on the sofa, and Penny immediately jumped back up and said, "I forgot the rest of the surprise!"

She was back in a flash with jumbo boxes of Raisinets, Good & Plenty, Goobers, a huge package of peanut M&M'S (my favorite), and three regular boxes of Jordan almonds. I gotta hand it to her, it looked like the concession stand in a movie house had spilled onto the battered coffee table.

Cherry said, "Oh, Penny, what a dazzling display! You've outdone yourself."

Penny smiled, reached behind her back, and pulled out another bag of candy.

"These are for you, Cherry. I read in a magazine how you—how did you put it—oh, yeah— 'absolutely adore chocolate-covered toffee.' So I got you a bag of Heath bars, too."

Cherry squealed, "Ooh, I *do* adore these! You're such a doll, Penny. Let's all eat candy 'til we get sick."

Opening the bag of peanut M&M'S, I said, "Last one sick is a rotten egg."

Penny said, "I saw this in a theater in Pensacola last summer and loved it. I think Coop will too."

Cherry asked, "Why didn't you drag this guy along with you?"

"Because we were, shall we say, living separate lives at the time. 'This guy' can be a real pain sometimes," Penny said with a laugh.

"And just how often would you say he's a 'real pain'?"

"Only when he's awake."

I said, "Hardy, har, har, Prevost. You know I'm the sweetest man in the world. Or at least, the sweetest man in the room."

Cherry said, "He's got you there, Pen."

Penny said, "Okay, I give." She hit "play," and the movie started. When Cherry's name came on the screen, we all clapped and whistled and hooted and hollered.

The first scene was in a wartime London hospital, with Cherry dressed in a nurse's uniform. She looked really good, her hair in one of those 1940 hairdos. I don't know what you call it, but it had kind of curled bangs, and was not quite shoulder length. She had a white nurse's cap on, and was looking really good—did I say that already? Anyway, the guy she was talking to in the hospital bed was dying, and when he kicked the bucket, she started crying and ran out into the street.

As the movie went on, it became clear that the dead guy was her fiancé, a pilot who had been rescued when his plane crashed over Germany. The first few minutes after he died, the movie flashed back to their romance, the crash, and all that stuff. It was actually pretty good, and Cherry was perfect for the part. Her acting was as good as anyone I've seen, and it was clear why she won awards for it.

I looked over at Penny, and saw she was already on the verge of tears. I told her to hit "pause," went in her room, got the box of Kleenex, and put it on the end table next to her. She took the box without ever taking her eyes off the screen, hit "play," and the movie continued. Cherry smiled at me as I sat back down.

There were some good action scenes, especially one where Cherry was on her way home and an air-raid siren went off. As she was running for the bomb shelter, she twisted her ankle, and fell down in the middle of the street. Just as the bombs started to go off all around, this big handsome British soldier came along, scooped her up, and raced to the shelter just in time. I have to admit, I didn't think they were going to make it.

But they did, and romance ensued.

Penny's tears had stopped by then, and my bowl of popcorn was empty. I had polished off all but a few M&M'S when the big dance number came on. Cherry's rescuer had been shipped off to Germany, and she was volunteering at the local British version of the USO, handing out food and dancing with the soldiers.

She had on a dress that showed off her legs and her curves really well, probably a little sexier than what the women wore back then, but hey, it was a movie. Believe me, I wasn't complaining.

As the band was warming up, an American soldier came over to Cherry, and said he wanted to give her a present. Wary, she said that she had a boyfriend, and wasn't sure that taking gifts from a stranger was a good idea. He promised her there were no strings attached, that he had something she would really like and he had no use for. Besides, he'd get more pleasure out of it than she would, if she'd only accept the gift.

Intrigued, Cherry followed him outside, where he opened a box and gave her a pair of genuine silk stockings and a garter belt with garters. She flipped out, gave him a big kiss on the cheek, and went in the ladies' room to put it all on. At that moment, the orchestra leader said, "This one's called 'In the Mood,'" the band started to play, and the joint started jumping.

Cherry came out of the ladies' room in her stockings, and looked even better, if that's possible. She found the guy who gave her the stockings, and they hit the dance floor. She made even the most difficult moves look easy, and that dress of hers flying up while she danced showed all the things a guy likes to see. It was easy to see why she never did nude scenes.

She didn't have to.

All of my objections to a dance scene in a war movie were forgotten after the first flash of Cherry's thighs. After a few minutes of her superb dancing and garter-belt flashing, I was ready to jump in a plane and fly to Germany myself.

During the scene, Penny and Cherry danced in their seats, and I tried to ignore them. I had my eyes glued to the screen so I wouldn't miss a single shot of Cherry's bopping and swinging. She was radiant, and glamorous, and all those movie clichés, but the main thing she was, was sexy as hell.

My candy ran out as the scene ended, so I stole the bowl of popcorn the girls had been sharing the moment they slumped back on the sofa, out of breath from dancing and laughing.

After the big-band number we all came back down to Earth, and watched the rest of the film in relative quiet. Cherry's character worked at the hospital, waited for word from her new beau, and went through all kinds of emotional stuff in the middle of the bombing of London. Her beau was in a couple of good battle scenes, and naturally was very heroic and manly.

Months passed, and her guy came back from Germany all shot up, and was brought to her hospital. It was touch and go for a while, and let's cut to the chase and say that he survived, they married and settled down in a house in Dover, and the Good Guys won the war.

The film ended as the couple put a little sign out by the white picket fence that read, "The Cliffs." A famous song played as the credits rolled, and Penny and Cherry cried. The song, of course, was "The White Cliffs of Dover."

It was the best chick flick I've ever seen, and I'm not just saying that because the star was sitting next to me the whole time. I actually enjoyed it. As Penny had predicted, there was enough killing and stuff blowing up to keep me interested. Not to mention how fascinating the wardrobe had turned out to be.

When it was over, Penny wiped her tears, and asked, "So, Coop, that wasn't so bad, was it?"

"Two thumbs up," I said. "Way up."

Cherry asked, "You really liked it, Cooper?"

"I really did, Cherry Page. Your acting was absolutely first rate, and your dancin'? Let's just say *wow*, and leave it at that."

Cherry smiled, and said, "I'm happy to see that my dancing is so appreciated. I had to take three-hour daily lessons for two grueling months before filming started."

I said, "Well, you were so good at it, I almost wanted to get up and dance myself."

Penny jumped up from the sofa and said, "I'm *so* glad you said that. There's still one more surprise to come."

She grabbed Cherry's hand, pulled her up from the sofa, whispered in her ear, and they headed for the bedroom.

57

THE PARTY HOUSE WAS IN A CUL-DE-SAC, AND THE DRIVEWAY WAS filled with cars. The circular end of the street was also filled with cars, some double-parked. Joe Don wasn't about to drag three big coolers filled with beer and ice from the nearest parking space, so he pulled up behind the last car in the driveway.

He got out his cell phone, to call Billy Bramlett, his ex-roommate with the Falcons, and tell him to come outside and help with the coolers. Bramlett, a three-hundred-pound second-string tackle who had played with Joe Don at the University of Texas, was the only man who could drink more longnecks than he could.

The two had cut a wide swath through Austin during their college years, and became well known as the hardest partying Falcons before Joe Don's career-ending injury. They didn't see each other much anymore, and that was why Billy had invited Joe Don to the party. The two had a lot of catching up to do.

Billy answered his cell with a loud "What!" and Joe Don told him to get his vast ass out to the end of the driveway, and help.

"On my way, J.D.!" Billy shouted into the phone, and within thirty seconds was ferociously shaking Joe Don's hand as they stood behind the Jeep.

"Whoa, man, you're breakin' my hand!" Joe Don said, laughing.

Billy hugged his buddy, and gave him a wet kiss on the cheek. The smell of beer was already heavy on him, and he swayed as he loudly asked where the damn coolers were located.

"They're right here, calm down," Joe Don said, laughing as he opened the back of the Jeep. "Grab a chest and lead the way."

"Aw, hell, J.D., I can do better'n 'at. Load me up with two of 'em."

"If you say so," Joe Don said. He lifted the heavy coolers one at a time and placed them on the huge outstretched arms of his friend.

Billy sauntered off as if he were carrying nothing, and said at the top of his voice, "The party's down around back by the pool—you cain't miss it."

Joe Don shook his head and chuckled at the sight of the massive man ambling towards the steps leading down to the backyard, grabbed the remaining cooler, and followed. By the time he had walked the length of the long driveway, he was breathing hard, and made a vow to get back into shape. With a grunt, he placed the cooler down and looked over the low white brick wall at the pool two stories below.

The big backyard was well lit, with strings of lights in the trees and bushes that surrounded the pool area. A large flat area twenty yards or so beyond the pool was the center of the action. A DJ under a large white open tent was playing thumping hip-hop at peak volume, and a dozen or so couples were dancing on a temporary parquet dance floor that covered the manicured lawn.

A long table outside the tent was loaded with food and beer, and a bartender was serving mixed drinks from a portable bar by the entrance to the tent. More lights were strung around the tent, and inside it, and a disco ball glittered as it spun around.

The backyard alone must be almost an acre, Joe Don thought to himself. He felt a pang of envy as he recalled again how close he had come to having a house in the neighborhood. He wasn't jealous, nor did he begrudge Quintavious his newfound wealth and success, but felt only emptiness as he watched the party from his perch high above it all.

Billy had made it down to the tent by then, and opened the ice chests after putting them down on the grass next to the big table. He grabbed a can and shook it vigorously, popped it, and began spraying beer over anyone who was within ten feet. He threw his big head back, let out a roar, popped another can, and swallowed the contents in one long gulp.

Joe Don knew that this would happen thirty or more times during the next several hours, and he made a mental note to stay away from the table whenever Billy was near it. He was wearing his best silk shirt, and didn't want it sprayed with beer. Dry cleaning stretched the budget a little too far for the time being.

Joe Don sat on the low wall with his back to the party for a few minutes, feeling sorry for himself before finally deciding it was time to get into the spirit of things. He opened the ice chest, pulled out one of his longnecks, and took a long drink. He turned and looked again at the party below, and realized he recognized four other players besides Billy, and counted only two of them friends. In the three years he'd been out of the game, a lot of guys had moved on to other teams, or like him, had ended their careers. Add the fact that married players hadn't been invited, and it was no surprise that he knew so few of the Falcons in attendance.

As was common at all the singles' parties, there was a surplus of young women of all races, all of whom had two things in common: They were very attractive, and they were very willing. Joe Don knew from experience there is a certain type of young woman who loves being around athletes, and who will do anything to be with them. *Anything.*

The women who attended the players' parties were different from the groupies who follow rock stars, politicians, or movie stars. The football groupies were wilder and crazier, no doubt about it. They had to be, to want such big, physically powerful, spoiled individuals as the young men of the NFL. Joe Don had always wondered if they had a need to be treated like dirt, or if they merely enjoyed it. Not that he had spent much time wondering about it, especially when he had been with one or more of them.

As he watched the party get wilder by the minute, he felt out of place, and the deafening music irritated him. By the time he was finishing his fifth beer, several of the women were skinny-dipping with two young Falcons in the deep end of the pool. By the sixth beer, the pool was half filled with players and women, all of them naked and noisy.

As Joe Don was twisting the cap on his ninth beer, two drunken beauties wearing nothing but bikini bottoms came up the grassy rise and asked why he wasn't down by the pool.

He said, "I'm workin' security. I need to stay up here."

"Oh," one of them said. "Okay," said the other, and they staggered off towards the front door of the mansion. One of them slipped and fell on her butt on the tiled porch, and they laughed as if it were the funniest thing in the world.

Joe Don watched the women as they barely managed to make it

into the house, and thought he was no longer in their league. He laughed drunkenly at his unintentional pun, and chugged his beer to dull the pain.

Below, the music was getting wilder and louder, and the unrestrained drinking was causing problems. Some of the women started loud arguments, and two of the players got into a wrestling match. They bulled each other around for a few minutes as the crowd loudly egged them on, and finally crashed into one of the tent poles, bending it and causing the tent to lean precariously, and bringing the music to a halt.

There was only a slight delay as Billy Bramlett went over and bent the pole back almost to its former state. He bowed deeply and almost fell over as the crowd whooped and whistled noisily in appreciation. The DJ came back louder, and the housewarming party got wilder, as some of the players and women paired up and went inside the house.

As all this was going on, Joe Don never once left his spot at the wall above the action. After he finished his tenth beer and tossed the bottle in the grass, he took one long, last look at the world he would never again be a part of and headed for his Jeep, leaving his coolers behind.

58

PENNY AND CHERRY CAME BACK INTO THE LIVING ROOM FIFTEEN minutes later. Each sported a ponytail and one of Penny's summer dresses; Cherry's was white, Penny's was yellow. Penny said, "Okay, Coop, time to dance for your supper."

I put on my grimace face, and said, "You know I don't dance."

Cherry frowned, and asked, "Don't you really, Coop?"

Penny said, "He never dances with me either, Cherry. He may not even know how—except for slow dances—so don't take it personally."

"Then we shall have to teach him. What say we pull the rug back, and make a dance floor."

"Great idea," Penny said. "Help me with the chairs."

I leaned back on the sofa and watched as they cleared the floor. I started to put my feet up on the coffee table, but they moved it in the middle of my attempt, leaving me with my feet sticking out in front of me. I dropped them to the floor, and crossed my arms over my chest.

Penny said, "Oh, don't give me that 'I'm not movin' off this sofa' look, buster. You're gonna learn how to dance tonight if it kills ya—or us."

Cherry giggled, and said, "Pen, cue up the dance scene on the DVD."

"Jolly good, old girl," Penny said in her new British accent, and in thirty seconds they were jitterbugging to the music, Penny taking the lead.

As if there was any other way it would happen.

They were quite a sight, Penny keeping up with Cherry's every move, both of them smiling and looking like the hottest babes that ever jittered a bug. There were no garter belts or stockings, but there was plenty of female flesh, what with their short dresses flying up all over the place. I was soon in a trance, watching them energetically move around the small room, in perfect step with each other.

When the song ended, they huffed and puffed, and hugged each other, then turned their attention to me.

Cherry said, "Go to the scene again, Penny. It's time for Cooper's first lesson." To me: "Come on, you, on your feet."

Penny said, "Okay, it's ready to go. Get up and join us, twinkle toes."

When I just stared at them, Cherry said, "Don't tell me you're too cool to dance, Cooper."

I continued to stare blankly, and Cherry whispered into Penny's ear. Penny nodded in agreement and said: "Coop, if you don't get up and dance with us right this minute, I'll arrest you and take you downtown."

"Now wait a minute, you can't just—"

Penny said, "Oh, yes I *can* just. I'm the chief of police, remember? What'll it be, dancing or jail?"

Since I'm a man who values his freedom, I said, "Okay, okay. I give. Who wants to take me on first?"

They looked at each other, and Cherry said, "I think you should do the honors, Pen. But take it easy on the old boy—don't hurt him."

"I'll take it nice and slow," Penny said, and started the movie again, the band swinging from the get-go.

I took Penny in my arms, counted to four, and we began to swing, man. Penny followed my lead as Cherry stood by watching, her mouth open as she realized that I knew how to jitterbug, and quite well, if I do say so myself.

Cherry yelled over the music, "Cooper, you're nothing more than a big, fat liar! You've known how to dance all along."

Penny was smiling her face off, and matching my every move. I've often wondered how women are able to dance backwards, but she made it look easy.

After the song ended, Penny hugged me tight, and we all applauded the band as if we were actually at the dance. I must admit, it felt really good to shake a leg.

We took a minute to catch our breath before Penny asked, "Where did you learn those moves, Coop?"

"I think the question is, Penny Prevost—where did you learn *your* moves?"

"My grandpa taught me when I was a little girl. He was a Seabee in the South Pacific during World War Two. Now, answer the question—where'd you learn to dance like that?"

"When Neal and I were at the academy, we used to go up to Myrtle Beach on our vacations." To Cherry, "Myrtle Beach is in South Carolina, a couple of states up on the East coast."

"Oh, I see," Cherry replied. "And that explains your dancing abilities how?"

"They had, and still have, a lot of dance clubs there. Beach music is what it's called, and that's where I learned to shag."

Cherry looked at me and asked, "That's where you learned to *what*?"

When I just stared, Penny jumped in with a grin, and said, "Cherry, you hafta realize somethin' about our boy, here. He has no concept whatsoever of popular culture." To me again, "In England, 'shag' means to have sexual intercourse."

I said, "Ohhh, I learned to do *that* at—"

"Never mind!" Penny said. "Another story for another time."

I continued, "Anyway, Cherry, the moves are very similar to the jitterbug, just slower. If you can learn one, you can learn the other."

Cherry said, "Well, Cooper, I'm truly impressed. You certainly have the moves. Fancy a go with me?"

"My pleasure, ma'am," I said, and we waited until Penny had the scene up on the screen.

We bopped through the number again, Cherry once more dazzling us with her dancing skill. Penny watched while perched on the arm of the sofa, again unable to keep from smiling.

When we were done, I collapsed on the sofa, and the girls fell down next to me on either side.

We sat for a while, and then Penny got up. She started the music, and pulled me back up to dance with her. After about a minute, Cherry asked, "May I cut in?"

"Sure," Penny said. "As long as you promise to give 'im back."

Cherry crossed her heart, said, "Promise," and we were off to the races again.

They were both much better dancers than me, but neither

said anything but complimentary things, and I was in shag heaven.

Make that jitterbug heaven.

When the song ended for what seemed to be the *eleventeenth* time, we all decided to go out on the porch to cool off. Penny and Cherry sat on the porch steps. I sat on the swing, and we silently watched the waves slide onto the beach. The temperature was perfect, and in a few minutes we were all cooled down.

After about ten minutes of talking about how much fun the dancing had been, Cherry said, "This has been simply marvelous, but I should turn in."

Penny said, "I'd better go in too." She looked at me with an "Okay with you?" expression on her face.

I nodded yes at Penny, and said, "Good idea. Bed—I mean, sofa—sounds good to me, too."

Cherry gave me a peck on the cheek, and Penny laid a sloppy kiss on me, licking my ear and laughing as she followed her new pal into the cottage.

They jitterbugged their way through the living room to the bedroom, and I stayed on the swing for a while, swinging and humming "In the Mood," and taking the night air.

Joe Don Kendrick was happy about two things as he pulled his Jeep into the driveway of his modest rented house in Brookhaven: He had made it home without incident, and had forgotten to turn off his front-porch light. The moths and bugs circling the old bulb were a welcome sight for a change. Fumbling in the dark for his house key would have been too much aggravation after the way the evening had gone. The frustration he'd felt at the party might have boiled over if one more thing had gone wrong.

For several minutes on the way home, a police car had been right on his tail. If the cop had decided to pull him over, it would have been a jail cell for sure. But luckily, when Joe Don had turned on to his street, the cop hadn't followed.

He turned off the ignition, and stepped out into the cool night air, his head still fuzzy. He was glad he'd left his ice chests behind; if not, he might have been tempted to drink more on the way home.

He felt the effects of every single one of the longnecks he'd guzzled before leaving the party without letting anyone know. All he wanted at that moment was to get inside his house, wash down three aspirin with a bottle of water, and watch TV until he fell asleep.

Joe Don walked on the concrete path towards the front door, and was ten feet from the porch when he felt a burning pain in his right thigh. Two seconds later, before he could figure out what was happening, he felt the same thing in his left thigh.

Suddenly sober, he looked down and saw blood spurting out of each thigh wound, and slumped to his knees on the grass next to the walkway. He tried to staunch the blood flow, but knew from his college biology class there were arteries in the thigh that meant certain death if severed.

And both of his were severed.

Another sharp sting struck the back of his neck, and suddenly in front of his face he saw a gloved hand holding the instrument of his death: A huge hunting knife, dripping with his own blood, clearly visible in the light coming from the porch.

His tormentor walked around in front of him as Joe Don fell forward, now on all fours, blood pouring from his thigh wounds at an alarming rate, and from his neck as well. He strained to look up at his executioner, and felt the knife slash his throat, but Joe Don Kendrick was beyond pain at that point.

The killer squatted down in front of him, and smiled at Joe Don's dazed expression, clearly enjoying the agony of the moment.

Joe Don looked into the eyes of the last person he would see on Earth, and thought his final thought:

"I know that face."

59

I WAS IN DEEP SLEEP MODE ON THE SOFA IN THE LIVING ROOM, WHEN a pair of soft lips kissed mine, and a hand slid under the waistband of my boxers.

My eyes still closed, I said softly, "Cherry, do you really think it's wise to be doing that right now? What if Chief Penny wakes up? She'll kill us both."

"Good one," Penny said, her lips now on my ear.

"Oh. It's you. I thought—"

"No, you *wished*," she said, laughing softly. "Come with me, I have something to show you. A little surprise I cooked up."

"Another surprise? At this time of night? Can't it wait until morning?"

On her knees beside the sofa, Penny tugged at my tee shirt, and said, "Trust me on this. I have reason to believe that you won't regret accompanying me. In fact, I can guarantee that you won't be disappointed in any way, form, or fashion."

Sleepily, I sat up, my eyes still closed, and leaned against her shoulder.

She helped me to my feet, and I opened my eyes. I could see in the dim light of the room that Penny was wearing her white satin robe that she puts on after swimming. It has short sleeves, and stops covering her at about midthigh. She quickly opened and closed it, and I could see that she was not wearing anything underneath. That woke me up immediately, and Penny was proven correct. I was not disappointed in any way, form, or fashion.

She took my hand and led me towards the front door, both of us trying to be as quiet as possible so as not to disturb our guest.

I asked, "Are you sure Cherry's asleep?"

"I've been up since we went to bed. Cherry went to sleep instantly, but I've been wide awake, starin' at the ceiling. All the dancing and excitement of our little party has me all keyed up. I can't get to sleep, can't even keep my feet from tappin'. For the last forty-five minutes, I've been setting up your little surprise, doin' all kinds of stuff, makin' a phone call, and movin' all over the house. I just checked on Cherry before I came to get you, and she hasn't moved an inch. She's sleeping like a log. A gorgeous, world-famous log. To answer your question, I'm sure she's asleep," Penny said, and squeezed my hand.

"I don't know about this. Should we really leave Cherry here alone?"

"Earl's out on the porch, armed and ready. The phone call I made was to him. I told 'im he could have a day off with pay and I'd cover for 'im if he'd come over and guard Cherry for a while so you and I could have a date."

"I like the way you think, Chief Prevost," I said.

"I thought you might." She picked up her raincoat from the coffee table, put it on, and said, "This little show is for your eyes only. Get your Glock—mine's in my coat—and let's go dance on the beach."

I got up, took my gun from the end table, and said, "Lead on." The screen door squeaked loudly as we tiptoed through it onto the porch, and we stifled our laughter like kids in church. Earl was sitting on the swing, his .45 in one hand and a shotgun in the other. He said in a low voice, "Hi, Coop. Don't worry, your secret's safe with me. Penny said I only get my day off after all this dies down, and if I tell, she'll make me work every holiday for the next five years."

I smiled and whispered, "Don't mess with her, Earl. She'll do a lot worse."

Penny said, "Watch out for our girl."

"Ten-four. Y'all be careful, and don't get caught," he said, and went inside, causing another door squeak.

Penny and I held hands as we walked down the steps, and when we got to the sand, she led me west of the cottage, towards a line of sand dunes. The night was cool but not uncomfortable, and there was a good deal of light coming from the moon, which had been full only a few days before. After we were down the beach a ways, Penny took off her raincoat, and did a turn. Her long black hair was down and gleamed in the moonlight, and she filled out the shiny white robe in all the right spots.

"Let's live dangerously," she said with a laugh.

When we got to the dunes, she pulled me over the highest one, and I got my surprise. There on the sand below was her beach blanket, a dark green king-sized velvet bedspread that had once been on her uncle Stan's bed in Pensacola. Stan must have gone through a hipster phase in the seventies. The thing looked like something out of a California swinger's pad, with fringe all around it. But it's the best beach blanket on the planet, without question.

On the blanket was a portable CD player softly playing classical music, and four fat candles set at each corner, blazing away. There was also a bucket filled with ice water, chilling a bottle of champagne that I knew for a fact had been in the fridge since I got back from New Orleans last year. Penny said it was only for a special occasion, and boy, did she turn out to be right about that. "Special" actually isn't a special-enough word for how the scene was set, but it's the best I can do. "Romantic" is not a word I use very often, but this was the definition of it, and maybe a little bit more.

We walked slowly down the dune, our feet digging into the sugary-white sand, placed our weapons down within reach, and took a seat on the velvet blanket.

Penny asked, "Want some champagne?"

"Don't mind if I do."

She reached behind the bucket and took two champagne flutes from a pillowcase. I took the champagne out and opened it the way a wine-expert friend of mine taught me. I undid the foil, twisted the metal cage from the cork, held the cork tightly, then slowly turned the bottle until a soft *pop* signaled that the champagne was ready to pour. Penny held the two glasses out in front of me and I poured, waiting until the foam went down before pouring in a little more. I corked the bottle and put it back in the ice water, took a flute from Penny, and made a toast: "Here's to the sexiest damn police chief in the entire world."

Penny said, "And here's to the *second* sexiest damn police chief in the entire world."

We clinked glasses, took a sip, and savored every drop. The champagne had been a gift from Susan, and was very—and I do mean very—expensive. Susan wouldn't tell me when I asked how much it cost, but Neal did after I got him alone. Let's just say it was ridiculous, and let it go at that. Dom Pérignon? Please. Cristal? I laugh at you!

I looked around at the candles, rubbed my hand on the blanket, and said, "Well, Chief Prevost. This is a side of you I never see at the office. Just exactly what did you have in mind, bringin' me out here like this?"

Penny took another sip of champagne, probably fifty dollars' worth, and said, "Look here, son. You just do as you're told, and nobody gets hurt."

"So *that's* how it is. You realize, of course, this is a clear-cut case of sexual harassment."

Penny said, "File a complaint and have it on my desk by Monday morning."

"Oh, you can bet I will. But right now, I'm not sure where all this is headed."

"Just *do what you're told.*"

"And nobody gets hurt?"

"You got it," she said.

"Whatta ya want from me?"

"Finish your champagne, put down your glass, and stand up right here in front of me."

Not wanting to get hurt, I emptied my drink in one pricey guzzle, put down my glass, and got to my feet.

"Closer," she said gruffly, and polished off her champagne.

I obeyed, and moved to within a foot of her face. She tossed her empty champagne flute onto the sand, and slowly began to pull my boxers down.

She said, "As for your sexual harassment case, I don't think you have a leg to stand on."

"It's not my leg I'm worried about."

Penny said, "Well, from the looks of it, you probably *could* stand on this."

"You keep doin' that, and I probably could."

"Shut up and lie down," she said.

"Yes sir, Chief."

I pulled off my shirt, and lay on my back on the blanket, feeling like a true swinging Californian. On the beach, long after midnight, with soft music, bright moonlight, and the taste of fine champagne. What more could a guy ask for?

Oh, yeah. That.

Penny started to take care of *that* when, still on her knees, she untied her robe, pulled it off, and tossed it beside me on the blanket.

Now naked as me, she leaned down and kissed me softly.

I pulled away, and asked, "What about the champagne?"

"What about it?" she said as she nibbled my ear.

"Well, it's a very expensive bottle of wine. Seems to me we should treat it with respect."

She said in my ear, "Lie back, and shut up."

I did as I was told. After several minutes, she stopped and sat up.

"That was amazing," I said groggily. "Talk about living dangerously."

Without a word, she put her leg over mine, took me in her hand, and slowly mounted me, taking her sweet time doing it.

"How's that feel, you lowly subordinate?" she asked, as she took me inside.

"Terrible. I hate it."

"Me, too," Penny said, and began to slowly move her hips.

Her hands were on my belly, and her hair had fallen down in front of her, blocking my view. I reached up and pushed her hair back over her shoulders, exposing one of my favorite sights: The tan line on her chest. I love the way her breasts are white at the bottom, and deep tan on the top. I also love the feel of them, and the way she reacts.

She leaned down, and as I raised my head up to kiss her, her hair fell onto my face. I had my hands full as her chest came down to meet mine.

Turns out it's not so bad being Penny's bicycle.

60

CHERRY WOKE UP IN THE SEMI-DARKNESS, AND FOR A MOMENT DIDN'T realize where she was. The curtains were open, and moonlight shone brightly through the window. She then remembered she was in Florida, lying in Penny's bed. She looked over and noted that Penny wasn't there.

She sat up and listened to see if she could hear anyone in the house. The silence almost convinced her she was alone, but she got up and walked slowly to the door.

Opening it inch by inch, she expected to hear Penny or Cooper's voice at any moment, but heard nothing. She took Penny's bathrobe from the hook on the door, put it on, and crept into the living room. She could see by the light of the TV that a man was sitting on the sofa, watching with the sound off. She froze when she realized the man wasn't Cooper.

Earl saw her, jumped up, and said, "It's okay, Miss Page! I'm a police officer. I mean, I work here. I mean, in Gulf Front. Penny called me to come over so she could, uh, go on a date with Coop on the beach, and it's okay, really. I'm Earl."

Cherry relaxed, smiled, and said, "How do you do, Earl. I'm happy to meet you. I'm also happy that you're a policeman and not a crazed killer. My heart stopped there for a moment."

"I'm sorry about that. I had the sound down so I wouldn't wake you."

Cherry said, "You didn't wake me. I just wanted a glass of water, is all. I'll get one and go back to bed."

"Yes ma'am, you're welcome to do whatever you want to. I'll be here 'til they get back, and you don't have to worry about a thing."

"I'm sure I don't, and thank you."

Earl sat back down, and Cherry went into the kitchen and pretended to drink. She ran some water and thought about Cooper and Penny and a date on the beach. The only sound in the cottage was the hum of the refrigerator and the ticking of the kitchen clock, a black cat whose tail was a pendulum.

She thought about the danger she was facing, but remembered her pledge to get on with her life. Besides, whoever had come to town and attacked Penny was long gone by now. She knew it might still be risky, if not insane, but she suddenly had the urge to go for a walk on the beach.

She walked back towards Earl, leaned into his vision, yawned, and said, "I'm off to bed. It was a pleasure to meet you."

"Same here, Miss Page, and don't you worry. You're safe with me here," Earl said.

"Thank you so much. G'night."

Cherry went into the bedroom, quietly dressed in the clothes she had worn that day, and waited in the dark. When she felt the time was right, she slowly opened the window, took the screen off, and laid it on the bed. She looked out, saw that she could easily climb down, and within seconds was on the ground.

It was a familiar feeling, sneaking out in the middle of the night to go on the prowl. Smiling at the thought of Poppy looking down from heaven, Cherry blew a kiss to the stars, and whispered, "Wish you were here, Pops."

She crept alongside the cottage until she reached the sand, and finding it almost dry, squished it between her toes, then trotted toward the Gulf. When she reached the water, she took a deep breath of the sea air and felt the gentle wind in her hair. It's so beautiful here, she thought, and played tag with the ocean the way she had as a child on holiday at the seashore. The water was cold on her feet, but felt wonderful, and she could taste the salt in the air.

When her eyes adjusted to the moonlight, she could see from her vantage point at the water's edge how truly isolated Penny's cottage was, almost like having a private paradise on a tropical isle. She looked to her right, and seeing nothing but sand, looked to her left. Down the beach about fifty yards she could see a faint light behind a line of sand dunes. She smiled as she realized what was most likely happening, but had mixed feelings about the situation. Happy for them, a little sad for herself, but most of all, she felt an overwhelming sense of curiosity.

Did she dare go over and try and get a peek? What if they caught her in the act, catching *them* in the act? How embarrassing that would be! Even as these thoughts went through her mind, she found herself creeping towards the dunes.

When she came to the line of dunes, at first she heard nothing. Then she heard something that stopped her in her tracks: The sounds of pure pleasure.

She heard oohs and aahs, and moans and groans, and the sweet tones of classical music. It was all too much! She backed away quietly until she was sure she was out of earshot, then trotted back to the cottage, her heart pumping wildly.

The excitement was almost more than she could bear. She had to talk to someone. She sneaked back to the bedroom window and climbed in quietly. She replaced the screen, turned on the bedside lamp, and found the bag that held her phone.

She sat on the bed and dialed Sally Allen's cell. Sally would be mad at first, but Cherry had come to a decision, and had to tell someone.

After four rings, Sally said sleepily into the phone, "This had better be good."

Afraid Earl might hear, Cherry said as softly as she could, "Sally, please don't kill me, darling, and whatever you do, don't look at the clock. I just had to call and tell you of the decision I've only just made a moment ago."

Sally said, "Cherry. My love. My dear. I'm sorry, but I shall have to kill you with my own hands. It's the right thing to do."

Giggling, Cherry said, "I have wonderful news, Sal. There's no turning back. I'm going to do it!"

"Do what, for the love of Zeus?"

"IT!" Cherry whispered.

Starting to wake up, and realizing what she meant, Sally asked, "You've found someone in *Florida*? After all these years? After traveling all over the world, almost every continent, you've found someone in *Florida*? Tell me you're joking, and I can go back to sleep. Please tell me that."

"Sally, I'm not joking. It came to me as I was on the beach. It's all so clear to me now!"

Sally asked in a slightly cross tone, "*What* is all so clear to you now?"

Cherry walked over to the window, looked out, and whispered, "I'm going to take Cooper as my first lover."

61

AFTER THE FUN, PENNY AND I LAY ON OUR BACKS ON THE SOFT BED-spread side by side, looking up at the stars. There was no need to speak, so we continued listening to the soothing classical CD, the perfect music for the situation.

The rain clouds had left the area, and the visibility of the stars was remarkable. Being away from the lights of the town, even one as small as Gulf Front, you get a spectacular view of the night sky from the beach.

We sat up. Penny retrieved the champagne flutes, and poured us each another serving. We drank slowly, and after another round, I noticed that the bottle was about half empty. I mentally toted up the approximate cost of each glass and smiled to myself. It was an incredibly lavish experience, but I knew that Susan would've been ecstatic to know how we used her gift. She and Neal have been push-ing me to propose to Penny for years; another few nights in the dunes, and their wish might come true.

As if reading my mind, Penny leaned into me. The wind had picked up a little, and the candles flickered, but neither of us felt the need to move or get dressed. It was getting cooler, but there was more than enough body heat left between us. Besides, the dunes acted as a windbreak, keeping most of the cool air from reaching us.

Sitting there on that velvet blanket, naked to the world, two of Gulf Front's finest were definitely living the High Life. I chuckled, and Penny asked what was funny. I said, "I was just thinkin' about what Neal says at a time like this."

"What's he say?"

"'Wonder what the poor folks are doin' tonight.'"

She laughed softly, and kissed my neck.

I said, "You know what, Chief Prevost? I'm beginning to really like this sexual-harassment stuff."

"Shut your mouth, and open it," she said, and started Round Two with another one of her overpowering kisses.

Sally Allen sat up as if launched from her pillow, and shrieked, "Cherry Leigh Page! Have you gone completely mad? *Coop?* Doesn't his girlfriend carry a gun?"

Laughing softly, Cherry whispered, "I don't care! I fear nothing at this point! She's wonderful, by the way, but I don't care about that anymore, either!" She paused, then asked, "Am I being horribly mean and selfish to even consider doing such a thing as this?"

"Yes, horribly so!" Sally said.

"What am I paying you for?" Cherry asked with a giggle. "I'm telling you, Sal, I simply cannot go on like this. I simply *have* to lose my virginity, and soon, or I'll go stark raving!"

Incredulous, Sally said, "Cherry Page! What in heaven's name will your mum say? You told me you two struck a bargain when she gave you the birds-and-the-bees speech: no hanky-panky before marriage, remember?"

Cherry pressed her forehead against the window. She remembered the half lie, but continued it by saying softly, "That bargain was made ages ago, Sally. Eons. And, besides, Mum said the first time should be special—that it should be with someone I had deep feelings for. If not the kind of feelings that lead to marriage, then at least to be in love. Now, I'm not saying that I'm in love; at least I don't think I am. But, I *am* saying that Cooper is special, and that I care for him deeply. He's a wonderful choice to be my first, and—and, well—if I don't have a man soon, I'll go 'round the bend. It's mad, I admit, but I feel like a bitch in heat. Or, at least what I suspect a bitch in heat might feel. I'm out of my mind! I'm going crackers! Help me, Sal!" she said, and collapsed back onto Penny's bed in a fit of giggles.

Now fully awake, Sally said, "I guess I'll have to be the mum here, and ask all the right questions. Let me think, I'm still asleep. Right. What would your mum ask at a time like this? Okay. Are you certain you want to go through with this? Are you absolutely, positively, sure?"

"Yes, Mum," Cherry said with a smile.

"Gawd, I was hoping you'd change your mind after I showed my disapproval. This is completely out of character for you, even as a film role. You, Cherry Page, a home wrecker?" She sighed dramatically, and said, "What else, then. Oh, yes, you say this boy is special?"

"Yes, Mum."

"And you have feelings for him?"

"Absolutely, Mum."

"And you'll be sure to take the necessary precautions?"

"No, Mum."

"You—what?"

Forgetting about Earl completely, Cherry laughed, and bellowed, "I don't know! I only know for certain that I'm going to have him as soon as we get back to the Ritz. What better place than a four-star hotel for my first time?"

Sally said, "Well, I'm not through with you, young lady."

"No more questions," Cherry said. "I've made up my mind, and it's written in stone."

Sally yawned loudly, and said, "Well, if that's the way you feel about it, I'm going to sleep. Call me when you've come to your senses."

"That's just it, Sal, I finally have come to my senses. And to think a lawman from America would be the first to have Cherry Page, the British Bombshell."

Sally said dryly, "G'night, bombshell."

"Night-night, Sally old girl. When next we meet, I shall have but a few hours of purity left."

62

GEORGE COATS AND QUEENIE, HIS GOLDEN RETRIEVER, WERE OUT EARLY for their morning constitutional, walking the same route they took every morning, barring rain. George owned a nearby music store, and never went in before ten, so there was no hurry. The pressures of meeting a payroll always seemed less of a problem in the predawn light. It was a foggy Friday, the grass wet with dew, and the street-lights were still on, a yellowish halo around them.

The Brookhaven neighborhood was quiet as always so early in the morning; it would be another hour or so before there were any signs of life. The lights of the small houses would come on one by one, and the noise of families getting ready for school and work would be heard up and down the streets. But George and Queenie would be back home by then, energized and ready for breakfast after their brisk stroll.

As the pair turned off of Malabar Drive and headed up Wentworth, Queenie suddenly stopped in front of the second house from the corner, sniffed the air, and stared at the front door. The big dog stiffened, whined, and began to try and pull George towards the house.

Trying not to disturb the neighbors, George said in a low voice, "Queenie! No! Stop that!" The dog never acted in such a manner, even when she spotted one of the many cats that roamed the neighborhood. George pulled back on the leash, hoping to distract her from whatever was drawing her attention, but Queenie was determined. She pulled harder still, dragging her now-angry master several feet into the yard before he could brace himself and stop her progress. He pulled hard on the leash again, wrapped the end around his arm, and dug his feet into the ground. This stopped the dog from pulling, and George relaxed, thinking that the situation was now under control.

It wasn't.

Queenie barked loudly three times, and a large crow flew from behind one of the bushes that lined the front of the house and settled on the roof directly above. The bird walked quickly back and forth for a few seconds, then finally perched on the gutter.

While this was happening, Queenie barked, whined, growled, and tried her best to haul George over to the bush the crow had abandoned.

Still worried about waking the neighbors, George continued to try and quiet the dog. But Queenie would not stop barking, so George looked up and down the street to see if anyone was around. Seeing nothing but the Jeep parked in the house's driveway, he decided to let the dog have her way before she woke the neighborhood.

The pair made their way across the short lawn, and George noticed several large, brownish pools of dried liquid on the grass and the concrete pathway. Hundreds of ants were moving around and through the puddles, and Queenie sniffed them for a moment. Then she whined and pulled George towards the bush.

As they got within a few feet of the bush, the crow lifted up slowly, flew from the roof over to a low branch of a nearby pine tree, and watched the dog and man intently.

Still trying to control Queenie and failing, George finally let go of her leash, and she hurried behind the bush, whining and growling low in her throat.

George asked, "Whatcha got, girl?" as if he expected an answer, then walked over and pushed his way into the bushes, his right foot stepping on the mutilated neck of Joe Don Kendrick.

Gagging at the sight and the smell, he grabbed the barking dog's leash, and pulled her away with newfound strength. This time, Queenie didn't resist, and they broke into a run and headed for home, where George immediately called 911 and breathlessly explained the circumstances.

63

WHEN I WOKE UP, IT WAS ALMOST DAYBREAK, AND I COULD SMELL coffee, but I didn't hear anything. No Penny and Cherry talking, no early-morning radio, no nothing. I sat up on the sofa, stretched, and ambled over to the open windows that look out onto the beach.

There in the water, up to their knees, were my two favorite babes, splashing water on each other, laughing as they tried to avoid getting wet.

They were each wearing one of Penny's bikinis, Cherry in white this time, and Penny in her orange one, which is my favorite since it shows off her dark hair and deep tan. It was a nice sight to see in the early morning light, and I went to Penny's closet and got a pair of my cutoff jeans to wear, then made a cup of coffee with cream in the kitchen. I figured it would be an even better sight to see up close, so I downed the coffee in three gulps, grabbed a folding chair from the screened porch, and went outside to join the girls.

The sun had just come up, and after the rain of the day before, the sky was a brilliant blue and perfect, not a cloud anywhere to be seen. It was going to be one of those ideal Florida Panhandle days.

I was a little shaky as I walked in the sand, but considering the goings-on of the night before, I wasn't doing too bad. By the time I got within twenty yards or so of the water, they had spied me, and waved and called out for me to join them. I waved back, declined their offer of a dip, and stuck my chair in the sand, all the while suffering their insults about what a sissy I was, and how gutless I'd become, and whatever else they said.

Some of their cruel comments were lost in the sound of the surf, and they gave up when I sat down and smiled at them like a dummy, obviously unscathed by the verbal assault. Penny stuck her tongue out at me, and Cherry thumbed her nose as they moved out into deeper water, all the while jumping up and down to try and keep warm.

Cherry finally took a headfirst dive into a small wave, and came up a few seconds later with her bikini top missing. Penny laughed and pointed at the unaware Cherry, and dove in herself, swimming underwater towards her new pal. Cherry finally realized she was topless, squealed, and immediately covered up with both hands before quickly sinking below the surface.

Just at that moment, Penny bounded up out of the water like a porpoise, the missing bikini top in hand, and attacked the half-nude Cherry, which turned out to be a mistake. The British Bombshell grabbed *Penny's* bikini top, gave a yank, and suddenly they were both naked from the waist up, laughing and wrestling in the chilly surf.

I watched the show from my folding chair, pretty much feeling like a sheik with a harem. I also felt more than a little privileged, seeing as I was in a very select group of men, maybe the only one in the group. I saw Cherry Page topless, and for quite a while. I mean, maybe her doctor and me were the only two guys in the world who could say that, and maybe *he* hasn't even seen her like that. Who knows?

One thing I *did* know: The day had just begun, and there I was, sitting on the beach in a folding chair looking at two beautiful women, sea-wrestling topless. One of them a famous movie star who didn't do nude scenes, and the other a gorgeous cop who did. On the beach at night, no less.

Another thing I knew: there was feminine pulchritude all over the place.

The two shameless hussies grappled with each other for several minutes, having a gay old time, no pun intended, before finally stopping to surrender their respective bikini tops. Well, actually, Cherry only pretended to surrender, and kept Penny's away as long as she could before finally giving in and handing over the orange strip of cloth.

All in all, it was a fun way to start the day, no question about it.

The main reason I'm relating this story about the beach scene that morning is to illustrate how quickly paradise can be lost. No, seriously.

Anyway, after they stuffed themselves back into their bikini tops, the two bathing beauties swam and dove and basically frolicked for another ten minutes or so, then ran towards me, the sun now fully up and shining on us all.

They found their towels, dried themselves off while their teeth chattered, and came over to sit down in the sand next to me after giving me what I'd come to expect whenever they came around: a couple of quick pecks on my cheek. Ah, the Good Life.

Penny asked, "Didja enjoy the show, big boy?"

"Show? What show?" I said. "I had my eyes closed the whole time."

Penny clouted me upside my head with her damp towel, and they each gave me a girl punch to the arm.

"Ouch, and ouch," I said, and asked, "Cherry, how 'bout that sandy bottom out there? Clean as a whistle, isn't it?"

"It's brilliant! And no seaweed whatsoever. Just like taking a bath. A rather chilly bath, but a bath nonetheless. And such gentle waves. What a beautiful spot you two have here. And this weather is simply extraordinary." Running the towel over her wet hair, she added, "I could easily spend the rest of my days in the Gulf Front sunshine, no problem a'tall."

She put her arms out behind her in the sand, leaned back, and offered her face to the glowing sun. Penny did the same.

I reminded Cherry, "Don't get too used to it, boss lady. Like you said, we can't have you goin' back to Atlanta with a face to match your hair."

Penny said, "Good boy, Coop, that reminds me." She handed Cherry the tube of sunblock she'd stashed with the towels. "Let me put some on your back after you do your face."

Cherry nodded and thanked her, took the tube, and rubbed sunblock on her face, legs, and arms. Penny took over and did her back for her, and I just closed my eyes and sighed, enjoying the smell of the sea and coconut-scented sunblock.

Cherry was right. I could easily spend the rest of my days in the rays of Gulf Front too.

No problem a'tall.

64

NEAL TOOK THE PHONE FROM A STILL SLEEPY SUSAN, AND WOKE UP quickly when he heard the tone of Agent Carver's voice.

"What's the bad news, Agent?" he asked, praying it wasn't Coop and Cherry who were the reason for such an early-morning call.

"You need to get over to Brookhaven on the double," Carver said. "I'm sorry to be the one to tell you. Joe Don Kendrick's body was discovered a short while ago in his front yard. I'm here watching the crime-scene people do their jobs. This has all the markings of another Computer Killer job, with a few new wrinkles. Kendrick's throat was cut, but there were deep cuts to each of his femoral arteries. And another thing, there was no attempt by the unsub to gain entry and use a computer. I don't know if you were aware of it, but Joe Don didn't even have a computer. The whole thing seems out of character to me, considering the way the other murders went down. This feels unplanned, spur-of-the-moment—even though it was brutally efficient."

Neal winced at Carver's choice of words, and said, "Go on."

"Well, my gut tells me that this was a warning. Or a show of complete contempt for the law, and well—maybe you. I think he wants you—and us—to know that he can get to anybody that's close to Cherry Page, and he'll stop at nothing."

Neal was silent for so long, attempting to process the information, that Carver finally asked, "You there?"

"Yes," Neal said quietly. "Barely."

"I can understand that. Like I said, Neal, I'm really sorry."

"I know you are, John, and thanks."

After several seconds, Carver returned to agent mode and asked, "You know how to get here?"

"Yeah, I know the way. Hold on," Neal said. He got up from the bed, grabbed a crutch, and hobbled out of the room with the phone, checking to make sure Susan wasn't listening, and said, "Gimme time to make some kind of arrangement to protect my family, and I'll be over there as soon as I can."

Carver said, "If you know where Chief Cooper and Miss Page are, maybe you'd better let them know what's going on."

"Maybe I'd better," Neal said, and turned off the phone. He softly closed the bedroom door, and leaning on the crutch, slowly made his way to the kitchen. He debated whether or not to use the coffee machine, worried that the aroma might wake Susan, and decided to settle for a Coke straight from the can. He took one from the refrigerator, sat down on the banquette that looked out on the back pasture, and leaned the crutch against the wall.

A few early birds sang brightly in the old hardwoods by the barn, and he heard Blue whinny. Neal thought for a moment about how much he missed his Sunday-morning rides.

He then thought of how devastated he would be if one of his girls or Susan were to become the next victim in the sick game that was coming ever closer to home. His thoughts also turned to the parents of the young ex-football player and how they were going to feel when they heard the horrible news of their son's death. And finally, he thought of Joe Don, who would never marry or know the joys of fatherhood.

He resolved yet again that the killer would not get away with these murders, and put out of his mind the many cases that had gone unsolved in the past. This case was personal now, and Neal would not rest until the killer was on Death Row.

After calling two of his men, and coming to the conclusion that they wouldn't be able to get out to the farm soon enough to guard his family, Neal gave up on the notion of going to the Brookhaven crime scene. He called Agent Carver and asked Carver to allow him to make a phone call to Joe Don's parents in Bandera, Texas. Neal didn't want them to hear the news from an FBI agent, or worse, the media.

He found the phone number on his computer, then realized it was an hour earlier in Texas, and decided to wait awhile. He had made similar calls as a homicide detective, and dreaded it, but felt he owed it to the big young man, who had become like a son to him in the short time they had known one another. Joe Don was the kind of kid anyone would like to have as a son, and Neal knew that it would be difficult to find someone to replace him at work, and impossible to replace him as a friend.

He also knew that he would be traveling to Bandera for the funeral, and that he couldn't leave his family alone. The killer was becoming more out of control by the minute, and the next target might be himself, or one of his loved ones. Someone would have to be there to guard Susan and the girls while he was in Texas, and Neal knew just who that someone was.

65

PENNY AND CHERRY DECIDED TO TAKE A WALK DOWN THE BEACH, AND after giving me my pecks on the cheek, they strolled off, heading west, away from town. My stomach was growling since I'd only had coffee for breakfast, so I decided to go in and make myself some eats.

I opened the front door, found my cell phone, and checked my voice mail. I had a message from Neal: *"Hey, bud, sorry to bother you, but . . . Joe Don's been murdered. It looks like our freak is strikin' closer and closer to home, and I feel like my family might be next. Carver is gonna put a rush order on the autopsy—no mystery with what happened—that way, I can fly the body home. I feel like I need to go to the funeral in Texas, so I really need you to come home and watch after my girls. . . . Of course, if you can't get here, then I won't go, but I feel responsible. (A deep sigh.) With my ankle, I'd feel better if you were guardin' them rather than me, anyway. I don't feel right about askin' any of my guys: they don't get paid enough. Besides, they're not police officers. Anyway, I've booked a flight outta here at seven thirty tonight, so if you could get back here by five or so, I'd appreciate it mucho. I'll get a car service to take me to the airport, so transportation is no problem. Call me as soon as you get this, and let me know what's what. Again, I'm sorry to mess up y'all's plans, but this is important. Tell Penny the next time we get together she can beat me up for ruining her time with you and Cherry. Okay, be safe, and I'll be lookin' for you and Cherry late this afternoon. Bye."*

See what I mean about how quickly paradise can be lost?

Vacation was obviously over. I wondered why Neal felt he had to go to the funeral, but decided that he must've been closer to Joe Don than I had realized. After thinking about it awhile, I figured it was the right thing to do, especially if I was there to look after the Feagin girls. Like he said, Neal wouldn't be at his best on crutches, and I'm sure he would have asked me to come back even if he wasn't leaving town. And I would have gone. I also agreed with him about his guys. They were underpaid, weren't trained, and I might have ended up having to look after them, too.

The first order of business was to get in touch with Neal, so I called and told him we would be there in time for him to catch his plane. Food was the next order of business, so I went in the kitchen and put six pieces of bacon in a skillet. As it sizzled, I got my stuff together. Penny would be disappointed, but she loves Susan and the girls as much as I do, so I knew she'd understand. In fact, if I tried *not* to go, she'd tear me a new one.

I spent the next few minutes packing my bag, flipping the bacon, and scrambling some eggs. I went out on the porch a couple of times to look for Penny and Cherry, but they were still out of sight. After I finished packing and had the bacon draining on paper towels, I went out on the porch and saw them about a hundred yards down the beach.

I yelled at them to hurry back, waving my arms. Within a minute, they were close enough for me to explain that Cherry and I had to leave. When I filled Penny in on the details, she said of course we had to go, to be careful, and to call as soon as we got there.

Penny was a real trouper; she put on a cheerful face and helped Cherry pack. She even made us a bunch of sandwiches and filled an old cooler with ice and drinks for the ride.

As Cherry and I slowly motored up the drive towards the highway, Penny blew us kisses and forced a smile. I waved out the window, and promised myself I'd make it up to her as soon as I returned to Gulf Front.

Maybe another night on that velvet bedspread in the dunes.

66

Reading the ad earlier in the morning newspaper that said: "South-eastern Discount Gun & Knife Show!"

Under the red headline was a map of downtown Atlanta featuring the Georgia World Congress Center, and the hours and days of the show. Time for another move, and this one was the most important one so far. It was such a fortuitous event for another meeting with a new friend!

Was it simply dumb luck, the way it had all come together?

The sunny Friday afternoon was perfect for the get-together, and the evening was sure to be the most fun of the last week by far.

Walking up to the entrance—there! The one who could be used to move the plan ahead, the one who would become the next and final piece of the puzzle!

This lamb had a dullness to the eyes that made it clear that there would be no problem manipulating the situation to the desired end.

Absolutely perfect.

Walking right up to the chosen one, appearing to be happy about the reunion, making eye contact, shaking hands, smiling. Yes, this was going to be even easier than it looked, and that was saying a lot!

Remembering the conversation earlier in the week about getting together sometime, guiding the lamb to a display booth specializing in antique revolvers. The dumb lamb-hands selecting a pearl-handled pistol, proffering it.

It's nice to come to a show with someone who's also really interested in guns. Now this is a beauty, and it feels so perfectly balanced, doesn't it? Is this—is this a pearl handle? I thought so. Yes, I have a pretty extensive collection, I guess you could say.

Protection? Yes, I have a few for protection as well—I also have a collection of knives. You know, it's good to have a blade or two *around just in case. I've been thinking of adding to my knife collection. That's one of the reasons I wanted to come to the show tonight (smile).*

Oh, you have a knife collection too, as well as a gun collection? Interesting! Great minds, I guess. Leading the lamb over to a booth which had knives of every sort laid out on a long table. These knives are works of art, don't you think so? The craftsmanship is beautiful. I can't imagine how many hours would go into creating something like this. Oh, really? That sounds like something that I'd really enjoy, watching them actually being made right before my very eyes. That sounds like a trip that would be worth the time and effort, for sure.

Yes, I know what you mean, people don't understand the fascination with knives, but I can't imagine being without mine. A lot of people don't feel comfortable having guns around, but knives are a different story, if they'd think about it.

Do you have a large gun collection? Really! That many? You must have to spend a lot of time keeping all of them oiled and clean. Oh, that's good. Having a housekeeper can really free up your time.

Walking down the long aisles, chatting, listening as if any of it mattered, pretending that the lamb was a fascinating creature.

I agree, this was such a good idea! Glad you mentioned your guns before, and glad we came down here. Not having anything special going on tonight, I appreciate meeting up with you again. And it's also nice to have the chance to relax and unwind after the last couple of days.

I guess we're pretty rare. You know how they say there aren't many Atlantans who were actually born and raised here——it's nice to meet another homegrown Atlantan. Oh, yes, I'm proud to be from Atlanta too. It's so exciting for a single person living alone, but I'm sure you know that.

I'm sorry, I'm taking up all your time talking when we should be concentrating on the guns. Okay, back to business. Stopping to examine another table loaded with rifles. What do you think of this one? Yes, I see what you mean. It really would be a better choice for utility rather than a collector's piece. Oh, yes, that one's more like it. I've never seen a rifle as handsome as that, you have excellent taste.

I hope you won't take this the wrong way, but I really enjoy your company. Are you up for a night out? Great; me, too!

Well, I'm certainly glad we decided to come down here tonight. Say, after we examine all the guns and knives, how about we go out and have dinner and maybe a drink or two? Do you have a favorite place? Oh, that's great! I love to listen to a really good live band. Country music? Yeah, I love country music too!

Is there any chance—now, you tell me if I'm being presumptuous —would you be willing to show me your gun and knife collections? Sure, I'll show you mine. Maybe tomorrow, if you're not busy? Oh, yes, I'd love to see your collections tonight, though—you have no idea!

Okay, let's get serious here. When we get tired of haggling with the vendors, we can go to the club. I'll follow you, and after dinner and a couple of drinks, we can go to your place, and you can show me your collections. I'm dying to see them!

67

As soon as Cherry and I were back in the metro Atlanta area, I called Neal and told him we'd be arriving at the Feagin farm within the hour. Friday-afternoon traffic was brutal, but we pulled into the long drive leading to the Feagin house with time to spare.

Neal and Cherry finally got to meet face-to-face, and before he headed out to the airport in the chauffeured car he had rented, we all stood and chatted in the big turnaround, Neal on his crutches.

Cherry shook hands with Neal, then took hold of my hand and said, "Cooper has told me all about you and your beautiful family. He obviously loves you all very much." She squeezed my hand when she said the word "loves," and Neal noticed.

He eyed me with his "You got something going on with this babe?" look, and I shook my head "don't" when I was sure Cherry wasn't looking.

Neal managed to keep from smiling, and asked Cherry, "How's our boy *Cooper* treating you? Did y'all have fun in paradise?"

She said, "Oh, Cooper has been simply wonderful, and Penny is an absolute living doll. I could move to Gulf Front and happily live there forever. It truly *is* paradise."

Neal eyed me again, so I quickly said, "Yeah, it's paradise most of the time, except we had a little rain."

He couldn't resist, "Well, a little rain can be quite romantic sometimes." He gave me another loaded look, and I glared back with my "shut the hell up" look.

Neal managed yet again not to laugh, and said, "It's an absolute pleasure to meet you, Miss Page, but I wish it was under different circumstances."

"I wish so too, Neal, and call me Cherry, will you?"

Neal smiled and nodded, then said, "I'm not looking forward to this trip to Texas, but—oh, yeah, Coop—Agent Carver is sending three agents over to help out tonight, so be on the lookout for 'em."

"Will do," I said, releasing Cherry's hand. "I'll take care of all your women. Just be careful, okay?"

"Yes sir, Chief. Okay, I better get goin'."

With that, Neal shook hands with Cherry again, headed over to the idling car, and clumsily climbed in the backseat. In a moment, he was out of sight, headed to Bandera.

Inside the big foyer, the Feagin girls were literally in awe of my movie-star boss at first, but after ten minutes at the kitchen table she had them calling her Cherry. Within twenty minutes, they were actually able to talk to her without staring wide-eyed. Susan and Cherry hit it off instantly, just like I knew they would. When Cherry went on and on about the delicious aromas in Susan's kitchen, the deal was done. I watched and listened as the five females laughed and talked and got to know each other.

There was still plenty of daylight left, and when the conversation turned to horses, Julie asked if the girls could take Cherry for a ride. I didn't like the idea of Cherry going off unattended, so I had to be the bad cop and deny all the fun. "Julie—girls—there's a maniac out there, and he may be closer than we think. No one is riding any horses around here until further notice. Got it?"

In one disappointed but resigned voice, they all said, "Got it," and the subject was closed. A minute later, the three girls and their new best pal were headed upstairs to do girl stuff.

After they were out of earshot, Susan said, "She's really somethin', isn't she?"

I acted as if I didn't know what she was talking about, "You mean Cherry?"

"Uh, *yeah*, I mean Cherry. Who else would I mean?"

"Just checkin'."

We walked into the big living room, each taking an armchair, and Susan continued, "I would think it's hard for a man like you— or any other man for that matter—to—well—to—what I'm tryin' to say—"

I asked, "Just what is it you're tryin' to say?"

She put on her mother hen expression, "I'm sayin' that Cherry is absolutely gorgeous, and completely attractive in the true sense of the word, that is to say, she attracts people to her. I mean, look at the girls. Shoot, look at me. We all fell in love with her the minute she walked in the door."

"And?"

"*And*. I could easily understand if a man fell under her spell." We could hear the girls whooping it up upstairs.

I said, "So you're worried that I've fallen under Cherry's spell, and you feel like it's up to you to bring me to my senses. That it?"

Susan squirmed, and said, "No, not necessarily that you've fallen under her spell. I thought maybe I caught her looking at you with more than friendship in her eyes. It's really none of my business, but—what am I sayin'? Of course it's my business! Penny is like a sister to me, or even like one of my own girls, you know that."

"Susan. Whatever you thought you saw, you didn't. Cherry and I are buddies, and Penny loves her to death, and just so you know, Miss Prevost and I have never been closer than we are right at this very minute."

"Good."

"In fact, just last night, on the beach, we opened that bottle of champagne you gave us, and—let's just say you would've been very happy to know what we were doing when we drank it."

Beaming, she asked, "How was it? Was it delicious?"

"Unbelievably so," I said. "And the champagne wasn't half bad either."

"Very funny."

Satisfied I wasn't having a torrid affair with Cherry, Susan leaned back and relaxed, and we listened to the occasional whoop from the girls. We avoided the heaviness of what was going on around us, and talked about the most mundane things we could think of. But I couldn't find any peace. Especially since I was wearing my Glock.

Susan said, "It's a good thing you're behavin' yourself as far as Cherry's concerned."

"Yeah?"

"Yeah." She stood and said, "It's a good thing, because—if you *did* happen to stray, after Penny got through killin' you, I'd dig you up and kill you again."

I smiled, and said, "You really do love me, don'tcha?"

"Damn straight I do."

68

FRIDAY-NIGHT SUPPER AT SUSAN FEAGIN'S TABLE IS ALWAYS SPECIAL, AND this one was no exception. Susan served up one of her classic meals, but for once in my life, my usually wide-open stomach was in a knot. All the ladies knew I eat a lot but they didn't give me a hard time about it; they realized I felt the pressure of being responsible for their safety. Call it women's intuition, or maybe better said, women's sensitivity.

Susan had cooked a mammoth pot roast and several of her legendary side dishes. At least Cherry enjoyed it all, and Susan gained another devoted fan of her culinary skills. After supper, the Feagin girls got out the Scrabble board, and Cherry joined them on the living room floor for a game. After a close match won by Jill, they broke out the Monopoly set and played until Julie was declared the winner, after being jokingly accused of cheating by both of her sisters. Susan and I watched and kibitzed, and I checked the doors and windows at least twenty times. By then, the FBI agents were stationed outside, and I talked to them twice, and in general drove myself nuts. Guarding Cherry was a breeze compared to having to watch out for all the women in my charge that night.

At ten thirty or so, we all sprawled out on the huge sectional and watched a DVD that Joy had recently bought. There wasn't a word said about watching TV, as everyone knew what a damper that could put on the evening if we happened to see a news flash about Cherry's situation. I finally began to relax, and stopped pacing and checking and checking and pacing, and sat still to watch the flick.

The film was *Cool Hand Luke*, one of my all-time favorites. I was a little surprised that the three Feagin girls knew about it, but it turned out that Joy had discovered the charms of Paul

Newman a few weeks earlier, and her new crush soon spread to each of her sisters. Susan and Cherry didn't need to be enlightened or persuaded; they both had a thing for ol' Paul. It was great to be normal for a while and before long I even felt good enough to sneak off to the kitchen and fix a gigantic pot-roast sandwich with potato chips and pickles on the side. Susan glanced at me when I returned with my foodstuffs, but Paul Newman was onscreen with his shirt off, so she paid me little attention, and for once didn't give me grief for denying her the chance to feed me.

It was close to 1 A.M. when the movie ended, and I announced that bedtime was nigh, no ifs or ands. Joy, Jill, and Julie went upstairs within a reasonable amount of time with a minimum of bellowing, and I felt very proud of the three young beauties. Not once during the evening had they been anything but cheerful and good-natured. I'm sure they wanted to know how Cherry felt about all the madness surrounding her, but they didn't ask questions or make nuisances of themselves. I was grateful for that, and I'm sure the fabulous Miss Page was too.

Susan had earlier made the guest room ready for Cherry, and she made up the sectional sofa for me after the girls went upstairs. She gave me a peck and retired to the downstairs bedroom, and the house was finally quiet. Maybe a little too quiet.

Every sound coming from outside made me twitch or jump, and I spent most of the night walking around, looking out windows, or trying to relax on the sofa, all with the lights on. I came up with all kinds of ideas and thoughts: Would someone close to me end up dead after all? What if the killer turned out to be a member of the cast or crew, like I had originally thought? What if Lyndon-Bowen, Cherry's slick producer, was getting even with her because she repeatedly spurned his slimy advances? And what about the FBI agents outside? Could the killer be an FBI agent, somebody involved with the investigation, or a police officer? Maybe a lady agent—or officer—jealous of Cherry? Everybody was fair game as I worried my way through the long night.

And another question preyed on my mind: Did the killer really believe all this stuff about Baal, or was it just a clever way to throw everyone off the track? Or—was I the killer, and simply too far gone to realize it? Okay, most likely it wasn't me, but I was running on fumes trying to figure out what was going on.

I finally dozed off around dawn, just like the night I had recently spent on watch at Penny's cottage. Thankfully, the night passed without incident.

69

AT 10:52 SATURDAY MORNING, AN ANONYMOUS CALLER CONTACTED the Alpharetta Police Department and asked to speak to the person in charge. The slower tempo of a weekend morning at the station in the suburbs of Atlanta was about to change. The caller claimed to have vital information regarding the Computer Killer.

The call was directed to Alpharetta police chief Darren Daniels, who was home riding his lawn mower in his large backyard, trying to get the job done so he could get to Home Depot before lunch. There happened to be a big sale going on that included two items he needed, or at least wanted badly, and he was daydreaming about all the fancy woodworking he would do once he owned the tools in question.

He was jarred back to reality when Carla, his wife of sixteen years, called him to the phone. He resentfully turned off the mower and walked slowly over to the back porch to take the call, frowning all the way. Carla went back inside after handing Darren the phone, not even vaguely curious as to why her man was being summoned on his day off. After sixteen years, she was familiar with the life of a police officer.

Chief Daniels brought the phone up to his ear and snapped, "Yeah." A strange, whispery voice greeted him, and Daniels covered his bare ear to try and better hear what was being said. It was difficult at first, but he focused and it soon became easier to understand. He listened intently for a few moments, and then said, "Who is this? This better not be some wild goose chase."

The caller hung up, and Chief Daniels was faced with a decision: whether to take the call seriously. He decided he had no choice but to consider it authentic, and he quickly called the station back to alert them of the call, and to see if the owner could be traced. It was later determined that the caller had used a disposable cell phone, making a trace impossible.

Daydreams of leisurely navigating the aisles of Home Depot vanished suddenly, and Daniels quickly went inside to get his car keys. Moments later, he removed his daughter's bike from behind his unmarked car in the driveway, and yelled at Carla to get the kids under control. He got in his car and headed for the location the caller had given him, uncomfortable in his dirty tee shirt and ripped shorts, cut grass clinging to his sweaty arms and legs.

He scratched at the itchy grass as he radioed the station and directed two backup cars to meet him at 2512 Flying Scot Way, a short drive from downtown Alpharetta. He knew the general area, but had never actually been on the road in question. A quick mental calculation had him arriving at the scene in less than ten minutes if traffic was not a problem. The roads were clear and the only difficulty he encountered was the sun hitting him in the eyes as he turned on to the main highway. He cursed the fact that he had forgotten his sunglasses, and pulled down the sun visor to block the blinding morning sun.

When he arrived at the location, Daniels pulled off the main thoroughfare on to a private dirt road that led to a secluded cabin, which stood next to a small man-made fishing pond. Stopping on the road after a few yards, he rolled down all the windows, and smelled the rich scent of the woods pouring into the car. He took a deep breath, calmed himself, and surveyed the surroundings.

After a moment, he gently stepped on the accelerator and slowly motored down the old tree-covered road. The tires crunched rocks and twigs on the dirt path, and a squirrel scolded him from a nearby pine. When he was twenty yards from the cabin, he noticed that the front door was slightly open. He stopped the car, turned off the ignition, and waited for backup.

In a matter of minutes, four young male officers arrived in two cars, got out, and proceeded as chief Daniels ordered: two went around back, and two followed the chief, all with guns drawn. What they found once they finally entered the cabin would have been a bigger shock had they not been expecting something out of the ordinary.

Chief Daniels called the station and after a brief discussion, instructed dispatch to contact the FBI and the task force assigned to the Computer Killer case.

70

At TWELVE MINUTES AFTER NOON ON SATURDAY, SPECIAL AGENT JOHN Carver answered his cell, "Carver."

A colleague and friend, FBI agent Craig Riley, said, "Hey, John. We hit pay dirt. I'll fill you in when you get here."

"Good news? You can tell a pal."

"It's definitely good news. Get out here and see for yourself. I can show you as quick as I can tell you."

Carver was instructed to report to an address in Alpharetta, which turned out to be a log cabin in a fairly remote section of woods. During the drive, Carver noticed for the first time that the trees had started to fill out, and realized how much the case had consumed his attention.

He was greeted by the local police chief, and escorted to the front room, which was now a bloody crime scene. Carver stuck his head in the door and took in the gruesome sight. He put on shoe covers, entered, and shook hands with a young FBI agent and his partner who were standing inside.

"Is the news as good as I think it is?" he asked.

The larger of the two agents said with a smile, "The news is excellent, sir."

Carver looked around the cabin and saw a small man of Asian descent lying on his back in the front left corner of the room, a gun in his right hand. The man had been stabbed in the chest, and his white button-down shirt was covered in blood. Carver knew he had been stabbed because a huge hunting knife was imbedded in his chest to the hilt.

Ten feet away, along the left wall, the body of a slender Caucasian man lay facedown on the floor. Dressed in a western shirt, jeans, and cowboy boots, the body was close to a small table on which sat a computer. A gray cowboy hat sat several feet away, the front brim smeared with what appeared to be blood. More blood pooled under the man on the floor, and his back was a bloody mess. His right hand was out as if reaching for the computer keyboard.

Carver spotted Craig Riley by the back door and called, "See Riley, what'd I say? All week long, I've been telling anyone who would listen the killer would turn out to be an Asian male. Yep, that's what I've been saying, an Asian was behind all this."

Riley walked over, smiled, and whispered loudly, "Uh, John. It's not the Asian guy. It's the cowboy type."

Carver asked, "Isn't that what I just said? That for the past week I've been saying it would turn out to be a cowboy?"

Riley said with a straight face, "It's all coming back to me, clear as a bell. Now that you mention it, I remember you said you'd stake your career on the fact that the killer was a cowboy type from right here in Atlanta, well over six feet, probably weighed about one eighty-five, was a Caucasian in his late thirties, and was gonna end up being found dead in a cabin in the woods. That's what I remember, John."

Carver said, "Kid, you've got a big career ahead of you. Mighty big."

Riley chuckled, and said, "Okay, here's what we have so far. The crime scene investigators found some hairs that Mr."—he checked his notes—"Mr. Hideki Nakamura was clutching in his left hand. They figure the hairs will be a match for Mr. William J. Tingle, our Caucasian cowboy corpse. Mr. Tingle left some fine prints on the computer keyboard. He served in the military, so we had his name, rank, and serial number in no time. Kinda nice to catch a few breaks after all those other crime scenes being so clean."

"They were spotless, all right," Carver said.

Riley continued, "Looks like Tingle broke in and was setting up his identity on the instant messenger, and Nakamura came home unexpectedly and surprised him."

"And you know this because?"

"Because all of the other victims were killed or restrained *before* the messages were sent. At least, that's the logical explanation for how Tingle was able to send all those other messages without being bothered. It also makes sense if you take into account all the other crime scenes were so uncontaminated. He killed or restrained the victims first, did his messaging, and cleaned up the scene afterward. Here, he left several prints because he thought he was alone and had plenty of time; this place is plenty isolated. And, he knew, or thought, that he would be able to clean up after he finished sending Ms. Page another message. But good ol' Nakamura caught him in the act, and did our dirty work for us."

Carver said, "Anybody been to Tingle's place? You said he's local, right?"

Riley replied, "Right. As a matter of fact, I'm waiting on a call from Giles—you know him? Jason Giles? I called him a half hour or so earlier and sent him over to Tingle's place. Not too far from here, just outside Marietta."

"Good deal," said Carver. "I don't know Giles, but I know *of* 'im. Good reputation."

"Yep. He's really on the ball."

At that moment, special agent Jason Giles and three additional FBI agents—Blaine, Hoffman, and Gupta—arrived at the Tingle home. Several horses could be seen grazing as the two government cars turned in to the long gravel drive that led to the ranch-style house. The agents parked and made their way to the front door. Hoffman and Gupta drew their guns, pointed them at the ground by their sides, and Giles rapped on the front door. Getting no response, he tried the door and found it unlocked. He and Blaine drew their weapons and the four agents cautiously entered. Giles loudly announced, "FBI!" and the men went quickly from room to room, shouting "clear" as they found each one empty. Until Blaine entered the kitchen.

He shouted, and when Giles came into the kitchen, he saw what had made his colleague call out: A small dark-haired woman of about forty lay facedown on the linoleum floor, dressed in a gray maid's uniform. A large amount of congealed blood pooled around her head and shoulders.

"Five bucks says she's illegal," said Blaine.

Giles pulled his cell from his pocket and called his contact with the Atlanta Police Department. "Bert. Giles here. Send the task force and some crime-scene guys out here ASAP. William J. Tingle residence, Marietta, thirty-two twelve something or other. Hell, I don't know—look it up. W. J. Tingle."

Agent Hoffman called from another room, "Hey, boss. We got gun cases and knife cases. There's a gold mine in here."

Giles and Blaine joined Hoffman to check out the cases, and Giles sent the youngest agent, Gupta, to the home office across the hall to look for evidence. After the men had all donned latex gloves, Gupta worked on the home computer while Blaine and Hoffman worked the gun and knife cases, which, luckily, were unlocked.

Before long, Gupta called from the office, "Got in the PC, boss. I'm all over it."

"Better him than any of *us*," Giles said, referring to the fact that as the youngest among them, Gupta was the man for the job. In fact, Gupta was known throughout the Atlanta branch as the resident computer whiz. His search of the PC turned up nothing more than the usual bookmarks and documents one might find on an adult male's computer.

Gupta abandoned the office and walked back to the master bedroom. He looked in the closet, then under the bed, and found what everyone was searching for: a laptop and a large briefcase, stashed far up under the head of the king-sized bed.

After he had been on the laptop for several minutes, Gupta yelled, "Jackpot!" and the other agents joined him. Their excitement grew with each passing minute and each bit of evidence.

Gupta found several websites that involved Baal and human sacrifice, and a document entitled "CP-Virgin" among the personal files. The most electrifying piece of evidence involved Agent Giles and a photo found on the bedside table. The man wearing a cowboy hat in the photo, William J. Tingle, was someone Giles recognized.

After the agents studied the evidence and material found in the bedroom for ten minutes, Giles went out on the porch and called Agent Riley, who was still at Nakamura's cabin.

Riley and Carver were standing out back of the cabin by the pond taking a cigarette break when Riley's cell rang. He said, "Riley.

Yeah. Tell me, J.G." He listened for a while, occasionally saying "yes" or "unh-hunh," then said, "Hold on." He and Carver tossed their smokes in the pond and walked inside. Riley went over to the kitchen table, sat down, and pulled out his notepad and pen. "Okay, give it to me," he said.

Carver went over to peer at Nakamura's corpse, and caught snippets of the conversation, intrigued when he heard Riley say, "No kidding? You know the guy? I'll be damned." Riley spoke and listened for several minutes and then said, "Great work. Lemme know when you get more. Thanks, buddy, talk to you later."

He put away his phone, walked over to Carver, and said, "Giles and his guys are at William Tingle's place, and they found a briefcase filled with all kinds of stuff about Cherry Page. Newspaper articles, tabloids, pictures of all kinds. Some of the photos had Cherry's face mutilated, that sort of thing.They also found a laptop, and when they checked its history, all kinds of Baal sites showed up, along with tons of Cherry Page sites as well. This guy has been doing the Baal thing for years, and following Cherry Page for months. They also found a shitload of knives and a huge gun collection. I bet there's some juicy DNA on some of those knives. Wanna take that bet?"

Carver smiled, and said, "No, I don't think I'll bet on anything about this case."

Riley said, "They also found some stuff that proves Tingle was actually serious about this 'Baal' business. It's definitely not just a smokescreen. And, get this. It appears that Miss Cherry Page is a virgin. A *virgin*. You believin' that?"

Carver let out a long whistle, and said, "That's pretty personal stuff. Not for public consumption, certainly. Back to Giles. He knows somebody? Somebody involved in the case?"

"Oh, yeah. Giles recognized Tingle from a photograph found in Tingle's house. Giles remembered where he'd seen him before."

"Where?"

"Giles was one of the agents working security at that charity benefit the other night—the one at the High Museum downtown—where Cherry Page gave a speech, remember?"

Carver nodded.

"Well, Giles saw Tingle at the benefit, even noticed him talking

to Miss Page and her bodyguard. J.G. remembered it all because
Tingle was the only guy there dressed like a cowboy."

Carver started to speak, but Riley interrupted, "Yes, Giles is
working on getting the surveillance tapes from the museum for a
positive ID."

Carver smiled and said, "You may actually make it in this FBI
business someday, Riley."

Riley returned the smile, pointed at the small Japanese man, and
said, "Tough break for Nakamura. Tingle got him with his knife
before dying himself from the bullet wound. From the bloody prints
on the keyboard and what's written on the computer, Tingle was trying to finish his message to Cherry Page when he collapsed. Gotta
give 'im credit—he was giving it the old college try right up to the
end. The way it played out, Tingle was close to Nakamura when
Nakamura shot him. Tingle was moving to stab him, and was able
to put the knife in Nakamura. Then, the gut-shot cowboy goes back
over to the computer to try and finish his message. That's what the
blood trail on the floor says anyway."

Carver didn't say anything for a moment as he looked back and
forth from one corpse to the other. Riley asked, "What's on your mind?"

Carver replied, "As you may have noticed, I'm losing touch. I
really missed the ball this time. Ten years ago, I woulda had my guys
at the High Museum, and we woulda nailed this sonofabitch Tingle
before anyone else got killed. Tingle was ripe for the picking. He was
right there. I don't know—I mean—there was some talk about these
murders being done by a group, or maybe even a female. This has all
been such a clusterfuck, and I've been—anyway, it's clear I was lost
from the get-go."

Riley felt sympathy for his colleague and quickly said, "Well, I
don't know about that, John. But as soon as the lab makes all this
official, I'm buying the drinks."

Carver stared at Tingle's corpse for a long moment, and then
said, "From now on, I'm going to just let the profilers do their work.
It's not like the old days, that's for sure. I mean, DNA wasn't even a
theory when I started."

"Hell, John, when *you* started, there weren't even fingerprints."

"Forget what I said earlier about your career. From now on,
you're assigned to permanent latrine duty at Quantico."

Riley asked, "Wanna see the computer? The message is ironic as hell."

"Sure, lead the way."

They walked over to the desk and Riley touched the mouse with a pen to wake it from sleep mode. There on the screen was the last message to Cherry Page from William J. Tingle, the Computer Killer:

This will be the last time I speak. Look for me, and you will see me. You will sikljnoaiq1

Riley said, "See? Tingle was dying as he tried to type, didn't even get a chance to finish his last sentence, just dropped dead. And look at the two lines I'm talking about: 'This will be the last time I speak.' 'Look for me, and you will see me.' He got both right. He sure as hell won't be doing any more speaking, and everybody will be seeing this prick all over the news for the next week, if not longer."

Carver smirked, and said, "I just feel so sorry for poor old Baal. He won't be getting his slice of Cherry pie after all."

71

AFTER A LONG NIGHT SPENT WIDE AWAKE, I GOT THE CALL FROM NEAL about what had happened at Hideki Nakamura's cabin. It was around two Saturday afternoon, and Susan was doing laundry and cleaning the kitchen. The Feagin girls had Cherry upstairs and were brushing her hair, getting makeup tips, and more girlie stuff. I was sitting on the living-room sofa watching a show about orangutans in Borneo.

Susan answered the ringing kitchen phone, assured Neal we were all still breathing, and told me to pick up the phone by the sofa. I said, "Hey. Everything okay in Texas?"

"As okay as it *can* be, seein' as I just got back from visiting the body of a man who's much too young to be dead. But that's not why I called."

"All right, then. Why did you call?"

"Well, bud—you sittin' down?"

"As a matter of fact, I am. And don't tell me anything that will ruin my day, understand?"

Neal said, "Man, are you ever off base. I've got news that'll make your day, and several other people's day as well. I'm talkin' *good* news, old bud-of-mine."

"Well?"

"You sittin' down?"

"Look, Feagin, P.I., we've already established my position. Are you gonna tell me this good news, or do I have to come out there and kick your bad ankle?"

"Agent Carver called." He paused.

"*And?*"

"And . . . they got the Computer Killer."

My mind went blank for a few seconds. Then I wanted to let out a whoop, but I restrained myself, and asked quietly, "You wouldn't kid your old bud, wouldja?"

"Serious, man. The guy's name is—was—William Tingle, and keep this to yourself. He was at that charity event you escorted Cherry to last Monday night. She even talked to the guy."

"She talked to the guy? You gotta be kiddin'."

"Nope. No joke. One of the agents remembers seeing him talking to Cherry and you. Did you notice a cowboy at the event? Supposed to have been the only one."

I went back to the previous Monday night at the High Museum in my mind, and there he was: asking Cherry if she liked country line dancing, and talking about dancing that night, and breakfast in the morning. "I remember him. Me and Cherry laughed about him and all the others who hit on her. *Damn,* man, this is a little spooky, knowing we looked that bastard straight in the eye."

Neal said, "He's dead as a hammer now, so don't give 'im another thought. He was found not too far from y'all actually. No more than five or ten miles from my front door. Let's not tell any of the girls."

"*That* will never happen, bud. I plan to keep all of this as far away from Cherry as possible, and I know you intend to do the same with Susan and the girls. They'll find out soon enough. Just give me a quick rundown."

Neal told me what he knew, about the crime scene at the cabin, and what Agent Giles had found in Tingle's house, the computer stuff, newspaper and tabloids, the whole nine yards. And what a whole nine yards they were.

After a minute or so, I said, "Whoa. That's enough for now. Wow. Let me process this for a day or two. I'm shaking a little, I'm so happy and keyed up at the same time. You can finish giving me all the details later."

"You sure?"

"Yeah. You and me will have a nice long talk about all this when things get back to normal. I don't wanna ruin the moment by hearing all the gory details. That will come, and too soon. Man. I'm at a loss for words, bud." I took a deep breath, exhaled, and asked, "So, you wanna talk to Susan?"

"Naw, you deserve to tell everybody the good news. After all, you're the one who had his ass on the line all week."

"Okay, thanks, but I didn't do anything you wouldn't have done if you could walk, you huge gimp," I said.

"Whatever you say, twinkle toes. But I owe you one for takin' care of my girls. Big-time."

"You don't owe me a thing. Let's change the subject. If that's even possible. Whew, this is too much." Another couple of deep breaths, then I said, "Okay, I can breathe again. Now—listen to me—Joe Don was doing what he wanted to do and I hope you're not feeling like you were responsible. Anyway, I'm sorry you have to go through all that funeral stuff."

"It's okay. Compared to what the Kendricks are going through, not to mention Joe Don himself, this wasn't much for me to do. I've made peace with what happened. His parents have been really nice. They said basically the same thing you just did. The kid wanted to be a private eye real bad, and it wasn't my fault, and they don't blame me for a minute." He sighed deeply, and said, "I just hope the funeral turns out to be beautiful, not like last year in New Orleans. I'm sure there are a whole lot of friends and family in Bandera to send him off. Still . . ."

"'Still' *nothin'*. His parents are right. There was nothing you could have done, and you know it. You're doing all you can, you're paying your respects. Now, shut up and get back home as fast as you can."

We said our good-byes and hung up, I called to Cherry and the girls to come downstairs, and then I told Susan to come into the living room.

When I had them all in a group, I smiled my biggest smile, and said, "Ladies, I have something to tell y'all."

When I told them the news, the screaming, crying, laughing, hugging, and general pandemonium went on for a good five minutes. The sense of relief I felt was tremendous, and there was a good deal of pride mixed in among the happiness, too. Cherry was doing her best to keep it together, and I was once again glad that she's an actress. She gave another wonderful performance, but I wouldn't have been surprised if she had collapsed into a fetal ball on the floor. As had happened before, I underestimated her; her demeanor made me very proud.

After it all finally died down, we turned on the news and watched as every local station and news channel told the tale of how the Computer Killer had been found dead at his final crime scene, and how wonderful it was, and all that good stuff. Atlanta policemen and -women were interviewed, and we saw several people me and Cherry knew, including Sergeant Traylor and other members of the task force. After twenty minutes of watching it all unfold, Susan asked me what my plans were, and it hit me like a cold glass of water to the face: it was time for me to go home.

I thought for a moment, and said, "Well, I guess I better call the airport and see about makin' a reservation for tonight. If there's a flight, I can be home for a late supper."

All the Feagin females looked at Cherry, and she said, "A reservation? You shan't have need of a commercial airline; you're a star now, remember? Let me call Sally for you, Cooper. She can take care of everything, and you can surely be home for that late supper. Would that be all right?"

"That would be great, if you're sure she wouldn't mind."

"I'm absolutely sure. You know how much Sally likes you. She'd be very cross with us both if we didn't let her take care of you one final time. I'll call her right this minute."

She walked over to the kitchen phone, and me and the Feagin women all took seats on the big sectional.

Jill said with a mischievous grin, "Uncle Coop, who is this 'Sally' person, and what have you been doin' with her? She takes 'care' of you? Hmmm?"

This caused the other girls and Susan to tease me about Sally, and I took it like a man, as if I had a choice. Thankfully, her daughters being there kept Susan from giving me another lecture about my relationships with women other than Penny.

After a few minutes spent defending myself, I saw Cherry hang up the phone. She came in the living room, sat down next to me on the sofa, and said, "Sally is very sorry, but the best she can do is have you on a flight for tomorrow evening at eight thirty."

This caused the Feagin girls to squeal, and caused Susan to give me a look that said, "You'd better behave yourself until you're on that plane, buster." It also caused me to relax and settle back on the sofa, finally able to unwind after constantly being on pins and nee-dles for the last several days.

Susan stood, and said, "Well, since no one's leavin' tonight, what do y'all want for supper?"

Everyone looked to Cherry, since she was the guest, and she took a moment before saying, "I hope that you all don't take this the wrong way—any of you. But I would *really* like to go back to the Ritz and have a long steam in the gym, and a quiet supper in the suite. Would you all hate me if I did that?"

There was silence for a few seconds, and then Susan said gra-ciously, "Of course we won't hate you, will we, girls? We complete-ly understand you wantin' to do that. After all you've been through? As much as we'll miss you both, we understand, don't we, girls?"

For a moment, the three girls looked like they didn't understand, and that they wanted Cherry to move in with them and stay forever, and that the last thing on Earth they wanted was for Cherry to leave. But they recovered quickly and said of course they understood, and whatever was best for Cherry was best for them, and they all gave her a group hug and she hugged them back, the four of them smil-ing and laughing and hugging in a pile on the big sofa.

This gave Susan another chance to shoot me a look, and I gave her a "What?" expression, all the while secretly glad that Cherry and I would be spending one more night together. I had to go get my stuff, didn't I? Besides, how often in a man's life does he get to spend time with an international movie star in a suite at the Ritz, for cryin' out loud?

That was the moment I finally admitted to myself that I needed to deal with the mixed feelings I was having about Cherry Page. On one hand, I felt great that Cherry was no longer in danger of her life. Not to mention Penny, and Neal and his family. Also not to mention me. It was a fantastic feeling to know that the FBI had captured the sick, dead bastard, but on the other hand, there was also the feeling of not wanting my new life with Cherry to end.

By that, I mean, what if I took Cherry up on her offer to become her permanent bodyguard and travel the world with her? Would a life with her be better than the one I have? Should I stay on with her, or go back home? It was a pretty big decision, and I only had a little over twenty-four hours to figure it all out, and decide how to proceed.

There was my life in Gulf Front to consider: I live in a little piece of heaven; I have a job I love; I have an incredible relationship with my incredible girlfriend about half the time; I'm surrounded by a terrific group of friends; I even have a really cool dog. *But,* does all that compare to the high life I could live with Miss Cherry Page?

I couldn't believe I was even thinking about all that stuff, but there I was, thinking it. It's not easy being a forty-five-year-old man with the maturity level of a twelve-year-old boy.

It came down to this: we knew who had been trying to kill Cherry, so the big mystery was solved.

But that left me with a new mystery to solve.

What the hell was I going to do with Cherry Page?

Part Four

Hollywood Ending

72

WHILE CHERRY GOT HER STUFF AND SAID GOOD-BYE TO THE FEAGIN women, I called Penny and told her the good news, and that I would be coming home the next night. Whatever I decided to do about the rest of my life, I would have to go home to Gulf Front and face Penny. She was ecstatic, naturally, about the news of the killer's death, and even shed a tear or two, something that she doesn't do very often. I felt bad about not telling her what I was thinking, but then again, I didn't really know what I was thinking. When Cherry was ready to go, I gave her the phone so she could talk to Penny while I got my stuff together.

Ten minutes later, Cherry and I said our long good-byes to the Feagins and went outside. After a quick talk with the agents who were guarding the house, and securing their promise that they would stay until Neal got home, we got in Neal's car.

Since we were technically still missing, I gave Cherry my cap and she put her hair up again and wore her shades so no one would spot her in the afternoon traffic. Twenty minutes later, we made it to Highway 400 and headed towards Buckhead.

I decided not to turn on the radio, and Cherry didn't object. After we had driven in silence for a while, Cherry leaned over, gave me a lingering kiss on the side of my mouth, and giggled as I tried to remain calm and drive.

"What was that for?" I asked.

"That's for being my hero."

"Oh. Okay. I just don't want you takin' advantage."

"There will be plenty of time for that," Cherry said. She looked straight ahead at the road, and continued, "Seriously, Cooper, I don't think I can express how grateful I am for all you've done. I've had to thank someone once before, for saving my life—Poppy—but never like this. So much danger, so much anxiety, for such an extended period of time. I'm at a loss. I need a screen-writer, at once."

"Cherry. *I* didn't save your life, or get your stalker. I was just hangin' around, ready to take a bullet, or a knife, or a hand grenade, or a bazooka, or whatever, for *you*, with no thought whatsoever for my personal safety. No big deal. I'm just a plain, truly heroic figure of biblical proportions, a simple man whose name shall live forever in the anals, I mean annals, of, um, time, and stuff like that. Really. You're embarrassing me here."

Groaning, Cherry said, "Did I say I was grateful? I meant to say, I'm queasy. Sorry I misspoke." She gave me another one of her girl punches to my arm, and said, "Thanks anyway, Cooper. I mean it."

"I know you do, and, you're welcome."

We drove in silence again for a while, until we hit a stall in the highway traffic, and moved only a half mile in the next fifteen minutes. I expected her to bring up the subject of my intentions, as in, what were they, and what was I going to do about taking her up on her offer to stay on as her bodyguard, and all that, but she surprised me one more time.

"Cooper, it's a shame you didn't get the five-hundred-thousand-dollar reward that Lawrence offered for the capture of my stalker. You deserve it, after all."

"Not really, but thanks for sayin' that. I'm just glad to have had such an adventure. And what an adventure it was."

Cherry said, "I'm glad I got to share it with *you*, instead of some dry old FBI agent. No one else would have made it bearable." She sat up straight, stuck her nose in the air as she had done last week, and said, "Right, then. So. Glad we had this little chat. Home, Jeeves."

"Yes, mum. Right away, mum."

A little more than an hour after leaving the Feagin house, we pulled into the lower parking lot of the Buckhead Ritz. Highway 400 had turned out to be not too bad, traffic-wise, and we had avoided being spotted, which was nice. But it was a different story when we got out of the Lexus at the Ritz. The now larger mob of reporters and paparazzi caught sight of us immediately, and started hollering and braying, calling out for us to stop and talk and pose for the cameras. Instead, naturally, me and Cherry ran to the loading dock entrance, laughing and waving to the throng. While we'd been on the lam, I had almost forgotten we were still big news, but their presence and commotion at seeing Cherry brought it all back in a flash. It turned out all the entrances had been under siege since the moment we'd left, waiting for Cherry's return, and only the fact that we were in Neal's car had made it possible for us to sneak in almost undetected. Cherry would have to face the horde sooner or later, but not right then. I was going to make sure of that.

We made it up to the suite pretty quickly, even with all the commotion we caused with the Ritz employees. The moment I opened the door to the suite, the phone rang, and Cherry answered.

"Yes, Sal, we made it. Oh, no, not quite yet, if that's all right? Tomorrow, perhaps? Yes, that would be much better. Thanks, girl."

She hung up and said, "The cast and crew want to throw a celebration party for me."

"I'm glad you put it off," I said. "I'm not up to it."

"Neither am I," she said, and kicked off her shoes.

I found a classical music station on the wall radio, and we both sprawled out in the parlor: Cherry on the sofa, and me on my bed by the window.

We sprawled and listened for quite a while, hardly speaking, and then started getting ready for our quiet night at the hotel.

Cherry had told a little white lie to the Feagin women about where she wanted to eat supper. Four hours later, Cherry and I were downstairs, seated in the Ritz's posh restaurant, after Will had worked his magic on her, and after I had showered and shaved and worked my magic on myself. Cherry was decked out in a black dress that showed lots of cleavage and her great legs, and I was choking in my damnable new tux again.

She had begged me to wear the monkey suit, and I did it because it might be our last night together. And because the studio had rented the hotel restaurant for the evening at Cherry's request so we could be alone. Her dress was by some big-shot designer, so I couldn't sit there in my tee shirt and jeans with her, could I?

There were a lot of people mad at us initially for ruining their evening at the restaurant, but I was sure that after they found out what was up, there would be no hard feelings. I have no idea how much it cost to rent the place for an evening, but since it wasn't me who was paying for it, I sat back and enjoyed the meal.

The restaurant in the Ritz Buckhead is paneled in dark wood and expensive-looking, with beautiful artwork all around. The décor is conservative, but it doesn't make you feel like you can't relax and have a good time. In one corner, a jazz trio played softly. There was a grand piano, drums, and one of my favorite instruments, a big stand-up bass. I love the way the bass looks like a giant fiddle, and the deep sound can make the hair on the back of my neck stand up. The group was hitting all the right notes, so to speak, playing great tunes that seemed to run together. It was the perfect backdrop, and Cherry moved her body to the music as we finished our salads and waited for the rest of our food to arrive.

"The music is so beautiful," she said, closing her eyes and swaying gently in her seat.

"I can agree with that," I said, picking up a roll and buttering it. "I can also agree with you about having supper in here. I'm glad you talked me into it, even though it must be ridiculously expensive."

"The studio can afford it, and besides, you kept one of their cash cows from being slaughtered. The least they can do is provide you with a good meal, yeah?"

"Since you put it that way, yeah, it's the least they can do." Pause. "You really think they consider you a 'cash cow'?"

"Moo."

I chuckled and took a huge bite of my roll; the last week had given me quite an appetite. At that moment, one of our three waiters brought a tray stand and a large tray with our main courses on it tableside, and began to serve.

He placed a plate with a lobster tail and broccoli on it in front of Cherry, and a plate with a thick porterhouse and french fries on it in front of me. Next, he poured more wine into each of our glasses, put some drawn butter down for Cherry, and placed a dish of sautéed mushrooms next to me. He then asked if we needed anything else.

Cherry looked at me with an "anything else?" expression, and I said, "This is great, thanks."

He bowed slightly to Cherry, and disappeared into the darkness.

The way the lights were set, Cherry and I were about the only things visible in the restaurant, including the band. They had small individual lights on their music stands, and that was about it. The effect was such that it seemed like me and Cherry were the only people in the room. It was definitely a night to remember, and was just starting, as it turned out. As we ate in silence, I thought again about the new unsolved mystery: the decision I had to make concerning my life with Cherry.

Or without her.

I quickly decided to change the subject in my head, so I started thinking about the past week, and the last year of my life, and how strange and exciting it had all been. My thoughts turned to women, of all things. I recalled the only real true love I've ever had, besides Penny, who may or may not be my true love. We're still working on that.

I met my possible true love in Tallahassee, the summer I graduated from the police academy. Gwen was eighteen and just out of high school, a leggy strawberry blonde with a face an angel would kill for. She had been accepted to pre-med at Harvard, and I knew she was way out of my league, but I was young enough to be hopeful. We met at a party a mutual friend threw on a Saturday night in mid-June, and hit it off immediately. We made each other laugh, and as the night wore on, tuned out the other guests. I may have been hopeful, but I was too scared to make a move on her. Gwen, however, was anything but scared, and after she made a move on *me*, we ended up back at the apartment I shared with Neal, sneaking in so he wouldn't catch us. We snuck in because if Gwen's parents had ever found out what we were about to do, I would've been a dead man, and she would have been in big trouble at home. Her father was a genuine pillar of the community—a bank president as well as a church deacon—and conservative to the extreme. In other words, our affair had to be kept secret, and that was fine by me. There were no public displays of affection, but there were plenty of private displays of youthful lust. We would meet at a motel when we couldn't use my apartment, and strained my bankroll to the limit.

It was money well spent.

I loved her in that way everybody loves his or her true love: that is to say, I wanted to be with her every minute of every day. She was my whole world, as trite as that sounds, and I'm sure everybody has felt that way at least once.

She made me feel so alive, and I experienced things for the first time when I was with her, things I've never experienced in quite the same way, even with Penny. For example, love songs were always sappy and stupid to me before Gwen came along; they were just dumb, and I made fun of them when I heard them on the radio. But that all changed dramatically when I met Gwen. All of a sudden, every one of those songs was deep and meaningful, and seemed as if it was written just for us. And after we broke up, every *sad* song seemed like it was written just for us.

Sound familiar?

Things were great that whole summer, and then one night the subject of marriage came up as we drove in my beat-up Volkswagen to the apartment after a movie. Her parents had left her alone for a week, and we were joined at the hip, and other places as well. It was around midnight, Neal was gone for the weekend, and heaven was suddenly a hot, cramped bedroom in the Florida Panhandle.

Still talking about marriage, and why people do it, we got out of the car and walked hand in hand up to the apartment. I put the key in the door, and my gorgeous Gwen said something that stopped me cold: "You know, Coop, as far as marriage goes, the only thing wrong with you is—you don't have a million dollars."

I turned to look at her in the dim light, expecting to see her sexy smile that would let me know she was kidding, but she was serious. I opened the door, she headed back to my bedroom as usual, and I knew at that moment there was no chance in hell I would ever be with her again after that summer.

That simple, that final.

We wrote to each other a few times after she moved to Cambridge, but by Thanksgiving, the fling was flung. I saw her once years later, right after I became police chief of Gulf Front. I was back in Tallahassee for a court appearance to testify in a trial involving a case I had been working on when I left and moved to Gulf. Gwen was home for a visit, shopping downtown with her mother. She didn't see me, and I've always wondered if I should have crossed that busy street and gone up to her. But I didn't have a million bucks, so I let the moment pass.

So much for true love.

As I sat in the Ritz restaurant, listening to the band and eating my steak, I also thought about other failed relationships, and how they affected my life. And then I thought about New Orleans and the beautiful blond FBI agent I had met there last year, and that brought me back to the past twelve months, which now included meeting Cherry.

Then I started thinking how amazing and exciting it would be to travel the world with Cherry Page, and what it would be like to actually have a relationship with her, and how it would taste to kiss Cherry Page with her lips dripping drawn butter.

"Well?" she asked, and I snapped back to the moment.

"I'm sorry, did you say something?" I asked dumbly.

"Yes. I said you look like you're a million miles away."

"More like a couple of feet."

"Pardon?"

"Nothing. How's the lobster?"

"Oh, Cooper, it's absolutely divine. You simply must try some."

She cut a big chunk of lobster tail, dipped it in butter, and slowly pushed her fork through the air towards me, aiming at my mouth. I obligingly opened up, she placed it on my lips, and I drew the lobster into my mouth.

"Mmm, mmm, *mmmmmmmm*," I managed to groan as I chewed. "That's incredible."

"You like? I think it's simply perfect," she said in that accent I love.

"You're right. It *is* 'puh-fickt,'" I said, trying to sound like her. I guess I didn't.

She said, "I wish I could say your Brit accent has improved, you Yank baboon."

I smiled like a baboon, took a swig of wine, issued a satisfied *aaahhh*, and went back to my steak.

Cherry called to one of our waiters, "Excuse me? Could you come over please?"

This time it was the youngest of the bunch, and he nearly broke his neck getting to the table. As he stared at Cherry, he defined the term "starstruck."

"Yes, Miss Page?" he squeaked. I had to turn my head and chew so I wouldn't laugh. He looked like a Trekkie who had just run into William Shatner at the laundromat.

Cherry asked, "Would you be so kind as to bring the chief a lobster tail?"

"Yes ma'am, right away ma'am," the kid said, turning and hustling off to the kitchen.

For the next few hours, Cherry and I were in our own little world. A very expensive little world, what with the three bottles of high-end wine we drank, and the dessert tray we used for a sampler after a long pause from gorging. We each had a bite or two of everything on the dessert menu, plus several cups of coffee called Jamaica Blue Mountain, or something like that. Like I said, I wasn't paying for it, and that was a good thing, because I'm not sure I *could* have paid for it. It was luxury living at its finest, and one of the best meals I've ever had. The conversation covered everything we hadn't had time to discuss in the last week, and was as pleasant and entertaining as it could be, not to mention stimulating.

After we were fully stuffed, Cherry said in a noticeably drunken tone, "What say we head upstairs to the suite? The night is young, and I have a surprise for you."

"You're the boss lady," I said, and groaned as I pulled my fattened carcass up and out of my chair, and went around to pull Cherry's chair back and help her up. Tipsy, she giggled as she stood, wrapped her arms around my neck, and drew me close.

"I say, old chap, did I mention there's a surprise waiting for you upstairs?" she said in my ear, slurring her words.

"Yes, mum, ye most surely did," I replied in my crummy British accent, and she pulled away so we could take leave of our private restaurant.

Cherry graciously signed autographs for the waiters, and the band stopped playing and came over to get one, too. The bass player, a large middle-aged black man, even asked me to sign one for him, and when I asked why, he pulled me aside and said in a low voice, "I been jealous'a you all week, man. That's the finest white woman on the planet. You my hero."

I signed his music sheet, and told him I loved his instrument, which got me a hearty laugh, and Cherry and I headed for the elevator, full of lobster, wine, and goodwill toward men.

When we got up to the suite, I looked around the room, but didn't see anything out of the ordinary.

I said, "Okay, you. What's the big surprise? Looks like the same old room to me."

Cherry took off her shoes and walked slowly over to the dining table, slightly off balance. She sighed heavily and picked up a new deck of cards that had escaped my attention.

"These are the surprise," she said, holding them out towards me.

"A deck of cards? That's the big surprise?"

As I started to take off my tux jacket, she said with a drunken smile, "You might want to keep that on as long as possible, old bean."

I stopped in my tracks and said, "Oh. Okay. I see now. You want me to look like James Bond in a casino while we play, right?"

She wobbled over to the sofa, sat down, and replied, "That's not what I meant, but I like the way you think."

My curiosity was getting the best of me. "Then, what *did* you mean?"

She tore off the wrapper, opened the box, and said, "Time for a friendly game of strip poker, Chief Cooper."

73

"NOW, CHERRY, WAIT A MINUTE HERE. YOU CAN'T BE SERIOUS. IF WE play strip poker, things might get a little outta hand."

"I'm relying on it," she said as she took the cards out. She discarded the jokers and the rules card, and asked, "Where shall we play? The table, or the floor?"

Resigned to the fact they she would get her way eventually, and not really being opposed to playing, and seeing as I had been sitting in a chair for hours, I opted for the floor, and we sat down in the middle of the parlor. I wasn't sure how the scene would play out, but the wine was making me feel like any decision I made would be the proper one.

Mystery, shmystery.

Cherry laid the cards out on the carpet and started spreading them around to mix them up. After ten seconds or so, she gathered them together, shuffled three times, placed them on the floor in front of me, and said, "Cut."

I cut the cards thin, to win, and she said, "Draw poker, nothing wild, nothing to open, and no drawing four to an ace."

As she dealt, I thought, This babe has played before.

I picked up my cards, looked them over, and kept a straight face as I saw the three nines. I also had a jack and a four.

"How many?" she asked.

"I'll take two."

She dealt me two, and said, "One to the dealer."

Hoping she didn't hit her straight or flush, I looked at my two new cards. A seven and a ten. If she didn't hit, I was the winner for sure.

"Whatcha got?" I asked.

She frowned, and said, "A lousy busted flush."

"You lose. Three nines," I said.

She smiled drunkenly and sexily, and it hit me: Cherry didn't want to win. She wanted to strip.

Holy macaroli.

I tried to get a look at her cards, but she quickly put them back in the deck as she said, "No peeking."

I decided that I needed to change my strategy as Cherry pulled her dress high up on her right thigh, and unfastened the silk stocking. I gulped at the sight of her slowly pulling the stocking off, giving me a show and another memory I'll have forever.

"I noticed you liked the stockings when we watched my film at Penny's," she said as I stared.

I realized if I was going to survive the game without being unfaithful to Penny, I was going to have to start losing, and fast. I also realized if things continued the way they were going, being unfaithful to Penny was almost a certainty. But did I really want to take advantage of a drunk woman?

Drunk Cherry handed me the deck, and said, "Your deal, copper."

I took the cards, and said nothing; if I had tried to reply, I'm sure my voice would have cracked like our young waiter's had. I shuffled, let her cut, and dealt the cards.

I picked mine up, and saw a pair of aces, a pair of deuces, and an eight. I asked how many she wanted, dealt her two, and took three after discarding the aces and one of the deuces. I was now drawing to a foot instead of a hand, and hoped my strategy didn't backfire on me.

It did.

I drew two eights and another deuce. That's literally almost impossible, but I was sitting there with another winner, barring a miracle draw by Cherry.

"Whatcha got?" I asked, but she was having none of that.

"Oh, no. It's your turn to show."

"Why do I hafta show? You didn't show yours."

"I think I showed plenty," she said with that same sexy smile. "Come on, now. Let's have a look."

I laid down my full house, and she showed me her pair of sixes.

"Looks like I lose again," she said, and pulled up her dress to repeat the silk stocking show on her left leg.

It was magnificent. And excruciating.

Great googley moogley.

She dealt the next hand, and this time I threw away a pair of kings, and got back nothing. It was her turn to show her cards, and luckily, she had made two pair.

"You lose, Cooper," she said.

"Yeah, yeah," I said, and quickly pulled off my jacket.

"Hey!" she said. "No fair. We're playing *strip* poker, remember? Now, put it back on, and take it off slowwwlllyyy."

I did as she ordered, and she whistled and clapped. I felt like a stripper must feel. I gotta admit, I didn't mind.

Even though I threw away two pair on the next hand, Cherry managed to lose, and she did something that I've seen in the movies, but never in real life: she took off her bra under her dress, pulled it out from the front, and waved it around like a burlesque queen before tossing it on top of my head. What is it with women and throwing their clothes on men?

Whatever it is, it was working. Seeing her tiddly from the wine, and braless, was, well—intoxicating. I needed to buckle down and lose, or there was going to be trouble.

After a couple of more hands, it was obvious we were both trying to lose. Me, so that I could keep her dressed and un-tempting, and Cherry so that she could strip and *be* tempting. What's the word I'm looking for to describe how I was feeling? Oh, yeah: Conflicted.

When neither of us even had a pair for three hands in a row, it was even more obvious that we were both trying to throw the game. But I was doing a better job of it, because I managed to lose all three hands, and keep her in that black dress. I knew if that dress came down, all bets were off, in a manner of speaking. I also knew that I still wasn't sure if I wanted to take advantage of a drunk woman, or not.

But a man's only made of flesh and blood.

Ten minutes and several losing hands later, Cherry was still in her dress, and I was down to one sock and my boxers. I said, "Okay, boss lady, I give up. You're clearly the better poker player. Time to close this game down before the local cops come in and bust us. We need to sleep off the wine, anyway, right?"

"Wrong. You still have a couple more hands to lose before we can quit."

I stood and said, "I just can't do that, Cherry. If I lose two more hands, I'll be completely naked and highly vulnerable."

She said, "Really? I hadn't noticed. Tell you what. I have a splendid idea."

Trying to look as cool as I could standing there in my boxers and one black sock, I took the bait. "And just what is your idea?"

She stood up slowly and almost fell over before I caught her in my arms. She looked me in the eyes, hiccupped, and said, "One hand, double or nothing."

I held her up and gently pushed her back a few feet until she was once again steady on her feet. Trying to talk some sense into her, I said, "Double or nothing won't work here, Cherry. What if I win? Do I put my clothes back on?"

"No, silly-goose Cooper," she said with the same sexy-drunk smile she'd been laying on me ever since we got back to the suite.

"Then what *would* happen?" I asked.

She put her hands on her magnificent hips and said, "If *you* win, I pull off all my clothes. But if *I* win—*you* pull off all my clothes."

74

In every man's life, there are defining moments, times that he remembers forever, times that shape him.

Like the first time you kiss a girl. I mean, a real kiss. With tongue involvement.

For me, that happened in the sixth grade. Monica Moser had a party, and me and her ended up alone in the cabana by her backyard pool. It was about nine o'clock at night, and the party was in full swing. Well, as full swing as you could get in the sixth grade back in those days.

Today's sixth-grade partying is another story; kids clearly grow up a lot faster now. It may not have been as wild as it would be today, but I'll never forget that first smooch. I wonder sometimes if Monica remembers that night. For all I know, she may have already been experienced in kissing, but I wasn't. Anyway, it's a good memory, and one of those defining moments I'm discussing here.

Then there's the first time a guy hits a home run, or scores a touchdown in a real game. By "real," I mean an organized game. My first home run came in a Little League game when I was ten. Mom was there watching, but my joy was tempered a little bit by the fact that my father missed it. But then, he missed pretty much everything in my life.

My first touchdown in high school was a twenty-four-yard run from scrimmage in the third quarter after taking a pitch on a sweep to the weak side. Touchdowns were few and far between if you played for Gulf Front High. Being such a small school, we only had nineteen players on the entire team. Obviously, a lot of us played both ways, and we usually lost by a wide margin. But, as long as I live, I'll never forget how good it felt to score the first time in a school game.

Another defining moment can be when you take a stand of some kind. Standing up to a bully, for instance. I drew a line in the sand waiting at the bus stop on the morning of the last day of school, fifth grade.

Dick Ingle, a big husky guy who was sometimes ornery and liked to pick on smaller boys, had taken Robbie Woodall's Brady Bunch lunchbox, and was keeping it away from Robbie, threatening to eat the contents right there at the bus stop.

Robbie was whining at him to give the lunchbox back, and trying to get it back, when Dick pushed him down hard on the sandy ground, laughing as Robbie tore the knee of his pants.

For some reason, I decided to get involved, something which was out of character for me at that age. Mostly, I just wanted to live and let live in those days, but something about Robbie's bloody knee made me take a stand. I firmly told Dick to give Robbie his lunchbox back. Dick stopped what he was doing, then came close, and towering over me, said, "Make me." So, I punched him hard in the stomach, "right where he almost had his operation," as he said later. Dick moaned, doubled over, and gave Robbie his lunchbox back, and I had another defining moment.

Then there was last night.

I wish I could tell you who won the double-or-nothing hand of strip poker, and which one of us undressed Cherry. I'm sure you'd like to know what the cards were, and how I played them, and all that stuff.

I wish I could give you a detailed description of how Cherry did a leisurely, sexy striptease, handing the two pieces of clothing to me as she slowly undressed, and how I felt sitting there watching in my boxers and sock.

I wish it was possible for me to accurately describe how her naked skin looked in the lamplight of the suite at the Ritz, the only light coming from a floor lamp in the corner. How her skin was creamy white, with a golden glow, and how her hair blazed red when the light caught it.

I wish I could tell you exactly how many minutes we spent in the parlor on the carpeted floor, exploring each other's bodies before we moved into the bedroom without saying a word. How we just went in there as if it was destiny, or something, and how she went into the bathroom as I waited on the bed.

I wish I could tell you about how quickly she sobered up after taking a short, cool bath, a shower being out of the question in her condition.

I also wish I could tell you how it felt to finally be entwined with her on that big bed of hers, the bed that had been nothing more than a really expensive sleeping bag up to that point. How it felt to see those famous green eyes up close, the way they flashed in the dim light of the bedroom, locked with mine.

I *really* wish I could tell you what happened between us on that bed. What I did to her, what she did to me. The sounds she made, the way she did things I didn't expect because of her lack of experience, and how she surprised me with her willingness and desire to please.

And, I wish I could tell you how it felt to be with someone as beautiful and famous as Cherry, how her fame actually made a difference, for whatever reason. And how easy it was to be with her in that way, how natural it felt, and how Penny never once entered my mind after Cherry's dress was off and in my hands.

Finally, I wish I could tell you what we talked about afterwards, the things she said, the things I said.

But like I always say: a gentleman never tells.

75

SUNDAY MORNING TURNED UP BRIGHT AND SUNNY, BUT I WASN'T AWAKE to see it, and neither was Cherry.

I finally woke up at five after noon, and seeing how heavily my boss lady was sleeping, I quietly called room service from the parlor. I ordered two huge breakfasts in case she might wake up hungry, and then jumped in the shower. To my surprise, I had no hangover at all, not even a little one. In ten minutes, I was washed and dressed. Twenty minutes later, breakfast arrived.

I went ahead with breakfast, knowing that after the past week—and last night—Cherry needed sleep more than her favorite breakfast fare. I was glad to have some time alone to think about all that had happened between us, and all that might still happen.

My plan for the morning was to go shopping, buy souvenirs for Penny and my friends back in Gulf Front, and of course, to buy a gift or two for Cherry. I really wanted to surprise her, and also thank her for everything. No, I still hadn't decided what to do about my situation with Cherry, and no matter what my decision was, I would have to go back to Gulf and face the music. Whatever the tune turned out to be, I owed it to Penny to do at least that.

As I ate, I looked through the brochures again, and found two shopping malls within walking distance of the Ritz: Phipps Plaza across the street to the left, and Lenox Square directly in front. I decided to go to Phipps first, to get Cherry's gift, because the store Every Thing British is located there. There's also a Tiffany's, and I figured I could at least do some window-shopping until I made up my mind about Cherry. Neal's office is there as well, and I wanted to take a look at it; after all, it was my idea for Neal to open an office there in the first place. Neal had said he was really happy with the location, and was glad he had taken my advice, unorthodox as it might be.

According to the brochures, of the two malls, Phipps Plaza has more high-end shops, like Tiffany's, Gucci, and Armani. Lenox Square is more my kind of mall, with a Macy's, electronics stores, and guy places where you can buy sporting goods and stuff. There was also a pizza place, and after all the walking I planned to do, I was sure to be in the mood for a good pie, so the shopping trip looked promising.

Ready to roll, I checked on Cherry once more, and saw that she was still dead to the world. I wrote her a note saying I would be gone for two or three hours and left it on the bathroom sink. I found my room key-card, placed the "Do Not Disturb" sign on the doorknob, and headed down to the bank of elevators.

Instead of going out the back way, I decided to go out the front door and have a little fun with the press corps that was still assembled in front of the Ritz. As I got off the elevator and crossed the lobby, I accepted congratulations from the desk clerks, and shook the hands of two bellmen who were saying what a great job I'd done guarding Cherry, and whatnot. A few people hanging around the lobby gave me a round of applause, and I gave them my best theatrical bow.

Outside, there was a crowd of forty or so reporters, and they attacked as soon as I was through the door. They all yelled, "Chief Cooper, over here!" and "Coop, look this way," and all that stuff, so I gave them the classic hands up in front of me to stop them in their tracks.

It worked, and they formed a semicircle around me, cameras clicking, and video cameras running. I pointed to a guy from CNN and nodded to him.

He asked, "How is Cherry doing?"

"Ms. Page is doing very well, and she can't wait to get back to shooting *Teaching English*," I said. Hollywood Coop, getting in a plug for the movie, even using the lingo of the cinema with "shooting." I laughed inside as I heard myself say it.

Immediate onslaught of questions until I pointed to another guy and nodded.

"What are your plans, Chief Cooper?"

"I'm goin' over to Phipps Plaza to buy some gifts for my friends back home."

Laughter from the corps.

He tried again, "No, I mean what are your plans concerning your future? Are you going to continue on as Cherry's bodyguard, or are you going back to police work?"

There was no way in hell I was going to let them know the truth about my indecision, so I replied, "I'll be goin' home to resume my duties as police chief. Ms. Page no longer needs a bodyguard. Next question?"

I looked to my left, and saw a familiar face.

"Kelly Ann, what in the world are you doin' here?"

Kelly Ann Rogers is the only reporter for the *Gulf Front Observer*, our little bimonthly newspaper.

She said, "First things first, Coop. I mean—Chief. I always wanted to say this." She threw back her shoulders, and said, "Kelly Ann Rogers, *Gulf Front Observer*."

Laughs from the reporters, then Kelly Ann said, "The world is dying to know, Chief Cooper. Tell us the answer to the big question."

"If I can."

"Was there any romance between you and Cherry?" she asked with a big smile.

I turned and looked right into a video camera that was about three feet from my face, and said, "No. There was no romance of any kind between Ms. Page and myself. As we Hollywood types like to say, 'We're just good friends.'"

More laughter.

She followed up by asking, "*Nothing* happened between you two while you were on the run?"

"All kidding aside, Kelly Ann—you know this better than anybody —I have a beautiful young woman in my life, and absolutely no need for another. Not even another as gorgeous and desirable as Ms. Page. Now go home and write what a fantastic chief of police I am. If I remember correctly, tomorrow's the next edition?"

"Sure is. I have a long day and night ahead of me. I have to hit the road and get home in time to print tonight. Grandpa and me will be up all night, but don't worry, we'll make it. Let me get a good picture for the front page—smile!"

More laughs as I posed while Kelly shot me with a small camera she pulled from her purse. I was really feeling my oats as I pointed to a guy from an Atlanta station.

"Chief Cooper, your life has been through quite a few changes recently. How can you just go back to where you were before all this happened?"

"Easy," I said with two faces. "It's all I know. This whole deal was a fluke from the beginning. It wasn't even supposed to be my job. It's been exciting and interesting, to say the least, and educational in a lotta ways, but it was nothing more than a fluke after all is said and done. I doubt I'll ever go through anything like this again. At least I *hope* I won't. No, I belong in Florida. It's my home, and I can't wait to resume my life as a lawman in a sleepy little town." I paused for effect. "Okay, one more question, then I need to get to my souvenir shopping. My fifteen minutes are up."

Laughs from the mob.

I pointed to a guy from Fox, and he said, "There's a rumor that Miss Page had met the killer. Any truth to that?"

I thought for a moment, and continued my exercise in mendacity, "No truth to that at all. He was simply a very sick individual who no longer matters, except maybe to the FBI profilers. Okay? Thanks guys—and gals. I hope I never see any of you ever again."

That got me my biggest laugh yet, and I went over and hugged Kelly Ann as the reporters gathered around. We all shared small talk for a moment, then they watched, photographed, or filmed me as I turned and walked towards Phipps Plaza.

A nude Cherry Page was in the bathroom brushing her teeth thirty minutes after Coop had left, when the phones in the suite began to ring. She quickly rinsed, spat, and ran to pick up the receiver in the bedroom.

"Hello?"

"Ms. Page?" a male voice asked.

"Yes, this is Ms. Page."

"Ms. Page, this is special agent John Carver of the FBI. I'm sorry to bother you. Is Chief Cooper there?"

"Oh, no he's not, Agent Carver. He's only just now stepped out to do some shopping. May I give him a message for you?"

"Well, his cell phone seems to be off—I can't reach him. It's not important, I just need to set up an interview. Do you have any idea when he'll be back?"

Cherry frowned, and said, "I'm sorry agent Carver, but I don't expect him back for at least two hours."

"That's okay, I'll call again in a couple of hours and see if he's made it back. Until then, I can keep trying his cell." He paused, and then asked, "Are you doing okay, if you don't mind me asking?"

"I'm doing *very* okay, Agent Carver, and I don't mind you asking a'tall. Not only that, I'm awfully glad to have this opportunity to thank you personally for all you and your people have done to bring this nightmare to an end. I shall never be able to repay you, but please know that I'm ever so grateful, and feel free to call on me if you ever need anything. Anything whatsoever."

"That's very kind of you, Ms. Page. And it was our pleasure to bring this man to justice, as well as our job. Now that it's all over, you just concentrate on making your movie, and enjoy the rest of your time here in Atlanta."

"I know that I will, Agent, and thank you so much again. If Chief Cooper calls, I'll tell him to get in touch with you immediately. If you don't hear from him, try back in a couple of hours. I'm certain he'll be back by then."

"Will do, Ms. Page." He chuckled, and said, "Pardon my pun, but I'm glad we can finally turn the page on this one."

Cherry chuckled too, and said, "You're forgiven for that one, Agent Carver."

"Thanks. Bye now, and you take care."

"I will, Agent Carver. You, as well. Bye-bye," Cherry said, and placed the receiver back on the cradle. She smiled to herself as she thought about what a joy it would be to get back to filming, and then giggled as she realized the only maniac she would have to fend off now would be her unctuous producer, Lawrence Lyndon-Bowen.

She spent the next couple of minutes flossing, and was tidying up the sink area when she heard a knock at the door of the suite.

"Just a minute," she called out, grabbed her robe from the hook on the bathroom door, and pulled it on as she walked to the suite's entrance. Expecting housekeeping, she looked through the peephole and saw a yellow mass of flowers in the hands of a deliveryman.

"Yes?" she asked through the door.

"Delivery for Ms. Page," the uniformed man said, and pulled the flowers to the side so she could see his cap. It read: "FTD."

Cherry opened the door and said, "Oh, how lovely! Tea roses!" She put her nose into them, and smiled at the thought of Coop remembering Poppy's favorite flower. "Come in, please, and put them on the corner table if you would. What a lovely surprise!"

"Yes, ma'am," the deliveryman said. He took the huge bouquet over and set the big crystal vase down on the table.

Cherry followed, gently ran a hand over the spray of yellow, and said, "There must be two dozen of them!"

"Three dozen, ma'am," the man said as he held out a clipboard and pen for her to sign. "Somebody must really like you."

Cherry signed, and said, "Yes, someone *does*. And I know just who that someone is."

The deliveryman pointed and said, "There's a card on the vase."

Cherry handed him his pen, tightened the sash on her robe, and pulled the small white envelope free from the vase and opened it.

The handwritten card read: *These should do nicely for your funeral. Welcome home. Sincerely, Baal.*

Cherry slowly backed away from the flowers as if they were a bomb set to detonate, fainted, and fell into the arms of the deliveryman.

76

As unable as I was to make up my mind about the women in my life, I was more than able to get out and about after all the indoor living of late. It was another gorgeous day in Atlanta, and I hummed to myself as I trotted across Lenox Road into the Phipps Plaza parking lot.

It was filling up, and there were so many expensive cars and SUVs that it resembled a high-end car lot. The majority of the vehicles were new, or almost new, and all of them seemed to have just come from the detailer.

There was a gorgeous white Rolls Royce that I just had to stop and take a look at; it was so clean and shiny it could only be described as dazzling. Looking into its spotless white interior, I felt a slight touch of melancholy as I realized that I would no longer be tooling around in the bulletproof Bentley. Then I smiled as I realized I might be back in it again, and soon.

Might.

I hummed some more, and headed to the mall entrance.

When Cherry came to, she was lying on her back on the sofa, and the deliveryman was standing over her with a look of concern on his face.

"Are you all right, ma'am? Can I get you a glass of water?" he asked.

Sitting up and making sure the robe covered her nakedness, Cherry said, "Yes, please. Water. That would be nice." She felt woozy as she tried to come to her senses, and when she did, she wished she hadn't. The words on the card flooded back into her mind, and she felt a shiver as she considered what they might mean.

Surely there was some kind of a mistake, or it was a bad practical joke. That was it, wasn't it?

The deliveryman brought her a glass of water from the pitcher that sat on the buffet table, and watched as she slowly drained it.

"More?" he asked.

"No, thank you," Cherry said. "Thank you very much. Give me a moment, and I shall go into the bedroom and get you a tip."

"I can't let you do that," the man said pleasantly.

Still slightly woozy, she asked, "Pardon?"

The deliveryman smiled sheepishly, and said, "Really, ma'am, I can't let you do that. It wasn't no problem. Besides, I never delivered to a famous movie star before, especially one as pretty as you."

Cherry smiled weakly, and said, "Nonsense. You worked hard, bringing that big bouquet all the way up here. I'll just go and get you a tip."

"I *said,* I can't let you do that."

Cherry felt a growing uneasiness as she looked at the expression on the man's face. He looked at her like a cat might look at a mouse that had stumbled into its path. She pulled her robe tighter, and said, "I don't understand. Why on Earth can't I get you a tip?"

"Because you might wanna use the phone to call someone while you're in there, and I just can't let that happen." He then changed the tone of his voice, and said, "Pardon my pun, but I'm glad we can finally turn the 'page' on this one."

A chill ran up Cherry's spine as she realized where she'd heard that voice.

She said, "It was you on the phone just now? *You're* Agent Carver?"

He laughed, and said, "Yeah, that was me on the phone just now. But no, I'm not Agent Carver."

77

I FINALLY MADE IT TO THE FRONT ENTRANCE OF THE MALL, WENT INSIDE, and was immediately impressed with the overall look of the place. Lots of highly polished granite and marble, all in soothing colors. Sunlight beamed down from the skylights in the high ceilings, and the place screamed "money." Or should I say it gently whispered it. Everything was immaculate, and it seemed there was a beautiful woman everywhere I looked.

The women were perfectly dressed, and had that air of confidence only unlimited credit can bring. If I hadn't been honing my acting skills all week, I would've felt like a fish on the dock. But since I had been living and traveling with a beautiful, world-famous movie star, I wasn't intimidated in the least. Besides, a few of them looked at me as if they recognized me but couldn't quite put their finger on who I was. That's what being all over the national news can do for you. I played it cool, and acted like being stared at by beautiful women was part of my everyday routine.

Tiffany's was on the lower level, and I took my time doing something I've never done. I went inside and pretended to shop for a ring. It was ridiculous on more than one level, but dough was the main concern. If you have to ask how much it costs, you can't afford it, right? I couldn't afford, so I didn't ask. The reward for catching Cherry's stalker wasn't mine to claim, so there was no money burning a hole in my pocket. There was a burning question, but I still had no answer, so I moved on.

As I walked around the downstairs level, I tried to get interested in the other pricey stores, but was just bored by them. There was one store that looked pretty interesting—Abercrombie and Fitch—but it didn't have the kind of stuff Cherry would find appealing, so I didn't bother going inside. I did make a mental note about the store though, that I would tell Neal to get my Christmas present there, seeing as it was so convenient for him. I'm nothing if not considerate.

When I'd had enough pointless window-shopping, I found the mall directory and noted the locations of Feagin Investigations and the British store. I thought I'd find Cherry's present first, then check out Neal's office, and finally head across the street to get souvenirs for Penny, Adam, Earl, and Mrs. Wiley.

The Brits were upstairs, so I took the escalator to the second floor, ready to go on the hunt for Cherry's gift. I wanted to get her something really special, a souvenir of our time together that would make her think of me every time she looked at it, and remember what a swell chap I am. Whether I stayed with her, or not.

Then I took into account the state of my *bank* account, and decided to settle for something that she wouldn't throw in the trash can as soon as I left for the airport.

The deliveryman pulled off his cap, and out fell a mass of blond curls. "Recognize me now?" he hissed.

Cherry froze. She recognized him, but couldn't place where she'd seen him. She said in as placating a tone as she could muster, "I feel as though we've met, but I'm sorry, I can't seem to remember."

"Let me tell you then," he said, and tossed his cap on the sofa. "I was at the charity benefit for your precious Poppy at the High Museum last Monday night. I was among the group of stupid men, including that moronic cowboy, who asked you for a date. I also told you we'd met in London last year at another of your Poppy charity benefits." He let the words sink in, and then asked, "*Now* do you remember me?"

Fear rose in her voice, but Cherry managed to reply, "Oh, yes. I remember. You said you had made your fortune in—oil, was it?"

"Dot-com stocks!" he spat, his face reddening. "How many times do I have to tell you? Dot! Com! *Stocks!*"

"Yes, I remember now. How smart of you to get out before the big crash!" Cherry said. She put her hands in the pockets of her robe so he wouldn't see them tremble.

The man walked around behind the sofa, and said, "My name is Kenneth Hammond, and I'm well-known not only as a brilliant software designer, but as an astute businessman as well. But all that meant nothing to you, Miss World-famous Movie Star. When we met in London, you blew me off as if I were just another fan, some zero you could ignore and send on his way." He walked back in front of the sofa, stopped in front of her, and glared as he said, "Well, let me tell you something, Miss Page. That was your first mistake."

I got off the escalator, and saw the sign for the British store straight ahead about a hundred feet away. I strolled towards it, hoping to catch the eye of a few more rich babes, but, alas and alack, it was not to be. Oh well. My fifteen minutes really *were* up.

The shop was smaller than most of the others, but it had a nice feel to it, and everything seemed pretty exotic, being as it was all from Great Britain. There was a section for English snacks—candy and crackers and stuff—and a big tea section, and a wall devoted entirely to Royal Family merchandise. Princess Diana trinkets were prominently displayed, and I wondered if she was still a big seller over there, too.

There was also stuff from Scotland, Ireland, and Wales, but mostly the goods seemed to be from England. I was checking out a black-and-white-striped rugby jersey when a nice-looking young woman came over and asked, "May I be of assistance?"

I immediately liked her for her British accent, and because she had that genteel manner that so many of Cherry's countrymen and -women possess. Her brunette hairstyle and small black eyeglasses reminded me of Sally Allen, and I knew I'd come to the right place.

I read her brass name tag, and said, "Yes, you can be of assistance, Daphne. I'm looking for a gift to give a young Englishwoman that will make her think of me every day. Nothing too expensive, but not a gimcrack either. Got any ideas?"

She smiled, no doubt at my bumpkinish American ways, and said, "I think I have just the thing. Would you follow me over here, please?"

"It would be my pleasure," I said in my best queen's English, and we walked over to a section that had silver tea services and porcelain cups and saucers on display.

She picked up a silver spoon, and said, "Perhaps your lady friend would think of you often if you purchased something she would find useful in her daily life. An antique teaspoon perhaps, or a silver tea strainer?"

"Hmm," I said. "I like the idea of somethin' related to tea, but antique silver may be out of my price range." I looked at the prices on the spoon and strainer, and saw that I was right.

There were some nineteenth-century teacups that looked good though, and as I checked them out, I saw it: A hand painted porcelain teacup and saucer with cherries on them. That was all I needed to see.

Another thing I could see was Cherry waking up and having a cuppa in her antique "Coop cup." Too good to be true.

I held the cup and saucer up, and said, "These are perfect. Can you wrap them as a gift?"

Daphne frowned, and said, "Oh, sir, I'm sorry. Those only come in sets of six. Would that put you over budget?"

Too good to be true was right.

I carefully put the cup and saucer down, gave her my best hangdog expression, and asked, "Isn't there some way you could sell me just the one?"

She bit her lip, and said, "I'm terribly sorry, sir, but you see, they're part of a set."

As I stared at the cherries on the cup, my newfound fame came to the rescue.

Daphne looked at me, cocked her head, and said, "Hold on. You seem awfully familiar. Are you the man I've seen escorting Cherry Page? Her bodyguard?"

I knew I had her then, from the excitement in her voice, and the look in her eyes. Gazing around as if I needed to make sure we were alone, which we were, I lowered my voice and said, "Yes, I *am* Cherry's bodyguard. Can we work somethin' out?"

She squealed a stifled, businesslike squeal, took hold of my arm with both hands, and exclaimed while hopping up and down just a little, "I knew there was something special about you the moment you walked in the door! I worship Cherry Page! Knowing that she has been right across the street this past week has been driving me mad!"

"Then you can help?" I said, and leaned closer in order to give her a full dose of my fame and star power. It worked.

Daphne pulled me over to the doorway that led to the back of the shop, looked around as I had done, and said, "The items you chose came in only yesterday, so I'm the only one to have seen them. Tell you what. I've one trick up me sleeve. I can *give* you the cup and saucer, and write it up as 'arrived damaged.' Then I'll just send the others back, and Bob's your uncle!"

I said, "But wouldn't they want to see the damaged pieces, for verification? I'll be more than happy to pay for it, I don't want you to get in trouble."

She shook her head, "I'll not hear of it. You let *me* worry about damages, and verification. It's a bit underhanded, but under the circumstances—I'll take care of everything. It shall be my gift to Miss Page and her handsome bodyguard."

I wanted to ask about my uncle Bob, but just kissed her cheek and said, "Daphne, you're a living doll. Tell you what. I'll make sure you get an autographed picture of Cherry. Maybe I can even persuade her to throw in a personal item too. Would you like that?"

Tears formed in her eyes, and she said, "Aren't cha kind? Aren't cha *kind*?" She picked up the cup and saucer, and said, "I don't really even think my boss, Mrs. Walsh, would be angry if she found out about our little scheme." She looked at me mischievously, and added, "Now that we know each other a little better, tell you what. I'll be more than happy to do this for you, but you must do something for me in return."

Uh-oh. Too good to be true again.

Her eyebrows were up as she waited for my answer.

"And just what exactly must I do for you in return, Daphne?"

She hopped a little again, and said, "You simply *must* tell me! Is it true what all the tabloids are saying? Did you really and truly have a romance with Cherry?"

I looked her straight in her British eyes, and said, "Sorry to let you down, Daphne, but, no, I didn't have a romance with her. She's waaay outta my league. And besides, my girlfriend would kill me if I tried anything with Miss Page."

Daphne was disappointed, but took the news with a stiff British upper lip.

"Oh, dear. That's such a shame. I was so hoping she had finally found a good man." She sighed, and said, "Maybe next time."

"Maybe," I replied.

She winked and motioned with her head for me to follow her into the back room. No one came into the shop as I watched her wrap the perfect present. While she worked, I decided to buy the rugby jersey for myself.

Now that I had Cherry's gift, I could go across the street to Lenox Square and buy stuff for Penny and my Gulf Front friends. When Daphne finished her wrapping, we walked out of the back, I picked up the rugby jersey, and we headed to the checkout counter to seal the deal.

78

CHERRY LOOKED AT HAMMOND, AND SAID, "I DON'T UNDERSTAND. What was my first mistake?"

Kenneth Hammond reached down to his boot and pulled out the biggest knife Cherry had ever seen.

"Understand now?" he said.

Unable to speak, Cherry tried to keep calm as her hands trembled in the pockets of her robe.

Hammond slowly waved the knife back and forth in front of his face, and said, "Take off the robe, and get on your knees here in front of me."

Cherry stared at the moving knife dumbly, then in his eyes, and realized she was in the presence of a psychopath. It was time to decide how to play the role of a trapped victim once again. But this time, Poppy would not be there to save her.

Cherry asked in a shaky voice, "Can't we talk and get to know one another without—without me having to?"

Hammond said with a snarl, "It's a little late for you to get to know me now, don'tcha think? You had two chances to do that, and you looked right through me, as if I didn't exist." He pointed the huge knife at her, and said, "Kinda hard to look right through me now, isn't it, Miss Page?"

His twisted smile took Cherry back to that terrible night in the London park. But as she sat on the sofa looking at him, something unexpected happened: Instead of being overcome with panic, she suddenly felt a calming influence come over her. It was as if Poppy were coming to her rescue again. Cherry gave in to the inevitable, much as she had that night in the park. But it wasn't out of a sense of resignation this time; the thought of joining Poppy in heaven gave her sudden strength. She consciously relaxed her body, refusing to show any more fear.

"You're quite right, Mr. Hammond. There is no reason whatsoever for me to try and get to know you." She took her hands from
her pockets, placed them in her lap, and said, "Get on with what you
came to do. Kill me, and get it over with. I'll certainly not give you
the satisfaction of seeing me beg."

Snorting a laugh, Hammond said, "I don't give a shit if you beg
or not, Miss Page. In fact, I *prefer* you let me lead you to slaughter
like the proverbial lamb. That's been the plan all along," he said, as
he polished the knife blade on his pants. "No more talk. Just keep
your mouth shut, and take off the robe."

When Cherry made no move to obey his command, Hammond
said, "You know, at first, I just wanted to get even with you for turning me down at the foundation dinner in London. And then—when
I got the hacker in London to break in to your computer—by the
way, he was the first to die—I wonder if they found him. Anyway,
when I learned all about you from your computer files—and I do
mean *all*—my plans changed dramatically."

Cherry continued to stare silently. It was clear he wanted to tell
her his plan, so she waited for him to continue. The longer he talked,
the better her chances.

Hammond moved back, put his hand on the table, and said, "I
bet you people have been wondering about whether or not I'm a true
believer in Baal, or if that was all just a crazy gimmick I was using
to make myself seem insane, or whatever."

Cherry said nothing.

"Well, let me assure you, Baal is *very* real, and he's the reason I
must have you in particular as a sacrifice." He turned one of the dining chairs around, and sat down facing Cherry. "Since we have quite
awhile before your idiot bodyguard returns, let me tell you why you
must die."

Cherry broke eye contact, and looked at the floor. Hammond
bristled, and said, "Look at me!" Cherry complied, and he continued: "When I cashed in my business, I toured Europe for the first
time. Paris, Rome, Madrid, sort of a grand tour. When I saw
London, I knew I was going to live there for the rest of my life.
Funny how things work out; if I had wanted to settle in Paris or
Rome, you'd be alive today." He smiled at his gaffe, and said, "I
mean, you'd be alive *after* today."

Hammond's smile faded as Cherry's gaze moved to the window. He continued, "Fifteen years ago, my business was floundering. I had the big ideas, but I was going nowhere. There were many months of struggle financially, and otherwise. And then I met a woman who changed my life forever. She showed me a world I didn't know existed. A world of worship, and true belief, and an amazing force that I could bring into my life simply by asking. She showed me how to follow the path that she'd found. That path—and it's one of *incredible* force—is Baal worship."

Cherry looked back at him, unsure of how to react. The look of rapture on Hammond's face as he spoke of his worship of a dumb idol would have been laughable had he not been serious. But one look into the maniac's eyes told her he was *dead* serious.

He went on, "As soon as I became a follower of the one true god, my life changed radically, almost overnight. The more dedication I showed, the greater the reward. My business took off like a rocket, coinciding with the boom in dot-com stocks so perfectly that within six months I was a millionaire many times over. Now, mind you, I had to do some things that seemed wrong at first, but the results spoke for themselves." He put the knife on the table, and continued, "These things *seemed* wrong, but I had to ask myself: are you really a believer? Or are you one of those small minds who jump from one New Age fakery to another? Well, I found out soon enough I was a true believer, and all it took was a sacrifice."

Hammond paused, and Cherry wanted to ask if by sacrifice he meant tightening his belt business-wise, or taking on another job, but said nothing.

He went on, "I ask you, Miss Page. What's a single human life worth in the overall scheme of things? Especially if it means untold wealth and power to the one strong enough to take that life, and give it to Baal?"

Cherry tried not to change her expression as she realized what he meant. It took all her skill as an actor to remain calm, and Hammond detected nothing in her face. He said, "You see, it has proven to be worth it. That young girl had no future anyway, and the power I got from her dying, it's indescribable. To watch her take her last breath on Earth, to see the blood run, to hold her warm little body in my arms afterwards. Pure exhilaration."

Cherry was stunned, but kept her face blank. She put out of her mind the fact that this man was totally delusional, and tried to stay in the moment. She wanted to ask how all this insanity related to *her*, and Hammond spoke as if he had read her mind.

"You know, when I first hacked—well, better said—when that poor fool O'Neill first hacked into your computer—I only wanted revenge. I intended to simply wreak havoc on your credit. Maybe charge a bunch of things to you online, that sort of thing. Maybe even screw up your bank accounts, clean them out or whatever. Just stuff to make your life a little hellish, you know? But then I discovered something from reading your e-mails that changed everything."

He looked at her smugly, expecting her to ask what he had discovered. Again, Cherry wouldn't give him the satisfaction.

Irritated, Hammond said, "You see, Miss Page, lately my business endeavors have begun to take a downward turn. It seemed that everything I tried—investments, takeovers, new ventures—turned to shit, and my bank account has shrunk considerably. And then it hit me. You are the answer to all my problems. Baal showed me the way back to power once again."

Cherry felt another shiver, and unconsciously tightened the robe in a vain attempt to protect herself from the creature sitting only a few feet away.

Hammond said, "The way it came together was pure magic. I was in a bind again, I needed guidance again, and I had already chosen a victim for the sacrifice. But then Baal showed me an even more powerful way." He paused for effect, and then said, "I found out from one of your e-mails that *you* were the perfect sacrifice."

When Cherry merely stared, he said, "Don't you see? You are the perfect sacrifice because you're—a *virgin*."

Cherry opened her mouth to speak, but Hammond interrupted. "I still think it would be best if you didn't say another word—*Cherry*," he said in a tone that made her skin crawl. "As I said earlier, I want to lead the lamb to slaughter without so much as a bleat. If you speak, I swear by Baal I'll kill you without the ritual." He added with a smirk, "Not only unblemished, but silent, too."

Resigned, Cherry made no attempt to talk her way out of what was surely coming, but calmly looked Hammond in the eye, and waited for her chance to reunite with Poppy.

He stood and said, "Take off the robe, and get on your knees here in the middle of the room. Down on all fours, my perfect little lamb. Baal waits for you to come to him. Once he has you he'll grant me the power I need."

I walked in the front door of the Ritz and was greeted again by the employees and guests who happened to be in the lobby, and I signed a couple more autographs. I even posed for a picture with an elderly couple from Germany.

I was glad my time in the spotlight was coming to an end, and I whistled happily to myself once I was on the elevator headed back up to the suite. Humming and whistling, that was me on that fine Sunday afternoon. The tune I selected to whistle was "Whistle While You Work," because I had done such a good job at finding the perfect souvenir for Cherry.

As I got off the elevator and turned the corner, I felt another little twinge of sadness as I realized again that unless I made a sea change in my lifestyle and decided to remain with Cherry, my remaining time at the Ritz could be measured in minutes. Even though I still hadn't come to a decision, the twinge became stronger as I stood in front of the door to room 521, and placed the key-card in the slot.

I entered the suite, called Cherry's name, and froze as I saw her naked body.

79

CHERRY WAS ON ALL FOURS IN THE MIDDLE OF THE PARLOR, AND A NAKED man stood over her, holding a huge hunting knife. They both stared at me, and I don't know who was more shocked, but I'm pretty sure it was me. The man roughly pulled Cherry to her feet, and backed her over in front of the closed curtains, his left arm across her breasts. He held the knife to her throat with his right hand, and pulled her face to his, cheek-to-cheek, lessening my chance at a head shot.

He growled, "Don't make a sound, Chief, or make a move towards the phone, or I'll cut her throat right where she stands."

Now, I'll admit, I have no training in hostage negotiation, but I've played poker for years. I quickly assessed the situation, and decided what my first move should be: I went into pressure mode, and raised the stakes.

"I have no intention of calling anyone," I said, then turned, and stepped over to the closet. I reached up under the spare blanket on the top shelf, took my gun out of its holster, made sure the safety was off, and aimed it at the man's head. "But I also have no intention of letting you get away, whether you kill Miss Page or not."

This caused Cherry to look at me as if I was out of my mind.

The guy said, "I'm serious. I'll slice her neck from ear to ear if you make a move."

I walked slowly over to the sofa, still aiming the Glock at his head, sat on the sofa's arm, and replied, "I don't think you understand. Like I said, you're not going anywhere, no matter *what* you do."

We were now about ten feet apart. He kept Cherry's face next to his, but loosened his grip on her slightly, and I felt I had made the right decision by putting the pressure on him. My heart was in my throat, and beating erratically like it does when I'm under extreme stress, but I gave him my best poker face.

He asked, "Do you have any idea who I am?"

I willed my voice to stay even, and said, "No, I'm sorry, I don't know who you are. I mean, I know you're obviously the—you're the—sorry, I just can't bring myself to use that idiotic name. Let's just say I know you're the man we've been hunting, how's that? As for your name, no, I don't know that."

He said, "Then let me introduce myself. Again. My name is Kenneth Hammond. We met at the charity ball last Monday night, remember?"

I recognized him at that moment; the blond curls gave him away. He was one of the dudes who had tried to put the moves on Cherry. The cowboy Tingle crossed my mind. They had both been at the charity event. That was probably how they had met. The Feds had it wrong, but their blunder didn't matter at that point.

I said, "Oh, yeah, now I remember. You were one of the guys that tried to get a date with Miss Page, right?"

"Right," he said, his lip turning up in a sneer. "Just another damn fool she rejected."

Cherry smiled slightly, and it hit me that she was amazingly calm under the circumstances. It also hit me that my arm was getting tired from holding the gun out, so I slowly let it drop to my hip, still aimed in the general direction of Hammond's face.

He said, "It looks like we have a standoff here."

"How do you figure that?"

"Because neither of us can do anything except wait."

I laughed what I hoped was a derisive laugh, and said, "Now, *that's* where you're wrong, Kenny."

"Kenneth!"

"Oh. Sorry. *Kenneth.* As I was sayin', you've got it all wrong. This is no standoff. This is my lucky day."

He smirked, and asked, "How can this possibly be your lucky day?"

"Because I'm going to get five hundred grand for information leading to your arrest. My job is done here."

He smiled as if I was a child who didn't understand big people's business, and said, "Your job is to protect Cherry Page, and at the moment, you're not doing your job very well."

I replied, "That's where you're wrong, Kenneth. My job isn't to protect Miss Page. My job is to kill *you.*"

That stopped him cold. As he struggled with the proposition that he had no bargaining power, I stretched lazily as if I didn't have a care in the world, my gun pointed at the ceiling. Turned out I was pretty good at hostage negotiating after all.

As he pondered this turn of events, I went into the only thing I actually know about hostage situations, Hostage Negotiations 101: Keep them talking. I've used the tactic before, last year as a matter of fact.

"So, Kenneth, where you from?"

He looked at me warily for a moment, then said, "Not that it matters, but I was born and raised in Atlanta."

I said, "And you work here?"

He looked distracted as Cherry squirmed slightly. He tightened his grip on her and said, "Yeah, my main office was here."

I nodded slowly, rolled my neck and shoulders, and said, "Kenneth, just one more question. Are you a homo?"

He snapped back to attention. "What?"

"I was wondering, because your first victim was a gay female impersonator. Did you have sex with him before you killed him? Is that why you're after Miss Page? Because you wanna be her?"

It was his turn to laugh derisively, and I have to admit, his laugh was much better than mine. In fact, it was downright evil. It actually gave me goose bumps. Say what you will about psychopaths, but one thing is certain: they really know how to do the derisive laugh.

He said, "Is this your way of trying to get under my skin, Chief? Or do you want to keep me talking till you can figure out what makes me tick?—the better to negotiate a peaceful resolution to our little hostage situation."

Okay. He was on to me. I forged ahead, "Yeah, I want a peaceful resolution, but I really *am* curious about your motives. And, I would like answers to some questions I have."

"Ask away," he said.

"Okay, thanks. What's your beef with Cherry?"

He said, "I thought I made my position clear in all my messages, Chief, but obviously I was wrong. Let me make it simple for you. Miss Page is the perfect sacrifice I need to give to Baal."

Now, *that* surprised me. "You mean to tell me this Baal business is real? You weren't just puttin' us on?"

His whole countenance changed. He looked like a brainwashed cult member as he replied, "I never joke about the power of Baal."

Cherry nodded slightly, as if to say, "He's serious."

I didn't know what to say, but Hammond did. He asked, "Why are you back so early, Chief?"

Now he had *me* off guard. I took a moment, then asked, "How would you know if I'm back early?"

He smiled and said, "I've been staying here at the Ritz since the Friday before you two arrived, Chief." He giggled a weird, high-pitched giggle at my expression, which now most definitely wasn't poker-faced, and continued, "How do you think I was able to spray that stupid bitch's room with all those fire extinguishers after I sliced her?"

I recalled the eerie sight of the poor woman from Minnesota covered in foam. "So you've been here all along. That makes sense. But how did you know how long I would be out today?"

"*Because*, Chief, I was out front with the news cretins and saw you leave. Then I called Miss Page and pretended to be Agent Carver. I had the flowers in my room, ready to go, and the cap and uniform jacket from the dead flower-boy drag queen, and, well—it all just fell into place with the almighty help of you-know-who."

I have to admit, the bastard had done a good job. It was my turn to do the same. My heartbeat had slowed to a manageable rate, and I was ready to start talking again. But before I could speak, he said, "You still haven't answered my question. Why are you here now?"

I pulled the gun closer to me, and replied, "Oh. Well, I forgot my wallet. It's in those tux pants in the bottom of the closet. I was shopping and when I went to pay for—something over at Phipps Plaza, I found I was without funds. So, I had to come back."

"I see." He looked like he was deep in thought, his eyes focused on my gun. I said nothing, letting him take the lead. After a moment he came back to the situation at hand, and said, "Well, we still have a standoff here."

Ball in my court.

"Kenneth, I want some more answers, if you don't mind. I may not get a chance to talk to you anymore after—I mean, you might be dead in a few minutes. So, tell me about Mr. Nakamura, and how it all went down in his cabin."

Hammond sighed as if I was the biggest pain in the ass he'd ever come across, and said, "Nakamura worked for me in my Atlanta office up until about six months ago. I had to let him go when I started having financial difficulties. He was just another cog in a machine set in motion by—"

"Don't tell me," I interrupted. "Our old pal, Baal." He looked miffed, but didn't react the way I wanted him to, just went back to his story.

"I knew about Nakamura's cabin, and it was easy enough to manipulate the scene. I had met up with Tingle again at a gun show Friday afternoon, and after I, shall we say, secured his cooperation, and spent the night at his house, I took him out there and broke into the cabin Saturday morning. Nakamura lives in a high-rise on Peachtree Street, and hardly ever uses the cabin, so I thought it was a good bet that it would be empty, and again, I was right. I called and told him I was a cop, that someone had broken into his cabin, and he was needed there immediately. I'm quite good on the phone."

"Yeah, I'm sure you are," I said.

"Anyway, when Nakamura came to the cabin, I waited till he was inside, killed him with the knife I left for the cops to find, and—this is the good part—put the gun in his hand and shot the cowboy moron at close range. I also fired a round into the wall for good measure. I must say, it was a job well done." He smiled at the memory, and said, "Can we get back to business here?"

"Just one more thing. How did you keep Tingle under control all that time?"

"Oh, we went out on the town, then back to his place. Once there, I slipped some Rohypnol into his drink. He was pretty heavily dosed, had been all night. He probably didn't feel a thing at the cabin."

I said, "Well, Kenneth. You realize, of course, that once there's an autopsy, the police and the FBI will realize it was all a setup. You understand that, right?'

Once again, he gave me the look that said what a pain I was, and said, "*Duh,* Chief. Why do you think I'm here now? Even though I made sure they would be working on a Sunday, I know they'll figure it all out soon. They will also undoubtedly find a stray fingerprint of mine here or there, on the pictures and tabloid articles or the laptop

I left in the cowboy's home, et cetera. In fact, they may already be on the way over here as we speak. That's why I have to sacrifice my perfect virgin, and get the hell outta here."

There it was. Time for my winning shot. I rested the Glock on my thigh, and said, "Wait a minute here, Kenneth." I paused for effect, as I'm wont to do when toying with a lawbreaker. "Did you say somethin' about a 'perfect virgin'?"

He gave me the pained look *again,* which was really starting to piss me off, and asked, "Are you really as dumb as you look, Chief? I told you. I know all about Cherry Page. *All* about her. I was inside her computer, remember?"

That didn't register, so I said, "Uh, Kenneth, I think I'm coming in on the end of a conversation we haven't had yet. What's this about you bein' inside Cherry's computer?"

He looked at me dumbly for a moment, then said, "My mistake, Chief, forgive my rudeness. It was Miss Page who I told about the computer hacker I hired to get all her personal and business information. Anyway, I know all there is to know about her, including the fact that she's a virgin. Don't you see? That's what makes her so special, so absolutely perfect, since any sacrifice made unto Baal must be a—what are you laughing at?" he asked, his face now showing anger.

It was once again my turn to laugh derisively, and I really laid it on thick. In fact, my laugh was so evil I wouldn't have been surprised if both Hammond and Cherry had gotten goose bumps this time. Of course, being naked, they might've gotten goose bumps anyway.

When I finally stopped laughing, I said, "Kenneth, old boy. My delusional friend. You've been wasting your time here. You see, Miss Page *was* a virgin, and the operative word is 'was.' You're a day late, and a half million dollars short."

80

HAMMOND LOOKED STUNNED FOR A MOMENT, BUT QUICKLY RECOVERED. "Nice try," he said. "You almost had me believing you there for a second."

Cherry smiled at me, obviously pleased by what I had said. She even looked somewhat relaxed, or at least as relaxed as she could be under the truly weird circumstances.

"Don't believe me, Kenny?" I asked with a grin, which grew wider as I watched him steam at the nickname.

He got that apoplectic look on his face again, then visibly calmed himself. He said with a fake smile, "Chief. Isn't it just a little too convenient that you deflowered my virgin only hours before I was to sacrifice her? Forgive me, but that sounds a little too perfect."

I stretched again, and said, "I really don't care how it sounds, Ken. The fact is, you kill her now, and you not only go to jail—or die where you stand—but you also get on the wrong side of Baal. You really think he's gonna give you any power for killing a common slut? Do you? Seriously? I'm no expert when it comes to human sacrifice, but I'm pretty sure a god won't take too kindly to being offered damaged goods. Am I right, Kenny?"

Cherry gave me a phony scowl for the "S" word, but I could see the smile in her eyes. Hammond stared at the floor, so absorbed in thought I almost rushed him. But I waited for the next move in our chess game.

It was a pretty good move.

He said, "Chief Cooper. You would receive a reward of a half million dollars for my capture, correct?"

"Correct. It's already in the bank, the way I see it."

He shook his head a little, and said, "Hmmm. That seems like an awfully small amount of money for someone who has done such a good—no, a *great* job."

I could almost see the wheels turning in his deranged, albeit fiscally sharp, mind. Hostage negotiations had turned into financial negotiations.

I said, "I don't know, Ken, a half million dollars? That's a lotta cash for a small-town cop like me."

He said, "Maybe so, maybe so. But what would you say to five times that? Or, even better, ten times that? Could you turn down an offer that would pay you five million dollars?"

That was my cue to do some more acting. I attempted to look like I was considering his offer, and then said, "I'm listening."

I have to say, it was weird, haggling over Cherry's life with a certifiably delusional psycho who was wearing nothing but his birthday suit, and her standing right there as his shield, naked as well. It reminded me yet again how bizarre my life has been for the last year.

Hammond looked confident once more, back in control. I'm sure he thought that once money came into play, the game was his to win. He persisted: "What if you were to let me go—just get dressed and walk right out of here—and what if you were to give me time to get the money together, then get it to you, and stroll off into the sunset?"

Once again, I have to give the guy credit. It *did* sound like a pretty good way to make an easy five mill.

I went into actor mode again, furrowed my brow, and gave Hammond my best "I'm really, *seriously* pondering your offer" look.

I finally said, "Mr. Hammond—Kenneth. I must say, that's a truly generous offer." A look of satisfaction slowly spread over his face. I went on, "But I'm not sure I can trust you. I mean, if I let you go, you might just walk outta here and never send me a dime. You see what I'm sayin'?"

"Chief Cooper. I give you my word. No, even better, I swear by Baal that I'll do exactly as I've said. You let me go, and I promise— I *swear by Baal*—that I'll pay you. Five. Million. Dollars. Now, you can't get a better guarantee than that."

As I listened to the nut bag, I wished for a moment I had been brought up differently. What if I had never learned about morality? What if I'd been raised by wolves? Five million big ones could have been mine, and all my worries would've been over. Except, of course, Cherry would've told Penny, so it was a very short wishful moment.

I looked at Hammond again as if I was considering his proposal, scratching my head, rubbing my chin, doing contemplative stuff, and he seemed to be buying it. He relaxed his grip on Cherry, smiled, and asked, "Whatta ya say, Chief? Do we have a deal?"

I couldn't think of anything to say, or come up with an idea of how to keep stalling. I only knew that this discussion was going nowhere. My thoughts drifted off to whether I should just try and shoot the bastard and get it over with.

I was calculating the odds as to whether or not I could actually hit Hammond in the head with a shot, when Cherry fainted dead away. Hammond struggled to hold her now dead weight up with one arm, and as strong as he was, it was a losing battle.

81

ONE MISSISSIPPI, TWO MISSISSIPPI.

That's how much time I had to decide what to do, and how to do it. We can debate whether my actions were clever or brainless, but at that moment, I had to move. I'm no James Bond, and am rusty with a gun after years in Gulf Front, so taking my best shot was out of the question.

I hurled my gun behind me over the sofa, dove at Hammond, and got his right wrist and forearm in a death grip. As I smashed him into the window with my shoulder, Cherry slipped from his grasp and slumped to the floor. I began to bash Hammond's wrist against the windowsill as hard as I could, and Cherry jumped up, ran into the bedroom, and slammed the door behind her. I realized she had faked her fainting spell, but I didn't have time to applaud her performance. I bashed Hammond's wrist on the windowsill several more times, each time harder than the last, but the knife was still securely in his hand. So I tried a new tactic: I stomped down on his unshod toes as hard as I could with the heel of my right sneaker.

He screamed in pain, but still held on to the knife. I stomped down again, this time even harder, and with all my might, pushed him with my shoulder into the window. I took my left hand off his wrist, grabbed his hair, and began banging his head against the thick window glass. The knife finally dropped as he struggled to maintain consciousness, and I kicked at it, trying to get it away from us.

Cherry was now doing some screaming of her own into the phone back in the bedroom, and that gave me a new jolt of adrenaline, knowing that I only had to fend off Hammond for a few more minutes before help arrived. I was really glad of that, because I don't normally wrestle a lot of guys to the death, especially naked ones.

I still couldn't quite reach the knife with my foot, so I stomped down harder on his toes and slammed his head into the glass again, and then again. The solid window meeting his skull stunned Hammond, but he managed to thrust mightily and push me away, separating us for the first time since I had jumped him.

I lost my balance and fell to the carpeted floor, saved only by the fact that he was wobbly and semiconscious. Hammond was a pretty strong guy, but so am I, and I was running on a full tank of adrenaline. He was dazed from the head trauma, and having trouble standing on his crushed toes, but he wobbled and tried to get to the knife, which was almost within reach.

I jumped up and slammed into Hammond again with my shoulder, knocking him away from the knife. I punched him so hard in the face with my left fist that I felt a bone in one of my knuckles crack. Pain shot up like electricity to my shoulder, and my arm went numb for a second. Hammond was fading into unconsciousness but was still reaching for the knife, his fingers twitching spasmodically.

I made a grab for his right wrist again, and he instinctively shot his left elbow into my temple so hard that I saw nothing but white light for a moment. I'm ashamed to admit it, but the blow almost knocked me out. Again, he had thrown me down and away, and I ended up flat on my side.

I got to my knees just in time to see him shake the cobwebs and focus on the knife, which was only a foot or two from his grasp. He was now between me and my gun, which was out of sight behind the sofa anyway. For a moment I wished I had taken a chance and kept my Glock, but it was too late for second-guessing.

I looked frantically around for anything I could use, and saw something I could reach before he got his hands on the knife: a big crystal vase filled with yellow flowers, sitting on the corner table.

Just as he unsteadily reached down and grasped the knife, I jumped up, took hold of the heavy vase, and swung it down like an axe right on that bunch of blond curls. Yellow flowers and water exploded around his head, and Hammond went down like a baby seal. Gasping for air, I stood over him, victorious, vase in hand, the undisputed champion of the Lunatic Division.

82

A MINUTE OR SO LATER, LEWIS, THE BIG BLACK SECURITY GUARD WE SAW almost every day, burst into the suite, gun drawn and breathing hard.

Physically spent, knuckle and head throbbing, I considered getting my gun, in order to help Lewis keep an eye on Hammond, but Lewis didn't need any help. Without a word, he quickly had the prone Hammond handcuffed, and was sitting on him, digging his big knees into the unconscious killer's back. My heartbeat was still elevated, but gradually returned to normal as I forced myself to breathe deeply and evenly.

Three hotel security men ran into the room, huffing and puffing, and began acting like genuine cops, asking me and Lewis every question they could think of that sounded cop-like. They stared at the sight of Lewis kneeling on the back of a naked white guy, and the big guard jumped up as if he'd received an electric shock when he realized what it must have looked like to them. Lewis quickly ushered the security men out into the hallway to keep guard of whatever was out there, and closed the door behind them. He then came back over and stood over Hammond, who was still busy being still.

I walked over to my bed by the window, pulled the topsheet off, and went over and covered Hammond with it; I had seen about enough of him by then. The bedroom door opened, and a barefoot Cherry stepped through, now dressed in jeans and a white tee shirt. Head down, she avoided eye contact as she slowly and silently walked over to me and opened her arms to be hugged. I wrapped my arms around her as she began to cry, softly at first, then in desperate, shaking sobs.

Holding me tighter, she said, "I'm so sorry, Cooper. I'm so *sorry!*"

Acting as if I had no idea what she meant, I said, "Cherry. Kiddo. What are you talkin' about?"

Still sobbing, she said, "I'm just so—sorry! I had—no idea—what else to do! I ran like—a scared—child. Not like . . ."

"Cherry. Stop. You did exactly what you should have done. What I *wanted* you to do. The last thing I needed was for you to get hurt. Why do you think I threw away my gun? I might've fired and hit you, or missed, and either way he would've been able to slit your throat, not to mention, you couldn't have done anything, anyway. If you had actually gotten your hands on the gun, you could have killed all three of us."

Cherry tried to laugh through the sobs, but didn't quite pull it off. She did manage to stop apologizing, but couldn't keep from sobbing softly.

I tried to lighten the situation by saying, "That was a neat trick, Miss Page, fainting like that. Quick thinking."

"I really *did* faint when—I saw the flowers earlier. When you read the card, you'll see why. It wasn't—quick thinking, really." Sob. Gasp. Sputter.

Her mention of the card didn't register with me because I was still thinking about how she had apologized a moment before. I had acted like I didn't know what Cherry was talking about when she was apologizing for her actions, but I *did* know what she was talking about: she meant that if she had been Penny, things would have gone a little differently. If Penny had faked a fainting spell, the nanosecond she was free, she would have run over behind the sofa, grabbed my gun, run back, and emptied it in Hammond's ear hole. All while naked. I thought yet again just how exceptional Penny truly is, and I also asked myself, what the hell was I thinking, even considering a life with Cherry?

The problem was, I *wasn't* thinking. Not with my brain, anyway.

Cherry said quietly, "You deserve a woman who can be there for you when needed, Cooper, not some so-called sex symbol."

The scent of her peach shampoo, the feel of her famous body against mine: the moment I thought I wanted had come, and the only thing I felt was protective. Not stimulated, not sexy, not crazed. Simply protective. I only felt what one would feel for a friend, or better yet, a little sister. That had been my original feeling for Cherry, and as it turned out, it was also the appropriate one.

The second mystery was solved, and I had my answer to the question about what I was going to do about Cherry Page: I would be her friend, and nothing more. It was a bittersweet moment, the feeling more sweet than bitter, but like I said, appropriate.

Lewis, clearly embarrassed by Cherry's emotion, said, "Y'all excuse me, folks. I need to call some people. I'll be right outside if you need me."

"Fine," I said.

He went out in the hall and closed the door behind him. Cherry went over and picked up a small white card that had fallen to the floor near the corner table. She handed it to me and said, "See? This is why I fainted."

As I read the card, Hammond stirred, groaned loudly, and opened his eyes. When he spotted me and Cherry, it all came back to him, and he glared at us. Even though I was glad to see I hadn't killed the sick freak, I couldn't resist giving him a little more grief.

"Kenny, you know what?" I asked.

He continued to glare, and once more his top lip curled up. Psycho Elvis.

I said, "Tell me one more thing, Ken-Ken. Why didn't you put the latch on the door? That was really dumb. If you had put the latch on the door, I might have opened the door, and seeing that I couldn't get in, decided that Cherry was in the shower, and gone back downstairs to wait. You might have been able to get away, or sacrifice her, or *something*."

Hammond said with a growl, "What's your fucking point?"

"My *point*, Kenny, is that if Baal is so almighty great, he would have reminded you to put the latch on the damn door. God certainly would have. Not only that, you brought a near lethal weapon for me to use on you, you dumbass. Don't you think a plastic vase would have been a better choice? I mean, come *on*. Talk about petards. Talk about hoist. Yep, Ken, the way I see it, you need to face facts: Baal really let you down. You might wanna seriously think about changing teams, buddy."

Hammond commenced to hurl abusive language and foul curses towards me at an alarming rate, and I covered Cherry's ears as she giggled.

I wasn't finished, "Yeah, Kenny, you might wanna consider worshipping the real God."

More cursing, more blistering abuse, more name-calling, all of it hurtful, and most of it untrue.

After Hammond finished cursing me and being really mean, I took my hands off of Cherry's ears. She looked me in the eye, and said, "Cooper, I really and truly want to thank you for telling our friend Mr. Hammond here about how you deflowered me last night. I feel that it may have been the very thing that saved my life."

In my best John Wayne voice I said, "Well, thank ya there, ma'am, but I was just doin' my job, is all. Just doin' my job."

Cherry carried on, "Maybe so, but obviously, I feel it was essential for Mr. Hammond to know that I am no longer a virgin." She paused and smiled knowingly at me, and I smiled knowingly right back.

Then she sighed, and said, "If only it were true."

83

I KNOW, I KNOW. I IMPLIED THAT I *DID* HAVE A TRYST WITH CHERRY, BUT if you recall, I never actually *said* I did. I stated several times that "I wish I could tell you," and "a gentleman never tells," but I never *actually said* we did the deed. I was just having a little fun. I don't really think of it as lying, but you might, if you have no sense of humor. But, in actuality, there was never anything untoward between me and Cherry. Truth be told, Cherry Page is still very much a virgin. That's the truth. I was always going to tell you, I was just waiting for the right time. Seriously. I was. So I embellished the story a little bit, big deal. I lied. By omission, I guess you could say. There, I said it: I lied.

So sue me.

Moving on, what really happened after the strip poker game, do you ask?

Well, five seconds after Cherry asked me to go double-or-nothing on one final hand to see which one of us would undress her, she became violently ill, and dashed to the bathroom as fast as her shaky legs could carry her. Thankfully, she made it to the toilet bowl, dropped to her knees, and voided the contents of her stomach as I held her famous red hair up.

Sexy, no? No. Definitely, no. So now you have all the facts.

Anyway, to change the subject: Have you ever been *really* embarrassed or humiliated, to the point that every single drop of blood in your body rushed to your face, clearly visible for all to see? Well, that was Hammond, as he realized that he'd been had. His face was so red, in fact, I was almost worried for him, blood pressure–wise. After a moment of going crimson, he turned his face away, and we never heard another word from him.

Within ten minutes, the Atlanta Task Force, several FBI agents, including Agent Carver, and various cops of all shapes and genders had made it up to the suite. Hammond was allowed to dress, and was then whisked away to the slammer as the law people got busy doing their jobs. Since they were going to be working the parlor as a crime scene, I called Sally Allen and told her me and Cherry would need to leave the suite, and asked if we could move to hers. She said of course, she could stay with Lynne for a while, so I called down and got a luggage cart to move my stuff out so I could pack to go home. I heaped all my clothes and suitcases on the cart, and took it and Cherry down the hall to Sally's room. I put Cherry and my pile of clothes in the bedroom, and closed the door behind her. There would be plenty of time for Cherry to give her statement to the law, since she wasn't leaving town like I was.

Sally was on the phone talking to Lynne, and when she got off, I said, "If you don't mind, keep everyone away for a while. Cherry could use a little downtime. And, Sally—would you do me one last favor?"

"Of course," she said, taking notes of my request before leaving.

I spent the next hour or so on the sofa with my cracked knuckle in a bowl of ice, listening to the radio. An exhausted Cherry called out from the bedroom that she was going to take a nap. At one point, I walked back to Cherry's suite to see how things were progressing. Agent Carver took me aside, and said, "Chief Cooper, I'm sorry about all this. If we had done our jobs a little better—or a lot better—you wouldn't have had to risk your life."

"Agent, please. You guys did a fantastic job. It was pure luck that I came back here in time. If I could keep up with my wallet, Cherry would be dead, so it's not like I did anything great. Let's all just be thankful we got Hammond, and let it go, okay?"

Carver smiled, and said, "I'm with you on that, Chief. But you did what needed to be done, and I want you to know how grateful the Bureau is, and how grateful I am, as well. Besides, now that you're a rich man, I want to stay on your good side."

He smiled at the look on my face. I must've looked like a dog that heard a sound no human can hear. "Excuse me, Agent?"

Carver reached over, put his hand on my shoulder, and said, "I talked to Miss Page's producer—Mr. Lyndon-Bowen—and he assures me you're getting the reward. Congratulations."

Wow. It hit me. Jackpot.

I know it's hard to believe, but until that moment, the thought hadn't crossed my mind that I would actually get the reward. Cherry had mentioned it on our ride back from Neal's house, but it didn't register. Even while I had been talking to Hammond about money, it didn't enter my mind as a reality; it was just a point of discussion in a conversation with an idiot. At that moment, though, it was real, and it had my head spinning for a few minutes. The sounds of the room died down as I considered the fact that I would be the second-richest guy in Gulf Front, after Mr. Milo. I might have to start using my full name, and demand to be referred to as Chief Samuel Cooper. Or not. Probably not.

I said a stunned good-bye to Agent Carver, went back to Sally's suite, and spent the next couple of hours thinking about my windfall, listening to the radio some more, and waiting for my boss lady to wake up. I finally heard her call to me, went in the bedroom, and found Cherry wide awake and sitting up on the bed. Smiling, she stretched lazily and said, "I am now ready to give everyone an audience."

I called Sally and told her that all was in place for the celebration, and to get the word out to the folks. Within a few minutes, Cherry's people who were staying at the Ritz had shown up and were crowding the parlor: Guinness, her director; Lawrence Lyndon-Bowen, her unctuous producer and my new benefactor; Sally; Will; Lynne; and some of the actors and crew, all excitedly talking and hugging. Lawrence congratulated me on my newfound riches, and actually seemed happy for me. My low opinion of him changed somewhat when he greeted me with a firm handshake and a genuine smile.

As soon as the well-wishers were all gathered, I went in the bedroom and brought Cherry out. Her colleagues burst into raucous applause as she made her entrance, and another hug fest erupted. Lyndon-Bowen had ordered champagne from room service, and the corks popped and the juice flowed. At one point, I looked over and caught Cherry and Sally off to one side, whispering and giggling. Sally kept glancing in my direction, and I wondered what they were saying. They wouldn't tell me, of course, so who knows?

I thought how incredibly poised Cherry was, and how well she had handled the life-and-death situation with Hammond, considering she's not a cop. Especially after what had happened in the last week, and more especially, the last few hours. We didn't have time to talk about it, but I made a note to ask her about her calm demeanor later.

Looking around the suite at the happy faces, I remembered the day we all met, and felt that pang once more, knowing I would never see those individuals again. But the bubbly had my spirits raised, and it was a time for joy, not pangs. Naturally, the cast and crew were buzzing around their star, but they all made a point of shaking my hand and offering congratulations and kudos. After a few minutes of revelry, I went out in the hall and called Penny. This time when I called, I knew what I was going to do: go home to my girlfriend and my real life.

"Hey Chief Prevost," I said. "You're not gonna believe this, but there's more to the story about Cherry Page."

She was stunned by my revelations, naturally, so I kept some of the tiny details from her, such as how I had wrestled a naked guy who was wielding a huge hunting knife, and the fact that I had a half million dollars coming my way. I held back on the financial news because I wanted to see her face when she learned of the reward. She didn't cry during the conversation like she had before; maybe she had no tears left. Anyway, after we exchanged a few lewd and bawdy comments about what would happen once we got our hands on each other, we hung up.

While in the hall, I also called Neal, who had heard from Agent Carver about the latest information, and we spoke for a couple of minutes while Susan and his daughters hooted and hollered in the background about my newfound prosperity. We laughed about my new status as a rich fat cat, and joked about what we would do now that I was in his and Susan's social class. He hadn't yet seen a photo of Hammond, and was unaware that the monster had been among the crowd at the benefit for Poppy's charity foundation, just as cowboy Tingle had been. Neal would later realize that Hammond had also been in Neal's office on the day Joe Don was murdered, and that Joe Don had seen Hammond too. When I found that fact out later, it made me sick to know that the big young man from Texas had undoubtedly recognized his killer. Neal and I hung up after more congratulations and promises to spend large amounts of cash.

It felt pretty good to be rich, I must say. Besides, it's not money that's the root of all evil. It's the *love* of money.

I don't love money by any means, but I do kind of like it.

84

AFTER EVERYBODY LEFT, CHERRY TOOK ANOTHER SHOWER, AND I STOOD at the window of Sally's suite, looking down on the late-Sunday-afternoon traffic. A slight rain was drizzling, and when the sun broke through from behind a cloud, it reminded me of the day in kindergarten when I had my first brush with authority. Five-year-old me was childishly drawing freehand with crayons, and my subject was a landscape of sorts. I had drawn the green grass, the blue sky, and the yellow sun, and was busy adding big purple raindrops when my teacher came over and soothingly informed me that it doesn't rain when the sun shines. What a dolt, I thought, or whatever a five-year-old Coop would have called her. She obviously had never been playing baseball in the summer with the older guys when a summer squall came in, bringing rain for several minutes as the sun continued to shine through. That moment was the beginning of my troubles with authority, I think. Of course, I'm authority now, so, whatever that means.

I was also reflecting on Penny and Cherry, and how they stack up against each other. No, not like that. I mean what each of them would bring to my life, and how I would be affected by my decision to turn down Cherry's offer to be her permanent bodyguard, and possible romantic partner. The thought of being in the movie world was daunting, to say the least.

Besides, I've always felt sort of sorry for Hollywood types in a weird way. They appear to have the world on a string, but then you find out that so many of them are simply lost. We're always hearing of some scandal, or one of them being in drug or alcohol rehab, or unending stupid things that one of them is doing, or has said. My point is this: over the past week or so, Cherry Page had shown over and over again that she isn't like those showbiz types at *all*.

There has never been a hint of scandal in her career, not even a hint of drug use, she's never publicly said or done anything stupid, and there's not a phony or pretentious bone in her extraordinary body. She doesn't mind being the center of attention, but she doesn't require it. Cherry isn't driven by the need to be loved by the public every minute, or to be a success as Hollywood measures it. She simply *is* loved and is a success by virtue of her virtues. She's down-to-earth, and special for so many reasons, but maybe the most special thing about her is that she's real.

But even as special as Cherry is, the problem, as I see it, would be the tremendous change in lifestyle that would occur if I took her up on her offer. In Gulf Front, I'm a big fish in a tiny pond. A tiny pond that just happens to be right next to one of the most beautiful beaches in the world. Cherry's world is a gigantic pond, and I would be the smaller of the two fishes in that pond. By far. I don't think I would be too happy with that.

On the other hand, if Cherry wanted to give up her Hollywood life and move to Gulf Front, that would be a different story. *That's* something to dream about. When I compare them physically as potential mates, it's a toss-up. And yes, I realize how shallow that sounds, and how conceited, as if they both think of me in the same way, but it's *my* dream, so there.

I also couldn't help thinking if I had met Cherry when I was younger, and if we were the same age, say, twenty-one or so, that everything might have turned out differently.

But, time being what it is, he said philosophically, all these thoughts came and went, my remaining Ritz minutes quickly passed, and it was time to get packing.

Literally.

EPILOGUE

INVIGORATED AFTER HER SHOWER, CHERRY SAT WITH HER BARE FEET under her on the sofa in the parlor watching me pack the larger of my suitcases, or should I say *stuff* the larger of my suitcases. The suitcase in question is an ancient Samsonite, bought more than twenty years ago, when I was at the police academy. It was now almost six P.M., and I had plenty of time to make my flight, but I wanted to get a move on. Good-byes are not one of my specialties; I try to avoid them whenever possible.

We were both ignoring all that had happened in the past week, and the mood was lighter than it had any right to be. Cherry laughed at my packing efforts, and it was great to see her happy and free of the fear that had been following her. There was a lot of denial going on in that hotel suite, but there was no denying the fact that I was leaving for good. We both knew it, and were okay with it.

Cherry covered her eyes as I crammed my clothes into the suitcase, and said, "You're going to absolutely ruin every article of clothing you own, Cooper! Won't you please let me help you with that? I'm a professional packer, I practically live out of a suitcase, and I'm offering you my services for free. Won't you—oh! I can't look! That poor shirt!" She laughed again, and said, "I'm going to buy you a complete new wardrobe, and have it shipped to you in Gulf Front."

"No you're not, missy," I said, still stuffing. "And besides, you don't know where I live, anyway," I said with a grunt as I tried to smash the clothes down into the suitcase.

Cherry said, "Hmmm. You're quite right about that." Pause. "Then I shall send it to Penny's beach cottage. I have *her* address."

"Well, I'll tell the postman not to deliver any big packages to Penny unless he checks with me first."

"Then I'll send it by FedEx, or whatever you call it," Cherry said.

I replied, "Well, then, okay, I'll get a job at FedEx, and become an executive, and stop the package from being delivered, and take the clothes and send 'em to starving kids in Bangladesh."

"Well, I don't have an answer for that. But I will, given time. I know another thing I'm going to send you. A computer, so we can e-mail and send instant messages. Penny, too, of course."

Continuing to try and close the suitcase, I said, "I can get my own computer, thank you very much." More stuffing and grunting. "Although it would be kinda nice to learn how to do all that stuff. And I know Penny will be e-mailing you and using that messenger deal every five minutes."

"And I'll be happy to hear from the both of you, each and every single time." She paused, her brow furrowed, and said, "But we shall have to come up with a username for you. Something that I'll recognize immediately. A name that means something to you."

"You mean like the one you chose—'pal of poppy'?"

"Precisely. How 'bout 'corny copper'? Or maybe 'penny pincher'?"

"Those are pretty bad," I said. "How 'bout, instead, let's see. I know—'idiot who did not shag cherry page when he had the chance.'"

Cherry cringed, and said, "Please, don't remind me. I'm so embarrassed by my behavior, you cannot imagine. I want to thank you yet again for not taking advantage, Cooper. I now know that having a real relationship is more important than having notches on my bedpost."

"Good. And if there's one thing I'm sure of, boss, it's that you'll find somebody. Trust me on that."

"How can I trust a self-proclaimed idiot who refused to shag me?" Cherry said with that sexy smile of hers. "You know, this talk about idiocy puts me in mind of something Joy said Friday night at the Feagins' house. She said to say it to you the next time you said or did something dumb."

"And just what did Joy tell you to say?"

"'Girls go to college, to get more knowledge; boys go to Jupiter, to get more stupider.'"

We both laughed, but I felt another damned twinge of sadness as I realized that I was really, finally leaving her. I thought maybe she felt the same way, and I was right.

She said, "Cooper, I can't believe this nightmare is finally over; I'm so happy about that, I can't express it. But, at the same time, I feel so very, very sad that you won't be here tomorrow when I wake up. Whatever shall I do?"

Still trying to pack the bastard suitcase, I said, "Well, you could always write your memoirs. I mean, you're young and all, but you just went through a helluva week. It would certainly make a good book."

Cherry said, "Yes, I suppose I could write a book about my life. It would most likely be well received, yeah?" She paused. "But what should the title of my memoir be?"

I pushed down with all my might on the suitcase, and said through gritted teeth, "How 'bout—*The Cherry Pages?*"

She shook her head, and said, "See? That kind of quick thinking is one of the many things I'll miss about having my own personal police chief." She let out a big, phony, theatrical sigh, and continued, "I suppose I'll simply have to go back to my dreary life as an international sex symbol and fabulous movie star."

I stopped manhandling the suitcase for a second and looked to see if she was serious. I should've known better. She laughed one of her sweetest laughs, and I had to join in. I was really going to miss Miss Cherry Page.

I then told some truths and some lies. "Well, I tell ya somethin'. I'm gonna miss having you for a boss, and I'm *really* gonna miss being in show business. Now that I've had a taste of the High Life, I don't know how I'll ever be able to live amongst the little people again. I mean, let's face it. There's not a single Bentley dealership in Gulf Front, and there's almost *no* paparazzi down there, except Mike Rogers, the old guy who edits our hometown newspaper and doubles as one of its two photographers. Or Kelly Ann, Mike's granddaughter, who snapped my picture for the front page earlier since Mike couldn't make the trip. And another thing: who's gonna cut my hair? Besides all that, what'll I do if I need to disappear? I just don't think it's right for a man to have to do his own makeup."

"I know. You've been quite the actor this past week. You could always go to Hollywood and find work."

Resting for a moment, I said, "I'm no longer interested in acting now that I've mastered it."

"Oh, no. Please don't tell me you're like every other actor on the planet. You feel the need to *direct*."

"Nope."

She thought for a second, and then said, "Oh, right. Silly me. Control freak. You want to produce."

"Nope."

"Well, *what* then?"

"Craft service."

She rolled her eyes, and said, "That will never do. You'd devour all the profit."

"Hmmm. Never thought of that. Oh well. I guess I'll have to give up show business after all."

Cherry watched as I sat on my suitcase again and continued the fight to close it. It was nice that the mood was light, and it made us both feel better. We talked as if all of the bad stuff had never happened.

Cherry said at one point, "I have a couple of confessions to make, Cooper."

"Oh, no. Don't tell me you were born a man. *Oliver*."

"Not hardly. But I'm afraid I did mislead you in some matters."

"Do tell."

"Well, remember at the beach? When Penny and I were wrestling and playing in the ocean?"

Remember? Do I remember when Cherry and Penny were wrestling and playing in the ocean? *That* little show was forever burned in my memory, on my brain, and on both of my retinas. For all time, throughout all eternity, till death do I part. I said, "Uh, yeah, I vaguely recall somethin' about you and Penny wrestling in the ocean."

"Do you recall that the top of my bikini came off, and that I was half naked to the world?"

"Let's see. You say your bikini top came off? Hmmm. Wait. It's coming back to me now. Yes, I recall that. Bikini top. Off. Half naked."

"I'm glad you remember," she said. "My first confession is this: I took the bikini top off on purpose."

Gulp. "You did not."

"Yes, I did. It was a brazen attempt to get your attention."

"Well, it definitely worked, you brazen-attempting hussy. You got my attention, all right. You also got my undying appreciation and devotion."

That got a good laugh, and she said, "Right. It worked, then. Good to know. One more confession, and I can let you go with a reasonably clear conscience."

"Okay, shoot."

"Remember again. At Neal's? When I called Sally and asked her to get you a seat on the studio plane?"

"Yeah . . ."

"Now, don't get cross with me, Cooper. Promise?"

"Promise."

"The phone call I made to Sally was an exercise in deception. It was a case of me using my acting skills to good advantage. I actually instructed her to get you on the plane *tonight,* so I could try one last time to woo you, and charm you with my ways." She fluttered her eyelashes like a floozy and continued, "Sally protested strongly, but went along after I begged and pleaded. Furthermore, it was I who requested that she reserve the restaurant, not the studio. I wanted you all to myself. Yes, I know, it was selfish of me. But, all that aside, think about this: did you really believe that Sally Allen would be unable to get you—or anyone else, for that matter—a seat on the studio plane within an hour or two? Sally could get any thing, any time, for any *one.*"

I had to smile at my naïveté. "My word, Miss Page. You're incorrigible."

"I know."

At that moment I was struck by exactly how *much* I was going to miss Cherry Page. A lot more than I had any real reason to, in fact. I once had a similar feeling as a teenager: when I was fifteen, I went with a national youth organization to Colorado over the Christmas holidays on a four-day skiing junket. I won the trip by having bought the winning ticket in a church raffle; otherwise, I wouldn't have been able to go. While in Colorado, I had a classic whirlwind teen romance with an older woman; a pretty sixteen-year-old babe from Indiana named Vicky, who was there with her group.

It was an innocent affair by today's standards, but I was completely nuts about her. We spent our days avoiding the slopes, since neither us could ski, and spent our nights by the big fireplace in the great room.

Anyway, when we both returned to our homes after four days in teen heaven, the romance naturally came to a crashing halt, and I was devastated. I missed Vicky in a way that was way over the top, especially since we had barely spent any time together. I missed not having her as if I actually *had* had her, so to speak, and it was crazy. That's the way I was suddenly feeling about Cherry: already missing her as if we had been in an actual romance together. Stupid, but there it was.

Naturally, after I'd been home for a while after my fling with Vicky, I forgot all about her; she became just another sweet memory. I knew it would be that way with Cherry, too, but I was feeling that twinge of genuine sadness yet again at that moment.

While I had been thinking about Vicky, I had also been stuffing my suitcase, avoiding talking for the time being. With a mighty thrust, punctuated by a final loud grunt, I finally got it to close. As usual, there were a couple of shirts and some socks that wouldn't fit inside, so I stuck them in a plastic bag I had kept for just that purpose.

Cherry jumped up from the sofa, grabbed the bag, and ran into the bedroom. "These are staying with me," she called out. "I must have *something* to remember you by."

She didn't know it, but she had something else coming to remember me by: the set of teacups and saucers with the cherries on them. The last favor I had asked Sally for was about the rugby jersey and the single cup and saucer Daphne had put aside for me at the British store. Sally assured me she would mail me the jersey, purchase the complete cherry teacup set from Daphne, surprise Cherry with it tomorrow, and send me the bill. Sally also promised to give Daphne an autographed picture of Cherry, plus a personal item as well. The teacups would be a nice surprise for Cherry, and would guarantee she would remember me fondly. Besides, I could afford it, now that I was a half millionaire. Before taxes, anyway.

While Cherry was out of the room, I placed my suitcases on the luggage cart, and answered the phone when it rang. The limo was downstairs waiting to take me to the studio jet, so I had only one last moment to reflect.

After the incredible ups and downs of the past week, it all came down to this: me and Cherry were both going back to our normal, everyday lives. Okay, so Cherry's life isn't normal or everyday, but the more I thought about it, the more my boring life in Gulf Front looked pretty damn good. In fact, I realized that I couldn't wait to get home and pick up my dog from Adam, see all my friends, and get back to a routine that didn't include daily danger. Most of all, I wanted to get my hands on the acting chief of police in Gulf Front, one Penny Prevost. I also wanted another bottle of champagne, the crushed-velvet bedspread, a sand dune, and a bunch of stars overhead. Another beach bash like the one we had a few nights ago, and who knows what might happen?

I mean, everybody's always telling me how I should marry Penny, and I'm sure that once they find out I'm a wealthy man, the voices will only get louder. I'll have to come up with a dozen new reasons to explain why I will remain unmarried, and express them quickly and continuously. That being said, nuptials are certainly not off the table of discussion in private. The problem is, I'm still not convinced that I'm marriage material.

I pushed the luggage cart over by the door, and walked back and sat on the sofa arm, now truly ready to go. When Cherry came out from the bedroom, she looked me in the eye, and seeing that our time together was finished, came over and took my hand. She squeezed it gently, then slowly led me to the door, and opened it wide.

I said, "Is there anything you need before I go, boss lady?"

"No thank you, sir." She looked at the floor, then back at me, and said, "For the last few hours, I've been trying to think of some clever way to express my feelings, some word or words that would bring our little tale to a proper end. I suppose if we were in one of my films, this would be the final scene where I would say, 'I only need *you*.' But this script has a different ending." She paused for a moment, and then said, "Lord, that was a corny thing to say, was it not?"

"No, it was a very *sweet* thing to say. And if the circumstances were different—well, I wish I had something unforgettable to say too, but I guess dialogue isn't my strong suit."

Then in one very last attempt at a British accent, I said, "I will say *this,* though, Cherry Page: I shan't forget you."

Cherry's eyes misted a little, and she said softly, "Oh, but you *shan.*"

"Shan't," I said, willing my eyes to stay dry.

Cherry smiled, leaned in, and whispered, "Shan."

And with that last dumb joke, we hugged and gently touched lips in a final kiss between friends.